THE RUINOUS SWEEP

THE RUINOUS SWEEP

TIM WYNNE-JONES

CANDLEWICK PRESS

Copyright © 2018 by Tim Wynne-Jones

Excerpt from *The Buried Giant* by Kazuo Ishiguro copyright © 2015 by Kazuo Ishiguro. Published by Penguin Random House.

Lyrics to "Carter and Cash," p. 383: Words and Music by Tobias Erik Karlsson and Tor Albert Miller, Copyright © 2016 MXM Music AB and Four Song Night All Rights for MXM Music AB Administered by Kobalt Songs Music Publishing All Rights for Four Song Night Administered by Songs of Universal, Inc. All Rights Reserved. Used by Permission. Reprinted by Permission of Hal Leonard LLC

While every effort has been made to obtain permission to reprint copyrighted materials, there may be cases where we have been unable to track a copyright holder. The publisher will be happy to correct any omission in future printings.

First edition 2018

Library of Congress Catalog Card Number pending
ISBN 978-0-7636-9745-7

18 19 20 21 22 23 LSC 10 9 8 7 6 5 4 3 2 1

Printed in Crawfordsville, IN, U.S.A.

This book was typeset in Sabon.

Candlewick Press
99 Dover Street
Somerville, Massachusetts 02144

visit us at www.candlewick.com

For Amanda Lewis.
Let me count the ways. . . .

The stormy blast of Hell
With restless fury drives the spirits on,
Whirl'd round and dash'd amain with sore annoy.
When they arrive before the ruinous sweep,
There shrieks are heard, there lamentations, moans,
And blasphemies 'gainst the good Power in Heaven.

—Dante Alighieri, *The Inferno,* canto 5

I slipped quietly past the guards, saying no farewells, and was soon a boy under the moonlight, my dear companions left behind, my own kin long slaughtered, nothing but my courage and lately learned skills to carry on my journey.

—Kazuo Ishiguro, *The Buried Giant*

PART ONE

THE SPACE CAPSULE

CHAPTER  ONE

The boy sat tight up against the passenger door. There was something breathing on the backseat. He hadn't noticed it when he'd climbed in out of the rain. He'd been too thankful, in too much of a hurry. But the shape of it had grown on his senses. From the corner of his eye he could see a pile of blankets. There—it moved! Something or someone.

"What's your name again?" said the driver.

Had he told him his name? He didn't think so.

"You got a name or what?"

Donovan. Dono.

"What's that?"

"Dono," said the boy.

"You don't know your own name?" The driver burst out laughing, his belly jiggling against the steering wheel.

Under the laughter, Dono heard a low moan from

whatever was buried in those blankets. He grasped the door handle. He had to reach Bee somehow. She'd be worried sick. Bee . . . Yes . . . Beatrice. *She* didn't call him Dono. Who was he to her? Turn. That's what she called him. Turn.

"Sorry, kid. Nobody's turning."

"What?" He hadn't said it out loud, had he?

"Too late for that."

Dono held his breath and stared straight into the darkness beyond the twin cones of light.

Are you.

"What's that?"

The boy shook his head. "Nothing," he said. Why were his thoughts leaking out of him like this?

There was something he needed to remember. It was the start of a question—as much as he could recall. Behind it was a whole world of questions.

"You're a quiet one," said the driver. "Strong, silent type, eh?"

Donovan shook his head. He couldn't think—mustn't even try, not here.

"You don't look like a ball player."

Had they talked about baseball?

"I mean with the long hair and all. What—you tie it back like a girl with a piece of string?" The man waited for a response. Got none. "You listening?" he said. Then he wobbled the steering wheel a bit—a power trip—just to show who was boss in this speeding car on this lonely stretch of highway on this moonless night. "Hey, a little company'd be nice. What do ya say, Dono or Dunno or whatever it is you call yourself?"

4

"Thanks," said the boy. "I'm just—"

"Boring as paint," said the man. He burst out laughing again. "Hey, just joshin' with you, kid," he said, and punched Donovan in the arm.

"Ow!"

"Whoa! Just a love tap, slugger."

Donovan reached up to rub his shoulder. He ached all over.

"Something wrong with you, kid?"

Yes. That much he knew. Something was very wrong.

"Just . . ."

"Just *what*? You on something?"

A good question.

"Gotta say, though, you got one helluva pair of shoulders on you! How's a guy supposed to know you're a wimp?"

"I'm not—"

"A sissy-boy?"

"I'm not *myself,* okay? Do you get that?"

"Well, forgive me," said the man. "Forgive me for picking up your sorry ass in the rain. Forgive me for having a warm car and a big heart." He patted Donovan's knee and chuckled. He left his hand there, one hundredth of a second too long.

Dono slithered away from the man's touch and began to weigh his chances. He'd had some tae kwan do. The guy was large but out of shape. He imagined he could take him if things got bad. Then again, he'd missed the class where you learned how to defend yourself in a speeding car.

Behind him, the blankets shuddered again. Just a drunk, he told himself. Sleeping it off. A drunk . . .

Then there was a low popping noise and a smell wafted forward from the backseat. *Jesus!* Dono pressed his face against the window as if trying to suck air from the darkness on the other side of the rain-splattered glass.

The driver chuckled. "God, I hate this job," he said. He shook his fat head. Donovan stared out the corner of his eye at him, his face red in the dashboard lights. Red? He looked at the dashboard. What kind of car had red dashboard lights? The flesh of the man's neck pressed against his collar, sagging over the frayed edge of it like dough left too long to rise. He turned his head Donovan's way and smiled wearily.

There was a tatty green pine tree hanging from the rear-view mirror doing nothing to quell the stench. The little paper conifer wobbled dangerously, as if the car's wheels were straddling some fault line in the earth and the Malibu was about to fly apart into a million shards of steel and glass and hapless humanity.

See. That was part of it. Something he wanted Bee to see?

"See what?" said the driver. "You see anything out there?"

"No. Sorry."

"Man, you are one weird customer," said the driver.

Donovan closed his eyes. He couldn't take much more of this. He was so tired. Too tired to keep his guard up. Words were seeping from him in a slow drip. What was he doing? How did he get here? He searched the empty highway ahead. He was running from something. That had to be it. He glanced back over his shoulder and saw only darkness out the rear window, and below it the darkness of something under wraps, something still breathing but smelling as if it had stopped.

Donovan faced the front and gripped the door handle more tightly. Dared to close his eyes.

"Here's the deal, Dono, my man. I got a job to do, okay? I don't choose the work. I just do my job. Wouldn't hurt to liven things up a bit. Tell me a bit about yourself. Your plans for the future." That made the man laugh again—laugh himself into a coughing fit. "What do you say, boy?"

Donovan squeezed his eyes more tightly shut. Saw lightning. Tried to shake it away, which only made his head hurt. *Are you?* There it was again: the question.

"Am I what?" said the driver, irritated now. Donovan clammed up. His mouth was closed; his eyes were closed. He resisted covering his ears, but the desire was there to make himself inaccessible. He wanted to be anywhere but here.

"Well, if that's the way you want it," said the driver. "Have it your way." And then the car started to slow down.

Dono's eyes popped open. There was nothing but forest on either side of the road. "There's this little rest stop up ahead," the man said. "Don't know about you, but I'm looking forward to relieving myself." He scratched at the wattles that hung from his neck as the speedometer needle drifted to the left. "Maybe you could give me a hand, eh?" he said, and then threw back his head and laughed.

"Oh!" said Donovan.

"That all you got to say? 'Oh'?"

It was the other thing he needed to tell Bee, just as soon as he could.

"I asked you a question, son."

"Shut up," said Donovan.

"What's that?"

Something trembled back to life inside Donovan, some struggling true piece of himself. "Forget about it," he said.

"I'm not hearing this."

"Yeah, sorry, you are."

"I did *not* hear anyone in this vehicle say for-get-a-bout-it."

There was a silence ripe with anger and resentment—the car shook with it. Any minute now it will all end, thought Donovan. The earth will open up and swallow us.

The man was breathing hard. "Ohhhh-kay," he said, drawing out the syllables, "you asked for it."

Suddenly the car swerved onto the shoulder and shuddered to a stop.

"How's this? Close enough to nowhere for you?"

Donovan nodded slowly. "Nowhere's good," he said.

And then before he could even loosen his seat belt, the guy was shoving at him with thick fingers and meaty arms, shouting at him, swearing at him. "The great outdoors, asshole," he said. "It's all yours." Finally the door shot open and Donovan fell out onto the gravel shoulder. The man threw the car into gear and started to pull away, howling with anger and frustration.

"Hey!"

Donovan twisted his foot free from the car and rolled out of its path as the back tires slewed in an arc toward him. The Chevy squealed to a stop, making the passenger-side door slam shut—*thunk!* Then the car swerved, churning up gravel, and shimmied back onto the rain-slick pavement.

Donovan sat in a heap on the cold shoulder, his foot aching, sprained or worse. The Chevy fishtailed down the highway, the horn blaring triumphantly, as if the driver had just won the world championship of fat losers. He was perhaps the saddest primate on the planet at that moment, with the exception of the boy he had left sitting in the dirt.

The car's engine roared, then the Chevy suddenly squealed to a stop. Donovan looked up. The back left passenger door of the car opened—right in the middle of the highway—and out of it shambled the thing that had been on the back seat. It rose on two legs under its shabby greatcoat of blankets, backlit in red. A thick and seemingly headless figure, stumbling, hobbling, and lurching toward the other side of the highway. The back door of the car slammed shut, and again the driver took off. Dono watched the faltering figure reach the edge of the embankment, sway momentarily, and then seem to fall down the slope out of sight, lost in darkness.

The Chevy's engine feebled itself into the distance, until it was a sound smaller than the slow wind shivering the trees and the din of the amphibious life all along the ditch, peeping their little hearts out. Donovan listened. How shrill it was. How urgent. A fog rolled in until there was nothing left of sound but frogs and the wet-lipped wind.

CHAPTER  TWO

The boy lay tight up against the side rail of the gurney. Surely they had not placed him there like that, pressed so hard against the railing? His face was contorted, as it must have been at the moment of impact. What had he seen in that blinding instant? Bee shook the image from her head, rested her hand on her heart, which was beating out of control. Calm down, she told herself. Don't try to imagine. Don't go there.

Be here.

She stepped closer to the bed. She reached out tentatively and rested her hand lightly over Donovan's chest, let it glide down like a feather until it hovered over his heart. It was there, beating, a survivor in an earthquake buried under the rubble of his broken rib cage.

"I'm here, Turn," she said. "Can you hear me?"

Monitors beeped, the room buzzed, ticked, clicked. There was a screen with green calligraphy that said the same thing over and over: you are alive, you are alive, you are alive. The intensivist had been less certain than the machine. Donovan was only barely alive. Unstable. Which meant she was allowed to be there, one of those good news/bad news things. The good news was she could stay as long as she wanted; the bad news was that might not be very long.

She sobbed involuntarily. Sniffed. Wiped her nose. *Get a grip, girl.*

"Turner, it's Bee."

Here was the medical rationale: because there was no guarantee he'd pull through, the benefits of having someone there with him—someone close—outweighed the distraction. And she was the only someone they could find so far. The cops were trying to track down Trish and Scott in the wilds of Algonquin Park. No, Scott isn't his father, Bee had explained. So they were trying to track down his father, as well, who wasn't answering his phone. Not a huge surprise. Until they found one parent or another, there was just Bee.

Bee and Turn.

Trish was his emergency contact number. The cop who had spoken to Bee had been scrolling through Donovan's phone looking for someone with the same last name as Donovan. There were no Turners other than Trish in his contacts. So she'd explained how Donovan had dropped his father's name, McGeary.

The cop scrolled to *M*. "Allen I. McGeary?" Bee had nodded. "Thanks."

"Don't be surprised if he doesn't pick up," she'd said before she could stop herself.

"What's that?"

"Never mind."

The cops had found Bee because of her text message to him, sent at 10:46, sitting in its little white balloon on Donovan's cracked cell phone.

Where are you?

She looked at him, felt for him ever so gingerly through the thin cloth of the blanket. "Where are you?" she said.

The duty nurse's name was Geraldine Ocampo. "Just Gerry is fine." And then Just Gerry smiled. "He was calling for you, honey."

"What?"

The night clerk had helped Bee out of her coat. She was out of breath and suddenly someone who had forgotten how to take off a coat. Then the clerk had handed Bee over to Just Gerry.

"Bee, right?" said Gerry. "It's one of the things he keeps saying."

"He can talk?"

Gerry wagged her head from side to side, not wanting to give the wrong impression. "Only sort of. Sounds. They come out of his mouth, and one of those sounds is you."

Bee covered her face.

"You sure you want to do this, honey? It isn't pretty."

Bee recovered. Nodded. "Yes."

Gerry smiled. "Reach out to him, okay? Just good stuff. Encourage him." Then she guided Bee into the semidarkness of the ICU and left her there with a pat on the shoulder.

So Bee sat on a hard chair, by a bed that looked like it was designed by NASA, and although it wasn't that cold, she found herself shivering and wished that the night clerk hadn't taken her coat after all.

"Ahhh . . . Ahhh . . . Urrr . . ."

His cracked lips moved and sounds came out. Bee gently squeezed his hand—the right one, which was scratched but apparently not broken. The left was in a cast. So were his legs. He was so broken. She bent closer. The chair scraped the linoleum, letting out a squeal. She flinched. His face did not seem to register the intrusive noise.

"I'm here, Turn. It's me."

Nothing. The slightest twist of his face, which quickly became a rictus of pain.

"I'm not going anywhere," she said.

Nothing.

A web of tubes carried liquids to Donovan's battered body, carried liquids away. There was so much of him that was liquid now. He was a wineskin. His strong bones broken; his muscled arms and legs flaccid. She imagined what was left whole of him as a tiny figure on a raft, rising and falling on a dark and swollen sea in the cavern of his body.

She looked around the dim, small room—too small— with all its machinery and blinking lights. It felt like a space capsule. A floating world not of the earth anymore but suspended above it, held in the planet's gravitational pull. She wondered that there weren't straps to hold him tethered to the bed lest he float away.

"Hu . . . Huuuuuu . . . Huuuun . . ."

She jerked in her chair. She had slipped away. She stroked his nearby hand.

Just Gerry had said to talk to him. Soothe. Comfort. Just Gerry was an optimist. She wore a little gold cross on a chain. A believer. Lucky her.

"Can you hear me, Donovan?"

His face contorted in a sudden paroxysm.

"It's all right, Turn. You're in good hands."

Right.

The ventilator was not hooked up. No intubation, which is why he could make any kind of sound at all. They hadn't shoved a tube down his throat through his vocal cords. "The doc who's on tonight isn't big on unnecessary extras," Gerry had said. "The RT will be monitoring him."

"RT?"

"The respiratory guy."

So Turn was breathing all by himself, which was something. An important something. He might not walk again, but he could breathe. She tried to imagine Donovan content just to breathe. Donovan, who lived to move fast, to hurl himself at things: fly balls and flung Frisbees. Her family had once had a long-legged mutt; Donovan was like that. Just walking with him was a workout.

"Ah . . . Are . . . Are . . ."

His mouth curled in. His tongue appeared, attempting to lick his lips. On the bedside table there was a cup with water in it, and Q-tips. Bee took one and dipped it into the water, then gently brushed the wet Q-tip along his lips. It was something she'd done when Nana D'Amato was in the hospital. His whole face seemed to move toward the moisture with the blind sense of a plant. Was it just her imagination? She dipped the Q-tip again and brought it to his lips.

"Are . . . you . . ."

She stopped, drew back the Q-tip.

"Am I what?"

"Are . . . you . . ."

"It's me, Turn. What do you want to say?"

She waited, the Q-tip hanging in the air above his lips.

"See," he said.

"See what?" She looked around as if there was something he needed, another blanket maybe.

She stared at him breathlessly. Nothing more came. Then she noticed his lips moving—hungering—and she gently dabbed them again with the Q-tip. Finally, his mouth closed. She put the Q-tip back in the cup of water and sat back on her chair, trembling.

There was so much she didn't understand. What had he been doing on Wilton Crescent? He was supposed to be at his father's and then join her at Bridgehead as soon as he could. But he'd gone home, for some reason, even though his mom and Scott were out of town. Maybe his big talk with his father had ended abruptly or had never gotten off the ground. She wouldn't be surprised. She hadn't wanted him to even try. She'd only ever met Al a couple of times but had loathed him immediately. She saw how he manipulated Turn. He tried it with her, too—tried to drag her into something. He spoke calculated words, sneaky words, words with barbs in them. She'd wanted Donovan to go see someone, professionally.

"Like your mother, for instance?"

"God, no."

"But a shrink."

They'd discussed—argued—what shape this help might take, but he was too independent, too determined. He'd solve this himself. "Listen," he'd told her, taking both her hands in his. "If I start talking to a therapist about my relationship with my father, it might go on for a decade."

And as far as he was concerned, that was that.

She leaned forward to look at him. How did he get himself run over fifteen yards from his own front door on a side street where you could count a typical evening's traffic on one hand?

"Oh," he said, startling her.

"Turn?"

"Oh."

Was it an expression of surprise at some new pain? She leaned in close again, gripping the rail with both hands, watching his lips move as if searching for something in the air before he spoke again. "Dad," he said. Or she thought it might be that; definitely there was a first *D;* she wasn't sure about the second.

She leaned forward. "What is it, Turn?"

"Dad."

"You want your father?"

His head quaked, like some kind of aftershock. She watched his face, willing his features to relax, the muscles to loosen.

"They're trying to find your father, okay? He'll come as soon as he can." She only hoped that was true. It was Friday, and Friday was pub night for Donovan's father. Well, any night was, really.

His hand suddenly flickered into life, as if he were playing a little arpeggio on the sheets. Then it lay perfectly still again. She patted it softly, softly.

"Dead," he said.

Dead. Or was it "Dad" again?

"What are you trying to say, Turner?"

There was no sign of recognition—nothing to suggest he heard her. She tentatively touched his face, tried to smooth out the worry lines on his forehead with her thumb. His face was the least damaged part of him. A livid bruise by his right eye and scratches from the bushes in which he'd landed. Then suddenly but slowly—achingly slowly—he lay his head in the cup of her hand, like a cat.

Did she imagine it?

"I love you," she whispered.

"Dead," he said. It was clear this time.

"No, you're not," she said. "We're at the General. You're safe now."

He seemed to respond. There was some kind of a feeble straining toward the words she was saying. And then his face moved away from her hand and he grew still. She removed her hand slowly from his face, sat back down, exhausted. She crossed her hands on her lap.

Her big black THEATER IS MY BAG bag was at her feet. She took out her phone and checked the time. It was in airplane mode so as not to mess with the high-tech equipment in the ICU. It was 2:30 a.m. She had phoned home from the lobby when she'd arrived to let her folks know where she was. She would stay the night if she was allowed to. She would phone again in the morning. She would phone work as early as she could to tell them she wouldn't be in. There was nothing else she could do. She wasn't a person who took to sitting doing nothing very well.

She should go talk to someone, wake up Daisy or Jen. But the only person she really wanted to talk to was this boy lying here half-dead, on his back, hard against the side rail, as if he would hang on to it for dear life if his bandaged left hand could only grab hold.

She dropped the phone back into her purse.

"Are you . . ." he mumbled.

She waited. "What, Donovan?" Nothing. "Am I . . . ?"

"Are. You."

She didn't ask again. He mumbled on indecipherably. There might have been words in the susurrations and murmurs, but Bee felt too tired to unscramble meaning from the sounds. Disheartened, she took a tissue from a box on his bedside table and wiped a line of drool from the corner of his mouth. Then she sat back down and closed her eyes to listen better, to listen with her heart. She dove into her bag again and found some hand cream, squirted some into her palm, and started rubbing it in. Had to do something.

"K . . . t . . ." he said. "Kill . . . t . . ."

She stopped rubbing. Froze. "Turner?"

"Kill . . . t . . . im."

Bee rose slowly to her feet and, resting one hand on the rail of his bed, leaned closer to his face.

"What are you saying, Turn?"

"K . . . KILL . . . DIM!"

He had raised his voice and she was so shocked she fell back into her chair, which rocked precariously for a moment before she steadied it.

Donovan's face contorted again and his one free hand scrabbled at the sheets.

"Bee? Beeeeeee!"

"I'm right here. Shhhh. I won't leave."

"Din . . ." he said. "Din'n meee . . ." he said.

"Didn't mean to," she finished the sentence.

"No," he whispered back. "No . . . no . . . no . . ." he said. And then his body seemed to cave in from the exertion and he was still again—so still she wondered if he was gone—as if these words had been a deathbed confession. She looked up at his monitor: the green calligraphy said otherwise. The space capsule was still hurtling through space with a live cargo.

Bee collected herself. These are just sounds, she told herself. He's hallucinating. Who knew what kind of meds he was on? *I'm* hallucinating, she thought, on too much coffee and not enough sleep. She calmed herself down a bit. Came to a decision.

She reached way down into her purse for her journal and a pen. She was a stage manager. Stage managers kept track of things. When everybody else is losing their heads, they know exactly who has to go where and to carry which prop. She never went anywhere without her trusty Moleskine and a good pen. Her father liked to say that the world was in dire need of more stage managers.

She wrote down what she had heard, trying to remember the sequence: the question "Are you?" asked twice, "See" something, "Dad" or "Dead"—one or the other, maybe both. She paused, looked at his face. He was motionless. Her eyes darted to his chest, waiting for it to rise, checking its movement against the monitor. Then she returned her attention to the page, but at first she couldn't make herself write down what else he had said. Then she did. Had to.

"Killed," he had said. "Killed him." There was no denying how plaintively he had called her name—as if he were lost. As if she were not there at his bedside. And there was no denying the melancholy pitch to his voice in what had seemed like an apology: "Didn't mean . . . Didn't mean to." Then she wrote a string of "No"s after it; she wasn't sure how many he'd actually said.

She sat back, closed the journal on her finger. She would record anything that sounded like a word from here on in.

She sat and watched. She thought of a favorite song of his and hummed it, very quietly. "Carter and Cash." Nothing. Gradually she felt herself go slack. She yawned, stretched, and settled. She drifted. She was in low earth orbit, a few hundred miles up, circling the globe, the seas and land masses slipping by down below if only there was a window in this tiny place to see them. She was lulled by the beeps and hum of the machinery that kept Donovan alive. She became a long, slim Buddha, sleeping upright on her chair.

When she awoke again it was to a hand on each shoulder. Just Gerry. "How you doing, Miss Beatrice?" She searched Bee's eyes, full of questions, as if she were the patient.

"I'm fine," she said.

Gerry gave her shoulders a squeeze and then turned to fuss with the IV tubing, the monitors and pumps, checked all the bells and whistles. She stopped to look at Donovan, her hand on her chest. "He say anything?" she asked.

Bee slipped her finger out of the journal and closed it. "Sort of," she said. "I couldn't exactly tell. He did say my name."

Gerry turned from her fussing. "Good," she said, her brown eyes glowing in the semi-dark. She stepped back from her patient, rounded Bee's chair, and picked up the clipboard at the end of his bed, on which she jotted some notes. Finished, she smiled again at Bee. "There's someone here for you," she said.

"Thank you," said Bee gratefully.

Gerry chuckled. "No, girl. I mean there's someone here to see you. Come."

CHAPTER THREE

Donovan lay his weary body down, breathing hard, letting the adrenaline dissipate, sucking up the pain in his foot. He shouted his anger into the dead forest, one earsplitting cry punctuated by the only word that could hope to channel his misery, a word with sharp-edged consonants at either end and a painful groan in the middle. The shout echoed, enough to stop the frogs from peeping. And then into the dismal silence that followed his cry, the peeping critters returned.

He sat up, scrubbed the gravel out of his hair, off the back of his hoodie. He glanced back into the impenetrable darkness. That thing. It would have heard his shout. Was it even now turning back, coming for him, drawn zombielike to the sound of human suffering? His eyes could pick nothing out. It would be upon him before he knew it was there.

No, he told himself. He'd smell it first.

He clambered to his feet, stood there, his hands on his hips, his right leg taking the load of his body while the twinge died down in his left foot. He patted his pockets, felt his wallet in the left back, felt his cell phone in the right front. Thank God for small mercies. He pulled out his phone. No charge. Right. No way of calling anyone. He knew that already, although he'd forgotten. He had tried to call her. Call Bee. He remembered that now. He'd been standing in a downpour. Then running. There had been a lot of running. Running from his father's place, running home to Wilton Crescent. Which is where the fat man had picked him up. No. That couldn't be right. Too far. And why would he do it: hitch a ride to nowhere?

To here.

He fumbled in his hoodie pocket and found his charger cable. Well, that was something. Now, if he could just find a tree with an outlet . . .

That's all there was: trees and wet.

He hopped over toward the bank that descended to the deeper darkness of the forest floor. By starlight he made out the shimmer of water. Flooded land, spring loaded. He could only guess that it was the same on the other side of the road where the thing had gone. He looked over his shoulder: no shambling blanket creature. Nothing. So he was on a kind of isthmus through hell. Perfect.

He closed his eyes. "Beatrice?" he murmured, summoning up her name and sounding it out. He could almost feel her there. "Bee?" He listened hard and swore he heard her. Surely he did, as if she were just on the other side of the air.

He opened his eyes, stared hopelessly at the dull face of

his cell. Clicked it harder, hoping to see her face doing her *Mona Lisa* routine.

"Bee?" he said out loud. Then he shouted it. "Beeeeeee!"

He had traveled Highway Seven to a cottage when he was young. Years and years ago, when they had still been a family. Was it the first time he'd ever seen anything dead? He remembered the bloated carcass of a raccoon on the roadside, with three kits, stragglers, arrayed across the road behind their mama like good little raccoon children who had been reduced to crow snacks.

"Are they dead, Mommy?"

"They're dead, Dono."

"Welcome to the country," said Dad.

There must be towns and villages, he thought. There were. He remembered one with a river running through it where they would go for groceries and the Dairy Queen and the library. But he wasn't sure what good a town would be to him right now. He looked in his wallet. He had a couple of twenties and his emergency Visa card, which, the minute he used it, would reveal his location. Your son was here, Ms. Turner, purchasing a not-so-happy meal; here, getting a room in a squalid motel; here, buying a ticket to Timbuktu.

The fog rolled in, courtesy of the slow, wet wind. There'd been intermittent rain all evening. Donovan was damp with it. He took a deep breath, drinking the air. He closed his eyes. His shoulders fell. He reached up, felt the bruise left by the driver on his left arm. He took another breath, felt the ache in his bones. The fog had clammy hands.

He took a piss off the edge of the shoulder, arcing phosphorescent gold into the dead water below. Then he crouched, painfully, and sat on the lip of the hill, his legs trailing down the weedy slope. He looked into the murk of the swallowed land, even now turning silvery in the mist. He strained to see lights through the trees, a house, a farm. Anything. He closed his eyes and let the fog massage his temples. He remembered dancing with a girl in middle school whose hands were almost this wet.

Then his eyes popped open. A car. Had he heard it or seen it through the membrane of his eyelids? Lights, like Morse code through the trees—dot, dot, dot; dash, dash, dash; dot, dot, dot—heading his way, coming from the east. He was on a long, slow curve, but there was nothing slow about the speed of those approaching headlights. He hobbled back to his feet, grimacing with pain. Not every late-night driver could be a pervert.

He could hear it big time now, the engine revving high, like the driver was in nineteenth gear and looking for twenty. Donovan hopped to the edge of the pavement as the lights rounded the bend, deep center field away. He faltered, the pain in his foot excruciating. He doubled over, then threw himself up tall, his right arm flying out, his thumb pointing over his shoulder, as the high-beam headlights cut through the fog, barreling closer, blinding him.

The driver seemed to see him at the last minute; he corrected his wheel to pass as widely as possible, but he was going too fast. The car careened across the road, then squealed back into the right lane, weaving along the solid yellow lines until the driver corrected one too many times. The car skidded on the pavement, spun out of control, and plummeted over the shoulder, tipping into darkness.

Flipping up

on end

and . . .

over.

A crash landing.

The engine howled and then stopped.

Donovan wasn't sure how long he stood there staring.

Did that just happen?

The headlights, still on, lit the pavement like a crosswalk. Donovan hobbled across the highway and along the shoulder with as much speed as he could manage. He stopped at the place he'd watched the zombie disappear over the lip of the shoulder. Some of the light from the crash spilled this far, but there was no body.at the bottom of the slope lying facedown in the muck. He moved on and finally stood above the crash site, looking down on the car's underside, an obscene sight: all those body parts you were never intended to see. A white Camaro reduced to a turtle on its back, water halfway up the driver's side window. There was music churning out of the radio. Hard rock.

A fresh surge of adrenaline coursed through him. He slip-slided down the gravel embankment into the weed-choked verge. Then he splashed through the shallow water and, bending over, peered into the car.

The driver hung lifelessly from his seat belt, upside down, one hand still clutching the steering wheel, the other hanging limp, resting flat on the ceiling below him. The ceiling light shone upward, giving the driver's face Halloween shadows. It was a little upside-down cocoon of a world of black pleather and winking lights and AC/DC.

The roofline was crumpled, deeply embedded in the mud. Donovan tried to open the driver's door but it was impossible. The other side was tipped up a bit, left to right, so he made his way around the humming, clicking hot body of the car. He was sopping to the knees now, slipping on the scree as he clambered back up the embankment around the front end of the car, then slid back down the other side. The top of the passenger door frame was free of the wet ground, the door unlocked. It took a two-armed effort, however, to open it, pushing mostly upward, heaving it open. Then he leaned into the cab of the car, trying to reach across the center console. He stepped on the upended roof's edge and the car began to tip toward him. He imagined the car falling on him, pinning his legs — submerging him under the black water. He jumped away and the car rocked back again. Settled. There was no way he could reach up to unlock the man's seat belt, but even if he did, what then? The man would drop like a sack — probably break his neck, if it wasn't already broken. Something was broken. The man was far too still. And looking at him, Donovan suddenly crumpled. He felt the pain of the crash surge through him. He doubled over, retched, but there was nothing in him to come out. He was empty.

He recovered, then leaned back into the car. He could reach the console. He stopped the music in the middle of a scorching guitar solo. The air filled again with the prehistoric sounds of night, modified only by hissing and popping, the death rattle of the flipped car.

He stared at the man, his knees pressed up against his chest, fetal in this metal womb. He tried to make the man breathe through a supreme mental effort. No luck.

The airbags hadn't deployed. He had no idea why not. Maybe this was the stretch of highway where nothing goes the way it should. Where fat perverts ditch you and a walking pile of blankets steps into the night and disappears and racing cars fly off into the trees and nothing is as it is meant to be. He watched the shadowy figure, grotesque in the dashboard light shining up into his limp and crumpled form, his grimacing face.

I've killed him, thought Donovan. All I have to do is stand by the side of the road, stick my thumb out, and people die. He hung his head and as he did, noticed a briefcase thrown up against the back corner of the ceiling, which was now the floor in this upside-down world. Water was trickling into the cab from the driver's side and was puddling, growing deeper, as the car settled. The briefcase sat in a pool of dank water. The ceiling light picked out details in gold. Donovan grasped the handle and lifted the briefcase out. Cracked from the impact, it fell open, and before he knew what was happening, stacks of money were falling into the oily black muck gathering in the car's interior. He slammed the top of the briefcase shut and lifted it clear. Then he stared back into the car. Several bundles of cash lay partially submerged, the bill on the top of every one a new hundred. The stacks were dense, perhaps two inches thick, wrapped in a mustard-colored currency strap.

Stacks of hundred-dollar bills.

Donovan gave in to shock. He stumbled backward until his heels hit the embankment, where he sank to his butt on the gravel. That's what gravity does, brings you down. Some ancient almost-man stood up some three million years ago to see if anything was coming, to see if there were fruit trees over yonder, maybe a stream, to check if there was a saber-toothed tiger looking for lunch. Gravity didn't like you standing. Gravity wanted to keep you in your place. But this almost-man all that time ago kept doing it anyway, standing up. Got into the habit. Gravity only laughed. Go on, stand up all you want, you'll fall eventually. You're mine.

Donovan hugged the broken briefcase to his chest. When he had caught his breath, he straightened the briefcase on his lap the right way up, the handle toward him. Slowly he opened it. There was nothing inside but money, two stacks deep, twelve stacks per layer, even though several of the stacks had fallen out into the car.

He managed to close the briefcase and lock it. Then he leaned his elbows on it and rested his head in his hands and stared out into the wet woodland. He closed his eyes again. Felt pain rake his body. Swore. Opened his eyes. The car's headlights suddenly went out. Gave up the ghost. He was in the dark again. Which is when he saw, dimmed by shadowy distance, a light, a light far across the other side of the forest.

He got to his feet, stepped down almost involuntarily into the mud, drawn to that distant light. In three steps the mud was up to his shin, just below his knee, but after three more steps it hadn't climbed much higher. The ground was soft on top but still mostly frozen, which was the cause of the standing water. Soon he had splashed his way under cover of the woods, leafless but dressed in fog. It felt as if the fog were in him, in his lungs, his head.

It was then that he heard sirens. Turning, he saw lights far off coming west along the highway, moving at a clip. Cops or an ambulance? No one had passed by on the highway to phone in the accident. But maybe this was a highway where everything just happened all on its own. No cause and effect. Randomness. The opposite of hope.

He should give himself up. He tried to think how that would work.

"I surrender."

"Why?"

"Because I did something bad. I'm not sure what."

"Did you flip this car upside down?"

"No, sir. Maybe. I don't know."

"What's in that briefcase?"

"Oh, right."

Something in him resisted. These fog-enshrouded woods would shelter him. He would disappear, just like the other passenger in the Chevy did. And if by chance the water got deeper as he made his way farther into the bush toward that flickering and ghostly pale light, then he would walk deeper into it, weighed down by what he had stolen, until he drowned and saved everyone a whole lot of trouble.

He set off. The coldness of the midnight water numbed some of the pain in his leg. He sloshed through the swamp, his chukkas sticking sometimes in the muck, squelching as he pulled them free, the ground not quite as frozen as he'd thought. By the time the cops arrived on the scene, he was well beyond the strobing light show taking place on the shoulder of the highway. He stopped behind a tree to look back. There were two cruisers. One of the cops was setting up flares along the road. Dono could hear the crackle of their radios in the liquid air. He watched for another minute or so and then set off again, away from the carnage, swinging the briefcase like a man off to the office: a man of seventeen with a gimpy leg and some dark crime weighing heavily on his broad shoulders, and what he guessed must be several hundred thousand dollars to think about.

There was something *else* he had to think about. Something he needed to tell Bee. He stopped. "Are you . . ." he said. But he'd lost it again.

CHAPTER FOUR

It was a farm, rendered ghostly by the night: a sprawling yard of dark buildings wreathed in smokelike fog, dominated in the foreground by a long, low-slung storage shed, backlit by a high-wattage yard light. Between the shed and the farmhouse, through the naked maples, he could see equipment strewn here and there, made almost warlike by shadows: machines with hulking limbs.

He stumbled. Got his balance. Looked down. He had tripped over a blanket lying in the wet grass. The other passenger had come this way, drawn to the light just as he had been. He looked up again and for one startling moment the image in his head clicked and he saw the spread before him in full summer light. He had been here! He couldn't remember when or why. As a child, perhaps. Yes. He shuddered at the shock of it.

There were lights on in the kitchen of the farmhouse, or at least what he suspected was the kitchen—suspected or remembered—because there was a side door into the lit room. As he drew nearer, he saw a porch with a bench up against the wall and work boots lying in the light oozing out the back-door window. He drifted away from the house toward the impressive storage shed. He stopped, leaned against the aluminum wall of the shed, April-cold—colder than the air. But it hardly mattered anymore. The chill was in his bones now. "I'm so cold," he said out loud, hoping that if Bee really were there somehow, she would hear him and cover him or lie beside him and hold him. He breathed deeply. He could smell her, the fragrance of her. He closed his eyes and felt her hand on his chest, registering its movement up and down as if she were counting his ribs. If he could just sleep . . .

But this was no place to drift off. He opened his eyes and looked around. If he was even to dare approach the farmhouse, he should probably stash the briefcase. He made his way back toward the rear end of the shed and there, a base-run away, was a trash heap: a place of junk and broken things. Approaching the pile, he could easily have imagined that it housed some kind of monstrous spirit all its own. It was constructed of spiked things and gears, iron claws and rotting axles, chipped blades, rolled and rusted barbed-wire fencing, twisted and demented-looking in what light spilled this far. And there, caught up in the barbed wire, was another blanket.

Such a strange trail of crumbs.

Around back of the trash heap, he dug into the dead

leaves a shallow grave for the briefcase, his newfound fortune, and covered it, grunting with the effort. He laid a rotten slab of particleboard over it. He stood up and surveyed his handiwork. He would need this money. He knew that much. Then he made his way stealthily toward the house, rubbing the dirt off his hands onto his hoodie, shambling, foot dragging—the walking dead following the walking dead—reaching the northeast corner of the house, where the windows were dark. He sidled along its length until stopped by a storm cellar. That's what he assumed it must be. He'd seen one sometime. Maybe here. A door on a forty-five degree angle to the ground, built into a low bunker. A door you had to lift up. He thought about the car door of the Camaro: all these doors all of a sudden that you had to fight gravity to open. He thought for a moment of entering the cellar and crawling into a safe dark corner to sleep. There was no lock on the door. Then he thought of being cornered there with no way of escape, trapped among the jars of pickles and dusty boxes of potatoes and root vegetables, all bound up in spiderwebs and choked with dust. He must have read that somewhere—what you kept in a storm cellar. Or had he been in one sometime? He *felt* a bit like a root vegetable. He thought of potato eyes—eyes that sprouted, feeling their way into the dark, looking for the light.

He passed the bunker and made his way toward the lit windows. He peered inside. Three men were playing cards. The window was cracked open, probably to let out the cigarette smoke that swathed their heads.

There was a bottle of Canadian Club half empty on the table and a couple of ashtrays piled high. Woodstove-warmed air seeped from the window. Not all the smoke was coming from cigarettes.

On the table were toppling columns of poker chips, and the air was full of the kind of banter that went along with Texas Hold'em. Each man held two cards; the rest were laid out on the table before them: the flop, the turn, the river. The talk, what there was of it, was drunken, loud between two of them anyway; the third had folded in more ways than one. He seemed to be asleep, his head on his arms in the space where his chips might have been if he'd won any.

In profile, on the right, sat a man with a gut that spilled over his studded belt. He had a tat on his left bicep, a bicep that was roughly the circumference of Donovan's thigh. His beard was coming in red, though his hair was a dirty blond with strands of gray in it. There was a massive mane of it, bedraggled and filthy, like he might have been rolling in the dust after bringing down the zebra he'd eaten for lunch. To his right and facing the window sat a skinny dude wearing an improbable leopard-skin vest—maybe stolen from a bad band sometime in the seventies. Under it, he wore a T-shirt that might once have been white. He was a man with sallow skin and a double band of thorns tattooed around each wrist. His skin was stretched too tightly over the bones of his face. His black hair was pulled back in a ponytail, the better to see the assorted bits of metal poking from his earlobes, his eyebrows, his lip. He had a scar down the right side of his face that bisected his eyebrow and curled in toward his mouth, almost as if he were smiling. But only almost.

Then there was the sleeper. Something about the top of his head, the balding in the middle, the shade of driftwood brown, the set of his shoulders . . . The man started and lifted his head from his arms as if he had just come back from a long way down. As if he had become aware of Donovan staring at him. He looked toward the window and narrowed his eyes as if trying to see the face on the other side—Donovan's face—frozen with shock.

"Dono?"

"For Christ's sake," said the lion.

"Are you in or out, Murphy?" said the leopard.

"Donovan . . ."

"Knock, knock!" said the leopard. "Anybody home?" His raised voice covered the gasp uttered by the boy at the window, who stumbled backward and fell down hard on his backside.

The third gambler was his father.

CHAPTER  FIVE

More cops, Bee assumed. Detectives this time, in street clothes but still somehow recognizable as cops. He and she cops. He, old school: tweedy kind of jacket, tartan tie, complete with stain, white shirt, gray slacks, brown shoes. The woman was in designer jeans, a pale-yellow top and Windex-blue faux leather jacket. She was wearing blue high-tops on her feet, and one of those feet was tapping. Bee clutched the front of her shrug closed as if maybe she had something to hide. The man had little hair to speak of; the woman wore her gingery-blond hair athlete-short and no-nonsense.

"Staff Sergeant Jim Bell," said the man.

"Hi, Beatrice," said the woman. "Callista Stills."

Bee shook hands. Bell's big hand was rough as sandpaper, his handshake slack, as if he were aware how easy it would be to crush bones. Stills's hand felt like Bee's—like she had just put on moisturizer.

"You look beat," said Stills. She smiled, but Bee felt as if this were the talking-to-youth smile she kept in her pocket until needed.

"I'm okay. Thanks." And here she was, trotting out the kind of lie you offer to people who pretend to care.

"The nurse was telling us he's talking a bit?" said Stills. "Donovan?" she added, as if maybe Bee had been bedsitting a number of patients.

Bee shrugged, an attempt to hide the fact that her brain had suddenly gone into high alert. She crossed her arms. Sergeant Bell had taken a step back and was leaning against the wall of the waiting room Gerry had led her to, through the locked doors of the intensive care unit. The doors had clicked shut behind her ominously as she'd left.

"Amazing to think he can talk," Stills prompted.

"It's not really talk, exactly," said Bee. "Mumbling mostly." And there was lie number two, definitely a different grade of lie.

"Okay," said Stills. "That's got to count for something."

Stills either didn't have a rank or hadn't wanted to reveal it.

Bee looked at Bell, but he was silent. This was obviously a job for the younger, hipper detective. And was the almost-chic look supposed to make her appear like one of the girls? Bee wasn't sure why, but she had taken an immediate dislike to the woman.

"It's kind of unusual for a hit-and-run victim in such bad shape to be in any condition to talk. So we were wondering if there was anything Donovan might have said that would be, you know, useful in any way."

"Useful?"

"Maybe shed a little light on what happened."

Bee rubbed her nose, looked around, and saw a box of tissues on a nearby table. Supporting actor Sergeant Bell beat her to it, handed her the box. She nodded her thanks.

"So no actual words?" said Stills.

Bee was glad she had left her journal in her bag back in the unit. She shook her head. "What's up?" she said.

Stills glanced back at Bell, who nodded, as if they'd rehearsed this. "Shall we sit down?" said Stills.

There was a little grouping of chairs, cushioned in tangerine-colored plastic. They sat.

"Do you have anything yet?" Bee asked.

Stills tipped her head, a noncommittal gesture. "We did a preliminary door-to-door on Wilton. No luck so far. It's a quiet street, rainy night, not a lot of traffic. We'll follow up on that, for sure." Bee nodded expectantly. "Something will come up," said Stills. "Crime Stoppers. You know. Somebody will have seen something."

It didn't sound like much to Bee. And it sounded as if Stills wasn't saying everything. Fine. Two could play at that game.

"A fair number of hit-and-runs turn themselves in," said Bell. "They drive home, sit for a while in the dark not sure what to do, try to sleep, can't. And—bang!—their conscience gets the better of them." He held out his hands as if he'd completed a magic trick and produced a perp. "See it all the time."

"So you don't have anything," said Bee.

"We're following up on a lead," said Stills, "but we'd—"

"A lead?"

Stills had blue eyes, a shade or two darker than her leatherette jacket. She was actually quite pretty, except she looked, right now, like someone who didn't enjoy being interrupted.

Bell leaned forward, settling his elbows on his knees. The word "avuncular" came to Bee's mind. "We've got a paint chip," he said. "That's what we've got."

"A paint chip."

"That's right." He held up his thumb and index finger about a button's width apart. "It's not much, but the fellows in forensics can do things with a paint chip."

"Really?"

"It's not like on TV. They can't tell you what the guy driving the truck had for supper. Not from a paint chip."

It was an attempt at gallows humor, but Bee didn't miss the one clue embedded in the sentence. "A truck?"

Stills glared at Bell. Bee didn't miss that, either. Bell glanced at Stills placidly and then looked back at Bee. "A truck, possibly: a pickup or an SUV."

"How do you know that?"

Stills's eyes seemed to vibrate with the effort it took not to roll them, but Bell ignored her. "He was hit high." With his hand, he indicated a spot halfway up his torso. "Fender height of a car is around twenty inches. The injuries, according to the clinical manager here we talked to, suggest first impact was higher. High enough, it might even be a lift job."

"A lift job?"

"A vehicle with modified suspension, new springs, shocks, and larger than stock tires. For better traction off-road."

"Jim, if you've just about finished . . ."

Jim held up a hand to call Stills off. "Know anyone with a red pickup, Bee?"

Bee's mind reeled. Suddenly, there was this flood of information. Was this detective suggesting the driver might not have been a stranger? She shook her head, tried to formulate a response, but Stills stepped in.

"Ms. Northway," she said, not quite able to hide her irritation at being sidelined. "What was Donovan's state of mind last time you saw him?"

Bee looked at Stills, trying to read her. "He was fine."

"When was that?"

"This morning, at school."

"Did he seem bothered about anything?"

Bee wondered if Stills could see the vein pumping in her forehead as clearly as Bee could feel it. "He was excited about getting together with his guys."

Bell produced a spiral-bound notebook and started writing. "Guys?"

"His team. He plays baseball in this adult league. Spring training."

"He plays ball?" said Bell.

"Yes."

Bell glanced at Stills, who nodded.

"How is that important?" said Bee. Bell just wrote in his notebook. Stills was clearly back in charge.

"Can you give us any names?"

Bee thought, shook her head. "It wasn't a scheduled

session. Training camp doesn't open for a couple of weeks. So it was just some guys. Sorry."

Stills nodded. "Other than that, was there anything going on? Did he have plans?"

There was only so much lying you could do before you got caught. The practice thing was true, and Stills seemed to know it. Bee was going to have to watch her step. She had a feeling she'd better start inching her way over into the truth lane. "This is the week he stays with his father," she said. "Once every couple of months."

"The parents are divorced?"

"Yeah. And his dad is . . . Well, he's an alcoholic and . . ."

Stills waited. "Yes, Ms. Northway?"

"They don't get along so well. So Turn, I mean Donovan, was going to tell his father that he wasn't going to see him anymore. Not until his father cleaned up his act."

That got Bell's nose out of his notebook.

"I see," said Stills. "And was this going to be difficult?"

Bee shrugged. "Donovan's old enough that he doesn't have any obligation to visit his father, let alone stay with him. He's stuck it out for a long time. He knew it was time, but . . . yeah, his father was likely going to make as big a deal of it as he could." Stills glanced over at her partner. "Listen," said Bee, "what does this have to do with Donovan's case? Somebody ran him down. His dad doesn't drive, so . . ."

Stills leaned forward and spoke very quietly. "All we'd like from you, Ms. Northway, is to let us know if Donovan said anything that might help us in our investigation."

Bee screwed up her face. "You mean something he saw when he was being hurled twenty feet through the air?"

"You just never know," said Stills.

As tired as Bee was, alarm bells were ringing inside her. She looked at Bell, who was leaning back in his chair, casual as could be, but there was nothing casual about his eyes, which were trained on her. What was this? Some kind of ambush? Why did it feel as if they *weren't* talking about the accident at all?

"Were you able to locate his father?"

That got a rise out of both of them.

"What makes you ask?" said Stills.

Bee shrugged. In theater class her favorite improv game was the one where you answered every question with a question. "What's going on?" said Bee.

"What has he said, Beatrice?"

"Why won't you answer me?"

Stills gazed at her steadily. "Ms. Northway, we are conducting an investigation. If you don't mind, we'd appreciate your answering the questions. Can you do that, please?"

Bee nodded woodenly. "He's mumbling," she said again, more convinced now than ever that she would keep what Donovan had said to herself. "Just noises, mostly pain."

From the expression on her face, Stills didn't believe her. Was it that obvious that she was hiding something? She folded her hands over her crossed knee.

"I'm sorry I can't help you," said Bee. "My boyfriend is in there dying and you want to know what was on his mind? As if . . . what? He was *looking* to get run over?"

She had raised her voice and a nurse passing by motioned with her hand to keep it down.

"Sorry," Bee whispered. Then turned to the detectives.

"Maybe I'm just really tired or something. Like freaked out, for instance. But I wish you'd let me in on whatever it is you're hiding from me."

"We're not hiding—"

"Yes, you are."

"Beatrice." Stills's voice was quiet, but she managed to turn Bee's name into a threat. "Excuse me. I am sorry for the awful situation in which you find yourself. But we've got work to do here. Trails can grow cold pretty quick. We're the ones asking the questions, okay? Do you get that?" She held up her hand to stop Bee from arguing. "Just answer me."

Bee nodded.

"A serious investigation is under way, and it is standard practice to keep sensitive information strictly on a need-to-know basis."

"A serious investigation of a hit-and-run," said Bee.

"That, yes. And another related crime."

Here it was. Bee tamped down a rising feeling of panic.

"We're just doing our job," said Bell, trying on the avuncular act again.

"And we are asking for your help," said Stills.

Bee swallowed. She was being obstinate. Obstreperous, her father would say. She lowered her eyes. "Sorry," she murmured. She was a girl who preferred being backstage, but she'd taken enough acting classes to manage a show of contrition. She looked up, swiped away a tear, and tried to look brave. The tear was real.

Stills's expression lightened, but only minimally. Her eyes were still hard, determined. "Donovan's mom is away?" Bee nodded. "With her boyfriend; is that right?"

"Scott," said Bee. "Her live-in boyfriend."

"Do they do this often?" said Stills. Bee was perplexed; it must have shown on her face. "Go off and leave Donovan with no contact information."

Bee's mouth gaped, then she caught herself and snapped it shut. She shook her head but didn't dare speak.

"Donovan's relationship with his father was troubled, from what you've said." Bee nodded hesitantly. "What was his relationship to his mother?"

"Excellent."

"And this boyfriend—"

"Scott," snapped Bee, interrupting the woman. "They've been together for, like, years."

"Okay."

"No, it isn't okay," said Bee. "This is ridiculous. It makes no difference where Trish or Scott are. You have a phone number for his birth father and can probably find his address—you're cops, after all. So something has happened to his father. Right?"

The detectives conferred, but this time it was a handoff. Stills nodded, frowning, and Bell sat up straight, tugged his slacks up at the knees. Then he flipped a few pages back in his spiral pad.

"Allen Ian McGeary. That the boy's father?" Bee nodded. He read out an address on Carling Avenue in Britannia, out in the west end. "Apartment number 304?"

Bee shrugged. "I've never been there, but that sounds right."

Bell closed the notebook. "Well, McGeary wasn't answering his phone because he'd had an accident, as well."

Bee could see in Bell's face that the word "accident" was a place saver, a euphemism. She turned to Stills, who looked as if she were trying to work up her youthful we're-in-this-together expression again. So Bee turned her attention back to Bell. "What kind of an accident?"

Bell held her gaze. "McGeary is dead," he said.

CHAPTER / SIX

There was broken glass everywhere. Beer bottles. Broken crockery that had once been a cheery polka-dot bowl. The floor was littered with popcorn, like a hailstorm indoors. His father's apartment. And Al sitting there in his La-Z-Boy looking up at him. Was that really fear in his eyes? Was he frightened of his own son? Good! About time! He loomed above his father, wanting to see him squirm—squirm and apologize. He had a baseball bat in his hand, a bat with a pulse of its own. Then suddenly his father's face cracked and he laughed. Just laughed.

They would come to the door, the lion or the leopard. They would see him sitting there, immobile, his arms pooled in his lap like some spineless Raggedy Andy. They would drag him inside and who knew what they would do to him: make him kneel before his father—kneel and apologize. Because now it all made some kind of mad and fantastic sense. The blanket-covered wreck in the Malibu, the stinking creature who had wandered off into the darkness ahead of him. His father. Passengers in the same car. Donovan shook his head.

No.

He had left his father's place in the west end. Run from him, from what he had done. And somehow he'd gotten all the way from Britannia in the west end to his home south of center town. And then left again. Just stepped into a car driven by a complete stranger.

His senses were shot.

The leopard called the man Murphy. Not his father's name. Not the name Donovan had changed to Turner, his mother's name, in an act of defiance that his father had shrugged off.

There was a roar from the lion and Donovan looked up expecting to see his face at the window. But there was no one there. The leopard was laughing. It sounded as if he'd just won another hand. The game was still on.

Donovan climbed slowly to his feet, and though every sensible bone in his body wanted him to get out of there, head back into the darkness, the least sensible bone in his body—the one between his ears—made him limp back to the window to that room, where the leopard was gathering the chips, where the lion shook his head and poured himself a generous helping of rye, and where Donovan's father rubbed sleep out of his eyes and slowly pushed his losing hand toward the dealer. There was blood on his shirt. Blood that had dribbled down from the cut on his chin, where he had fallen . . .

Al's chin smacked the edge of the glass coffee table and his head jolted back, toppling him over. The room swam and tumbled. Someone yelled at Donovan; his father's friend Rolly Pouillard, the apartment super. He couldn't hear a word Rolly said. Only the sound of the roaring inside his own head.

Donovan stepped drunkenly away from the kitchen window, bent down, his hands on his knees, then threw his back up straight again, afraid he would topple over headfirst and never stop falling. He rested his hands on his hips, a runner safe at second — only just — after a headlong slide.

He knew he should leave but he couldn't. He felt as if it were somehow out of his control. He was supposed to be here. *Back* here, where he'd been before, as a child. He shook his head and stumbled to the window a third time. Stared inside, saw his father's stunned face.

"You in?" said the leopard, leaning toward the man they called Murphy. He nodded, and the lion poured him a drink and Murphy downed it in one shot. His head trembled from the jolt of it, and he took a long breath and stared at the table with the eyes of a man who wasn't entirely sure where he was. It was an expression Donovan had seen too many times on his father's face to count.

"Read 'em and weep," said the leopard with that half smile on his face that wasn't really a smile but an accident.

Then Donovan heard a car. He ducked and turned in time to catch a fleeting glimpse of it on the side road before it disappeared behind the bulk of the shed. Quickly, on shaking legs, he made his way back to the storm cellar and crouched in the dark behind the bunker wall, holding his knees in tight to his chest. He had seen enough of the car to recognize it was a police cruiser.

The cruiser pulled into the yard and stopped near a mud-stained pickup. The driver turned off the engine. There were two officers, but neither moved. Donovan could see from the ambient light that the driver was radioing headquarters. Backup? Then the right side door opened slowly and the passenger cop stepped out. He was wearing a flak jacket. He looked carefully around, as if there might be snipers on the henhouse roof, the barn, the huge shed. Gunmen behind the dark skeletons of the farm machinery littered around the yard. His partner opened his door, got out, closed it quietly, and joined the other policeman in checking the yard. If the boys inside the farm had noticed they had visitors, none of them made an appearance.

Cautiously, their hands on their service pistols, the officers approached the kitchen door. They weren't crouching or sneaking up, just watchful, alert.

One of them stepped quietly onto the covered porch. He examined the boots lying on the decking, lightly toed one with his shoe and then looked back at the other cop, who nodded as if to say he'd noticed, too. He knelt down, pulling a penlight from his gadget belt to examine the boots more carefully. Then he flicked off the light, replaced it in its holster, and shook his head at his partner, the answer to an unasked question. He stood up. The leader rapped on the door, the passenger stood back at a good response distance. Donovan heard the sound of a chair scraping the floor, cowboy boots clumping across tired floorboards. Then the door opened inward. The light from the kitchen spilled out, animating the first cop's face. "Evening, Mervin," said the cop.

"Hey, if it isn't the boys in blue," said a deep voice with all the consonants worn off at the edges.

"Can we have a word?" said the cop.

"Kinda late for a social call."

"Just want to ask a question or two."

"Well, Jeezus H. Christ," said Mervin. "You guys and your questions."

The screen door reluctantly swung outward and Donovan saw the lion's thick-wristed arm hold it open. The first cop stepped into the room. His partner followed him in, letting the screen door snap shut behind him. And then the inner door closed. Donovan slipped from his hiding place and headed back to the open window. Part of his brain said to turn tail and run. But his aching foot vetoed the running part of that idea. And by now another voice in his head was saying, Let's face it, Dono, you're bat-shit crazy—this whole thing is crazy—but maybe somebody will say something enlightening and you will learn what the hell happened and why you are here and not in your bed asleep. So go listen. Get yourself arrested.

"Any you boys see the accident up on Seven?"

"Does it look like we been out and about?" said the leopard. He was leaning back in his chair, his hands out to his side all innocent-like and a snide look on his long-ago injured face.

"You didn't hear nothing?" asked the second cop.

"We heard a lot of moaning from our host here, Mr. Green," said the leopard, indicating the lion, who reoccupied his seat, which strained under his weight. They all got a laugh out of that, even Mr. Mervin Green.

"Bad night, Merv?" said the cop.

Merv took a swig of his whiskey, shrugged. "Might've been if we was playing for money. But that'd be gambling, Harry."

The lead cop chuckled and sniffed the air. "Smell that, Pete?"

The other cop nodded. "Oo-ee! What brand of tobacco you fellas smoking?"

Donovan noticed that the ashtrays were all empty now.

"If you're talking about illicit substances, I don't see none," said the leopard, not in the least perturbed. "But you're here 'bout an accident. What kind of accident would that be?"

"Guy flipped his car," said the lead cop, pointing north.

"Hurt?"

The cop nodded.

"Bad?" said Merv. He sounded hopeful, as if bad would be entertaining.

The cop nodded again. He'd been leveling his gaze at the three of them, one after the other, while his partner scanned the room, taking in the pizza boxes, the low fire in the wood-stove, the coats hanging by the door. He reached out, touched the sleeve of the nearest coat. Not wet. That's what he was doing. And now Donovan knew what the boot inspection had been about: looking for signs of mud. The third man at the table was resting on his arms, seemingly dead to the world.

"So, no liquor run? Nothing like that?"

"Hey, officer—" said the leopard, leaning forward so that the front legs of his chair made contact with a *clunk* on the floor. "Cameron," he said, reading the lead's name tag. "Have we met?"

"Harry Cameron," said Merv. "You remember Harry, Oscar."

"I remember a pip-squeak of a guy named Cameron back in high school," said Oscar, scratching the barbed wire around his wrist as if it were real. "In the stamp club, I think. Maybe the chess club? Think I stuffed him in his locker once."

Cameron chuckled. "Ya think?"

"You grown some since then."

"Grown a thick skin, Oscar."

Oscar chuckled.

Then Pete tried to get the conversation back on track. "About the accident," he said.

"Does it look like any of us is in a position to drive a vehicle?" said Oscar.

Constable Cameron piped up. "As I recall, Oscar, you've been known to drive under the influence."

The leopard nodded. "Damn straight. And I lost my license. When I got it back, I took the vow." Merv laughed out loud, a low, smoke-stained roar. The third player was roused from his sleep or inebriation or death—whatever it was he was dealing with. He stared at the table with such intensity it was as if his gaze were the only thing keeping it from floating away. Cameron noticed that, too.

"Don't know your friend here," he said.

"Murphy," said Oscar. He leaned across the table and poked the man in the arm. "Say hello to these here fine, upstanding law enforcement officers."

Murphy glanced up at the cop, who stood less than a yard away. He nodded in greeting and then resumed staring at the table.

"New in these parts, Murphy?" asked Cameron.

The man nodded. "He's just passing through," said Oscar. "Said he liked to play cards, and I said, 'Well, that's good, because I love to separate a man from his money.' "

Everyone laughed. Clearly the cops were not there about gambling—or weed, either, it seemed.

"This accident," said Oscar. "Something missing?"

Cameron stared at him sharply now, then turned to his partner with his eyebrow raised before returning his attention to the skinny man in the leopard-skin vest. "What makes you say that?"

Oscar smiled on both sides of his face, but it wasn't a pretty sight. "You said the guy was hurt bad. Sounded like maybe you meant dead." He rubbed his chin with his right hand. "And since you didn't mention no other car, just the one, at first I wondered if maybe you was looking for a witness. But now I don't think so."

"No?"

Oscar leaned back again, never taking his eyes off the

cop. "I'm reckoning you've got yourself a crime scene up there."

"Go on," said Cameron.

"Don't rush me," said Oscar. He looked at the cop, looked down at the chips piled high in front of him. "This guy get rumbled or what?"

Again, the cops exchanged glances, which made Oscar chuckle and rub his hands up and down his vest.

"As a matter of fact, it does look as if there is some merchandise missing. And you just guessed at that?" said Pete.

"Oscar's got the vision," said Merv, tapping his forehead.

"So what does your 'vision' tell you, Oscar?"

"That you guys think we had something to do with it, whatever *it* is."

Cameron tipped his head sideways. "Let's run with that, okay?"

"Come on, Constable," said Merv, picking up his cards and then throwing them back down, as if yet again he'd drawn baby numbers. "That ain't why the police are knocking at our door late on a Friday night."

"Really?"

"Well, you aren't exactly strangers," said Merv. "Always looking for an excuse to drop by anytime, day or night." He sniffed. Picked up his cigarette pack and tapped one out.

"He's right," said Oscar. "Weren't no 'accident' brought you here."

Cameron accepted the challenge, chin up. Then he turned his attention to Murphy.

"You know anything about it?" he asked. Murphy didn't

acknowledge the question. "Hey," said Cameron. He poked the man's shoulder. Murphy flinched but didn't look up.

"Your friend here stoned?" said Cameron, turning to Oscar.

"He's just a quiet one, officer. Leave him be." He reached across the table and patted Murphy's hand, which lay there, holding a red chip between his thumb and finger. There was red on his thumb, too, as if it were the chip that was leaking blood, not the man.

"Which one of these good ole boys gave you the bloodied chin?" Cameron asked.

"Hey!" said Merv, pushing himself away from the table. "You don't come in my house accusing us of violence, you hear? Does it look like there's been any kind of fight here?"

"Calm down," said Oscar. Then he looked at Cameron. "Murphy's been with Merv and me the whole time. He got himself a bloodied chin before he arrived, cleaned it up, and it opened again. Nobody's been taking shots at nobody. I can vouch for that."

Cameron smiled and turned to his partner. "Take note of that. Oscar Shouldice just 'vouched' for the validity of a statement he made."

Now Merv really growled, deep down in his chest, and shook his lion's mane.

"You got something you want to add?" said Cameron, looking at the lion. The constable had his thumbs tucked in the front of his belt and his fingers were beating out a little rhythm on his shiny pressed pants: busy fingers wanting something to do, something to wrap themselves around. The top of his gun holster was unbuckled.

"We didn't *see* nothing. We didn't *do* nothing," said Merv. "You got no call to be here."

He was about to say more, but Constable Cameron held up his hand, stopped him. "Hold your water, Merv. We're just asking around. No cause to get perturbed."

"Huh," said Oscar. "I think my good buddy Mr. Mervin Green here thinks this is looking a whole lot like harassment."

Cameron stared at Shouldice, who stared right back at him, unblinking.

Oscar Shouldice and Mervin Green: the cops knew these guys by name. A den of thieves, thought Donovan. But there was someone missing, wasn't there? He shook his head. He'd been here and there was . . . there was someone else. No. He couldn't get to it. Just thieves and a hitchhiker with a bloodied chin. A hitchhiker who suddenly raised his head and stared again toward the window. Donovan backed away. He didn't think he made any sound, but the last voice he heard from the window was Constable Cameron's.

"Anyone else around?" he said.

Oh shit!

That was Donovan's cue, but for a moment he couldn't move. It was if he were standing in mud. The will was there but no strength. Finally, he made his legs work and hustled back to the storm cellar entrance. He threw himself down behind the bunker just as the door opened, first the real door, then the screen. A gust of wind stirred up last fall's dead leaves nobody had gotten around to raking. A loose section of gutter rattled overhead. Donovan clenched his fists and held his breath. The door closed. Donovan breathed again.

After a moment, he checked, keeping his head low, to make sure it wasn't a ruse—the officer only pretending to reenter the house. The porch was empty, but Donovan had heard enough to know that hanging around was far from a good idea. And getting himself arrested wasn't really anything he was prepared to do just yet. It would require giving up, and he couldn't do that. Something deep inside his injured body told him to hold firm, get a grip. There was something pressing that he had to do. He just couldn't recall what it was.

He slunk back the way he'd come, staying tight to the house. Then he sprinted, as fast as he could on his gimpy ankle, back to the trash heap. He'd have been tagged out easy, running like that. Sent back to the dugout with his tail between his legs. He crawled behind the rusted pile of clutter. If they came looking, they'd find him. There was nowhere else to go other than back to the woods, and no energy to get there anyway. There was a broken-down fence to clamber over and the swamp beyond that and a stretch of lonely highway. He couldn't go back. It was not an option. And going forward didn't seem like much of one, either. A trash heap, in fact, seemed about the most fitting place to be.

CHAPTER SEVEN

Bee seldom cried. She loved theater but she didn't have much time for drama. She was happier solving other people's emotional meltdowns than having them herself. Her mother was a shrink; maybe she got it from her, but she didn't want to be a therapist or a counselor. She was a stage manager. Which meant, as far as she was concerned, making sure no one ever had to have a meltdown in the first place—not on her set. She anticipated disaster. She adapted quickly. When an actor's brain went off-line, she was there with the missed cue. On her stool backstage in the corner with her headset on, she called the show, her voice calm and secure, her manner deliberate, her directions precise. Other people could have the spotlight. She was happy to be the one to make sure it was focused in exactly the right place.

But she cried now. No histrionics, little more than a hiccup to start it off, but that seemed to open the floodgates. She sat there, back straight, and let her tears wash her tired face.

Again, Bell was there with the box of tissues, and Bee hungrily pressed tissue after tissue against her leaking eyes, her leaking nose.

She muttered a thank-you and covered her face with her hands to hide from Bell and Stills, who took up a station across from her. She wanted to count to a hundred, look up, and find them gone.

Hide-and-seek. That's what this was going to be now.

"Drink some water, kid," said Bell. She took a bottle from him — who knew where it came from — and did as she was told. "I'm sorry to be the one who had to break it to you."

Bee sniffed. Stared at the two of them. Sensed that with Stills, there might be a veneer of concern, but piling up behind it was an avalanche of questions.

"What happened?" said Bee.

"That's what we're trying to sort out."

"Must have come as a shock," said Bell. "But you didn't know him well?"

Bee shook her head. Sniffed. "No. Like I said, I've only met him a couple of times. It's not that." She blew her nose. What was it? He was a drunk, a waste of time, but Donovan stuck religiously to the custody arrangements made for him when he was just a kid, when Al was still a working newspaperman and capable of something like responsible conduct. Now he was dead. And Donovan was hanging by a thread to life. It was a rainy spring night, April the fifteenth, and people were dropping all over the place.

And there were those words in her journal.

Not just Donovan's but her own, from before: her worries for Turn, her fears. It was, after all, her journal, a place where a girl could pour out her most troubling concerns.

That brought her around. She became aware of Callista Stills's hand, filled with more fresh tissues, hovering near her face. New tissues for old. The detective gently uncurled Bee's fingers, took the soggy paper mass from her, and replaced it.

"Thanks," said Bee. "I'm sorry."

"It's a lot to take in," said Stills. She managed a tight little smile, then walked off to locate a garbage can and some hand sanitizer. She returned, took her seat across from Bee, close enough that Bee could smell the medicinal odor of the sanitizer. "Can we go on?" she asked.

Bee nodded. Didn't have the energy to obstruct them right now. But she would be on her guard.

Bell picked up where he had left off. "From what we can tell, Donovan arrived at his father's apartment around eight o'clock. You say he was at a baseball practice?"

"Yeah. Britannia Park. It's about a mile from his dad's apartment."

Bell nodded and added a note. "He left the apartment about a half hour, forty-five minutes later, and then came *back* around nine thirty, somewhere in there. Were you in contact with him at any point? Did he phone?"

Wait. What was that? Bee stared at him, her forehead drawn. This sounded odd. Why would he leave and come back? Her gaze drifted to Stills. Then she slowly shook her head. They waited. She sniffed, cleared her throat. "He'd never phone me at work."

"Even if there was an emergency of some kind?"

"My cell phone is off-limits at work. I mean I can phone him on my break. I just can't take calls. It's the rule. If there was a real emergency, I guess he could phone Bridgehead—the coffee shop where I work. He's never done it." She looked from one to the other of them, suspicion blooming. "You guys have his phone. You could see if there had been any calls."

"The battery was low, near dead. He got your text message somehow, but he didn't make any calls out," said Bell.

"But Donovan could have contacted you some other way," said Stills. "Or come and talked to you, work or no work."

"He didn't."

"You talking about the Bridgehead in the Glebe?" Bee nodded. "It's what? Six or seven blocks to Wilton Crescent from there?"

Bee nodded. "You can ask at work. Ask anyone. He didn't come there tonight—I mean, last night." Again Stills held her gaze as if waiting for her to crack, but Bee was thinking about something else—something Bell had said. Another clue.

"How do you know any of this?" she said, deliberately turning her attention to the sergeant.

"Excuse me?"

"His comings and goings. When he got there, when he left?"

"There are witnesses," said Bell.

"Witnesses," said Bee. "As in plural?"

"Uh-huh. But we're looking for corroboration."

Bee's hands dropped to her lap, like two birds falling from the sky from one shotgun blast. She looked up at the detectives, shaking her head. "Silly me. And here I thought you were looking for some maniac who ran Donovan over and left him for dead. Now he's suddenly the chief suspect in a murder investigation?"

"Nobody said that."

"He was murdered. His dad, I mean."

"Nobody said that, either."

Bee gave up. They weren't going to budge.

"Bee, Donovan was there in the apartment. *Anyone* who was there is a suspect until we can clear them."

"And who else was there?" said Bee.

Stills ignored her. "Ms. Northway, we don't know very much."

"That's for sure."

The outburst earned Bee another full-on glare. She threw up her hands to either side of her head but wasn't about to apologize.

"We are still looking into the hit-and-run," said Bell. "It's a major crime. But we can't ignore the connection."

"Fine," Bee said, and threw herself back against the hard surface of the seat. You want petulance as a side order to obstreperous hostility? Got it. She glanced at Stills and then looked away toward the picture window, the lights of the city, the wet blackness of the early morning long before light.

Stills got up from her chair and squatted in front of Bee, nose to nose, or at least it felt that way. "It's our job—Jim's and mine, plus a whole crew of crime scene investigators—to figure out the connections, if there are any. It's what we do, okay?" Her voice was low, even. "Sometimes we have to get up in a person's face about it. I don't want to do it that way. But you've been resistant, defensive. And that only makes us wonder why."

Bee looked down at a tear in the tangerine-colored plastic of the chair. She wanted to say she wasn't being defensive but stopped herself. It was one of those things you can't say. Way too lame. So she rejoined the staring match with Stills. No blinking. No bursting into hysterical laughter. No screaming. Stare her down, if you can. Don't let her know about the journal with Donovan's words copied out in it. Don't let her know what else lurks in that journal. Don't think about the damn journal.

Bell piped up, his gravelly baritone cooling things down a bit. "We have reason to believe Donovan was very mad at his father."

"Who told you that?" Bee said, then immediately rolled her eyes. "Sorry, I forgot. I'm the one answering the questions."

"So . . . ?"

"His father's a scuzzbag."

"*Was* a scuzzbag," said Stills.

Then Bell said, "Anything change lately? Any escalation in the hostilities that you know of?"

Bee crossed her arms. Wanted to shake her head. Couldn't.

"You mentioned Donovan was going to talk to him about not visiting anymore," said Stills. "How was that likely to go down?"

Bee shrugged. "It wasn't likely to go down well, but if

you mean would it end in violence, I honestly don't think so."

"Donovan not prone to temperamental outbursts?" Bee waited one second too long before she looked away. "What is it?" said Stills.

"Nothing."

Stills sighed. "I think we can both agree that that's not true."

"Beatrice," said Bell gently, fulfilling his good-cop role. "We've got a chaotic crime scene. We've got witnesses to say there was more than one violent interchange."

Bee turned her attention back to Bell. "Well, what do you want from me, then? I wasn't there. Like I said, check at work if you don't believe me."

"We're not suggesting you were," said Bell.

"But you seem pretty sure he was in touch with me."

"We have to look at every angle," the sergeant continued. "There are discrepancies in the information we've been able to gather so far. Time problems. There's room for doubt. And what we want from you is any help—any information at all—that might clear Donovan."

"Or point the finger at him."

"Enough!" said Stills. She stood up to her full height but didn't step back so she loomed over Bee. "Do you know anyone else who might have had reason to harm McGeary?"

This was something else. Something new. Bee wanted to say anyone who met him might want to do him harm, but she figured this was not a time for flippancy. The man was dead. She looked up at Stills, her eyes sharp and waiting. "I think his girlfriend was leaving him." Stills nodded, but not as if she knew this already. It was a nod that said go on.

"Donovan's father goes—*went*—through a lot of girlfriends, but this one had been around awhile."

Bell was writing. Whoever they'd talked to hadn't said anything about this.

"You know her name?" he asked, his pen poised over his notebook.

She thought. It was something dumb. "Kali," she said. That was it.

"Last name?"

Bee thought. "Something Irish. O'Connell, maybe? No, O'Connor."

Bell wrote the name down. Stills continued, "Good. Thank you. Anyone else?"

Bee tried to think. There were a number of characters Turn had described in his father's merry band of losers. But they were *friends,* weren't they? She pounded her forehead lightly with the heel of her closed palm. No one came to mind.

"Sorry," she said. "I can't think of anyone else, but he could be really nasty." She swallowed. "He was good with words. No, that isn't it. He wasn't *good* with words; more like a suicide bomber with words strapped to his body. When he went off, people could die. Oh . . . I'm sorry. I guess that wasn't appropriate."

"Go on," said Stills.

Bee sighed and then remembered something Turn had said to her. "Apparently, Al was good about ditching people, but he didn't like people ditching him. Maybe things really went bad with Kali."

Stills tipped her head to the side, questioning.

"What?" said Bee.

"Or Donovan?"

"What do you mean?"

"Well, wasn't Donovan ditching him, in a sense?"

Bee pressed her lips tight together. She felt swindled.

"If, as you say, McGeary didn't like people leaving him, then how's he going to take to his son pulling the plug?"

Suddenly, Bee was spent. Couldn't go on. It must be close to four by now, she thought. Her head fell forward on her chest and her hair formed a curtain covering her face. She closed her eyes.

"Bee?"

"I'm done," she said. Then she realized she wasn't done. She wasn't going to field any more questions, but there was something she needed to say. She cleared the curtain of hair from her face, tucking it behind her ears. "Donovan really puts a lot into being a gentleman. His dad was smart, educated— whatever—but he'd become this sarcastic, mocking, totally foul human being. Donovan was all about taking the high road. His father would play on that. See if he could rile him. But Donovan was onto him. He knew what his dad was doing. He would just ride it out. You know?"

The nod from Bell was way too hesitant. There was no nod at all from Stills. She had been walking around, but now she resumed her chair across from Bee, beside her partner. Her face was stony.

"What?" said Bee. Then she wished she hadn't.

Bell closed his spiral notebook and put it in his sports- jacket pocket. He clicked his ballpoint closed and stuffed it in the breast pocket of his shirt. The two detectives rose.

"Thanks for your help," said Sergeant Bell, trying to

sound upbeat and missing it by a mile. "I hope Donovan's condition improves."

Stills nodded. And then they walked away. But she stopped and turned around. "If he says anything, I trust you'll let us know." Then she walked back to Bee and handed her a card she seemed to produce from thin air. INSPECTOR CALLISTA STILLS it read. She gazed at Bee, waiting for a reply. Instead, Bee shifted her gaze to Bell.

"Have you got a card, too?" she said.

It was a calculated gesture of pique. Bee wasn't quite sure what had made her do it. Bell, meanwhile, fished in his pocket and came over with his card.

"Thank you, Staff Sergeant," said Bee. She never once looked at Stills, but the inspector's glare was leaving scorch marks on her cheek.

Bell stepped back as Bee pocketed the two cards.

The inspector leaned in very close to Bee's ear, as if to share an intimate secret. "We *will* be in touch," she said.

CHAPTER EIGHT

There must have been a cool wind coming out of somewhere because dropping down behind the garbage pile, Donovan began to feel something like warm. He had heard once that when you had hypothermia, the last thing that happened before you froze to death was that you began to feel good and toasty. He was too exhausted and beat up to feel anything like euphoria, but he'd take this feeling right now over shuddering any day, whatever the consequences. He leaned back against a forty-gallon barrel. It must have been full because it didn't shift with his weight, only sloshed a bit. Rainwater, he guessed. He closed his eyes, took in a long, slow breath, and let it out, felt almost at peace. Glad to be off his feet. At least he wasn't running anymore and he could take stock, try to make sense of those fleeting glimpses brought on by seeing Al at the card table—glimpses of what must have happened back at his apartment. They began to coalesce into images. Like Polaroid photographs, the glimpses gaining more color and detail the longer he held them steady in his mind's eye, until bit by bit he was able to string together something of the story.

He had been at his father's place, out in Britannia. He still visited him, wasn't sure why. It wasn't court mandated anymore. Maybe he had thought he could change his father. He wouldn't be the first misguided son with a messiah complex. The thing was, his father was changing *him*. It had taken Bee to recognize it, to see what the visits did to him.

"I'm not saying stop seeing him," she'd said. "But you need some help, Turn. You need to talk to someone."

It was his temper.

"You're not afraid of me, are you?" he'd said.

"Not at all," she'd said. "I'm afraid *for* you."

So he'd made up his mind. He'd make the break. He didn't need a therapist to tell him the old man was bad news. "I'll do it," he'd said. "This week. You wait. Dad and I will have The Talk." The look in her eyes was not encouraging. "You don't think I'm up to it?"

"Weren't you the one who said nobody dumps your father and gets away with it?"

"It's an ego thing," he told her. "He turns it around so he's the one doing the dumping. Either way—dumper or dumpee—I'm out from under. *Finito. Hasta la vista.*" He had dusted his hands as if, after all these years, it was all going to be as easy as a lob to first for the final out. Bee wasn't so sure. He should have listened to her.

Because he and Al didn't really talk anymore.

Funny YouTube videos, action movies, draft choices, and player deals: a truly rich relationship. For instance, Donovan never brought up the twelve-step program that always stalled for his father at step number two: recognizing a higher power that could restore sanity. The highest power Al McGeary recognized was Al McGeary.

"See someone, Turn," said Bee on the phone during her work break. He had been at the park. Spring training. That's when he saw his cell battery was low. "Gotta run," he said.

He played in an adult baseball league, tier one, the youngest player on his team. Their season didn't start till May, but a few of the guys had gotten together under the lights out at Britannia Park, smacking balls around, digging the winter out of their bones. He was going to talk to his father when he got back.

"Sounds ominous," his father had said that morning.

"Just be here."

"Where else would I be?" said Al.

"I mean be here and sober."

"Now it really sounds ominous."

"I'm serious."

"Got it."

"Sober."

"As a proverbial judge."

So Donovan had gone straight to his father's from practice, walked in sometime around eight, and heard the laughter: a party.

Shit.

He leaned his forehead against the hall closet door. Turned out it was just one other person, but that was one person too many, Dad's friend Rolly. Dad and Rolly were three sheets to the wind. Which meant six sheets to the wind between the two of them. That was a lot of sheets.

But "sheets to the wind" was too fresh an image to describe the kind of inebriation these two could get themselves into. Donovan had once found a book with 2,231 synonyms for being drunk. There were some good ones: "Sir Richard has taken off his considering cap" was maybe his favorite. "He's kissed black Betty" was another. Donovan was pretty sure he'd seen 2,231 examples of his father soused. Anyway, when he got to the door of 304, Al was good and glazed, glazed and segued, half-canned, round the corner, and in uncharted waters. In a word, gone.

And it wasn't as if Donovan cared anymore. Not really. If he'd been able to think about it rationally, he might even have seen how eloquent his father was being. You want a father-son talk? Here's what I think about that.

He should have just left.

What had he been thinking?

Al made some off-color joke and Rolly laughed like someone in the last stages of emphysema.

Donovan's heart banged against his ribs dangerously.

Get out of here. Split! Don't even stop to collect your shit.

He'd go to Bridgehead and wait for Bee to get off work. No. Not an option. Anyone else could chat up the baristas, just not boyfriends.

Peals of laughter from the front room.

Go to Bridgehead anyway. To hell with the rules! Buy a maple macchiato, get yourself a cream mustache and go all Clark Gable on her . . .

"Breaking news, Rolly. The lad is leaving me."

Donovan's attention was dragged back to the moment. "What's that?"

"Donny T. He's throwing me over. Clearing out."

"*Non.*"

"Ah, *oui,* Monsieur Pouillard. At least that's what I think he's got up his sleeve. Assuming he can find the balls to do it."

"I had not known things were so bad."

"Bah! Things are what they are. He's high-strung, like his mother. For all his brawn, he's really a mama's boy." Al stopped, sucked on the neck of his bottle—Donovan could hear him, hear the glugging, the sigh of contentment, the burp. "You can bet *she's* behind it, Rolly. The whole thing reeks of one of Mama Trisha's stratagems. Consolidating her moral victory."

Don't wait to hear where this is going. You think he didn't hear you come in?

"Here's to Trisha the Virtuous," slurred Dad. There was the tink of bottle necks, more glugging, and then he said, "Yep, this is definitely one of the old girl's cunning stunts."

Rolly's death rattle of a laugh followed. "Cunning stunts, eh?" he said.

"You betcha," said Al. "That's my ex for you, such a stunning—"

"Shut up!"

Donovan wasn't sure how he'd gotten there, but there he was, all six foot two of him, standing over his father in his easy chair.

"Hey, it's Downtown Donny T. You whack another one out of the park, sonny boy?"

"Shut it, Al. Just shut the fuck up."

"I was asking how your practice —"

"I heard what you were saying."

"Uh-oh," said Rolly, backing up into the dining area.

"Not sure what you're getting at, Donovan."

"What you called Mom."

His father raised his arm as if it weighed a ton. He waved his hand in the air. "Didn't call her anything."

"You were just about to."

"Oh, that. Hey, an old joke. A little play on words. Get over yourself."

And the bat came down.

Smashing the bowl of popcorn on the table beside the La-Z-Boy.

"What the —"

And the bat came down on the beer bottles.

"Jesus!"

And the bat came down on his father's crystal whiskey glass so hard that a piece of it pinged off the TV screen across the room.

His father's hands grabbed the arms of his chair and he leaned toward his son, his face a ferocious red — a junkyard dog at the end of its chain. And then, just as suddenly, his muscles went slack and a lazy smile creased his face. "Oh golly. Did I forget about our little talk?" He smacked himself in the forehead and then threw himself back in his chair, laughing his drunken head off.

Donovan stood there. He'd finished last season batting .315. He was stronger now—had hot hands, and right this minute they were hotter than anything.

Al leaned forward, all condescension and brass. "What's on your mind, son," he said, and the look on his face was calculated, a come-on, a dare.

"Apologize," said Donovan, his voice shaky but not his resolve.

"You're the one breaking things, as Rolly is my witness."

"Apologize," said Donovan. He took his eyes off his father just long enough to glare at Rolly. Rolly was smart enough to keep his mouth shut.

Donovan stepped closer to his father, leaned in close. "Stamp your foot twice, Al, if you get what I'm saying."

Thunk!

Donovan awoke to the sound of a door closing, startling him back into the land of the living—or this facsimile of it. A moon had appeared from somewhere, a good-size moon, remarkably similar to the one he regularly took for granted in that other land he occupied up until . . . was it only a few hours ago?

He sat listening. Would he even hear footsteps on the spring-wet grass, the soggy blanket of dead leaves? He turned, careful not to make a racket, and on his knees peeked through a chink in the trash-pile wall. No one.

He turned back, wrapped his arms tight around his chest. He had drifted off. He was shivering, but it was only partially from the cold. His heart was beating so hard he was afraid it might bust right out of him. He turned again toward the farmhouse, afraid someone might hear his heart and come looking for him. Do him in. Undo him. That's why he was here, wasn't it? This was the Country of Payback. He threw himself hard against the cold steel drum. Water sloshed out and trickled, freezing, down his neck. He struggled to catch his breath. Struggled to calm himself down. He sat there feeling the cold water seep into the elastic band of his underwear. He closed his eyes and willed himself back to his father's apartment in the city, made himself watch what happened next.

CHAPTER NINE

His father hurled himself up out of his chair and Donovan sprang back, but he needn't have. The old man teetered there, as if standing on the bow of a ship in a storm. Then his eyes rolled back into his head until there was nothing but blood-shot white and he went down like a sack of flour.

His chin caught the edge of the coffee table, hurling his head back. And there he lay on the carpet amid the unseasonal snowfall and shards of broken crockery and glass, his arms flung outward but the rest of his body all cramped up between his chair and the heavy coffee table.

"Dad?"

The bat dropped from Donovan's hand and he dug his cell phone out of his pocket. "Shit!" Low battery. He turned to Rolly, who was staring at his friend with his tongue between his teeth, as if there were something wrong with the picture but he'd be damned if he could figure out what.

"Rolly! We've got to phone 911."

Rolly tore his attention away from Al to refocus as best he could on Donovan. When he finally had him in his sights, he glared. *"Tabernac,"* he said. "Look what you done."

Then Al groaned and they both turned their gaze on him. His hand lifted feebly from the floor and gesticulated, then fell back again.

"Your phone, Rolly," said Donovan. Rolly patted his pockets, shook his head. "Then where's Al's? He's having a heart attack, for Christ's sake."

Rolly held up his hand like the world's saddest traffic cop. "It's not his ticker," he said.

"But he—"

"His ticker's fine!" shouted Rolly. Shouting made him lose his balance, and he reached out a hand for the dining room table to steady himself. The empty bottles sitting there jiggled. "He just stood up too fast. I see it before."

Donovan stared at his father, who was still breathing. He wanted to believe Rolly, but he didn't think Rolly had worked in the ER anytime recently.

"I'll go phone," said Donovan.

"Yeah, you go," said Rolly, flinging his arm out in the general direction of the door. "You done enough damage 'round here." Donovan stared at the man. He was finally moving, shuffling like he was eighty instead of forty-something, shuffling around the couch toward Al. He glanced at Donovan and shook his head. "You got some nerve, kid, talking at your old man like that."

Donovan stepped backward. Felt dizzy, stopped. Looked again at his father. Blood trickled down Al's unshaven chin onto his T-shirt. But then his eyes flickered open, took in his son, looked him up and down. Donovan watched a grin worm its way onto his father's face.

"Vamoose!" said Rolly.

But Donovan only stared. And then he went to his father, knelt beside him, and whispered in his ear. The words weren't for Rolly to hear, just his dad. "You got that, Dad?" he said. His father nodded slowly.

"*Fiche le camp!*" Rolly shouted.

And Donovan got to his feet, shaking.

"Back to mama," said Al, waving. "That's a good boy."

"I'll handle this," said Rolly, who had taken Donovan's place at his father's side. He wrapped his arm under Al's shoulder to lift his limp torso into a seated position.

And Donovan left, slammed the door behind him, good and hard so that it echoed down the hall. He ran—couldn't get out of there quickly enough.

He heard a door open, the next-door neighbor no doubt; the one who called the cops whenever the noise level got too high in 304. Donovan didn't turn to look. He crashed through the door to the stairwell. The elevators took forever and he just wanted out.

Thunk!

Another door. On his knees again, Donovan peered through his spy hole. A woman, silhouetted by the yard light, walked from the big shed toward the house. She stopped before she reached the porch and turned to look in his direction, as if she had heard something. He cringed—curled in on himself. She couldn't possibly see him, could she? When he dared to look again, she was still staring his way, and the yard light gave her whole body an aura, like a full-on halo.

Then she turned toward the house, climbed the steps to the porch, and entered. The screen door opened, the kitchen door opened. The screen door shut, the kitchen door shut. And Donovan was alone again.

He took a deep breath and resumed his seat, his back against the oil drum. Then he gasped, went cold all over. Not five yards away stood a man. He had his back to Donovan, staring out toward the forest, his arms limp at his sides, a long moon-shadow off to his left. Donovan sat perfectly still. Had the man heard his intake of breath? It didn't look like it. Had he walked right past the trash heap without seeing Donovan there, another piece of wrecked machinery?

Donovan's hand moved carefully to his right, where the broken handle of a spade stood like a rotten tooth. He wrapped his fist around it, lifted it slowly, quietly. He turned his attention to the weapon, enough to see that the spade was still attached, rusted and chipped but heavy enough. Then the shovel dislodged something that clanked, and when Donovan looked up, the man had turned to face him. He walked toward Donovan, shuffling drunkenly. He was wearing saggy sweatpants and a short-sleeved T-shirt, and Donovan knew who he was even without being able to see much of his face. In the light of the right bracket of the moon, he recognized that stumbling gait, the body left to go to seed.

"Dad," he said, but the man did not answer. Then, as he

grew nearer and nearer, Donovan gasped again and drew his knees in tight to his chest. His father stopped two paces away and stared down at the boy in the trash heap.

"Here, let me help you out," said the man. He shoved his hand into his pocket and pulled out a lighter. He lit it and held the flame up to his face, the better to see the damage there. This was not Murphy, the cardplayer. This was not the man he had left in apartment 304 back in the city. He was battered beyond recognition, his nose a bloodied stump, an eye caved in, livid bruises. His father lifted his hand to his mouth and cupped it there. Then his lips parted and three teeth tumbled out into his waiting palm. He closed his fist on the teeth and then threw them aside.

"This is your work," he said.

"No!" said Donovan.

"Sure it is. Was your bat did it."

"No. I never —"

"It's what you wanted."

"I ran. Ran away."

"But you came back."

"No!"

"Yes!"

"Not to do that."

"Then what? To apologize."

"Yeah . . . Yes."

Al laughed, shook his head. The action made his body falter. It looked for a moment as if he might fall, and Donovan drew himself in tighter. Then his father clicked his lighter shut, shoved it into his pocket, leaned forward, his hands on his knees. "You can't take back what you said, you know. What you whispered to me, all private and personal—just for my ears. You can't ever take that back."

"No," said Donovan. He shook his head. "But I didn't do *that* to you." He pointed at his father's face, his arm shaking.

"Sure you did." Though his words were garbled, there was humor in his voice and a moon glint in his one remaining eye. "There were even witnesses. Remember?"

And instantly, Donovan did.

He was back in the apartment again, alone with the corpse of his father. He was standing, staring at the body of this man lying, not on the floor the way he'd left him, but on his La-Z-Boy, reclined all the way back, his body contorted, his face a hideous shambles—a World War I landscape—his jawbone cracked, his cheekbone poking through. A face from a nightmare. Then the apartment door flew open and Kali walked in. Kali and some stranger. Kali stopped and covered her mouth with her hands to stifle a scream.

The apartment went out like the lighter had done a moment earlier. There was just the two of them again, him and his father.

"I didn't do it!" Donovan cried. "I didn't touch you!"

"The bat, Dono," said his father.

The bat. His bat. It had been leaning there against the coffee table, its sides wet with gore.

"But . . ."

"You can run all you like, son, but you can't outrun the truth." Then his father took the lighter from his pocket again and flicked it on for one last look. That's what Dono thought he was up to, but instead his father was scanning the ground.

"Where'd you put it?" he said.

"Put what?"

"The money."

"I—"

"Don't bother lying to me. I don't want it all. Just some. Just . . . just enough." His father straightened up, as best he could, and stared at Donovan. "I need it, okay?"

Donovan shifted aside, got shakily to his knees, turned, and lifted the rotten piece of particleboard upon which he'd been sitting. He dug out the briefcase, opened it, turned it toward his father, and then moved away a yard or so. The lighter picked out a distorted smile. Al kneeled before the briefcase and grabbed a handful of bills, shoving them in the pocket of his sweats.

"Just because you're dead," he said, "doesn't mean you don't need this stuff."

"I'm not dead," said Donovan.

"Who said I was talking about you?"

Donovan swallowed, watched his father take another handful of cash. He watched the breeze grab at it greedily, and some of the bills flew off into the night before Al could shove the bundle into his pocket.

"This is how you know you're in hell," said Al. He held up another bundle of hundreds, shaking them at Dono. He chuckled. "You can bet if there's a heaven, the angels don't have pockets."

He stopped. Maybe his own pockets were full or he'd just had enough. He climbed to his feet, almost pitching forward, regained his balance. He stared at Donovan one more time, shaking his head, then, flicking off the lighter, he turned, stood for a moment, swaying as if the wind might be enough to knock him over, before shambling toward the forest, the swamp.

Laughing.

He was laughing. Donovan watched until he couldn't see him anymore, until he faded into the darkness. Even then he could hear the laughter. Then nothing.

"I killed him," said Donovan to no one.

Somewhere in the night an owl called. He guessed it was an owl. Something out hunting. He listened. Imagined some scurrying rodent squealing as its feet left the ground, squealing at the rush of air under huge wings, squealing and writhing just before its back snapped under a powerful beak.

CHAPTER TEN

Bee stood there as Inspector Stills and Sergeant Bell waited for the elevator, neither of them looking back at her. What had changed? The elevator dinged and chugged open. Then it closed on the detectives, dinged again, and was gone. She tried to put together the lengthy sequence of questions and her responses, the knowing looks from one to the other, the sudden coolness when she'd explained to them about Donovan being a gentleman and taking the high road. There had been violence: "a chaotic scene," Bell had called it. There was something they'd said—something at the center of her unease—something that tied these random thoughts together. What was it?

He plays ball.

Bell had glanced at Stills then, and she had nodded. Nodded gravely.

She told Donovan all about it. She sat in the twilight of the ICU, leaning forward in her chair, her voice level and pitched low. Keeping it cool. No drama. Poor guy didn't need any more drama. But he did need to know where things stood in case he had something to say.

"I believe in you, Turn," she said. "Trust me. Let me help you."

She watched him for any sign of understanding. Nothing. So she talked on, told him everything the detectives had said, everything they had insinuated, let him know the score, counting on his fighting spirit to rally.

"Give me something to go on," she said. "I'll do the rest."

He was not at peace. He was motionless, but beyond the bruises and abrasions on his face, she saw that he was troubled.

"Whatever happened, Turner, I'm on your side." She said it over and over again. Nights and days went by, months, years, millennia. For, after all, they were not on the earth anymore, but in a windowless space capsule circling the globe in minutes.

"If you can hear me at all and if there's anything I need to know, I'm listening."

She waited, to no avail. There was no flicker of an eyelid, no minute raising of a finger from the bright-white sheets. No low groan she might interpret as "I hear you."

"You did not hurt your father," she said. "Okay? I know that about you. That isn't what happened. Do you hear me?"

Her gaze drifted to the green calligraphy readout, as if it might actually spell out a denial. "You are alive" was all it said. Some consolation.

Had he really rested his head in the palm of her hand earlier? Probably not. She offered him her hand again, gently stroked his cheek. He neither welcomed it nor turned away.

But words did come from time to time. She began to think she could see them forming in his face. See his lips quiver as he prepared to speak. The same words she'd heard earlier, words not much different than swallows and whimpers—with way more vowels than consonants. Her father had torn his rotator cuff a couple of years back, and for months he would utter little moans when he forgot and reached too high for something on a shelf or tried to tuck in his shirt. "Uh"s and "Ow"s and "Argh"s. Sometimes he would spontaneously groan handing a bowl of pasta across the table. She wished her father were there right now. Both of her parents. She had never felt so alone. So far away from home.

"Ji-uh," he said.

Bee was jarred back to full consciousness.

"Ji-uh?" she asked, reaching into her bag for her journal.

He seemed almost to shake his head. "Ji-eee," he said.

She wrote it down and underlined it. "Go on, Turner. Anything, okay?"

"Ji," he said.

"Okay," she said. "Jim?"

He thrashed weakly, but enough to make his point. She went through the alphabet: jia . . . jib . . . jic . . . jid . . . jiff . . . jig . . . Jill—"

"Jill!" he said, pouncing on the word. She had to imagine the *L*s but they were there.

"Jill," he said again. And then nothing. Another few earth orbits. "Ji-eee."

"Got it," she said. She leaned close to him. "I'm writing this all down," she told him. "Everything you say, Turn."

She listened and watched and saw his lips move. "Jill."

"Jill?" she asked.

"Jill-eee," he said, as if correcting her.

And she said, "Jilly?"

His eyes flickered. She gasped as if "Jilly" might be the Open Sesame word. But his lids didn't open. Instead, he went still again. Exhausted.

Bee was no longer tired. Her circadian rhythms did their thing, reminding her that twenty-four hours earlier, she had woken up to her phone's irritating alarm. Five o'clock. She'd kicked off the covers after only a moment's hesitation, padded to the kitchen to make some sweet tea, then hurried back to her bed to curl up with *Adventures in World History* to prep for a quiz that morning. While she could sleep in till all hours given the chance, she had come to realize that her brain was especially clear in the wee hours. I am a morning person, she had thought, which didn't make much sense if she intended to make a career as a stage manager. She didn't mind that she worked the Friday evening shift. She would have time to go home from school, shower, eat something, have a little rest, and go to work. She could make a cappuccino with her eyes closed, and she could smile and apologize to the girl who had asked for low fat and whip her up a new one in no time flat. And there were other benefits to getting up early. Breakfast with at least one of her parents. This Friday morning it had been both of them.

Twenty-four hours ago.

Funny how the world could change like that.

Gerry came in and Bee quietly closed the journal, leaving her thumb in to mark her place. The nurse laid her hands on Bee's shoulders again and squeezed. "That must have been tough," she said.

It took Bee a moment to get what she was saying. "The interrogation?"

Gerry nodded. Bee nodded. Gerry seemed to be waiting for more but Bee was in no state to share. Gerry seemed to understand. She went about her work.

"My shift ends at six," she said. "Maybe yours should, too, yeah?" She turned to face Bee. "You need to go home, girl. Get yourself a shower." She nodded encouragingly, modeling the response she was hoping for. Then she turned to look at Donovan. She glanced back at Bee with her fingers holding the cross around her neck. "He's not going anywhere," she said.

But that was the point, wasn't it? He might.

"What if he dies and there's no one here for him?" Bee whispered. "He'd be all alone."

Gerry did her the honor of taking the question seriously. She rested one hand on her hip while her other kept hold of the cross.

"Well, if he's been conscious, then he'd know you were here with him for half the night, so how could he begrudge you some downtime? And if he isn't conscious—wasn't, not one bit—then, honey, it won't matter anyway."

Bee thought about it. "That's not a very good answer," she said.

Gerry's face melted into a sad smile. "I'm a nurse," she said. "You want a better answer, there's a chaplain on duty."

Bee held up her hands in surrender. "It's okay," she said. "I know you're right." She slipped her finger out of the journal and placed the little Moleskine back into her THEATER IS MY BAG bag as Gerry continued her survey of the patient and his machine. "No word about his mom?" Bee asked. But even before Gerry shook her head, she knew there couldn't have been or she would have been told.

"You get home to your own mama," said Gerry as she left the room. "Get some sleep."

"I will," said Bee. "Promise." But she waited until the swinging door closed again behind her.

"You heard her, Turn," she said. "You're not going anywhere. Got it?" She stood and gazed at him, then turned to leave. She had only walked three steps when he spoke again.

"Jilly," he said.

CHAPTER ELEVEN

He ran. He looked back at his father's apartment block. They were coming through the door, Kali and the stranger. He wasn't sure how he got out of the apartment, how he slipped past them, but he did—a runner avoiding a tag at home plate. Safe! But not safe—not even vaguely—not if they caught him. They'd kill him if they caught him for what he did. He didn't remember doing it, but they weren't going to listen. He ran across Carling Avenue, four lanes, Friday-night busy. He timed his run; cars zipped past him sending rooster tails of rain to drench him, honking their horns, their brakes squealing. Somehow, he made it to the median. Some-one shouted, "Idiot!" He ignored them, looked back the way he came, saw headlights pulling out of the apartment drive-way. There was no entry to the eastbound lane so the vehicle had to turn west. It was a pickup, he'd seen it downstairs when he'd come back to the apartment. He looked to his right, dashed from the median to the south side of the thoroughfare. More honking, more braking.

"Moron!"

"You out of your fucking tree?"

Yes, he thought. Definitely. He ran eastward, glancing back from time to time for a bus. He saw the pickup pull a U-turn at the first intersection west of the apartment. He ran, then turned to face the headlights and threw out his thumb. No one stopped. It was raining, bad. He ran again, pulling up his hood. Then he turned, stuck his thumb out, ran some more. The traffic crawled, but the pickup was gaining on him, changing lanes, coming on fast, and still no bus. There was never a damn bus! He ran, turned, threw out his thumb, and finally a crapped-out van swerved across two lanes to pull up at the curb. The passenger side window powered down to the smiling face of a dude with dreads. "Need a lift, man?" Donovan pulled open the door, closed it hard behind him.

Al's girlfriends came and went; they never lasted. Donovan had learned something about patience in that regard. No matter how loud they were, or witless or messy, how much they tried to befriend him—or come on to him when his father wasn't looking—they eventually saw the light. The latest had been Kali: Kali O'Connor. She had lasted longer than most. Kali O'Connor: aging hippie from somewhere out in the boonies with I'll-take-you-home-again-Kathleen hair, red as the pickup Donovan had seen parked outside the apartment. Maybe even from the same paint source. She had aspirations to write. To her, Al wasn't an out-of-work journalist; he was someone who had published, a font of wisdom. That's what she had thought until she learned what everybody learned after a while: how infrequently the fountain was actually turned on. How little dribbled out of it.

Kali had left, a month or so ago, as far as Donovan could remember. But it was her, all right, her and some beefy, grim-looking guy he'd never seen before. Flat-faced and sporting a mullet, with a low center of gravity and the swagger of a barroom scrapper. His father's slide from grace had landed him in a country tattered around the edges and peopled by all manner of fallen comrades: addicts and losers and bar-stool prophets; the let-down, it-wasn't-my-fault crowd. Folks mostly waiting for the ax to fall. Or the bat.

For the third time, Donovan woke up, this time without the alarm of a door slamming. He peered into the dark, praying his battered father was not returning. A man with a face made as ugly as the words that came out of it.

He looked at the briefcase. Closed it, snapped it shut, flinched at the noise the locks made.

Just because you're dead doesn't mean you don't need this stuff.

Was he dead? Could you even ask the question if you were? Then again, his father had looked like a walking corpse: a funeral waiting to happen. No, Donovan thought. I'm not there, not yet. This might be a kind of hell he was in, but it was hell on earth. He gazed up at the sky. Surely, there was no moonlight in hell.

He reburied the briefcase under the rotten particleboard. Gone. Out of sight, out of mind. Was that what he had done with his father's murder? Had he buried it down so deep he couldn't recall what really happened?

Back to mama. That's a good boy.

He'd done exactly that, fled to his home. But when? Was it when he left the apartment the first time? He shook his head. That made no sense. He and Mom and Scott lived in the Glebe—nine or ten miles from his father's place. There's no way he'd have gone all that way home and then come back. So later, after the second time, after escaping Kali and her friend in the pickup.

He slowly shook his head, trying to piece it together. There was a hole in his memory. A black hole with all the gravity a black hole tended to have. He tried to peer down into it, then stepped back from the edge, afraid of being dragged into a darkness that could tear you apart, reduce you to atoms.

He thought of his mother. Had to fight not to sob. She wasn't at home. She and Scott had gone camping. And now that door opened, too, and he remembered.

"In April?"

"No black flies," said Scott.

"And no bears," said Trish.

Scott threw up his hands. "Whoa, now! I can't guarantee there'll be no bears."

Then Trish pounded on Scott's chest with both her fists until he gathered her into a hug. They were laughing about it, about canoeing in Algonquin Park when the lakes were only just free of ice and there were no tourists and it would be just them and the wilderness.

"There may be bears just coming out of hibernation and hungry," Scott said, and got another beating for it.

"You guys are totally nuts," Donovan said.

"Uh-huh," said Trish, beaming. "You want to know how crazy?"

"I'll bite," said Donovan.

"*This* crazy," said his mother. She extricated herself from Scott's embrace, found her purse, and took out her cell phone. "Watch this, fellas," she said. And she placed the phone gently but resolutely on the kitchen island.

"You're leaving your phone," said Donovan.

Trish nodded.

Scott laughed. "You're kidding me, right?"

Trish shook her head.

Scott and Donovan exchanged mock-startled expressions. "Mom, your phone is, like, crack. You won't make it twenty miles without going into serious withdrawal."

"Break out in a cold sweat," said Scott.

She folded her arms. "I'm doing it. Cold turkey."

Scott clapped. "So I get you for a whole long weekend with no business associates? Sweet."

Trish's face broke out in a radiant smile. "My two gorgeous men," she said. "Do you really think there's anything I can't do?"

Scott pretended to give it some thought. He looked at Donovan. They conferred. Then they both shook their heads. "Woman strong," said Scott. "Woman bigger than handheld device."

"Yes!" said Trish, flexing her biceps. "Hear me roar." Which she did, a mama lion.

Donovan could see the cell phone on the kitchen island. He was standing alone in the house. They had gone. They had gone camping and it was night and he was alone in the house and his father was dead. He *had* gone home. But he didn't phone 911, because . . . Because his mother's phone was password protected—thumbprint protected. And there was no house phone. No other phones in the whole world. Besides . . . Something happened . . . He was home, then he wasn't home, which made no sense, and . . . everything went blurry.

"You are . . ."

There it was again.

He had talked to someone. Why couldn't he get hold of this?

"See?"

But he couldn't—couldn't see a thing: nothing but a sudden onrush of light and then blackness. And then . . . He groaned. He imagined himself back in his father's apartment all alone picking up the pieces of broken china and trying to make them into a bowl. And into that bowl he would place every kernel of popcorn. Then he'd piece the beer bottles back together painstakingly, and the crystal scotch glass. And then his father. He'd put his father back together and make him whole again. Maybe when you killed someone this is what happened. You killed them again and again, and the memories came without rhyme or reason and you couldn't escape them and yet the memory of actually *doing it*—that was $T = 0$. Someone had explained the big bang theory to him . . . well, they'd tried to. There was nothing and then there was something. And the something came out of nothing at the precise moment that Time equaled zero. When everything began. Or maybe when everything ended?

He heard a sound behind him and flipped onto his side to peer through his spy hole. Someone was at a lit upstairs window of the farmhouse. A woman. She had opened the window and was peering out. She hugged herself against the cold, then shut the window. Now she pulled down a shade and he watched her shadow withdraw from the bright rectangle.

He got to his feet—couldn't sit there another moment. He walked, out from behind the trash heap, tentatively toward the house, his eyes on the lit window. He saw a silhouette of the woman again, distorted, passing by. The shadow passed the shade again. He held his breath, waited, saw her profile, tantalized. Then her light went off. So anticlimactic: the allure of a woman's body in silhouette, gone. He shook it off. Without taking his eyes off that newly dark window, he made his way toward the door in the shed. That must have been where she was coming from when he saw her cross the yard. He placed his hand on the doorknob, turned it. The door was unlocked and he slipped inside.

CHAPTER TWELVE

He had dared to hope it might be warmer than outside but it wasn't, not really. However, it was drier. He couldn't turn on a light, but he had a plan. This lunatic flight from reality had to stop. He needed to go home. He had panicked. There was no blame in that. And . . . He shook his head again. No use trying to make sense of it. Go home.

Somewhere in that shed there must be an electrical outlet. There were lights after all, even if he didn't dare to turn them on.

He wanted to charge his phone, just enough to get word to Bee. Suddenly the ache of missing her, of wanting to tell her—tell someone—cut through the multitude of dull aches in his body, the cuts and bruises, the shivers that felt as if they would rattle him to pieces. The warmth he had thought might be hypothermia had deserted him. "So I'm not dead," he said, in case anyone wanted to know. That was something. But Bee not knowing where he was or what had happened—making her worry like that—that was the worst ache of all. She would know what to do. If he could just reach her, that would be the start of everything becoming bearable again, whatever else was going to happen.

He stood stock-still, his hand on the inner doorknob. Skylights let in what there was of the moon, and that tricked out all the things stored here, gave some shape to the crowded darkness. He heard a faucet dripping somewhere. He waited, every sense alert, taking in the looming shadows, until he felt he could walk. Just to his left a pile of empty pallets was stacked against the west wall, right beside the door, a stack almost as tall as he was. He leaned against the stack, gripped the edge of the wood as if his feet might suddenly be swept out from under him. Anything could happen. Nothing would surprise him.

He sniffed: weed. He'd smelled it at the kitchen window, and the cops had noticed it right away when they arrived. It was stronger here. A heady aroma. Sweet, almost comforting . . . Well, maybe under other circumstances. But the last thing he needed was to have any more of his mental powers compromised. He was running on empty in the brain department right now. And he had a task to perform.

Across the expanse of floor, he thought he saw a desk. It would probably prove to be something else, but its desk-ness drew him forward, and he walked tentatively toward it, putting one foot before the other uncertainly, feeling ahead like a blind man into the darkness with one hand out front and one guarding his crotch. His toes felt ahead for the gaping hole there that would take him down to Hell Central. But there was no hole, not so far. The way was clear, free of rubble. His senses told him the place was kept neat. A neat shed; that should have been a clue.

He reached the desk-like shape, and it *was* a desk: an old wooden desk, by the feel of it, and an old wooden wheely chair. He pulled the chair out on its rollers, swiveled it toward him, and leaning forward, felt the cushion. It was vaguely warm. The woman must have been sitting here, however long ago it was. He gingerly sat down. The chair squeaked under his weight but in a comforting way, and Donovan groaned involuntarily with happiness at the softness of it. He leaned back and the chair leaned with him. He rotated the chair to face the desk and carefully felt its surface. A wide, old office desk with an expansive pitted top. His eager fingers located a stapler, a ruler, some kind of book with a spiral spine. Pencils, pens. A small bowl he picked up and felt: a container for paper clips with a magnetic top. It all felt wonderfully tangible and prosaic and real. And everything was dry, which was a victory of some kind. He felt the base and neck of a desk lamp. He found and followed the electric cord, standing and then kneeling beside the desk, finding the wall outlet. There was a free socket below the lamp's plug. He withdrew the charger from his hoodie pocket and the cell from his left pants pocket and connected them. He plugged in the phone.

The charging message came on: a battery woefully empty but soon to be full—or full enough. "Bee," he said, as quietly as a prayer. He would tell her that she had been right. That he needed help. But no—first of all he had something else he needed to tell her. Ask her. A question: *"Are you . . ."*

Oh, why wouldn't it come to him? Never mind. It would be enough to even hear her voice.

He rested the phone on the desktop. In its glow he could see that the wood was a warm golden-brown, old but well tended. And although the floor was concrete, there was no dust. So the woman, or somebody, worked here a lot, he gathered. He got to his feet again and moved around to the front of the desk, where he sat down. He would wait here. He folded his arms on the desktop, then let his head fall forward onto them. His eyes closed, tired of trying to see things in the dark. Tired of running. Tired of not knowing.

And then the lights came on.

CHAPTER / THIRTEEN

Wilton Crescent should have probably been called Wilton Comma. It was barely two blocks long and where it began to curve, it actually became Oakland Avenue, so where was a crescent in that? It started out at Bank Street across from the stadium and no one but residents would be likely to turn onto it at all, unless they were going to immediately turn left onto Queen Elizabeth Lane, which led down to the parkway along the canal. It was part of the southern boundary of the Glebe. She smiled, remembering an early conversation with Donovan.

"What is a glebe?" he'd asked. "Isn't there a bird called a glebe?"

"That would be a grebe."

"Right. So . . ."

She'd stopped and looked at him. "You live here," she said.

"Yeah, but I never thought about it until now. Which is your fault."

"My fault?"

"Yeah. You're making me question everything."

If it was a compliment, it was a sly one. She had smiled anyway, wanting to take it as flattery.

"You know what it means, don't you?" he said.

She nodded. "It's a Scottish word meaning church lands. This area used to be called the glebe lands of Saint Andrew's Presbyterian Church."

He had nodded knowingly. "That makes it official," he'd said.

"What?"

"You know everything."

Bee shook the memory from her mind. *If only,* she thought.

A driver who continued down Wilton might easily suspect it was a cul-de-sac, unless he or she was one of the few dozen people who lived there, in modest houses stretching, in the last block, along only the north side of the street. The south side gave way to a wooded slope with pleasant views between the trees and shrubbery of Brown's Inlet directly below, a tamed and lovely pond that didn't, as far as Bee could tell, actually empty into the canal. She wasn't sure how it got the name "Inlet."

This is where she drove not long after lunch on Saturday. She'd slept like a log and then woken up with a start at eleven wanting only to head back to the hospital. It was all her mother could do to get her to shower and eat something. There was still no word from Trish Turner. No word from the hospital, although she wasn't sure they considered her family enough to contact, even though she'd left her name with the ward clerk.

"You're his amanuensis," Bee's father had said over fresh bagels from Kettleman's.

"Should I see a doctor about it?" she asked.

He chuckled as he slathered mustard on the corned beef in his sandwich. "A scribe," he said. "A fancy word for it."

"Amanuensis," said Bee, liking the sound of it. "If all you've written down is less than a dozen words, do you still get to call yourself an amanuensis?"

Her father considered the question seriously and then shook his head. "Probably just stick to scribe," he said.

She didn't care. It was something to do. She wasn't sure she could sit in that blinking, beeping, ticking room without some task to perform, however menial, however sporadic. The space capsule seemed so far away from her sun-splattered kitchen. For after a night of rain, the sun had come out of hiding and was ready for interrogation. Where were you on the night of Friday, April fifteenth? A foolish question to ask the sun, which, after all, had a foolproof alibi. But such was the cast of Bee's mind that she saw everyone as a suspect right now. Everyone but Turn.

As much as she was in a hurry to resume her place at his bedside, amanuensing or scribing or just scribbling — whatever it was — she turned onto Wilton on her way to the hospital and pulled over to park as soon as she found a place. She locked the car door and set off on foot. In only minutes

the sky had darkened again, and, just like that, the promise of a sunny Saturday was compromised, the sun trapped
behind a leaden veil, a lot of veils—a regular harem of veils.
She prayed for a wind to blow the veils away. The stillness
disturbed her. The sound of her boots on the sidewalk disturbed her. She stopped and closed her eyes, breathed in
deeply the new greenery, the sweet fragrance of the rain-wet
street. Whatever else was happening, the earth was breaking
free from winter's stranglehold. She wondered whether she
should dig up a handful of dirt to take to Donovan. A whiff's
worth: aromatherapy.

She passed Donovan's house, the windows shuttered. No
lights on. No one home. Donovan's house: just three doors
up from the accident scene.

The sight of the yellow crime-scene tape made her forget
about spring awakenings. Made her wish she hadn't wolfed
down her brunch. There were no cop cars there, only two or
three neighbors with dogs on leashes, standing on the periph-
ery of the tape, staring down the hill, talking in low murmurs. Maybe someone would know something. She moved
closer.

From what she could piece together, he had been hit facing the vehicle. A vehicle that, thanks to Staff Sergeant Bell's
slip, she knew might have been a pickup, a red pickup. A red
pickup so high off the ground that instead of throwing Donovan up over the hood had launched him into the thicket on
the hillside above the inlet.

There were tire tracks on the grass verge by the curb on
the south side of the street. The vehicle had humped itself up
onto the grass before stopping. The tracks went only a yard

or so. She stared at them, muddy from the rain. Was there enough of a pattern there to distinguish a make of tire? Bell hadn't said anything about that, just the paint chip, a paint chip not as big as her baby fingernail, embedded in Donovan's clothes somewhere. She shuddered. She looked at the burnt rubber on the road, where the back tires had squealed to a stop, or was it that they'd squealed as he backed up and split the scene, the tires spinning and spinning as the vehicle sped away, heading up toward Bank Street?

She looked around. Someone must have heard something. Seen something.

She turned to look down the street, the direction in which the truck or whatever it was must have come in order to have climbed the curb in this manner. The corner, where the comma ended and Oakland began, was less than twenty yards away. The car had to have been coming from that direction, and yet that meant rounding the curve—a tight curve, almost ninety degrees. No one—no one in his right mind—could have come around that curve fast enough to launch a boy into orbit. He'd have heard the vehicle squealing as the driver held the turn.

So how did it happen?

There was a path at the juncture of Wilton and Oakland that continued down through the trees to the inlet.

Might the vehicle have been parked on the path? It was paved and wide enough. That would have given it a more or less straight trajectory toward the point of impact. But what was a vehicle doing on a pedestrian pathway? Unless it was waiting for him.

Waiting for Donovan.

But that was ridiculous. Who would do such a thing? Donovan's enemies included pitchers he'd burned for a home run, infielders who'd gotten in his way when he was sliding aggressively into base. Oh, there were guys at school who hated him, no doubt: What was there not to hate? He was good-looking, pleasant, smart, and talented. But school grudges didn't usually escalate to murder. She shivered at the thought, swore at herself for even thinking it. It *wasn't* murder. Not yet. Hopefully it wouldn't *ever* be murder because he was going to wake up and be with her again. The point was that it was inconceivable there could be anyone who hated him enough to do this.

"Probably drunk," one of the dog walkers said.

Bee wondered. It didn't seem likely. A drunk driver would have had even less control; he would have never made it around Oakland onto Wilton. He'd have ended up flying down the hill himself, crashing into a tree.

"Or stoned," said someone else. "Probably wearing headphones. Stepped right into it."

Bee froze. They weren't talking about a drunk driver: they were blaming what happened on Donovan. Suddenly, she couldn't stand to be there for another minute. She shoved her hands into her pockets and headed back toward the car.

"Fucking idiots," she said as she passed the gawkers.

"Hey!" said one of them. And his hideous little dog started yapping at her.

"Show a little respect," the other one called after her. "Someone died here."

CHAPTER / FOURTEEN

He assumed that the woman standing at the door was the one he had seen leaving the shed. He had watched her at her window shade half hoping for a peep show. She shut the door behind her. Donovan did not move. He wasn't even sure he could. What he could do was get the cell phone out of her sight line by sliding the chair to his right.

"You didn't waste any time," she said.

He looked at her. She was leaning against the door. The door was red. She was blond, her hair short and manageable. She was wearing blue jeans and a denim jacket over a pale-green print T-shirt. She was probably in her midthirties, he thought. There was something about her, he . . .

"Cat got your tongue?" she said.

"I didn't take anything," said Donovan.

"No," she said. "I can see that."

"I just needed to get inside out of the . . ." He couldn't begin to say what it was he wanted to get away from—pretty well everything.

She nodded as if she understood. "And charge up your phone," she said.

The fallen look on his face seemed to amuse her but not for long. Her expression grew stern. "Was it you who killed my dog?"

He would have thought nothing could surprise him. He was wrong.

"Excuse me?"

"You heard what I said."

"I didn't see a dog," he said. "Didn't hear a dog."

"Which, you've got to admit, is surprising on a farm."

Donovan tried to swallow, found he had nothing to swallow. His mouth was bone-dry. Had there been a dog that other time? He had been here before, it was just . . . He shook his head, not able to connect the dots.

The woman leaned back against the door. Her hands were in her back pockets. As far as he could tell, she didn't have a weapon on her. She wasn't as big as he was, but she sure didn't look worried. And he hardly looked dangerous. He tried to imagine gimping over to her and taking a swing, knocking her out and running off into the night. Ha!

"I don't know anything about your dog, lady." His voice was a grave, shadowy thing. "Honest to God."

Her right eyebrow rode up about a quarter inch. It was the only change to her expression. Then she nodded toward the back of the shed. He followed her gaze. In the shadows, there was a king-size freezer, surrounded on one side by a stack of oversize tires and on the other side by a generator. Donovan had to look twice before he saw what she wanted him to see. She flipped on another light and there was no doubt. A dog. It was lying on the top of the freezer, unmoving.

"The bowhunter," she said. Donovan didn't understand. It was as if she had spoken to him in another language. "Bowhunter," she repeated, and drew an imaginary bow, letting an invisible arrow fly straight at him.

He swallowed hard. Looked back at the lifeless dog. A big black Lab by the look of it, and now he saw it—an arrow, embedded in the dog's neck. He turned to look back at her. "I've never even held a bow and arrow in my life."

"Liar," she snapped. Then her face softened. "You don't remember, do you."

He shook his head.

She laughed but there was sadness in it. She looked over at the dead dog for a good long moment. If there had been grief, she was mostly over it. She turned her attention back to Donovan; her gaze was level and hard.

"You must have been the fellow who robbed the car up on the highway," she said, kicking herself off the door. She walked a few steps toward him. Strode. She strode toward him, all business. Then stopped three strides away. Her hands were at her sides now.

Donovan had never been much of a liar. If his father had inspired him in any way, it was to not follow him down that road. He wasn't sure if he nodded or not. The woman chuckled in any case.

"So, where is it?" she said.

He waited, tried to think if there was anything he could

do. He wanted to close his eyes—maybe click his heels while he was at it. Then he nodded with his chin toward the outside.

"Uh-huh," she said. "I'll need a bit more information than that."

"The trash heap," he muttered.

"What was that?" she said, cocking her ear, putting her hand behind it. "I work a farm, kid, I'm around a lot of heavy machinery, not to mention a lot of loud mouthed stupid men, so I don't hear so good."

"The junk pile. I buried it."

She nodded. "Good place for it," she said. She looked to her right, where there was a giant spool of some kind of yellow conduit lying on its side. She went and perched on it, and Donovan's baseball brain kicked in. He was at third, and home was that red door, and the catcher had just peeled off toward first after an errant throw from the outfield.

"Don't get any ideas," she said, as if she could read his mind. "You've got a gimpy leg. You've got a good body but you're at the end of your rope. And, like I said, I work a farm. I'd have you hog-tied in about thirty seconds, you try running on me."

It was almost a relief. Donovan didn't have much desire to move.

"You don't want to run from me anyway," she said, her voice calmer. "I can be a help. You need help, right?"

He nodded, wondering now if she could read everything in his head, whether he thought it or not.

"So, next question," she said. "What's in it?"

"Excuse me?"

"Whatever it is you took."

He hadn't heard the rest of the conversation in the kitchen with the cops, and she hadn't even been there, unless she was listening from another room. He didn't expect the cops had told the men much more than he'd heard.

"You going to tell me or do I have to smack you around a bit?" Now both her eyebrows were raised. "Better still, I'll get my brother to do it for me: Mervin, the one with the mane of hair? Goldilocks. Only problem is he just doesn't know his own strength. Might likely pulverize you and we'd just have to take you back to the swamp there and weigh you down with a concrete block." She leaned on her knees. "It wouldn't be the first time."

She smiled as her words hit home. Donovan wasn't sure how much of what she said was true, but he remembered Mervin Green, all right, with arms like oak branches, a loser at poker with a short fuse.

"It's money," he said. She nodded. "A lot of money," he added.

She rubbed her nose with her hand. It was a muscled hand with bitten-down nails. She was pretty, he guessed, in a hard way. Life wasn't easy on her.

"You assessing whether I can do the job?" she said.

He stared blankly at her. "Sorry?" he said.

"Get you to where you're going," she said.

"Oh."

"The money will help."

"Listen," said Donovan, suddenly standing up. "I'll show you where it is and then I just want to get out of here and go home."

She had stood up the instant he did and cut the angle

toward the door in case he was foolish enough to make a dash for it. "You're not going anywhere," she said. "You won't stand a chance without me."

His shoulders sagged. His head drooped. "I really don't know what you're talking about."

"Of course you don't. How could you? But you made it back here, which is a start."

He stared at her, racking his brain. "Do I know you?"

She nodded. "It'll come to you."

He had thought he recognized the place. There had been that snapshot when he'd first seen the house up close—seen it as if by day, a flash of memory that went out as quickly as it appeared.

"Don't fight it," she said. Now her smile softened again and he knew he had met her before—this softer version of her.

"And hey, you've got the stump money," she said. "That's good, however you came by it."

"The what?"

"Trust me, Donovan," she said. She nodded as if showing him how to say yes.

"It all just . . . happened," he said. "I was hitching and this freak dropped me out near here and then this car was coming way too fast and when he saw me he lost control and next thing I know he's in the ditch."

She nodded, but the look on her face made him wonder.

"Do you know something I don't?" he said.

She nodded. "The money's a good sign. It'll be all right," she said. "You'll see."

He shook his head. "I doubt it. I don't know how you

know my name, let alone how you knew I was here. I don't even know where 'here' is."

"I saw you right off," she said. He stared at her. "When you fell on your butt outside the window? It's a wonder the others downstairs didn't hear you. I was up in my room." She pointed back toward the house. The room he'd seen the light in. Figured. None of this was going to go his way. "I guessed you'd still be skulking around, which is why I left the door unlocked." He nodded slowly, realizing he'd walked into a trap. She smiled again. "Hey, I'm used to herding cattle."

She seemed to have some plan for him, to have been expecting him. It made no sense. He needed out. He needed Bee—for her to come and get him. Then he needed the police—to tell them what happened. Tell his side of the story—what he could remember.

"Ma'am," he said. "Could I use your phone?" She shook her head. "Please."

"The line's down, kid."

"Don't you have a cell?"

She didn't answer. Stonewalled him. Not so much as a gesture one way or the other. Right. He cleared his throat. He'd have given his right arm for a glass of water. "I don't know what's going on."

"You want to get home," she said.

"Yeah," he said hopefully.

"I don't know," she said. She was frowning now.

"I'll do anything."

Her frown deepened. He couldn't bear to lose her now. "Please," he said. "Whatever it takes, I'll—"

"Shut up!" Her face darkened.

"No, listen—"

"I said shut up!" Her voice had gone quiet—quiet but sharp. Which is when he heard what she was listening to: the sound of motorbikes. Not just one or two. More like a herd.

He stood up, petrified, and gazed in the direction of the yard, where they seemed to be gathering.

"This could get messy," she said.

And then there was the unmistakable sound of gunfire.

CHAPTER FIFTEEN

The front of the shed faced the yard. It was two garage-doors wide, and there were narrow windows fitted at eye level. Outside, there were at least a dozen bikes—big Harleys, operated by men built with the same kind of dimensions as their rides: large, with a lot of grunt power. They were running this way and that, hiding behind the vehicles in the yard, with guns aimed at the house.

"Come on," said the woman, grabbing Donovan by the sleeve of his shirt, pulling him back deeper into the shed toward the side door he'd come through. She locked it and then her hand slid down the wall, behind the pile of wooden pallets, where she must have flicked some kind of switch because a motor started up. She grimaced at the noise of the engine, looked anxiously toward the yard, then returned her attention to the pile of pallets.

Outside there was return fire from the house and shouting and all Donovan could think of was where to hide. He saw a ladder at the back end, near the freezer and the tires and the dead dog. It led up to some kind of a loft. He headed toward it, but the woman grabbed his sleeve again. He tried to tug himself free.

"When they show up with guns, they don't plan on anyone getting out alive," she said.

"But we've got—"

He stopped, his eyes growing wide. The stack of pallets was rising off the concrete floor. They were piled on some kind of a lift, like in an auto body shop. And just like the pneumatic hoist in a body shop, it was moving way too slowly.

Bam!

A bullet smashed through the steel door, ricocheting off the floor not a yard from Donovan's feet. He backed up then realized he was moving away from the rising pallets, which, he could see now, was their way out, for there was an entrance: a circular hole in the floor just smaller than the size of the pallet, about a yard or so in diameter.

"Come on!" The woman waved him toward the metal staircase that spiraled down around the oil-slicked central piston. The lifted pile stopped at about four feet and she was already ducking down under it. There was another shot through the door, and again Donovan sidestepped where it had hit and made his way toward the stairs.

Then he remembered his phone. He raced back to the desk and grabbed it, pulled it free of its cable just as a third shot pierced the metal-clad door.

117

The woman's head was just visible at floor level. She had stopped and was staring at him, astonished. Then she shook her head, and he saw her stab at a red button on the wall and the motor started again. The lift was going down.

Donovan raced for the stairs. The lift was descending faster than it had risen. Gravity—never gave a guy a break. More gunshots, forcing Donovan to back away.

"They're in here, too!" someone shouted from outside the door and then there was nothing for Donovan to do but race to the rapidly diminishing escape route and slide on his belly under the hoist. Grabbing the handrail of the staircase with both hands, he pulled with all his might and his legs followed him in, just as the pallets alighted on the concrete floor with a quiet smack.

He hustled to his feet and clambered down the stairs, reaching the bottom just as the door to the shed above crashed open, followed by a spray of gunfire.

He stood at the foot of the staircase next to the woman.

"Assault rifles," she said quietly. "Bullpups."

Then, placing a finger to her lips and with a nod of her head, she stepped through a door at the bottom of the shaft into a room of brilliant light. Donovan followed, too dazed to do anything else, and she shut the door quickly but quietly behind him. She reached past him and smacked a series of light switches on the wall, pitching them into darkness. But not before Donovan saw where they were. It was a grow room. The giant room, as wide and long as the shed, was a frigging weed operation!

Above them, men spilled into the shed. He felt the woman's rough finger touch his lips, reminding him not to make a sound. She needn't have bothered. He was struck dumb. She leaned in close to his ear.

"The name's Jilly," she said. "Follow me."

CHAPTER / SIXTEEN

She took Donovan by the wrist and led him, like a blind man, down the central corridor. There was a tincture of light coming from somewhere, enough to see a forest of marijuana. Which explained the heady aroma up in the shed. But down here, in the belly of the beast, he could feel the cannabinoids really working on him.

At the north wall of the underground bunker, there was a door Jilly pushed through, dragging Donovan along. She closed the door behind them, sealing off the last little bit of light. She let go of his wrist, leaned against the wall, and took a deep breath.

"The smell can really get to you," she said. He nodded. Not that she could see. "It's the nutrients we feed the plants that'll kill you, though," she said. "I don't work down here without a gas mask."

There was another blast of gunfire upstairs. Jilly laughed. The kind of laugh you let out when you've bobsledded down an Olympic run for the first time—by mistake. "You know," she said, "when the cops eventually get here, they'll survey the wreckage and say the place burned down because of us tampering with the wiring to get enough juice to grow the plants. They won't say a damn thing about the ten thousand shell casings they find. Just another grow op, up in smoke." She laughed again. "But, oh my, will Lanark County be feeling good tomorrow!"

Donovan wasn't exactly sure if he understood anything she said. What he understood, standing there in this closet, in the darkest darkness yet, was that he had been saved from a bunch of maniacs by a maniac. It was a lose-lose situation.

"You rested up?" she said.

The question could not truly be answered.

"Follow me," she said. She took his arm, another door opened, and his nose was assaulted by the sweet smell of wet earth. "Duck," she said, and then he felt her hand pressing down on his head, just in time to avoid a low ceiling. Reaching up protectively, he felt a wooden beam. She closed the door behind them and locked it. Three different locks slammed into place. Then she scrambled about and next thing he knew a flashlight came on. They were in an underground earthen tunnel. There was a locker just inside the steel door through which they'd come, and from it she took a shoulder bag that seemed already partially packed, plus a firearm that looked as if it were straight from *Star Wars*.

His eyes must have given away his stunned surprise.

"Oh, this," she said, grunting as she swung the strap

over her shoulder. She patted the weapon affectionately. "It's an FN P90. It's what they've got. Gotta fight fire with fire," she said. Donovan nodded as if he'd been thinking the same thing.

There was a loud crashing sound from somewhere above and he scrunched his shoulders even more than they already were, standing in a tunnel not quite five feet high. "Shouldn't we be, you know, going?"

Jilly was staring up at the ceiling. She nodded. "But only so far," she said enigmatically, and then started down the tunnel, bending low. Donovan mostly crawled after her, stayed back a few feet just in case the assault weapon dangling from her shoulder went off by mistake. If it did and he was killed, at least he would already be buried. It wasn't a comforting thought.

In only a few minutes they reached the door at the end of the tunnel, by which time he was desperate to get out. He'd always had a bit of claustrophobia, but until tonight, he'd never realized just how severe it was. There was only compacted dirt above their heads. Dirt—tons of it—held up by thick beams and plywood. His hand reached out for the door, like a runner reaching for the ribbon at the end of the race. She slapped him down.

"Not yet!" she said. She had gone from a crouch to actually sitting on the smooth dirt floor. "Sit!" she said. He did. He wondered what her next command might be. Roll over? Play dead?

Donovan stared at the assault rifle, lying across her lap now. It looked futuristic and deeply troublesome.

"A 'bullpup'?" he asked.

She nodded. "You settled yet?" She was shining the flashlight at his face. He shaded his eyes and nodded. Then she turned off the light. "Don't want to give anybody a clue where we are," she said.

Donovan just swallowed, wishing he had a clue. He folded his legs and rested his hands, knotted, in his lap, like a kid in kindergarten at storytime. The door beside them let in dribbles of cold air. He breathed it in hungrily, desperate to push the door open and see the night.

Where were they? As far as he could reckon they had been moving east, toward the concession road. Leaning toward the door, he could pick up the sounds from back at the farm: gunfire, but only now and then. More crashing sounds. What he wanted to hear was the roar of motorcycles revving up and leaving, going back to wherever they'd come from. If they were Satan's Choice, then it was time they went back to Satan's garage, wherever that was.

"A bullpup's what you call an automatic weapon with the action and magazine behind the trigger in the buttstock."

Donovan said, "Oh," and left it at that. Lesson over. She'd said she ran a farm and he couldn't help wondering how many other farmers kept machine guns in an underground locker. He wasn't sure how long they were going to be there, but even if it was, say, a few days, he doubted whether his conversational skills were up to actually talking to Jilly. Conversation, when it was any good, usually had to do with having something in common. The only thing he had in common with her, as far as he could tell, was that their lives were equally in danger from a dozen or so gangbangers outfitted with weapons of destruction.

"I'm trying to figure how I'm going to get you to where you're going," said Jilly.

"Oh," said Donovan again.

"After the cops left, I took a little trip up to see the accident on Seven. The car was still there in the ditch, and I'm pretty sure I recognized it."

"Really?"

"This slimeball named Lucan, who's the dry cleaner for those guys back there destroying my family home."

"The dry cleaner?"

"The one who washes their dirty money."

"Oh."

"The cops know Lucan, and they know who controls most of the dope sold in this neck of the woods. They also have a pretty good idea that we have our own little operation and that those pagans back there don't like it." She chuckled. "We don't like them, needless to say."

Donovan thought suddenly about his English teacher, who would get his shorts in a knot about people saying "needless to say" since if it was, then you shouldn't be saying it. He didn't think Jilly would appreciate a grammar lesson, though.

"This is the way it works," she said. "There has to be money to pay Charlie. There's just no way around it. You needed that money and there it was."

Donovan didn't say anything. Didn't think there was much point.

Jilly sniffed. Sniffed again and groaned. "Can you smell that?" He realized that he had been smelling it ever since they sat down. Smoke. "Those one-percenters out there are torching my farm right now."

"One-percenters?"

"Yeah. Satan's Pagans. The S-Pops, I call them: Satan's Pissed-Off Pagans. That's who we're up against."

Donovan thought about the "we" in her statement of war, but he didn't have much time to give it his full attention because next thing he knew she was in his face. She'd leaned in—one leaping shadow across the tunnel—and grabbed his shirtfront in her fist. "Level with me," she said.

"Honest, I don't—"

"I don't want to hear 'I don't.'" She shook him like a rag doll.

"Okay, okay. That guy in the Camaro—"

"No, not that."

"Then what?"

"Murphy."

"Who?"

"You know. The guy playing cards with my brother and Oscar. Who is he? Murphy wasn't his real name. Just something Oscar Shouldice came up with for the benefit of the cops." Donovan nodded, and although it was pitch-dark, she was close enough to register the gesture. "So, is he who I think he is?"

"He's Allen Ian McGeary. My father."

She let go of his shirtfront. "Yeah, thought it might be." She threw herself back against the earthen wall. "I only caught a glimpse of him. I tend to keep out of the way when the rye and cards come out. God, has he ever gone to seed."

Donovan stared at her, and in the almost total darkness a memory began to stir.

"So, did you kill him or not?" she said.

"I . . . I don't remember. I guess I must have. I mean he's dead, isn't he?"

"Most certainly." She laughed dryly. "But I can't help thinking he's taken a long time getting around to it."

Donovan swallowed. "You knew him," he said.

"I knew him. Knew you, too, kid," she added.

"We came here," said Donovan. "When I was little."

"See, I told you. It's coming back, right?"

Coming back wasn't how Donovan would have put it. Thawing, maybe. Slowly. Very slowly.

"No?" said Jilly. "Oh well. Anyway, that's what brought Al here, I guess. And so that's what brought you here after him and then that brought those one-percenters here after you. Which is why—"

"Wait a minute. What are you saying?"

"You stole the Pagans' money less than one mile from *my* operation, which is why the cops came around earlier, followed by the S-Pops. Wouldn't be surprised if the cops tipped them off: torching our operation would save them a whole lot of paperwork and taxpayers' money. The cops like it best when the enemy neutralize one another. You know what I mean?"

He didn't. He was hopelessly lost.

"Well," she said with a sigh. "There's nothing else to do. We had to get the money one way or another."

There was silence. Nothing more to say. And then into the silence that had permeated Donovan's mind crept a feeling of terrible uncertainty that he had to share with somebody. "I'm not sure if I did it. Killed my father."

"Oh, here we go—"

"No! It's not what you think. I'm not trying to worm out of it. It's just I can't piece it all together, what happened."

He expected her to chastise him again, but she remained quiet. After a moment, Donovan closed his eyes, which had the effect of setting free a tear that was waiting there. He felt it course down his cheek.

He cleared his throat. "I'm dead, too, aren't I."

She didn't speak for a moment. "No," she said at last. "You're a traveler in a land that is part memory, part dream, and with all the vestiges of the kind of pain only the living can feel."

He wasn't sure what to make of what she said other than to take a little bit of hope and courage from her words. Was that why Al had laughed like that as he stumbled off into the night? Was it because after all those years of "feeling no pain," finally he really *wasn't* feeling any pain? He let out a ragged breath and then the quiet closed around them.

And then into the quiet came the sound of motorcycles starting up: one, two, three, and then too many to count. They were going. The sound of them leaving came closer and closer as they turned out of the yard and headed north on the concession road toward the highway. In only a moment they were passing so nearby, the tunnel door actually shook and Donovan covered his head expecting the passageway to cave in from the vibrations.

Then they were gone. Jilly pushed open the low door and they both scurried out into the moonlit night. They were standing in a little copse of ironwood trees and dense, tangled shrubbery, mostly prickly ash, hard by the split-rail fence that bordered the eastern end of the property. The moon was low on the horizon now, and there was a hint of false dawn. Birds were starting to sing in the trees above their heads. But there was a sound much louder than the birds, a crackling noise, a splintering noise. Turning toward the farm they saw the flames: the house, the shed — it was all going up in smoke and cinders, pulsing red like a heart ripped live from the earth.

CHAPTER / SEVENTEEN

There was no way to pull a U-turn on Wilton—too narrow—so Bee was forced to drive the length of it, which meant passing the dog walkers. Nor could she pass them at speed. It would be a blasphemy to drive too fast, here of all places, not to mention deadly trying to make the turn onto Oakland. The outcome was not surprising. One of the men made a fist at her as she passed, his face red with indignation. The other called after her, words she could barely hear because of the throbbing of blood in her ears. She was heading along Oakland, which curved up toward Bank Street, when she thought about what he had said.

Someone died here last night.

What did he know? Bastard! Then suddenly she slammed on the brakes. Had there been news? She hadn't even thought to check the radio. She gulped in air as if suddenly the car was a bell jar. She clung to the steering wheel. She had her phone. She could Google it. But she just sat there not wanting to know.

No one would have contacted her. She was nobody. Just the girlfriend. It was coming on a year, this unlikely union: theater girl and jock boy. He was all about basketball in winter and baseball in summer. Balls. It was all about balls: chasing them and hitting them and heaving them into things and running, running, running. But he wasn't just a jock. "Is anybody just one anything, really?" he had said to her early on.

"A wise jock," she'd said, and watched the temper brew on his face until he realized she was teasing him.

He'd come to see her last show and raved about it. Insisted she was the star, no matter that she was never seen. "Those curtains opened, like, perfect. And the lights—I couldn't take my eyes off the lights."

"Shut up," she'd said, weak from laughter.

"There was this prop—what was it? Oh yeah, the bowl of fruit. I knew, soon as I saw it, you'd put it in the guy's hand. It was so . . . so *there*."

"I don't do everything," she said. "There's a team."

"But you're the captain, right?"

She liked that: captain. When she was stage managing *him*, he'd call her that: Captain Northway.

He read books she recommended and wanted to talk about them. He had thoughts he wanted to think. He had a wonky sense of humor. And, yes, he was gorgeous, lithe and strong and gentle. He was a boy who could have easily rested on his laurels—his prowess on the field or court, his well-sculpted ass. But he wanted to make something of him-self. Be someone.

"You've come to the right person," she'd said. "I'm all about 'be.'"

It only took a moment for the smile to blossom on his face. "Cool," he had said, nodding. "And I'm all about 'do.' We're perfect."

A car beeped, and looking in her rearview mirror Bee realized she was holding up traffic. She waved and the car beeped again.

"Prick."

She put the car back in gear and puttered up to Bank, deliberately slowly. She waited at the stop sign, too long, until Mr. In-an-Almighty-Hurry-on-a-Saturday-Morning beeped at her again. Then she turned south toward the hospital.

Be and Do—Bee and Turn: a perfect couple? No. Because there was Turn's shadow self. His temper. He hated it. Hated that he lost it so easily. He was working on it, he swore. But whatever had happened last night, one person was dead and another was hanging on for dear life. Somewhere in all of that was Shadow Donovan.

She could not and would not believe he could have killed anyone. But if he had—if it was an accident, say, or . . . well, she didn't know what. If it was true, then she knew what would happen next, when he lost it and then came back to the land of the living: his remorse, his shame.

Enough to step in front of a truck?

She shook her head. No, she wouldn't believe it. He loved life way too much.

She was tired. Not like the way she was tired last night.

More like existentially tired. She had slept soundly enough but only for four hours. And now, because her spirits had fallen, she was immediately reminded of the journal. She had written a lot about Donovan and Shadow Donovan in that little maroon Moleskine, and without having to reread it she knew there was enough there to convince anyone he was capable of doing damage to his father. *She* didn't believe it. And it wasn't just mindless loyalty, either. There was a deep goodness in Donovan that would stop him short. She was sure of it. She gripped the steering wheel tightly.

Killed him.

He'd said that.

She couldn't think about it. Not now. It was too frightening.

She pulled up to a red light at Riverdale. And sitting there, suddenly a terrible, terrible thought occurred to her. *His bat.* He'd been at baseball practice. He'd have had his lucky bat with him. *We've got a chaotic crime scene. We've got witnesses to say there was more than one violent interchange.*

Bee took a deep breath. A sob caught in her throat. She pressed her fist to her lips. Tried to force from her mind the image of Turn with a bat in his hand, swinging in a huge arc.

No. Regroup. Another deep breath.

"Act two," she said. "Places everybody."

The red light changed to green and she pulled onto the bridge across the Rideau. The sky was growing darker. Bee watched the cloud shadows lengthen on the turgid water of the river. She leaned forward to look up through the windshield at God, assuming he was up yet. "No pathetic fallacy, thank you very much!"

"What do you mean I can't go in?"

The new ICU nurse's name was Winters. No first name on her tag. Probably "Frigida."

"You're not on the list," said Winters for the second time, as if maybe Bee were hard of hearing. She flipped the pages on a clipboard. Back and forth, back and forth. "You're family?"

"Not exactly. But I'm the only 'family' he's got right now, until his mother gets here."

Winters straightened up, cracked her back. "Can't help you," she said. "Rules are rules."

"Gerry Ocampo can vouch for me."

"Geraldine Ocampo is a nurse."

"And the lady at the desk, the unit clerk. I don't remember her name."

"And who's not on duty now. Anyway, I need a doctor's say-so."

"Well he did say so," said Bee.

"What doctor?"

Bee pressed her fists against her forehead, not surprised to find that it was throbbing now. "I can't remember. He was hardly here."

"Dr. Choy?"

"Yes! Dr. Brian Choy."

Nurse Winters shook her head. "He didn't leave instructions."

"But he told Gerry when I was there that it was okay."

"Well, he should have signed off. Sorry." She turned to go.

"No, wait," said Bee. "Dr. Choy said the patient was

unstable and that's why it was okay to be there. Because . . .
Because he might not make it."

Winters frowned. "You do realize that poor lad has suffered major cervical-spine trauma."

"I know that. But he was talking."

Winters raised her eyebrow with impressive disbelief.

"He was," said Bee.

"Well, that may be so, but he's certainly not talking now."
Somehow Bee didn't believe Winters. Her eyes gave her away.

"You have to really listen," Bee said, and earned a wintery glare.

"Miss Northway. I can assure you he won't be talking now."

"What's that supposed to mean? What's happened?"

"I'm not at liberty to tell you. It would be violating patient confidentiality."

"I had clearance last night."

"That may be so, but all I'll say to you now is that he's stabilized."

"I think—"

"This isn't about you. What *you* think or need is of no consequence right now."

"He was trying to tell me something. He is still talking, isn't he?"

"Not in any discernable way."

"The cops," snapped Bee. "Two detectives asked me to monitor anything he said. They're trying to find out who ran him down."

"Please lower your voice."

"Sorry. Ma'am. Nurse."

"When Mr. Turner recovers, your detectives can take all the time they want with him. My job is to help him do that—recover—and right now he needs as much peace and quiet as he can possibly get. Unless otherwise instructed, he is to be left alone. Now I'm sorry, but I've got work to do." She turned to leave yet again.

"Nurse Winters?" The nurse stopped but didn't turn. Probably building up an icy blast with which to transform Bee into a snowgirl. Slowly she pivoted from the waist.

Bee held up her journal. "He did speak. Really. I wrote down what he said. The cops asked me to." It was a bent truth more than an untruth. Bee pulled from her journal's pages two business cards. "The detectives who were here last night," she said, holding up the cards for Winters's inspection. For the briefest of moments, Bee thought the detectives' business cards had trumped everything. Wrong.

The nurse approached Bee, ignoring the cards held out to her, her gaze fixed implacably on the girl. "I'm sorry that your boyfriend was in an accident. I'm sorry he is in my intensive care unit. Now I would like you to leave."

"But—"

"When his *mother* gets here, she can decide whether you may enter. Until then, I'd thank you to let health-care professionals do what we're paid to do."

She held Bee's gaze another few seconds, daring her to blurt so much as another word so that she would have the excuse to Taser her. Bee held her gaze without apology and without tears. Finally, the woman left.

Bee stood there shaking, not sure if she would scream or just implode. Through a supreme act of will, she stayed where she was, banking on the fact that Winters would not turn around a second time. She didn't seem like a woman who was used to being disobeyed. Bee waited, stock-still, until the only other nurse in the vicinity moved on to some other soul on life support and the unit manager was digging in her filing cabinet and the old volunteer gentleman who had greeted Bee at the door was busy greeting someone else, and then she took a deep breath and made a beeline to Donovan's room.

CHAPTER / EIGHTEEN

And so, like some failure in evolution, they headed back to the swamp. They recovered the money first. "What happened?" said Jilly, seeing the half-empty briefcase.

Donovan shrugged. "My dad," he said.

She nodded. "Figures." She stuffed the remaining bills into her backpack and, when that was full, her pockets. Then she chucked the briefcase into the trash heap and they trudged down toward the slime.

"Look," said Donovan, stopping at the edge of the woods. "I'm going to hit the road, okay?"

"Like hell you are," said Jilly.

"No, seriously. I've got to get back . . . you know. Home."

She looked him up and down. "Planning on hitching?" she asked. "Good luck."

She was right. He was a filthy wreck, an escapee from the quagmire—a bogman. "Look, I'll walk if I have to."

She shook her head and moved on. "You set foot on that concession road, you're dead meat."

He stared at the empty road not a hundred yards away, then turned back to her.

"Did you happen to count the bikes leaving here?" He shook his head. "Well, there were ten. But there was an even dozen that were dispatched to do the deed."

Donovan swung his head toward the inferno. He saw no movement other than the flames trying to outdo one another at licking the sky. Then he turned to Jilly again. "Maybe they're dead," he said.

She shook her head assuredly, as if she knew for sure. "They left a couple behind to clean up."

"But the cops will come, won't they? A fire like that?"

"You obviously weren't listening to me," she said. She smiled patiently and combed her fingers through her hair. "The cops won't come until they're good and ready. The firemen won't come at all." She surveyed the inferno and then reached into her breast pocket and pulled out a little container of Tic Tacs, sprinkled a couple into her hand, and then offered them to him. He took a couple. Breakfast. "See, around here," she said, "the firefighters are all volunteers. Assuming anyone saw the flames—and that's a big if—and assuming that this same anyone bothered to sound the alarm, they'd know whose place it was and just go back to bed. The ground's good and wet, no chance of a brush fire spreading. That's the only thing they'd be worried about."

Then before he could say anything more, she was off

again and he had to scamper to keep up. The earth dragged at his every step.

"Where are we headed?" he asked.

"You'll know when we get there," said Jilly.

He wondered if that would be true.

They headed west, the fire over Donovan's left shoulder and the highway on their right. So close—a few hundred yards away. And Ottawa was . . . what? Sixty or seventy miles east, at a guess. They were walking parallel to Seven, and he couldn't for the life of him figure out why he didn't just swerve off and take his chances out there, but he followed, like some tame creature on a rope. He imagined he'd get maybe twenty yards before her bullpup bit him, good and hard.

There were cars on the highway by now, one every few minutes, with their headlights on in the gloaming. Commuters, he guessed, heading east to the city. He didn't know what time it was and then realized he had his iPhone, at least partially charged, and surreptitiously pulled it from his pocket to check. It was at 30 percent but there were no bars—none at all. Somehow he was not surprised; as if there was likely to be any communication in a swamp. It was five o'clock. He'd been up something over twenty hours. In no other twenty-hour period of his life, short of being born, had so much happened.

Meanwhile, Jilly trudged on ahead with her sci-fi shooter flapping against her bulging backpack. "Damned one-percenters," she muttered.

"What does that mean?" he asked.

"The Pagans: a pack of one-percenters."

"I don't understand."

"Ninety-nine percent of bikers are law-abiding citizens."

She didn't go on, but Donovan wasn't quite so numb with tiredness that he couldn't do the math. In fact, he didn't feel as tired as he had earlier. He was so far beyond the Pleasant Land of Tired that the idea of it didn't really compute. He also noticed that his foot didn't hurt anymore. Maybe he was high from exposure to all that weed. He sniffed the air. Soon all of the county would be.

"Didn't you tell me that Mervin was your brother?"

"I did."

"So . . ." he said and let the single word just float there to see if she could guess where he was going with it.

She stopped. Leaned against a tree and turned to look at him. "Mervin and the others—they can look after themselves."

"But all that gunfire."

She shrugged. "The Pagans like to make a lot of noise. Mervin isn't all that smart—I inherited all the brains in the family—but he's got enough horse sense to lie low."

Donovan looked back toward the homestead. The fire was burning itself out: a low glowing on the horizon, like a false sunrise with dark angles, black sticks where walls had once stood. How low would Mervin have had to go?

Jilly turned westward again, swinging her right arm in a wide circle to wave him on. "Westward ho the wagons," she said. "Pick it up, kid."

But he didn't. Maybe I'll just stand here and become a tree, he thought. Grow some leaves. How hard could it be?

"Move it!" she shouted.

After a while they stepped out of the submerged land onto more solid ground. The way ahead rose toward a bare hill, and soon enough they had cleared the drunken forest, though not without having to make their way through prickly ash that tore at their clothes and, finding flesh underneath, seemed all the more determined to feed on his blood. Jilly seemed oblivious of the thorns. Oblivious of anything but her task. And it seemed he was her task. His guide.

They stood in a field of wild grass, new growth coming up between the gray, winter-weathered stalks. The hill was laced with low-slung juniper bushes. Juniper. He remembered juniper, but it was a dim memory at best. He saw a berry amid the green and picked it. He rolled it in his fingers and sniffed it. Gin. It smelled like gin. A memory came to him of smelling that smell for the first time. Not the drink, the berries. He looked up at the woman marching on ahead. He seemed to remember her being there, too, just like this, leading the way. How could that be?

"Come on, Dono," she said. She pointed up the hill and on they stomped, at a brisker pace, until they reached the top and stared down on a wooded vale and a dark river. The trees were not yet dressed, but there were buds on every branch.

"Is that Mordor?" Donovan asked.

"What?"

"You know, where we throw the ring into the fires of the crack of doom?"

Jilly didn't seem to know what he was talking about. Or maybe, he thought, she just didn't have a sense of humor. Either way, Donovan shrugged and shut up. They headed down and soon found themselves walking through a grove of low and gnarled trees. Apple trees. An orchard, but abandoned, by the look of the underbrush. A few apples clung to the branches, blackened and shriveled. No Eden, that's for sure.

At the river's edge, Jilly finally sat down and, grateful, Donovan joined her, groaning as he stretched out each leg in front of him.

"I guess you only look like you're in good shape," she said.

He wanted to say he was in great shape for slapping a ball over the left field wall or running from third to home, but even as the words occurred to him, the thought of home blossomed in his head and then just as quickly shriveled like a dead apple. The thought of it plugged up his throat. She leaned over and patted his knee. People kept doing that. "I didn't mean nothing by it," she said. "I know what you've been through."

Behind them, the sun was rising. It hadn't made it over the hill, but there was already some warmth in the air. And smoke. "I'm sorry," he said, "about . . . you know . . ."

"My house burning down?" He nodded. She shrugged. "Happens," she said. He gazed at her, not sure he could have heard her right. "It's whatever it takes," she said.

"What do you mean?"

"To get you here," she said. "It's never easy."

"Oh," he said. It was no kind of answer. She glanced at him and something in her eyes warned him off: you don't want to go there, her eyes seemed to say. So he turned away and stared at the river, a whole other kind of water than what they'd journeyed through in the swamp, alive and moving.

"What do we do now?" he said.

"We wait," said Jilly.

She was staring across the river. Donovan saw smoke rising in a thin stream up into the lit air. Smoke from a chimney. And sure enough, he caught sight of a small house through the foliage on the other shore. No lights but a telltale shimmer of reflected sun on a window. Every sane person was still asleep. The low hills across the river were deeply wooded, but there were other houses, now that he adjusted his gaze, here and there, indeterminate in shadow. Cottages, from what he could tell, ramshackle.

"The dog will probably see us first," said Jilly.

Donovan inspected the other shoreline, about a fly ball to shallow center field away. He didn't see any dog. He didn't see anyone up and about. It was . . . he checked his cell phone. Six thirty.

"Where are we?" he said.

"Off the grid," she said, eyeing his phone with a wry expression. He tucked it back in his pocket and then decided to roll up his pant legs and see what damage the prickly ash had done—see if he'd picked up any blood-sucking travel companions.

"It's an island," she said, tilting her chin toward the far shore. "The river is like a moat."

There should have been something to say to this. But after opening several compartments in his brain and finding them empty, Donovan went back to examining his bloodied calves. He was tracing a long scratch on his left shin when it occurred to him what this river was. This is where you crossed over, left behind the land of the living. He looked up at the island across the dark water. It didn't look like hell. He looked down again at his bloodied legs. "Is this it?" he said to himself, and he was about to ask Jilly when he heard barking.

Jilly smiled. "Told you." She pointed to a black dog dancing on the other shore, barking his fool head off. "Minos," she added, waving to the dog, who immediately turned tail and raced up into the woods. Jilly got to her feet and slapped the grass off her butt. Donovan stared up at her.

"Charlie's dog," she said.

"Right," said Donovan. "Of course."

CHAPTER NINETEEN

Charlie came to them on a boat with Minos sitting in the bow. It was a wide-bellied rowboat, long and wooden, and Donovan thought he'd seen one like it somewhere but he couldn't think where. Then he remembered: it was Ratty's boat in *The Wind in the Willows*. His mother loved that book and she read it a lot, and he had a feeling he liked it because he liked who she was when she read it to him.

It had taken the dog long enough to wake his master. The sun was peeking above the hill behind Donovan and Jilly by the time Charlie launched his craft and began to make his way across the water toward them. As the boat pulled free of the shadow of the willows that lined the other side, Donovan saw that there was a kind of figurehead on the front of the rowboat—a skull. Nice.

Charlie was dressed in a wrinkled shirt. His sleeves were rolled up to reveal strong forearms working the oars rhythmically. His shirt had once been blue, by the look of it, but had been sun dyed, like his torn jeans that held about as much blue in them as the early morning sky. His feet were bare, as if it were July not April. Bare and very white. If his clothes had seen too much sun, Charlie didn't seem to have seen any; his skin looked like marble, all the more so for the shock of long, dark, unruly hair that crowned him King of the River.

There was a current. It was deceiving, and Charlie was such a good oarsman he seemed to navigate it without any trouble, but it was there all the same. Donovan watched a branch float by the boat, heading south at quite a clip. Not a river you'd want to swim across. Donovan couldn't help checking out his options. He wasn't exactly chained up in leg irons, but running was about the last thing he could think of doing. For now anyway. Jilly looked at him and smiled. Her smile was a kind of leg iron, come to think of it.

Charlie was strong, loose-limbed. With one last heave, he lifted his oars from the water and smiled over his shoulder at Jilly as the boat bumped up on the mud of the east bank.

"You are a sight for sore eyes," he said. He didn't even seem to notice Donovan, and when Donovan looked sideways at Jilly he saw a blush creep up her neck and her cheeks.

Before the raft had even made land, Minos leaped out, landing in the water, then racing up the bank to run in mad circles around Jilly, barking and wagging his tail and shaking the wet out of him. Donovan stepped back. He'd never much liked dogs. Especially big, noisy, black dogs.

Minos didn't seem to notice him any more than Charlie did. Meanwhile, the dog's master had jumped ashore, his
white feet squelching in the mud. He wore wooden beads
around his neck. He was handsome but for the pallor of
his skin. And though his hair was so black it had a bluish
sheen, his chin was remarkably clear of stubble. Unnaturally
smooth, like porcelain.

Jilly reached down and tugged him two-handed up the
grassy bank and into her arms. Donovan watched them
embrace before deciding to look at something else—anything
else. There was certainly lots of time for a good look around.
He resisted the urge to cough. Meanwhile, the dog sat at
Jilly's side, his tongue lolling, barking now and then between
affectionate whimpers as if to say, I've missed you, too, I've
missed you, too!

"Long time no see," said Charlie, finally pulling himself
away. "I saw the smoke on the way down."

"Yeah, well," said Jilly, as if her farm burned down on
a regular basis. Was that what she meant when she'd said
"Happens"?

The smile on Charlie's face lessened a few watts. "You
okay?"

She nodded. "I'm alive," she said, sounding as if it weren't
so much a miracle as a burden.

"The Pagans?"

"Who else."

His shook his head as if she'd said they were having
trouble with mice again. Then he turned his gaze on Donovan, and the gravity of his expression deepened, as if this
stranger had only just materialized there and his presence had

something to do with Jilly's misfortunes. Which Donovan had to admit was true.

"And you are?"

"Donovan." He was going to say his last name but stopped.

Charlie nodded by way of a greeting, not offering his name let alone his hand. But his arm pulled Jilly closer, in a proprietary way that made Donovan want to say, Listen, Charlie—if that's your real name—I never touched her!

The ferryman turned his full attention back to her. He did not let her go but, having glanced back over her shoulder toward the hill, she gently but firmly disentangled herself from his arms. "We should get moving," she said. It was the first time Donovan had thought that she was truly afraid the Pagans might be on their tail.

Charlie nodded. Then he peeked at the backpack. "That looks serious."

She nodded, smiled. "Yeah. And there's a little something from me, as well." She took her assault rifle off her back and handed it to Charlie while she slipped out of her backpack. Then she exchanged the pack for the gun. He took it in both hands.

He placed it on the ground, flipped the top back, and pulled out a fistful of bills. He nodded. Glanced at Donovan with a more kindly expression on his face. "This ought to do," he said.

"Go deep," she said. So he dug his arm down through the money until he reached the bottom of the pack. Slowly, carefully, he dragged out his find and held it up to the light.

It looked to Donovan like a dime bag of weed. "Nice," said Charlie, elongating the vowel tenderly.

"It sure ain't schwag," said Jilly. "For you, only top-shelf. Aged. Very smooth." She strapped her weapon on her back, stared again up the hill, then glanced at Donovan with an expression he couldn't read. The closest he could get was, What? You're still here? Something in him made him step back as if she were releasing him, but then her expression changed again and she shook her head slowly, back and forth. So he checked his movement, gave up yet again. There was a whole lot of giving up happening. It wasn't like him. He was usually the one who marched up and down the dugout urging on his teammates when they were behind, even if it was the bottom of the ninth. He wasn't sure what inning he was in anymore.

Charlie held the baggie for the dog to sniff. Minos barked excitedly and wagged his tail, which made Jilly laugh, despite her now obvious unease. Donovan watched her glance anxiously up the hill again. She patted the dog's shiny black head. "Good dog," she said.

Donovan felt like a third wheel. Here was this happy family celebrating the return home of Mommy with the groceries — not to mention tens of thousands of dollars — and he was just . . . what? Nobody. Next to invisible. Unwanted on the voyage. He looked back longingly, not toward the farm but northward. If all Jilly could picture on the other side of the hill was marauding gangbangers, Donovan saw a new day dawning. Across that hill, now sleek with sunshine, and through the swampy forest was the highway to home. The clouds were clearing; the day might get hot, or at least good and warm. He could walk a bit and his clothes would dry and then he could try hitching or call Bee as soon as he got some bars and she could come and get him.

"Hey!" Jilly was staring at him. By now, without really knowing it, he'd backed off a long way. "Where you think you're going?" He shrugged. She swung the assault rifle around and pointed it at him. He threw up his hands, shocked to fully realize what he should have known all along: he was her prisoner. "Come here," she said.

"You don't need me. I'm just—"

"No, you're not," she said, shaking her head. "You're staying."

"But why?"

She stared at Charlie, who shook his head with a disgusted look on his face, as if to say, Some people just don't get it. Then Minos, who had been sitting obediently at his master's feet, jumped up and came barreling toward Donovan and raced around him again and again and again, as if wrapping him up in rope.

"You see, man?" said Charlie. "The dog wants you to stay."

Donovan stared at Jilly, dumbfounded. She had pointed the gun at him. He'd thought they were . . . well, he wasn't sure what he'd thought. Maybe not friends, but . . . And she'd done that to him as if she were delivering the merchandise, nothing more. He squinted, his mouth open in an unasked question, and watched as the hard look on her face turned into an expression of the deepest sympathy. "Sorry," she mouthed. And in her face now, he understood something: the hardness was how she got through this.

There was a village among the trees. No paved roads to speak of, just tire tracks through the grass, trails and paths, some paved with stones set in sand. Handmade houses. Creations of the wood-butcher's art, nestled in leafy glades, crouching in ferny hollows, shot through with light from the rising sun. There were hand-carved or painted signs over some of the doorways: THE SECOND CIRCLE, FRANCESCA'S END, LOWER LIMBO. On the road nearest the river, several of the buildings were boarded up; summer homes, Donovan guessed. But as they walked the curving, rutted road up the hill, they passed a dome and a resurrected barn, a house built around a giant bark-stripped tree. Houses of salvage, chicken wire and tin, slate and off-cut lumber. Crouching houses, leaping houses on stilts, houses covered with hand-sewn canvas and sapling ribs. Houses made of train ties and fieldstone and junkyard mismatched windows.

If he was dead, he didn't feel any different—any *less* alive—than he'd felt for the last umpteen hours. When would that happen, he wondered? And the answer came to him unbidden: when he felt nothing at all.

This place—he felt it, all right. If it was a dream, it was one he'd had before. He had been here and was here again.

Despite the birdsong and the growing warmth, he shuddered. A colony of improbable cabins set in the woods against a backdrop of a steep cliff. From the water he had eyed that sandstone cliff above the treetops, the yellow rock face warming in the sun. There had to be a way up to the top. If he could get away, he'd find a path. Up there, surely there would be a signal. But he would have to pack that thought away for later, when and if he could recover enough energy for such a venture. For now there was just this sleepy village and a body that had never felt so bone weary, one he felt that he was carrying around like excess baggage rather than living in it.

The three of them and the dog came, at last, to a yurt—eight sided, as far as he could tell—with a roof of cedar shakes and with window boxes filled with last year's desiccated flowers. At the door, Charlie played butler, bowing low and waving Jilly and Minos inside but staying Donovan with his hand. He pointed out back to a shed. He was about to enter the yurt himself when Donovan spoke.

"Did someone come through last night?" Charlie closed the door softly and turned to him. "More like early this morning?" said Donovan.

Charlie nodded. "Man," he said, "you sure messed him up good."

Donovan didn't have the energy to refute the statement, let alone proof to the contrary. "Where'd he go?" he said.

Charlie stared at him, but his gaze softened a bit. "I just get them here, man." He shrugged. "After that . . . well, there are all kinds of paths." He threw out his arms expansively.

Donovan looked around. "But it's an island, right? How big can it be?"

Charlie pushed his hair back out of his face. "Maybe not so big in, like, area," he said, "but, when you add the dimension of time . . ."

Donovan stared at him. Had he missed something? Had Charlie lit up a spliff when he wasn't watching and was now talking Canabian?

Charlie laid a big-knuckled hand on his shoulder. "There're paths, man. Trails you gotta take. Shit you've still got left to do. Right?"

It took a moment, but Donovan nodded. Yeah, sure . . . all kinds of paths. Why not? Then he turned and looked back down the long, slow hill, where he could catch, from this vantage point, only a glimpse of the river.

"Don't get any ideas," said Charlie.

Donovan turned to face him. Charlie's pale-gray eyes said more: *Don't even think of leaving.* If that meant rowing back across that river, Donovan couldn't imagine it, but the look the man gave him made him shudder.

"Get some rest," said Charlie. Then he left him there, on the stoop. Donovan waited for a good minute or two. It wasn't just exhaustion, inertia. He was hoping against hope that the door would open again and Jilly would be smiling there, waving him inside, where there would be fresh bread and farm eggs sizzling in an iron frying pan. Honey in a ceramic pot and coffee percolating on the stove. When a good few minutes had passed, he took a deep breath of the pine-scented air, which would be all the breakfast he was going to get. It gave him just enough energy to make his way up the narrow path to the shed, lost in the gloom and up against the rock face of the cliff. He craned his neck and stared up. It seemed far too high to climb.

CHAPTER TWENTY

It wasn't a work shed or gardening shed, as he had supposed. It was actually just one huge bed—well, a mattress anyway—from wall to wall to wall, with just enough floor inside the door for an old stick-back chair to sit on to take off his muddy chucks and peel off his stained and reeking socks. The pine floor felt smooth and refreshing on his bare feet. The windows were open and the curtains billowed in the chilly breeze. The deep sill was lined with old hardbound books, shells, and pretty stones. He closed his eyes and stood there for a moment, just enjoying a silence that was filled with newly born light and a kind of sweetness that came from he wasn't sure where. Then, with his last bit of energy, he undid his belt and clambered laboriously out of his drenched and clinging jeans, his sopping boxers, and, last of all, his shirt, stained and torn and bloody.

He crawled across a handmade quilt and slid under the covers. His head hit the pillow as if it had been guillotined from his aching body. His last thought was of childhood and a cottage with flannel sheets.

It wasn't here but somewhere near. The flannel sheets, the light, the piney air. He knew these sensations. He was six? Somewhere that smelled like this. And . . . And his parents arguing through a too-thin wall. His mother crying. A screen door slamming.

Donovan drifted down, down, down into a vision of his child-self alone on a dock, watching dragonflies patrol the waters. He saw a fish leap and splash down into silver. Waves radiated from that disappearing act until they lapped feebly at the posts of the dock, his naked toes. He recalled his mother calling him for supper. Everything was okay except that Dad wasn't there. They ate alone, him and Mom. He remembered getting up from the table.

"Dono, where are you going?"

"Just to the window."

"Sit down, please."

But by then he'd seen what he needed to see, and he came back immediately. "Sorry," he said, and he dug into his food again. The canoe was gone.

Bee was with him, lying behind him, naked and spooning. He snuggled into her, felt her right hand find its way slowly, slowly across his shoulder, stop before sliding down his collarbone and then onto his chest. Felt her breasts press into his back as her fingers roamed his chest hairs. He groaned with pleasure. Then she was kissing his neck; he could feel the compression of her lips, the wetness of each kiss, until her fingers pushed back the hair to expose his ear and her eager tongue explored that cavity, flicking in and out.

I'm too tired for this, he thought, even as the one part of his body that never did much thinking rose to attention.

I'm too tired. Tired of running. Tired of wanting. Tired of fire and muck and surly strangers. I want to go home . . . Home to—

His eyes shot open. The flannel sheet he was clutching in his fist, the billowing curtains, the books along the window's ledge—nothing he had ever read. And these fingers on his chest with their bitten, black-polished nails.

He froze.

"Shhhhhh," said a calming voice from behind him. A woman's voice. He cautiously turned to face her and she pulled back, the better to see him and for him to see her in her nakedness.

"Wha . . ."

"It's okay," she said.

"But I—"

"Don't know me? Does it really matter? Isn't *this* all that matters?" Her hand slid down his chest, across his stomach, and disappeared under the covers.

"Wait!"

"But why?" she said, taking hold of him.

Why? A difficult question, one requiring a lot of concentrated attention. He closed his eyes, not up to the mental challenge. He groaned again. His penis, always the keener, had known the answer right away to the question that his brain couldn't handle, like the kid in class who's always throwing up his hand and saying, Me, me. Ask me—all attentiveness and knowing. The only answer his penis seemed to know was, Why not?

"No!" he said. "No!" And he pulled himself away and up on his elbows, gasping for breath. He grabbed the sheets and dragged them up to his chest. She only smiled, pulled her mane of auburn hair out of her face and smoothed it behind her shoulders. She was not a girl but a woman maybe twice his age, still smooth-skinned, with full breasts and a tattoo of a dragonfly perched above where her heart would be. There was also a tattoo of a salamander, delicately colored, appallingly realistic, curved down her belly as if darting toward the warm shelter of her groin.

She had Charlie's pale, almost iridescent white skin, dappled by the blue light seeping through the tie-dyed curtains. She rested on her haunches, her back straight, her fingers intertwined almost primly in her lap, but too decorous somehow, as if she were posing—on display. And he was drawn to her despite everything that told him not to be.

"There is only now," she said, her voice like syrup. Then she placed her fists on the bed and leaned toward him so that the long muscles in her arms stood out and her breasts swung freely—temptingly. "There is only this," she said, crawling on her knees until she had straddled his legs.

Her eyes closed, her neck arched, her mouth opened with longing, and Donovan felt his resolve slip away—like a boat caught in a sudden offshore breeze. He was stranded. Overwhelmed. None of this was real, and you weren't responsible for what was not there. What happened in hell stayed in hell. His hand reached toward her, toward her breast, wanting to touch the dragonfly . . .

And then he saw the millipede.

It was on her neck, and at first he thought it was another clever tattoo, hidden until that moment by her wild hair. But it moved down and down until it disappeared under her right arm. He snapped his hand back while she groaned in anticipation, her eyes still closed, waiting. He blinked. Had he dreamed it? Was it a hallucination? If it was, then so was the spider that shinnied down a strand of web from her hair onto the bedclothes and scuttled off. And the sow bug that appeared on her forehead. Her thick auburn hair quaked, alive with movement. Donovan pulled away until he could press his back against the log wall as her face drew nearer and nearer. As he watched in horror, a thick, black worm slithered out of her mouth, over the bottom row of her tiny, neat teeth.

He screamed.

He screamed again and, tugging on the bedclothes, covered his head. He squirmed under his flannel tent, sure that the very bed was alive with vermin.

"Go away!" he shouted. "Fucking go away!" He didn't stop shouting until he realized he was alone. He dropped the sheet from over his head and opened his eyes in time to see the door gently closing. But as he watched, it opened again—just a whisper—caught in the breeze, as if the little shed were breathing. He listened and was sure he heard the sound of laughter.

CHAPTER / TWENTY-ONE

It was growing dark when he woke again. Not full-bore night, but the dusk that gathered first under the boughs of pine trees at the foot of a sandstone cliff, blocking out the west-leaning sun. Donovan sat up and trained his eyes on the door. It was properly closed now. Someone had been there recently, by the looks of it.

And by the smell of it.

He craned his neck to see past his feet. There was a tray on the floor at the end of the mattress: a plate piled high with sandwiches, a bowl of fruit, a tall glass of some reddish brew with a creamy head, another bowl of something, still steaming. The aroma captivated him. Smoothing aside the covers, he crawled across the bed and stared suspiciously at the fare. The glass was frosty cold. He brought it to his nose and sniffed. Beer, sweet and hoppy. Suddenly he was overtaken with thirst. If it was poisoned, so be it. He drank. He tipped the glass on a steeper and steeper slope, as if he were drinking against the clock, as if his life depended on finishing this glass before the illusion ended. But it wasn't an illusion. He brought the glass down hard on the tray. His mouth hung open, beer drizzling down his chin and dripping onto his naked chest. He belched gloriously. Then he stared into the steaming bowl. Soup, thick with vegetables and chunks of meat. He breathed in tomato and herbs. His stomach rumbled. He belched again. He had eaten a couple of Tic Tacs sometime in the early morning, and before that . . . He could barely remember before that.

He sat naked, crossing his legs, and leaning forward, he carefully lifted the soup toward him. He saw nothing suspicious, nothing with legs, and anyway the peppery smell was driving him mad. If anybody was going to mess with him here in Lower Limbo, it wouldn't be poison, he thought; more likely some psychotropic drug—or an aphrodisiac, judging by his visitor. He shuddered at the memory—part repulsion, part insane pleasure denied. Some soup slopped hotly onto his inner thigh. Swearing under his breath, he lifted the soup bowl away from his body, then with one hand he pulled the bedcovers over his lap. He brought the bowl back carefully, grabbed a spoon, and dug in. Let them drug him senseless; how much worse could life get?

When he had finished the soup, he mopped up the broth with a thick slice of bread. He ate a sandwich of some rich semisoft cheese with avocado slices, cucumber, and bean sprouts. The fruit bowl contained a pomegranate, halved, revealing its ruby-red seeds; bananas; apples; and plums.

There were walnuts and squares of chocolate mixed among the fruit. Greedily, he helped himself. And then when it was done—when there was hardly anything left—he lay back down, his arms flung out to the sides, and waited for whatever was to happen next.

What did they want from him? Were they fattening him for the kill? Who was that woman, so beautiful and so lived-in! Did he know that face? He was afraid he did, and afraid he'd remember who it was if he gave it any more thought. She frightened him—her need. Who could ever satisfy it?

He sat up again, energized and resolute; he had to get out of here! Which is when he noticed his clothes. They had been washed and, by the look of it, ironed. They were folded carefully over the back of the chair. His shoes had been cleaned of muck, and when he reached out to touch them, he found they were dry. So if this place was some kind of purgatory, at least they did laundry.

His cell phone! He grabbed his pants. Not in the pocket. *No, no, no!* They couldn't do this to him. Then he saw it, the glint of its silver edge. It had been tucked safely into one of his shoes. He opened it. No bars. Not down here. But there was still most of the juice he'd managed to top up back at the farm.

Dressed, he stepped out into the failing light. He could see man-made lights already twinkling between the trees, although it was not quite dark. Then his sight traveled far over to his left, and about halfway down the hill, in a meadow at the end of a long driveway, there was a large building he hadn't noticed on the way up. It was brightly lit now, and seemed to be some kind of community center, for he could see a crowd congregated inside, and if he listened he could hear a congenial-sounding hubbub. Pathways led down to it from all around. He saw a couple and a child. The man had a mandolin strapped to his back. The child—a girl—ran ahead in a long white dress, did a wobbly cartwheel, and then called back to her parents excitedly, "Did you see that? Did you see that?"

Saturday, thought Donovan. It's Saturday night.

He walked down the shed's narrow path until he was at the yurt. He listened at a curtained window. There didn't seem to be any sound coming from inside. He thought of Minos. Was it worth peeking inside the door to see if Jilly and Charlie were there or not? No. He looked down the sandy road he had half stumbled up this morning. Nothing but tire tracks, really. He saw no one around. He heard distant laughter, from the meetinghouse, he supposed. Then someone started playing a guitar. A fiddle joined in, and finally voices rose in a cheery kind of folk tune. At the chorus, others joined in. It all sounded jolly, and Donovan wondered if everybody had been enjoying the well-aged gift that Jilly had brought in her backpack. Or were the contents of the backpack all just for her rowboat lover boy?

This was his chance. He turned and, craning his neck, looked up at the cliff face that had seemed far too steep this morning. He surveyed its length. A path at its base disappeared into the shadows between the trees. He took off along the path, glancing back furtively to see if anyone had seen him. No, all the paths of Hippieville led to Party Time.

As he'd hoped, the path curved around the cliff, and in not more than five minutes he saw what looked like a way up. It was just a narrow gash in the undergrowth that grew thickly against the sides of the cliff face, a trail, though not one used with any frequency. He climbed. The cliff blocked out the setting sun, but it was not so dark that he couldn't feel his way forward—upward—a foothold here, a handhold there. Slowly and with many stops and scratches, he made his way until he was able to look down on the tops of the trees and the crazy patchwork rooftops here and there of the little community in the woods. *Here be hobbits!*

He could catch glimpses of the river between the trees.

Distant thunder rolled. The sound surprised him, made him turn and press his back against the rock. His breathing was labored. His freshly pressed shirt was already sweat stained. More thunder, and he scanned the sky for lightning. Nothing. Not yet, but he could make out rain clouds approaching, heavy with a darkness blacker than the encroaching night.

He turned back to his task, and as he climbed, the breeze freshened. It would be cold up top. You never knew in this part of the world at this time of the year. Thunder suggested rain, but if the temperature dropped just enough, it might even snow. He'd seen snow in late April. Oh, but please not tonight. Or if it had to be tonight, *not just yet.*

With a final push and a last bit of a crawl he made it to the top and clambered to his feet on the plateau. There was an area of flat stone and beyond it grasses bending in the wind, bushes rustling, trees shushhhhing and waving, their tops still lit by sundown.

Lightning in the eastern sky. He counted: one Mississippi, two Mississippi . . . and got all the way to ten before he heard the rumble of thunder. From here he could see Highway Seven way off to his left heading east and west. He thought he could almost see the light spill of the city far off in the distance, but it might only have been wishful thinking.

He found a boulder to sit on and pulled out his cell. He opened the phone and there she was, Beatrice, with her brown eyes, a golden comma in the left one, not so much a twinkle as something molten. It was one of the few pictures he had of her smiling; not that she was dour—not that at all—only that she didn't tend to smile for the camera. She was downstage beautiful but with the mind of a stage manager: the one who got the lights focused and the curtains opened. The one who called everybody to places exactly when it was time. She had let him hang out backstage once during a dress rehearsal, though he'd had to sit on a stool in a corner and not move. From the shadows he had watched her at work, the show behind the show. The woman behind the curtain. Beatrice with her extravagantly thick hair pulled back in an all-business bun at the nape of her neck and her headphones on. God, she was gorgeous in headphones. He had watched her in the wings, her face capturing a little limelight that spilled from the stage, but a face that was made for deeper things. And yet somehow she had seen something in him worthy of smiling for—something worth believing in, beyond his ability to smack a ball around. Sometimes when he was with her he almost thought so himself.

Three bars. It ought to be enough.

He dialed and the phone rang and rang and rang and—

"Donovan?"

He almost couldn't speak, he was so glad to hear her voice.

"Are you there? Can you hear me?"

"I'm here," he said. "Except I don't exactly know where here is."

"Oh, Turn," she said, and she was crying now. He'd never heard her cry.

"Bee, I'm so sorry. I've been trying to phone . . . This is the first time—"

"Where are you, Turn?"

"I don't know. I don't know. Bee . . ."

"It's okay. Calm down."

"I've sort of been kidnapped. There's this woman, Jilly, who I almost feel I know. It's a long story. I . . . I—"

"Come back," said Bee. "I need you back, okay?"

"I'm trying, really hard, I've—"

"It's all going to be fine."

"Something happened," he said.

"I'm here," she said. "I'm listening."

Lightning flashed. Thunder cracked loudly, not more than five Mississippis away.

Donovan struggled to steady his voice. "My father," he said. "I killed my father. I didn't mean to. I don't remember what happened . . . some of it, just not everything."

"Shhh," she said, her voice a soothing whisper.

"There was something . . . Something I had to tell you."

"Okay, go on. What was it?"

He closed his eyes. "You are," he said.

"Yes. What?"

"I can't! I don't know what it was."

"It's okay, Turn. Shhhhh. Stay calm. I'm here. I'll stay here."

Donovan wiped his face with his hands. The sweat was cooling there. The wind was brisk, coming from the east, like Bee's voice was coming from the east and like the storm. All of it coming at him, exposed on the top of this headland in the sky. He tucked his free hand in his armpit, pressed the phone to his ear. "There was this fight," he said. "Rolly was there. And Kali showed up, too, which is weird because I thought they'd broken up. But anyway, that was later. She was with this guy. I didn't know him. There are these conflicting stories in my head. Are you there?"

"Yes," she said. "I'm listening."

"I'm scared, Bee."

"Shhhhhh," she kept saying. And her voice was like a quiet lake tide lapping on the shore.

"Bee? I'm so sorry."

"Just come back," she said.

"I'm trying. You have no idea." He laughed—it burst out of him. But he stopped just as quickly, because the sound coming from his mouth sounded insane.

She didn't answer, not right away. Then it thundered again, making him leap up from his sandstone throne, the noise so loud, so near.

"Don't leave me," he said.

"I won't."

"You are . . ."

"Yes. Right here. You'll be fine. You are strong, Turn."

He summoned up all the strength there was in him. "There's a storm," he said.

"Just come back, Donovan Turner. Do you hear me? Come home."

"I need you to do something for me," he said. He looked at his phone. He didn't have a lot of battery left. "Get the cops to phone me. If they call, maybe they can GPS my location. I'm on some kind of island, on a hilltop. They could send a helicopter, it's big enough—"

"Shhh . . ." she said. "I love you."

Then the heavens opened and the connection was lost.

CHAPTER TWENTY-TWO

If it was possible for him to look worse than when she'd left him, he did. He was agitated. As the frigid Nurse Winters had told her, there were ice packs piled around his exposed ankles and draped across his shoulders like football pads. His legs twitched, his free hand twitched, making a feeble fist. She tried to take his hand and he flinched. He tossed his head from side to side, straining against everything that held him down.

"Donovan, it's me," she whispered. "I'm not supposed to be here but I am." He stopped thrashing. It wasn't a coincidence! He could hear her; she was sure of it. "You missed me," she said. "That's why you were thrashing around, right?"

He groaned, long and deep. His hand rose and fell, his head shook from side to side against the ice bags. He was talking to her without words, expressing some huge need.

"You have something to tell me," she said. And immediately he stopped thrashing. He groaned again. "Something urgent," she said.

She turned to the door, heard someone wheel something by, heard the jiggle and tink of glass containers. She turned back to him. "Donovan?"

He writhed in his bed but stopped again, his broken body railing against the movement.

"Donovan? Are you there? Can you hear me?"

"I . . . hee . . . nosh . . . uuu . . . heee . . . is . . ."

"Oh, Turn," she said.

"Bee . . . so . . . sor . . . phooo . . . furti—"

"Where are you, Turn?"

"I . . . do . . . no . . . dono . . . Bee . . ."

"It's okay. Calm down."

"I . . . sor . . . k . . . na . . . thersis . . . wooo . . . Ji . . . Ji-eee . . . I fee . . . no . . . slongsto . . ."

"Come back," said Bee. "I need you back, okay?"

"I . . . tryhar . . . I—"

"It's all going to be fine."

His hand was twitching worse than ever. "Som . . . ha . . . hap . . . happen . . ."

"I'm here," she said. "I'm listening."

She watched his throat constrict, the muscles tighten like wires, his face contort. "My fath . . . I . . . k . . . kilt . . . my faaa . . ." He shook his head from side to side. "Di'n mean . . . Don . . . remem . . . som . . . of it . . . not . . . evthin . . ."

"Shhh," she said, her voice a soothing whisper.

"Therwa . . . som . . . te . . . te . . . you . . ."

169

"Okay, go on. What is it?"

His brow furrowed. "You are . . ."

"Yes. What?"

"I . . . can . . . cant." With an almost inhuman effort he managed to change "can" to "can't." Then he swallowed. "Don . . . Don't . . . whas."

"It's okay, Turn. Shhhhh. Stay calm. I'm here. I'll stay here."

She touched his face and, like before, he pressed his cheek into her caress. Then a string of unintelligible sounds poured from his mouth, all vowels without the basket of consonants to hold them together. Then silence. Then "You there?"

"Yes!" she said. "Yes. I'm listening."

"I . . . scare . . . Bee . . . " He began to keen, his voice a vessel of pain.

"Shhhhhh," she said.

"Bee? I . . . so . . . sor . . ."

"Just come back," she said.

"I'm . . . try . . . you ha . . . no . . ." Then his face seemed to erupt with anguish, the cords in his neck tightening. *Oh God,* thought Bee. *What am I doing to him?* Then the muscles of his face let go, slackened.

"Don . . . leeme . . ."

"I won't."

"You are . . ."

"Yes. Right here. You'll be fine. You are strong, Turn."

He swallowed, and his eyes, though they were closed, scanned the room blindly. "Therestor . . . stor . . ."

"Just come back, Donovan Turner. Do you hear me? Come home."

"Nee . . . somf . . . me . . ." He stopped. Then a slurry of sound fell from his lips, none of which she could make head nor tail of.

"Shhh," she said. "I love you." She wanted to see a smile break out on his face, his hand reach out for her—any sign at all. But it was too much to ask for. He had done as much as he could.

"What is it?" she said. "I'm listening."

She stroked the back of his hand. This time he didn't resist.

They had taken away her chair. It was in the corner, but she didn't bother going for it. At any moment, Winters would storm in and probably have her arrested. Every moment was precious.

"I don't believe you killed your father," she whispered.

Sounds poured out of him then, garbled and jumbled and meaningless, guttural—filled with razors and stone. Bee's stomach roiled watching him struggle. He withdrew his hand from her touch. That boy, the one lying almost peacefully last night—he was gone. She dared to hope this was a good sign. He is a fighter, she thought. He is recovering.

"*Someone* killed your father. That's what you were trying to tell me, isn't it?"

He groaned, whimpered. More sounds clattered from his mouth, but nothing connected to thought.

Bee leaned closer, wrapped her hand around the guardrail,

and whispered into his ear. "You have a story to tell me," she said. "We have to know your side of the story."

"You . . . are," he said, the word distorted, filled with air, but recognizable all the same.

"Yes," she replied. "Go on."

"You . . ." He stopped. She waited. But patience was not an option.

"Who, Donovan?"

He thrashed his head from side to side as if to say she had asked the wrong question. Was that what he was saying? She waited. His forehead creased. Whatever it was he was trying to say, he was agonizing over it.

"Ka," he said. "Ka-ee . . ."

"Kali?" she asked. He closed his mouth; she watched him swallow. Then he opened his mouth but no sound came out. She reached for the Q-tip and moistened his lips. He sucked on it, and after a moment she recharged it with more moisture and he sucked again, parched.

"Kaaaa," he managed again.

"Kali killed your father?"

"Nonononononononono!"

She stepped back from his bed, as if blasted back by the force of his denial.

"Not Kali," she said. "Got it."

"Bo," he said, interrupting her.

"Bo?"

"Bo . . . hu . . . hun."

"Bo," she said again.

"Bo . . . huh . . . hun . . ."

His hand flailed in the air and fell to the bed. His face contorted, but she had the feeling it was as much the frustration of trying to speak as the racking pain of his body, one aggravation compounding another. He groaned with a misery that cut her to pieces. She whimpered. She stood back, afraid now that she was actually making things worse. Winters was right; she had no business being here. She took another step away from the bed. She should go, let him rest. Later. She would come back later.

"Bee," he said, and she was at his side immediately.

"I'm still here," she said. "But you should rest, Turn. You need to rest and knit yourself back together."

"Ji," he said.

"Jill," she repeated. "Jilly."

"Jilly."

"Jilly."

She watched his face, wanting desperately to see him nod, but the cords of muscle in his neck were strained as if some huge blackness were passing up through him. His face was frozen in concentration.

Bee dug in her purse and pulled out the journal, flipped through the pages to where the ribbon was, and wrote down the sounds exactly as he had said them. Kali was connected to this whole thing. And someone named Jilly.

She heard voices just outside the room, glanced nervously toward the door. She lowered her head to his ear. "I can't stay, Turn," she said.

"Bo . . ." he said. "Bohun . . . bohun . . . er."

She wrote it down. Wrote and waited. He opened his

mouth wide and what came out was a stifled sob, what might have been a howl had there been enough air in him to make such a sound.

Then pain seemed to explode on his face, like terrible black waves inside crashing against his skull.

"Oh no," she said. "Oh, Donovan."

Then the doors behind her flew open and someone was saying her name over and over.

CHAPTER / TWENTY-THREE

He stood with the cell phone pressed against his chest, covered with both his hands. But he didn't stop talking. He had to tell her about Kali and the man who showed up with her at the apartment. Who? The idea came to him out of the night sky as bold and bright as lightning.

The bowhunter.

The one who had killed Jilly's dog. Could there be a connection? He didn't know or care, he just needed to talk to Bee, tell her all the things going on in his head. There was so much—so much to tell her. He shuddered into the blast of wind and rain in his face, his words shaking and trembling, until he could talk no more for fear of drowning. His mouth was full of the storm. He needed to get in out of the downpour. It buffeted against him, pushed him back away from the ledge. Behind him the trees, batted about by the wind, sounded like an ocean. He looked back toward them. Presumably beyond that wall of trees was the other side of this island. She had said that, hadn't she? Jilly. She'd called the river a moat, as if the whole place were man-made, imagined into existence. He was drawn to the trees—no, *pushed* by the huge, flat, slapping hand of the wind. He wanted *off* this island! But for now, he only wanted shelter. In the trees he'd be out of the rain. Then lightning crackled in the sky, followed instantaneously by thunder, making him duck and reconsider stepping in among the trees. Didn't every kid get that drummed into his head when he was little: don't stand under a tree when there's lightning? But the thing was, standing here so high up he was a lightning rod all by himself. He needed to get down off this rock, but he couldn't leave, not until the cops called. She had to do that for him. He bowed his head, shivering now in the blasts of freezing rain.

Phone. Please phone.

A minute passed. The wind howled, the rain was like sticks beating on him. The phone vibrated in his hand. Then his Death Cab for Cutie ringtone started up, hardly audible with all the elements acting out around him. He pressed the phone to his ear. "Hello?"

He listened. Nothing. Mumbling chatter. Laughter. Someone calling out a muffled name he didn't recognize. A rattling sound of glass tinkling against glass. Someone had pocket dialed. He held up the phone beaded with rain to check the number, and suddenly it was yanked from his hand.

"Wha—"

His arm was locked behind him in a steely grip.

He struggled. He was strong, but his assailant was stronger. He must have pocketed the cell phone because the next thing Donovan knew, the man had him in a full nelson and was pressing down on his neck. Donovan slipped, sticking out his foot in front of him just in time to avoid falling on his face. The man was saying something, his mouth up hard against Donovan's ear—growling something, pressing him harder and harder, doubling him over. He could feel the man's teeth against his ear.

"Think we don't know what you're doing?" the man said.

Donovan brought his hands together, cupping his fingers like two C-hooks, and pressed them against his forehead to alleviate the pressure on the back of his neck.

"Think the bowhunter isn't onto you?"

He pressed harder and Donovan groaned with pain. Lightning flashed and he glimpsed the tattoos on the man's wrists—all that he could see of him: two double bands of thorns.

It was the leopard. "You're not going anywhere, kid. You're staying here, where we can keep an eye on you," he said. "We need you dead."

We need you dead.

Which meant he wasn't dead.

Not yet.

Hope welled up in Donovan, gave him strength. With a grunt he lifted his right foot and smashed it down hard on Shouldice's instep. Once, twice. Then he swung his foot back upward between the man's legs and heel-kicked him in the groin. The leopard howled with pain and his finger slipped—just a bit—enough for Donovan to step beyond the man's right foot, plant, and then swing his left leg so that his foot was behind the leopard's right leg. With every ounce of energy he could summon up, he twisted, and Shouldice's left arm flew free. For just a second, Shouldice, still holding on with one arm, was lying exposed across Donovan's knee. He punched him three times hard in the groin and took him down. The leopard writhed on the ground and Donovan backed off. He had to get out of there now, while he had the chance. He started toward the path, slipping on the rock. Got his balance, only to be pulled down. The leopard had grabbed his ankle. Donovan kicked and kicked—kicked himself free. Then slid away, only to be tackled again. They rolled on the rock, Donovan using the other man's momentum to get on top of him, only to be rolled over again. The man was wiry and filled with the power of crazy. Donovan could feel his strength slipping away.

The leopard straddled him, his knees painful on Donovan's upper arms. "You're going down!" he shouted in Donovan's face, louder than the rain. "You hear me?" he said, his mouth all teeth. And then, just in case Donovan hadn't heard him, he punched him hard in the face. Donovan turned his head and took the brunt of it on his left cheek. The right side of his face was pressed hard against the gritty rock. All the fight went out of him. He struggled even to stay conscious. The rain battered his stinging skin. The sky was crashing all around him like crumpling metal. Then the leopard's hands cupped his chin so he had to look up into the man's face, dark one moment, then in a flash of lightning all too visible and ugly with rage and punctured flesh and that smile that was not a smile but a memory of a knife fight. It was a face insane with anger, as if his blood were boiling — as if fire were pumping through his veins. His hair had come loose from its ponytail. He was a wild man. He laughed and then took Donovan's head in both his hands and cracked it back against the stone.

Donovan went completely limp. It was over. He could feel what was left of his life slipping away from his grasp — his not-yet-much-used life. He could only lie there, sopping wet, bleeding and hurting, and watch his life step up and out of him and walk away.

The leopard felt it, too, the life seeping out of his victim. He clambered to his feet. Almost lost his balance, regained it, then he stood shakily, straddling the boy, towering above him. Skinny as he was, he looked like a colossus. Donovan had been almost a man up until a few moments ago, but now he was a boy again, defeated and surely dying. The leopard leaned over at the waist, with his fists on his hips so his face was directly above Donovan's. "You're gonna love it here. Man, do we have plans for you." He unbent himself to his full height and flung his head back to laugh up at the stormy sky.

He shouldn't have done that.

With what Donovan figured might be the last move he would ever make, he pulled in his foot and then smashed it into Shouldice's right leg. The man toppled over, stumbled to regain his balance, and then stood, his arms flung out to either side. Another lightning strike revealed his horrified face, his wheeling arms. He was standing on the very edge of the precipice. Their fight had brought them to the brink. The leopard was there one moment and then gone, leaving only his scream behind.

CHAPTER / TWENTY-FOUR

He was back in his father's apartment. He closed the door behind him. Undid his shoes and parked them on the rubber mat by the door. Dumped his cleats there as well. He could hear his father and someone else. Rolly. Drinking. He lined up his cleats next to his chucks. Listened to them laughing.

What did they possibly have to laugh at?

You don't live here, he told himself. You are a visitor. You are only passing through. You won't ever live like this. You know that. You are not *better* than him, but you are better than *this*.

Then somehow he was bringing his Louisville Slugger down, again and again on bowls and bottles and the whiskey glass he'd bought his father for his birthday—had his father's initials engraved on it. The irony of it.

He smashed and smashed and smashed, but when he came out of this frenzy there was only broken glass. Not a man with a broken face—a pulverized face—a face reduced to pulp. A dead man. He had not done *that*. He knew it deep inside his bones. If nothing else in the world made sense, this at least did.

He was cold. Colder than he could ever remember being, as if the rain had turned to snow after all, and he was buried in it. He had to move or he would freeze to death. He shook his head slowly, back and forth, back and forth, hating the pain and yet craving it—making it come again and again. You could only feel pain like this when you were alive.

He had not killed his father. Al's wretched ghost had lied to him. Big surprise! They could not pin that on him. He felt the revulsion grow inside him. Felt it like a wave shuddering up from his gut, rising in him until he burst awake, flinging his body sideways just in time to puke. The vomit erupted from him, splashing on the wet rock. All that food he had eaten so ravenously, flying out of him, again and again until finally it was over and he lay back down on hard, wet bedrock, his breathing shallow, aching all over, but still— miraculously—alive.

He wiped his face of splatter, barely able to hold up his arm. Then he lay there, letting the wind feel him up, tearing at his shirttails. He lay there and let the rain spit on him.

The storm was moving on. The rain only came in gusts now. There were trees on the clifftop and trees below him so that if he closed his eyes it was as if he were suspended in a place that was somewhere between the earth and another earth.

He forced himself to sit up again. Felt woozy for a moment and hung his chin on his chest. When he had the energy, he lifted his right hand and tentatively explored the back of his head. His hair was matted with blood. He winced with pain as he touched the wound and then, holding his hand close to his eyes, tried to see if the blood was fresh, attempting to see whether he was draining away or whether the hole in him was closing, scabbing over. The rain made it hard; everything was wet. He had no idea how long he'd been out.

What he did know was that he'd been hit by a truck — or felt like it anyway. The thought made him dizzy, even lying down. He felt the way a really bad hangover made you feel, lying in your bed with the room helicoptering around you, out of control.

He clambered to his feet, groggy as hell. It took him several efforts. He hustled himself, as best he could, *away* from the ledge. He found the boulder he'd sat on earlier, waiting for the police to call, a call that could not reach him now for the simple, earth-shattering reason that the man he had just pitched over the cliff had taken Donovan's cell phone with him. He sat down heavily. Then he leaned his head on his folded arms and started sobbing.

Eventually, he climbed down off the cliff. Backed down mostly, lying against the rough slope, letting himself slide, stopping himself with a foothold here, a handhold there. Until the steepness tapered off and he found himself at last standing on level ground, his arms numb, his back on fire, shredded. He stood, still dazed, deep in the shadows of pine trees and cedars, on the grassy trail that had led him around the cliff. He looked up dizzily and saw the top of it black against the less dark sky. Clouds scudded in the wake of the storm like nosy spectators following a riot at a safe distance. Where the clouds parted, he caught the odd glimpse of a renegade star. Then he looked down the trail, back toward Hippieville, Lower Limbo—whatever the place was called. Somewhere along there he'd find the leopard, if his fall had brought him all the way back down to earth. He might be caught on some ledge, bent around some tree branch. He might be alive. Doubtful, but then anything like certainty had taken quite a workout in the last twenty-four hours. For all Donovan knew, the leopard might have flown away. This island seemed a place where leopards might fly.

He found him, wingless, fifty yards later. It was so dark that he almost stumbled over the body. It lay spread-eagle, facedown. One of his legs was bent the wrong way. Donovan squatted and reached out to touch the man's back. If he discounted his father at the gambling table and then the hideous specter of him at the trash heap, he'd never seen a dead man, let alone felt one, but he knew—his fingers knew—that the man was no longer of this world.

Donovan felt the man's back pocket. He tugged out a wallet from his drenched jeans. He couldn't see anything, but he could feel his way to a few bills. He might need them. He had killed the man; he somehow didn't think robbing him would land him any deeper in hell when he got there. He was in no hurry. Then he heaved the man over, shocked at the dead weight of him, and felt his front pocket—had to be the left one, because it was his right arm that had snagged Donovan by the neck. He recognized a familiar shape, fished his hand in, and dragged out a cell phone—his cell phone. It was cracked but still lit up to reveal Bee smiling in a life he scarcely found possible to believe he had once lived. There was Italian blood in her on her mother's side: the thick fall of dark hair, the hint of coffee in her skin. There was just enough juice left in his cracked cell phone to see her. He kissed the screen. There were no bars, no chance of another call down here at the cliff's base, and no energy to climb up there again. Not ever.

He pocketed the money and the phone. He took a deep breath. He had to get away from here. He had to get out to the highway, get home. He had let Jilly lead him, too tired to resist. It had seemed right somehow. Not now. Not anymore. She had made it seem as if he had to do her bidding. How had she done that? Why had he trusted her? Well, it made no matter. She had abandoned him, and he felt no qualms about taking off—the sooner, the better. He looked back along the trail; presumably it would find its way around the cliff and on the western side there would be another river or the other arm of the same river. He had no idea how far it would be—how wide the island was. Better to stick to what little he did know. So he stepped over Oscar Shouldice—very carefully—and headed toward Charlie's place and the sandy wheel-rut road down to the river crossing. Looking back a few paces along the trail, the carcass was already lost in shadows.

After another hundred yards or so, he heard music. Not strumming and fiddling anymore but electric guitar, smashing drums, and a tectonic bass that seemed to come from somewhere down inside the earth. Stepping out into the clearing, he could see that the party at the meeting hall was in full swing. He passed the sleeping shed, Charlie's octagonal yurt, and walked down the hill they had walked up that morning.

There were lights on in the woods here and there, and there was the blaze of light from the meeting hall. He hoped most everyone was there, dancing up a storm; that or safely tucked in bed at home. He didn't want to run into a single soul. Doubted he had any fight left in him, should it come to that. He had one very simple plan. Didn't think he could come up with a plan B or any kind of evasive action. He walked in long strides, letting gravity pull him back toward the river.

"Donovan?"

The voice came from behind him, soft, barely distinguishable from the breeze in the trees and the underbrush. He stopped.

"You haven't forgotten me, have you?" said the voice, a woman's voice. And then a woman's hand was on the small of his back, flattened, rubbing gently up and down, soothing the skin grated on his rock-slide escape down from the cliff. He closed his eyes. What the leopard had not been able to do to him might be accomplished by this soft hand. An arm curled quietly, soothingly, around his middle. He felt her lay her head against his back. He was groggy, tilting forward and back, forward and back, ready to fall if it were not for the delicate arm around his waist.

"I have to go," he said.

"You can't," she said.

He knew who it was. And now her other hand slipped under his shirt and caressed his right flank, making him flinch at first from the abrasions there, then calm down again, settle into her hand's touch for it was cool, so cool.

"I have to get back."

"No," she said. "Shh," she said. "You are here now."

"No."

"Yes," she said plainly, without any attempt to convince him—as if it were merely a statement of fact. "There is such a long time ahead of us. It needn't be spent alone. The waiting . . ." She stopped and he felt her body press against him, but not hungrily as she had done that morning. It was more a desire to hold on to something, as if he might support her just as he felt she might support him. "The waiting doesn't have to be without tenderness," she said.

She kissed him between his shoulder blades. He heard the sound of her lips, felt the shape of them through his sopping shirt. Then she must have taken the material of his shirt in her teeth, for he felt it pulled away from his skin. He thought of the vermin on her, the things living in her mouth.

"Don't," he said quietly. "Please don't."

Her teeth let go but her other arm snaked around him, reached up until it cradled his right cheek, where the leopard's fist had landed. He let his head lean against her hand, hold him. It was heavenly and awful.

"Who are you?" he said, though what he meant was "What are you?"

"You knew me," she said, "but it doesn't matter. Nothing matters anymore. Matter doesn't matter." She laughed gently, then smothered the laugh in his shirt. "You are dead, Donovan. You can't grasp it yet, but—"

"No," he said.

"When you do get it—give into it—things will get a lot easier."

He wanted to argue. The leopard had told him he was alive. But he had no strength in him to fight this woman. He listened to the night: the band playing a ballad muffled by the trees and the wind and the water lapping. Water. The river was nearby. He had to get to the water, get to—

"You must be dead," said the woman, "because I am, and we are talking together, you and I. Holding each other—"

"No, only you are holding—"

"Don't," she said, and pressed herself against him, her fingers massaging his skin so that he cried out in pain, which she smothered with more shushing and kisses on his back. And her hands grew tender again, coaxing him to relax, to give in, to stay.

"I killed myself," she said.

He was caught off-guard by what she said. "Why?"

"Why doesn't matter."

"Of course it does."

"I don't remember," she said.

"How could you not remember?"

"Do you?" she said. His head hurt. What was she saying? "Let go of your pain," she coaxed him. "Let go of caring. It's too heavy a burden. Be with me. There is so much I can teach you about forgetting."

He closed his eyes, daring to imagine what that might be. He could turn around in her arms and hold her. Find out. But he resisted the temptation. His head tilted forward, his chin to his chest again, as if the whole night was one of resignation that never quite took. He wrapped his arms around her arms so that he drew her as close to him as he could, loving the feel of her body against his back, wanting this embrace, letting it charge him, give him the energy to go on, regardless of what she was saying. He must go on. He could not stop now.

"Thank you," he said softly.

"Then you'll stay?"

And now he unwrapped her, like tenderly taking off an article of clothing. He turned, and taking her arms, he gently pressed them to her sides and stepped away from her. There was a light over the doorway of a cottage in the trees nearby. There was an overgrown and mossy path down to the rickety broken gate where they stood. He wondered if this was where she lived. In the light he could see her clearly. She had seemed so huge looming above him this morning on his bed, but she was really not so tall. She was dressed in a simple black shift, the hem of which wavered around her knees, pulled at by the wind. Her legs were like birch saplings, white even in the semidarkness. Her feet were bare, her hair was a tangle, her face beautiful with hope, her hair glinting red.

"I'm not dead," he said. "Not yet."

Her face fell. But when she looked up into his eyes, there was no rancor, no resentment in what she told him. "That's what they all say."

CHAPTER / TWENTY-FIVE

She backed away from him, not out of fear but out of surrender, defeat. There was sadness in her eyes. She rubbed her lips with the inside of her wrist, and he saw even in the dim light from the porch the marks that had brought her to this place between worlds. He took her wrist in his hand and kissed the scars. He did not fear her anymore but only felt a deep sense of sorrow. She left him, and passing through the broken gate, she walked up the path to her house. It made him think she had abandoned hope before this; it came so easily to her. He almost called her back — out of pity, not longing. But the door closed on her without a look back.

There're paths . . . Trails you gotta take. Shit you've still got left to do.

He took a deep shaky breath, turned, and headed down to the river. It was around the next bend, if he remembered correctly. Yes, there it was. There was the faintest glimmer of light on the surface from who knew what source. Maybe a river at night could make its own light. This river anyway.

He looked up into the sky. There was no moon. Perhaps it was too early. But a part of him wondered if there was no moon on this side of the river. All the more reason to cross over.

Back at the social club, the band launched into some hard-edged rock song from the sixties or seventies. Neil Young, maybe. Distorted guitar. Right, he recognized the riff and the lyrics came to him. "Hey hey, my my."

He found Charlie's boat in the long grass, just where they'd left it, but now the grass was battered down by the rainstorm. He climbed aboard into a half foot of water. The boat rocked, the water sloshed. He climbed back out and stood looking down at it. There was as much river in it as there was for him to cross. Too much to bail. He'd need to tip it over. He grabbed the gunwales and started to tip it, but—oh, it was heavy. A wooden boat. A long wooden boat and he was such a long way from being at full strength. The water slopped from side to side, splashing up at him. He wiped his face. Stood up and crossed his arms, stuck his hands under his armpits for warmth. In the background the band was rocking out.

Exactly!

He pressed down hard on the gunwales and then lifted—Rock it out! Again and again, feeling the equilibrium shift. It was like pushing a car from a snowdrift, putting your shoulder into it, letting it fall back. Push, lift, push, lift. And now *lift* with all your might—with all the might that made you still something of the earth and not some phantom dweller on this island in the middle of Nowhere.

And the boat tipped. At its highest point, he felt it begin to fall away from him and he let go. The weight of water did the rest. Over it went with a loud *whoosh,* followed by a flat, hollow *thunk!* only he could hear, thanks to the grunge coming from the party.

When he had righted the boat again, he gathered the oars from the grass, placing each of them as quietly as possible into the oarlocks. The guitarist was on a wild, cascading fuzz-box solo; nobody would hear a boy on a riverbank unless they were within a few paces. He stopped for a moment, looked around. Then he climbed in, hurrying now, and immediately slipped and fell down hard on his backside.

His flailing arms managed to dislodge one of the oars, which clattered in after him so that the quiet was shattered. He didn't stop to listen. As quickly as his aching body could manage, he found his seat, restored the oars to the locks, and then . . .

His head drooped. He was still on land. Too much on land to shimmy the heavy vessel into the water.

This was not going well.

He climbed out again and headed to the prow, lifting it with a grunt that seemed to come from his very toes, and the boat slipped into the water so quickly on the wet grass that he fell again and almost lost hold of it, grabbing the painter just as the bow smacked the water's surface. He held on to the rope as if his life depended on it. The river had other ideas. It tugged the boat south. Which, when he thought of it, was the direction everything seemed to be going.

The current he'd sensed rather than seen that morning was strong now, fed by the gusting wind, the river heavy with the storm, flooding its banks, its powers renewed. With both hands, he hauled the boat back to the shore and slithered into it, shoving off as best he could, holding on to both gunwales as the boat spun lazily counterclockwise, finding the flow, rocking from his shifting weight, bucking a bit, settling in. He sat and applied his arms to the task of turning the boat to face the far shore. He pulled and pulled on his left oar and somehow managed to bring the boat around. Then he planted his feet firmly on the cold floorboards, bent deeply at the waist, and plunged both oars into the water, pulling for all he was worth to fight the river's authority.

There was only death over here, he thought. That's why Jilly had brought him. She had been his guide to the underworld, except he wasn't ready for that. He had fight left in him. All he needed was to make it back across the river.

It was only sixty or seventy yards. He could do it. Had to do it. He didn't care if he floated downstream a bit—which he was doing whether he wanted to or not—just as long as he eventually made it across. He plunged the oars in again, pulled and grunted with the exertion, matching strength to strength with the river's persuasive drag. Diagonally would have to do.

After only three or four pulls he had to stop and take a breather. Adrenaline had kicked in yet again with the promise of escape, but he was running on empty, a term that had taken on new meaning. How empty could you ever become? The damage suffered on the clifftop was deep. His muscles felt detached from his bones, as if it at any minute they might all snap. He had vomited up most of the sustenance he'd taken in, and it had come from only that one meal. He rowed some more, ached, groaned, dug in. Then he paused for breath and looked over his shoulder into the dark of the fields on the other side to measure how far there was left to go. A glint of something caught his eye. He stopped rowing. He scanned the far shore.

Men. The dark shadows of men.

Large men. Five, six . . . more . . . he couldn't tell. Wasn't sure what was solid or the product of an overextended imagination—an over*turned* imagination. He was almost midriver and the boat had drifted, clockwise this time, in just this short moment of his discovery, facing downstream and picking up steam. But he didn't dare row now. The music from the club had faded into the background behind the wall of trees that stood sentry along the island shore. The rock and roll dimmed under the wind and the water. Still, he was afraid the metallic sound of the oars in the oarlocks would carry to those shadowy figures assembling on the far bank.

He slithered off the bench, low into the boat, and let it drift away from the gathering. He was flotsam now. Just another storm-torn branch caught in the current. He peered over the stern. It looked as if the men were launching a boat of some kind themselves. Yes, four or five of them tumbled into it, not soundlessly but without any talk. A raft, maybe four yards long, sitting low in the water with the weight of its silent cargo. They shot across the water while another raft appeared and was soon filled and ready to go.

An invasion.

Lightning a long way off lit up the low and heavy cloud

cover, enough for Donovan to catch a profile or two of the men still left on shore. There were still others arriving down the long, slow hill. And it was clear to him who they were now, from the weight of them and the long hair flying in the wet air and the ragged beards and torn-off sleeves and weapons strapped to their sturdy backs. The Pagans were looking for their money.

CHAPTER / TWENTY-SIX

He was floating away, the river drawn toward some distant sea, without any way of knowing what side of the river he would eventually land on, assuming he would ever land at all. Having stopped rowing, his body had lost all desire to continue. It was a miracle he had gotten this far. The rest was out of his power. He moved on, two hundred, three hundred yards from the landing place, turning in a slow circle, the current strong enough to spin the boat, which he had noticed when it was upside down had little in the way of a keel. Lightning glimmered, but all Donovan caught sight of ahead was the skull on the bow of the vessel. The skull's back was to him, but he knew it was smiling. It was all a skull could do. From relief, maybe?

He rested his hands on the cold seat. He closed his eyes. Somewhere up ahead he would find his strength and muscle the boat over to the other shore, but for now he just needed to rest.

The easterly gusted above him—around him—pushing the boat back toward the island shore, but by now far enough downstream that he had rounded a thickly wooded point of land and the site of the invasion was lost to him. Then suddenly there was a huge jolt that rattled Donovan's bones and pitched him to the deck. The boat had hit something. Its momentum was stopped dead just for a moment, then it began to list to the right and slip forward again to come to rest at last in a marsh of bulrushes.

It was quiet here, still. Somewhere a few feet away the river rushed on its course to wherever, but in this backwater there was only the gentle sloshing of the deadened waves against the hull of the boat, a somnolent lapping sound, soothing.

And the frogs again. The peepers.

He could not see the shore. He leaned over the gunwale, tried to judge how deep it was but saw only black, smelled only stagnation. He manhandled one of the oars out of its lock and lowered it into the water. It didn't go far into the sludge. Like a blind man, he felt along the oar's shaft until he came to the wet, then lifting the oar, he measured how deep the water was: seven hands, up to his midthigh, more or less. He could wade ashore. He couldn't really *see* the shore, but he could hear it, the wind making havoc in the willows. He sat, slumped on the bench, and tried to summon up the energy to climb out of the boat and wade through who knew what kind of mud and crap toward nothing more substantial than the sound of earth. Who knew how deep the swamp floor really was?

Then the shooting started.

It sounded almost innocuous. *Pop, pop, pop*: fireworks a long way off. Then he heard the screams. He slid down onto the floor of the rowboat, the hold of it, and slithered on his backside to the farthest corner in the back. The explosions and shouts and screams went on and on, distant but blood-curdling. As far away as it was, he covered his ears, as if the dying were all around him.

Jilly! She was there. He imagined her dancing with Charlie and then the doors flying open and the Pagans entering, guns blazing. In his ravaged imagination, Donovan watched her, twirled around and around by machine-gun fire, a whole other kind of dance. He curled up into a fetal ball, his teeth chattering. It was his fault. And if that wasn't enough, it *kept on being his fault.* He should never have run—should never have come here. He wrapped his head with his arms to block out the sound of the killing.

He awoke to a splash. His eyes flew open. It was light. Gray dawn, everything shrouded in a heavy curtain of mist. His mouth was open. There was spittle on his cheek. He wiped it off, closed his mouth, swallowed hard. His throat was dry.

Something was moving nearby. He looked over the gun-wale and watched a black nose, poking out of the water, head past the boat, leaving behind a V of tiny wavelets. A beaver, he thought, but too small. A water rat—something like that. It must have seen him for it dived suddenly and was lost to view. He leaned his chin on the gunwale and waited, but it never came up that he could see. He smiled to himself. It had seen him. He was pretty sure of that. And that was good, wasn't it? It meant he was real.

He listened to the morning gathering itself around him. Birds chittering, some land animal nattering. A *clonk, clonk, clonk* that he guessed might be a woodpecker. He stared east. He didn't think he had ever thought just how wonderful morning was, even if there was only a silvering of the sky to indicate that there might be a rising sun back there somewhere. He couldn't see the eastern shore of the river. Couldn't see beyond the marsh grass and bulrushes. And that made him feel safe. Safe as Moses. Except for one undeniable problem.

He was still on the wrong side of the river.

A red-winged blackbird sat on a bulrush only a few feet away. He watched until it, too, seemed to notice him and flew off. A wise decision. Stay with me, man, and there's no telling what will happen. But, oh, for a pair of wings with red epaulets. Sadly, he was earthbound. Correction: waterbound.

He was sitting in several inches of water. Had it rained again? He didn't think so, not this much. He crawled to the bow of the boat and stared over the side. There was a hole. He looked back the way he'd come and saw a boulder some ten yards upstream. The culprit. The crack wasn't big, but when he reached down he could feel the water bubbling in. He rested his arm on the foredeck and his head on his arm.

I wake up to this?

After a moment, he lifted his head and looked into the gloom of the near shoreline. It was as far away as first base. Time to disembark. Either that or do the right thing and go down with the ship. But that was only true if you were the captain, he thought. And he was not the captain of this ship, just an ill-fated passenger. Then he heard a noise in the underbrush and looked again and there was someone coming. A figure moved out of the shadows into the light at the shore.

Jilly.

He heaved himself over the gunwale and lowered himself to the cold bottom, gasping as the water reached his crotch. But that was as far as it went. Holding on to the edge of the boat, he took a tentative step, then another. He stopped, returned to the boat and grabbed the painter, and tried to drag the boat to shore behind him. No go. The waterweeds were too thick, the weight too much, and his strength sadly diminished. He dropped the line. Charlie's boat would sink there. The skull just smiled back at him. He turned again toward the land and the woman who'd brought him here.

It was like moving through motor oil, black and viscous. But with each stride it was less deep, and finally he waded ashore. The southern end of the island, he guessed. She had stepped back to give him room to clamber up onto dry land, as if, like a dog, he might shake the water off. She leaned against a tree. She had changed. She was wearing a blue dress with embroidery across the chest. A party dress, he guessed. She wore a yellow cardigan over it against the morning cold. She must keep stuff at Charlie's, he thought. She was holding something in her arms. She pushed herself away from the tree and handed it to him, a soft old gray blanket. He took it and draped it around his shoulders.

"You're alive," he said. She nodded. "What about the Pagans?"

She rolled her eyes. "They always do that," she said disgustedly. She folded her arms. "One of the things about being alive is knowing that the Pagans are going to come."

"I don't understand."

"It happens again and again. They sweep down, all unsuspecting, and kill every living soul in horrible ways. Happens over and over. The folks here, they die, then they forget about it and go on about their business until the next time."

He gazed at her, his head filling up with questions like Charlie's boat was filling up with dirty water.

"What?" she said.

"Your place," he said.

"What about it?"

"When I apologized for, you know, bringing down the Pagans on you, you just shrugged. Like it was no big deal."

She shrugged again, but in her eyes he could see that she knew where he was going.

"It'll be there when you get back, won't it," he said. She nodded. Then he looked back across the river and frowned. "But it's over there," he said, not wanting to say what "there" was any more than he wanted to accept what "here" was.

"Some places are so near to the other world they kind of operate on the same principles. If that helps at all."

Donovan looked down at the wet earth and shook his head. She came closer and took him tenderly by the arm. He looked up and stared at her. She had done something with her hair: there was a flower in it. "I *do* know you."

"I brought you here, Dono."

"I mean from before."

Her smile was radiant. Maybe the sun had come up behind

his back, snuck up on him when he wasn't looking, and now it was shining fully in her face. He actually turned to look, but no, just a curtain of silvery gray. He returned his gaze to her to find some of the glow had gone. She was still smiling, but she was troubled.

"Remembering can be hard," she said.

"Yeah," he said. "There's this hole in my memory."

"Don't sweat it," she said. "We remember what we can bear to remember."

He looked down at the ground again and shook his head slowly. "I know this much. I didn't kill my father."

"Good," she said. "Then this journey has been worthwhile."

He looked at her, puzzled.

She shrugged. "I'm your guide, Dono. Guess I wasn't doing all that good a job. I came looking for you yesterday in the sleep shack. You were dead to the world. Sorry, bad choice of expressions. Then the next time I looked, you were gone."

"I had something I needed to do," he said.

"Bee?"

"Yeah. I had to reach her."

Jilly nodded as if she understood. "I figured it was something like that. You were saying her name in your sleep."

"So not entirely dead to the world."

She smiled again. Then she looked past him toward the dawn, squinted as if the light must be growing—dazzling. It wasn't, as far as he could tell, but maybe her eyes were more sensitive. "I kept looking for you at the dance, just in case you showed up. I'd have sent you packing if you did, knowing what was coming. But you figured it out yourself."

"Not really. Dumb luck."

She looked beyond him again. "You were trying to leave," she said.

He followed her gaze to the boat, which was sitting significantly lower in the water now.

"Charlie's going to love that," he said.

"Don't worry about him."

"I'm not," he said.

"But you are worried. Your face is one big worry."

He shuddered, wrapped the blanket closer to himself. "I'm not getting out of here, am I."

"I don't know." She shrugged. "I'm not in charge. When someone turns up on my doorstep, I know to bring them here." She reached out and squeezed his shoulder. Her hand was strong. It hurt, but it was a good hurt. "You've hung on a long time. Longer than most."

Donovan grimaced. "What am I supposed to make of that?"

"It means there's something you still need to do."

Shit you've still got left to do.

He looked at her. Her eyes were shining, and he didn't bother to see if it was the sun because he knew now that the light was coming from inside her. It gave him a kind of hope. "I couldn't kill someone," he said. Jilly's hand had been resting on his shoulder. Now it traveled down his arm to his hand, which she took in hers. "Come on," she said.

He hurt all over and he was freezing cold and he was

starving, but her hand in his felt wonderful. This was what being alive meant. What more proof did he need?

There was a path of sorts, an animals' path, narrow and ill-defined, but something to follow. Jilly dropped his hand after a bit because they had to walk single file. He followed after her, as docile as a lamb, and after a while the path opened up to an overgrown and drenched garden surrounded by a falling-down fence, along which grew magnificent sunflowers with their heads lowered, daunted by the night's downpour. There were dewdrop-laden tomatoes and behemoth zucchini. There were bushes weighed down with green and yellow beans. There were carrots and beets, everything luxuriant and well tended. He smiled. He remembered helping with the weeding.

He lifted his eyes. Beyond the garden stood a house, a small house—just a cottage. Not a dwarf's cottage, either, with fancy painted shutters. Not a yurt or anything fanciful: a small, brown-stained, wood-sided cottage with a tar-paper roof and a woodstove. He could see smoke curling up into the leafy birch trees.

But that was odd.

There were leaves on the trees here, more golden than green in the sunlight. Because now there was full sunlight, and he and Jilly stood in dappled shadows. He realized he wasn't cold at all anymore. Jilly held out her hand, as if she had read his mind, and he handed her the blanket. She folded it carefully and then held it to her chest, her arms wrapped around it. She nodded toward the cottage and her eyes asked him if he recognized it. He nodded. It was coming back to him.

The roofline sagged, bowed in the middle. His eyes traveled to the left, knowing before he saw it that there would be an outhouse at the back end of the garden. There, right there, with a sickle moon carved into the door. He had been to this place before, when he was young. When they were still a family.

All those many moons ago.

CHAPTER TWENTY-SEVEN

Bee sat in the waiting room where she'd met with Bell and Stills. It had been empty then; it was busy now, late afternoon on a Saturday. A different place altogether than in the small hours of a rainy morning. Thirteen hours ago. A lifetime ago.

Her head was buried in Scott Yarabee's neck, sobbing and accepting tissues from him to clear away the worst of what was spilling out of her face. His arm encircled her shoulder, his voice was low and calm. His sweater smelled like wood smoke. Trish was with Donovan.

"You go," said Bee. "I'm fine."

"I'm good," he said. "Anyway, I'm afraid I might run into that she wolf." That was how Bee had introduced the on-duty nurse, inevitably bringing to Scott's mind Shakespeare's "winter of our discontent." Bee pulled away, coming up for air in order to wipe her nose again. Beside her, a little boy was revving his plastic car's engine— *"Vrrrrrm! Vrrrrmm!"*—while his baby sister yowled in her stroller and their mother nattered to someone, seemingly oblivious to the combined decibel level of her children. Bee dove her head back down into the comfort of Scott's shoulder. He patted her head.

"I'm not a puppy," she said.

He got them both a coffee. Trish had been in the ICU for an hour now. "You should go be with her, Scott. I'm fine, really."

"Let's finish our coffee," he said. He took a noisy sip and gagged. "Which might be sooner than expected."

Even as he said it, Bee gagged as well.

"Machine-made cappuccino," Scott said, and somehow imbued the three words with a world of discontent.

Bee got up and walked over to the trash can to deposit the cup and its putrid contents. She remembered Inspector Stills taking her soggy tissues to the same trash can the night before. Then she returned to Scott and stood in front of him. "Just go," she said.

"Hey," he said, standing up and taking her face in his hands. "You've been holding the fort, Ms. Beatrice Tomato Northway."

"Stop," she said, trying not to smile. She removed his hands from her face. She didn't press him. He was not a man who would be pressed. Instead he told her about the cops chasing them down in Algonquin Park. They were canoeing but had left an itinerary at the park offices. They hadn't gotten far.

"We fell asleep to the sound of the wind in the pines, the water lapping on the rocky shore, the baying of wolves. We woke up in the dark to a helicopter. It was like something from *E.T.*" They left the tent pitched and hitched a ride back to where their car was parked. He would have to go back to recover whatever the bears hadn't destroyed.

"Local OPP gave us a police escort as far as the end of his jurisdiction. First time I've ever driven at warp speed on the Trans-Canada."

He sat and stretched out his legs, his hands pressed together between his thighs. He was one of those happy-faced men. She imagined that he would look like he was smiling even in his sleep. But now his brow was filled with consternation. Their rude awakening, the long drive home, and what they found in the ICU had obviously taken a toll.

He moaned. "I'll never get her to go anywhere ever again without her cell phone," he said. Then he took Bee's hand and gave it a squeeze. "Thank God you were here for him," he said.

She nodded, then looked away. "I need the ladies' room," she said. She walked away, head bowed. Seeing them, Trish and Scott, had relieved the pressure of being Donovan's sole support, but all her strength and resolve had abandoned her now, left her exhausted beyond belief. She washed her face repeatedly, splashing cold water in her eyes, then drying her face on the horrible brown paper that seemed more tree than towel.

When she came back to the waiting room, Scott was gone. Good, she thought. Trish needs him more than I. But the woman with the noisy kids wasn't quite as oblivious as she had seemed.

"Something's happened," she said.

"Excuse me?"

"Your friend. They came to get him. One of the greeters."

Bee turned and faced the doors to the ICU. She saw a solemn-faced doctor in scrubs buzzed through the swinging doors into the unit. The doors clicked shut behind him. She heard a clangor in her head, sirens as loud as an air raid. She saw Donovan rise from his bed into the dim mechanical air of his chamber, watched the wires and cables and tubes fall away, saw the capsule of his room suddenly fall out of orbit and drift off until its glinting surface was lost in dark matter.

CHAPTER / TWENTY-EIGHT

He passed through the garden, everything bent from the storm but not beaten. There was a sandy path that led around to the front of the house and to a gate. He passed through the gate. He seemed even to remember the slight screech of it as he pushed it open and closed it behind him.

"Always close the gate or the rabbits and deer will eat us out of house and home." He smiled. His mother's voice had come to him out of nowhere. He stood gazing at the screened-in porch. He turned and there was Dad's car, the Subaru wagon with the busted front bumper. And there was the water, sparkling, for there was no mist here—not on this side of the island. The river was wide and green except where it was mottled gold in the morning light. The red canoe was tied to the dock. He smiled. His father was home.

He heard sounds inside. He walked to the screen door and opened it, felt the slight tug and click of the spring catch releasing the door to his grip. He stood for a moment on the threshold, then his mother's voice came to him again.

"Don't just stand there letting in the mosquitoes."

He hurried inside and let the screen door close behind him. *Click.* At the last second he had stopped it from slapping with his butt. He stepped into the dim front room. Mom was at the counter washing up. She was in jean shorts and a pale-peach-colored top with loose sleeves she had to keep rolling up. Her hair was up and held in place by a chopstick. She was humming a song by Duran Duran, her shoulders bopping along. He knew the song, "Come Undone." Sometimes she would sing the words and hum the parts she didn't know or was too preoccupied to remember.

"Hey child, stay wilder . . ."

He liked that part. She would sometimes say that to him with a big grin on her face and he would cover his ears because she didn't have a very good voice. He would scrinch up his nose and beg her to stop and she would laugh all the more and sing all the louder and tickle him. But now she was just singing to herself.

Dad came into the front room from the darkness of the little bedroom. There were two bedrooms: one small and one smaller—not much more than a closet. But it was big enough for Donovan, as tall as he was for a seven-year-old. Dad was in shorts, too, his legs tanned and strong. He was wearing a spotless white T-shirt. His face was newly shaved, his hair tousled and still wet from a shower.

"I'm heading out," he said.

Mom didn't answer, but her hands stopped moving. She stopped singing as well. Her shoulders stopped bopping.

"I'm going to paddle up to that creek I was telling you about," he said, gathering his watch from the arm of a huge old armchair. "Might be a while. Have no idea how long it is," he said, as if she'd asked a question. He chuckled. "If I'm not back by dark, call the emergency response team."

Mom's shoulders relaxed and her hands started to move again. She picked up the song where she'd left off.

Dad turned for the door then something made him stop. For one astounding moment Donovan thought his father'd seen him standing there in the doorway, a spindly silhouette, framed in morning light, but it wasn't that. Dad made his way back through the front room to the kitchen area and gave Mom a peck on the cheek, squeezed her arm.

She inclined her neck for him to kiss, but he didn't. He turned and headed for the door.

"Hope the fish are biting this time," she said.

He stopped and slowly turned. "What's that supposed to mean?"

Mom only whooshed a strainer out of the soapy water and clanged it down into the drying rack. Dad made a sour face and headed toward the door.

Donovan stepped aside to let him pass, but he didn't want to. He wanted to stop him. Wanted to stand his ground, grab on to his father's hairy wrist and hold on tight. But he couldn't, couldn't have even now, when he was ten years older and taller than his father—ten times stronger. It didn't matter. You can't ever stop your father.

Donovan took one last look at Mom and then followed his father outside, watching him half run down to the dock, in such a hurry to get away.

There was no fishing rod in the canoe. Had Donovan noticed that before, when he had stood here all those years ago? His father bent down, grabbed the gunwales of the canoe, and expertly pushed himself off from the dock, out into the dappled green, settling onto his wicker seat without a fuss, picking up his paddle. The paddle was made of cherry-wood. Donovan knew that because he had given it to him. Well, Mom had bought it for him to give to his father. She had given Al the canoe.

"Follow him," said a voice behind Donovan.

He turned. It was Jilly. She had moved up the hill, up toward the head of the trail that led from this secluded cottage back up the island to the settlement. She nodded her chin toward the dock. "Go," she said.

He turned and, surprisingly, his father had not left the dock. He was just now reaching down to grab the gunwales, preparing to kick off. But . . . Donovan turned to her.

"Go, Donovan."

"There's no boat," he said.

She laughed. "Well, walk," she said.

He turned again, in time to see his father bend down, grab the gunwales a third time. Donovan looked back at Jilly for direction. "Like Jesus?" he said.

"No," she said. "You are part fish, you know. We're all part fish. We came from the sea. We never lose it, really."

"I'm not much of a swimmer."

Again she shook her head. "Walk," she said.

This was getting nowhere. He turned, scanned the shore for a bridge, a spit of land, the slippery wet surface of a stepping-stone. But he knew this beach, this stretch of river. The water got deep quickly.

When he turned back to her, he gasped because she was right behind him. She took him lightly by the shoulders and turned him around to face the dock, the red canoe, his father, who still kept leaving and not leaving. "Follow him," she whispered in his ear. Then she kissed the back of his head and gave him a gentle shove.

Somehow he understood now. He walked down to the beach and stepped into the water. He turned, hoping for a nod—something to let him know he was on the right track—but she was gone this time, and he was filled with uncertainty.

"Jilly?"

He turned yet again to the dock and was not surprised to see his father reach the canoe, bend down to grab the gunwales, as if he would always be stepping into the red canoe.

"Boy!"

Donovan turned back toward the forest in time to see the brush part at the trailhead. The lion stepped out. He was as unkempt as ever, dragging weeds and bramble in his wretched clothing. His body was pockmarked with bullet wounds. Smoke drifted from some of the rude holes in his chest and head and legs. He swiped the air in front of his bearded face, clearing the smoke, while a bleeding hand pushed aside his mane of hair, picking out leaves and branches and throwing them aside.

Donovan stood ankle deep in the river.

They sweep down, all unsuspecting, and kill every living soul in horrible ways. Happens over and over.

Now the leopard arrived, pushing aside a branch and stepping up beside Mervin, dragging his badly twisted right leg. His face was smashed in from his fall from the cliff, his nose a black mess of congealed blood. He made a face at Donovan and then, reaching down, straightened his knee as best he could, so that it was the right way around. He hitched up his pants and crossed his arms as if to say, You have a lot to answer for, kid.

"You seen Jilly?" asked the lion.

Donovan nodded. "She was here," he said. The two men looked around and then returned their attention to Donovan. He shrugged. "I don't know where she went. She *was* here. Then she was just gone."

There was an angry shout from still farther up the path, behind the two men. They didn't turn, just kept a weather eye on Donovan as if he might also disappear if they didn't pin him down with their gaze. The new voice belonged to Charlie. He pushed his way urgently between the two men. He was carrying his dog, Minos. The big black body lay across Charlie's arms. There was an arrow in his neck.

"The bowhunter," said Donovan. It just came to him. Like what had happened to Jilly's dog.

"We've got to find him," said Charlie.

"We've got to find Jilly first," said the lion.

"No," said Shouldice, raising his arm and pointing at Donovan. "The first thing we've got to do is destroy him."

Which is when Donovan turned toward the river and

waded in. Not in any great hurry. They weren't going to follow him. They called after him, but he didn't turn around. He was going to take Jilly at her word, believe in his fishy past and just go. Glancing sideways, he saw his father take off from the dock—at last for real—and glide out onto the golden-green water. It was as if he had been waiting for Donovan—as if he would have waited as long as it took for him to enter that river. He shot ahead with strong, sure strokes and Donovan followed, walking forward until his head was underwater.

"You ain't getting away that easy!" yelled the leopard.

"Where's Jilly?" yelled the lion.

"Damned bowhunter!" yelled Charlie.

He could hear them all, even down here, but he paid them no mind, just walked on the sandy floor of the river. At one point he looked up and saw the canoe passing over his head. He had gotten ahead of his father. He waited, then followed, like a man walking on the moon in graceful, long bounds.

This stretch of the river was mostly weed free and Donovan made good time. He breathed normally, didn't think too much about it. When everything was impossible, a little thing like breathing underwater didn't seem that remarkable. He kept his head cocked upward at the dark hull of the canoe just ahead of him, not so far that he lost sight of it. It was beautiful down here, really. The sunlight streamed into the depths, gilding what weeds there were, swaying in the gentle current. Fish darted about, too busy chasing minute particles of drifting breakfast to pay much heed to this gangly stranger in their midst.

Then the water grew shallow. In a matter of moments, Donovan's head pushed through the skin of the river. He shook the water from his hair, and there ahead saw his father glide into a grassy shore, where a woman was waiting. Donovan dug his fists into his eyes and wiped them clean. The woman bent down to catch the prow of the canoe. She was young, wearing sandals and a long summer dress that looked as if it had been spun out of sunlight. Her hair was long—longer than when he had last seen her. Longer and bleached by the sun. And his father was hopping from the canoe into shallow water and splashing in it like a child in a rain puddle, which made her laugh and hold out her arms, and then he was in her arms and they were embracing.

Donovan stood, waist deep now, and watched as they turned toward a little cottage up among the trees.

"Dad," he called. He waded in toward the shore. "Dad!"

His father didn't hear him. Didn't know he existed at that moment, or that anything existed other than this woman that his arm was wrapped around. But the woman heard Donovan. She turned and smiled at him, a sweet, sad smile.

"Jilly," he said. Then everything went black.

PART TWO

THE BOWHUNTER

CHAPTER TWENTY-NINE

"But you guys were winning, Dono," said Max. "Way ahead."

"It was still a crap call," said Donovan.

"The ball was totally outside," said Daisy, "but still—"

"And what do we do on a called strike three?" said Max, cutting her off. "Let me remind you, Dono, my butthead friend: The batter pauses for just a moment. He looks out into the distance, beyond the scoreboard, stoic, silent. In this way, he registers his complaint—"

"His disappointment at the ump's obvious ocular impairment," said Daisy.

"Exactly," said Max. "And then he leaves the batter's box, walks slowly, manfully, and proudly back to the dugout."

"Instead of—"

"That ump never calls me fair," said Donovan. "I don't know why."

"Well, you sure showed him," said Max. "I can't think of a better way to make your point than getting ejected from the game."

"Tickets?" They had reached the front of the line and Bee handed over hers and Donovan's to the girl.

The Cineplex Odeon. A Saturday night in the summer of 2015.

Bee squeezed Donovan's arm, shook it, trying to shake a smile out of the tightness in his face. He knew the drill: shake it off, make the effort. Something like a smile cracked the surface.

Their destination? *Paper Towns.* High school train-wrecks, thinks Bee, wondering if maybe the new Judd Apatow might have been a better choice.

"I am totally overdoing it tonight," said Daisy.

"Popcorn and Maltesers and a drink," said Max. "Combo numero uno."

"Uh, no, actually number five," said Daisy.

"That's a regular-size popcorn. I thought you said you were totally overdoing it. Didn't she say she was totally over-doing it?"

"Uh-huh," said Bee. "But she meant totally overdoing it in a Daisy-size way. What are you drinking, Daisy?"

"Uh, Evian?"

"Told you."

And then there was the jostling and joking that Max and Daisy seemed to have abundant stores of as they argued over who was paying. Bee bought herself some Skittles. "Anything?"

she asked Donovan. He shook his head. "Come on," she said. "Live it up." She tugged on his arm again, managed to shake another crumb of a smile out of him.

"I'll grab a latte," he said and then walked away to the coffee place across the lobby.

So it was going to be like that. She watched him go, shoulders hunched, hands in pockets. As she turned back to the counter, Daisy flashed one of her Big Sympathy smiles. "It's not as if they lost the game," she said.

The douchebags had been drinking.

"How do you know they're douchebags?" whispered Daisy to Max. "I mean, and not just jerks?"

Max sipped on his Coke, swallowed. "According to the Urban Dictionary, a douchebag has surpassed the level of jerk and asshole but hasn't quite reached motherfucker."

"Enlightening," said Bee, but she was looking across the lobby to where Donovan had just paid for his latte and was heading over to join them. And between him and them were the douchebags, who seemed to have no other purpose in life, right at the moment, than to spout douchebaggery at anyone who passed within hailing distance: different kinds of douchebaggery for girls than for guys.

"Uh-oh," said Max under his breath.

"Do something," said Bee.

But it was already too late.

"Eww! What's that, fagboy?" said DB-1 as Donovan passed by.

"So frothy!" said DB-2. "Looks like cum in a blender."

That got them going—laughing their heads off. It should

have gotten Donovan going, too, but he stood and waited until they stopped.

Somehow, DB-3 had managed, in his addled brain, to link Donovan to Bee and Daisy and Max. "Shouldn't you be saving that stuff up for your girlfriend, dude?" And just in case this remark was too subtle for Donovan to interpret, he made as if he were jacking off.

Next thing he knew, he was lying on the floor howling, with his face bloodied. And Donovan was standing over him, having miraculously not spilled even a drop of his latte.

There might have been retaliation, but Max handed off his mountain of junk food and made his large presence known to DBs-1, -2, -3, and -4, who finally got his chance to join in the banter. "D'ju fuckin' see that?" he said.

And then security swooped down and guided Donovan out of the theater, with Bee and the other two friends tailing along, balancing popcorn and drinks.

"Go see the movie," Donovan said. "Please."

"Yeah, right," said Max.

Donovan made no attempt to resist the removal. Bee knew he wouldn't. The guards were just doing their job, after all. And whatever it was that exploded in him, there would be no follow-ups, only remorse. Only regret that it had happened. Again.

CHAPTER THIRTY

She looked back through her journal to August 24, last year, eight months ago. They'd gone to see Turn play. It hadn't gone well. He'd been thrown out of the game in the sixth inning. Max had disappeared with him and helped to jolly him out of his funk enough to get him to the movie theater that night, but that was as close as it got. She shook her head, turned the page.

She was sitting on her bed. It was seven in the evening and she was in her pajamas. She'd never gotten out of them all day. Mom was allowing her a grace period before she went into professional therapist mode. They were giving her space. She just wasn't sure if there was enough space in the whole world for her to find a way out of this.

She squeezed her eyes shut, pressed her thumb and forefinger into the sockets. She leaned into the pressure until the darkness was filled with little squiggling jolts of light. She was so tired.

There was a knock on the door.

"No, Dad," she said. "But thanks anyway."

There was a pause before he spoke. "You really can distinguish my knock from your mother's?"

"Yes, Dad."

He knocked again. More of a rapid rap this time.

"Close, but it was still recognizably you."

"Startling," he said. "The breadth of your talent never ceases to amaze me."

His attempts to chivy her out of her depression were sweet and, mercifully, short. They weren't really frightened for her, she didn't think. No one was on red alert. No one was counting the Advil tablets or ridding the house of razor blades. She was reliably sane. She was sad, not suicidal. She was also mad. Mad at herself and mad at Donovan and mad at his hapless dead father and mad at the unknown driver of a possibly red pickup truck.

She looked at her notes, the attempts to understand Turn, to come to terms with him. They stretched way back. They had been together almost a year and her first worried entry was as early as June of last year. She shook her head and flipped the pages to the last entry she had made, an entry of utterances—a sound poem. She got up. She went to her desk, sat down at her computer, and opened a new document. She titled it. And began to type. A poem, if that's what it was.

The Last Words Of

The last words of Donovan Turner as transcribed by his amanuensis, Beatrice D'Amato Northway

Are you?

See

Dad

Dead

Killed

Killed him

Bee?

Beeeeeee!

Didn't mean

No, no, no, no

Jill

Jilly

Kali

No, no, no, no, no

Bo

Hun

There was more—stuff she'd missed when she'd crashed his room behind Nurse Winters's back. So much stuff but not much of it really comprehensible. So this was the distillation of it: sixteen or seventeen words, if you didn't count repetitions.

She'd scribbled some notes in her journal. When he said, "Didn't mean . . ." she had finished the sentence for him, as if he had meant to say, "I didn't mean to." He had said "no" right away, as if it might really be a response to what she'd said, but that could be taken two ways: "No, I didn't mean to kill him" or "No, you've got it wrong. That wasn't what I was going to say at all." She wasn't sure anyone else would interpret it that way.

There were other interpretations to "killed him," as well. Donovan hadn't necessarily been confessing that *he* killed his father. He said "killed him," which could have meant someone else killed him. And the word "no" could be taken to mean it wasn't him who did it.

Bee leaned back in her chair, the little maroon journal closed in her lap, staring at the words until the screen saver kicked in: a photograph Daisy had taken of Bee and Turn at Daisy's cottage last summer. They were sitting on a rock in their bathing suits. She was reading a book. He was untangling a fishing line. Neither of them was staring at the camera; they were each happily engaged in what they were doing. She loved the picture. She wondered how long she would leave it there.

She picked up her journal and flipped to the heading "April ninth." Seven days before Donovan died. She read what she had written and the scene came back to her.

"I'm going to end it with my dad."

"Excuse me?"

"What I said. You were right, as usual. It's gone on way too long. I'm doing it."

Bee lay back on her bed, the phone to her ear. "I'm almost afraid to ask what that means."

He laughed. "Sorry, totally bad choice of words. We're going to talk. And I'm going to say, you know, I won't be coming anymore. You're a bad influence, et cetera—all that stuff you said."

Bee closed her eyes. "That wasn't what I said—"

"No, I know. But you were right. I mean, I get it."

Why wouldn't Donovan really listen to her? She tried to keep her voice low and even. "I still think you need to see someone, Turn."

"And what's the first thing a shrink will say? I need to break with him, climb out of the snake pit. So I do that—I can—and we go from there, right?"

She couldn't speak.

"Bee?"

"I'm here. I'm just afraid it's not going to be easy."

"Of course not, or why would I still be putting up with his shit? I just needed a shove. Thanks for that."

She chuckled darkly. "You mean threatening to leave you? I was only—"

"Not true. You *were* kidding in one way, and in another way you weren't kidding. I am just so, I don't know, preoccupied with his crap."

"Like obsessed, for instance?"

"Right. I get it. And it was really brave of you to lay it on the line. I can't go on like this. So now I've got to, you know, step up to the plate."

"Always the baseball analogies," she said.

"Yeah, well."

There was a pause. A long one.

"He'll set you off, Turn. You know he will."

"He'll try. Yes. That's the test. And I'm ready. No, seriously. I won't let him. You're right, he's a manipulative bastard—"

"I never said that."

"You didn't need to. It's true. He plays people. But I can beat him at his own game."

She froze. "What does that mean?"

"Okay, okay. Bad choice of words again."

"Donovan. Don't—"

"I'm going to prove this to you," he said, his voice game-ready. "I am going to rock this."

The boyish streak of optimism he got from his mother. He could go into the ninth inning down a hundred runs and still fully believe they could win. He could make everyone on the bench believe it, too. "You know what I love about baseball?" he'd said to her early in their relationship, when she would have had to say that there was nothing about baseball she loved other than maybe Cracker Jack.

"Do they even have Cracker Jack?"

"What?"

"Like in the song, 'Buy me some peanuts and Cracker Jack.'"

He stared at her with an expression that led her to believe he had no idea what she was talking about.

"You were saying why you loved baseball."

"Right. Do you know why?" She shook her head. "There's no game clock." He held out his hands as if inviting applause.

"There's no game clock. That's it?"

"Exactly," he said. "There's no two-minute drill to work on. No Hail Marys, no desperate flinging the ball from mid-court. An inning can last for eternity, the runs piling up and up; the sun could rise and set a hundred times and the game would not be over."

She had smiled at that image. She did not possess a single sports gene, as far as she knew, but she did have genes that responded to boundless confidence. "Are you saying it's not over till it's over?" she had said, and he had nodded like an eight-year-old, with his eyes bright and his whole face shining, as if she had made up the line herself.

That was then.

"Okay," she said. What else could she say?

He took a deep breath. "I'm going to make you proud of me," he said.

"Turn—"

"I know, I know. That's not the point."

"But do it soon. Do it when you're fresh."

"Tomorrow evening. Soon as I get there."

"Okay." She hated the uncertainty in her voice.

"Come on, Bee. Trust me."

And as a theater girl, she said, "Break a leg."

He winced at that. A wince she could hear over the phone.

She had trusted him. But he couldn't talk to his dad Sunday because . . . Well, she couldn't even remember why now. And Monday went by and Tuesday, too, and when she and Donovan met at school Wednesday for lunch, she pushed him up against the lockers, hard enough for him to say, "Ow!" and she said, "You can't do this. Don't you see? There's no shame in that. He's your father. He's bigger than you even though he's two inches *shorter* and half-rotted-out inside. He'll always be bigger than you in your head." She poked him in the forehead to push home her point.

"Take it easy," he said.

"No, because you won't listen." Then she was up in his face, her body pressed against him, holding him in place, needing only some tacks to pin him to the wall, her favorite poster boy. "You. Need. To. See. Someone."

"I'll do it."

"You'll see someone?"

"No, I'll talk to him! End it."

And she said, You're not listening, and he said, I don't want you to leave me, and she said, Don't try to talk to him because he OWNS language, Donovan, and he knows all the words to destroy you and the ninth inning can go on for frigging ever but he'll always beat you because—do you know why?—because he's a bully, Donovan. And you're not.

There was a knock on Bee's door, raising her from the memory. "There's someone here to see you, honey."

"I'm not in."

"It's a detective and I already told her you were."

Inspector Stills.

"Alone?"

"Yes. She seems nice enough."

Her mother, professional psychologist, sadly misjudging a well-put-together face and vaguely hippish attire.

"Just a minute."

"Good girl."

No, not a good girl, thought Bee, a girl who pushed too hard, a bully herself. Demanding harridan, harpy, crone, virago. Pick one.

She went to close her computer and realized she hadn't saved "The Last Words Of." She called the document "Essay topics," in case anyone came sniffing around. She hid her journal under her mattress and then, as she left the room, wondered at how common a hiding place that was.

CHAPTER / THIRTY-ONE

Sergeant Stills was in black slacks and a black turtleneck under her blue leatherette jacket. She wore a thin gold necklace. Classy. She was also wearing heels, which suggested to Bee that the detective wasn't planning on any chase scenes, not on foot. Her makeup was good. Did they learn that at the police academy? Hard edged, no nonsense. Just enough mascara to turn her blue eyes into lethal weapons.

Bee had quickly dressed into what her father called, a little unthinkingly, her "widow's weeds." She preferred to think of her outfit as basic mourning: black tights, black funnel neck, black turban headband. She wore no makeup. Her own brown eyes seemed drained of whatever luster it was that sometimes made them glimmer. They were dirt brown, set in a face that looked, by her own assessment, like the hoarding around a construction site in winter.

Stills was sitting in the living room with Bee's mother, who rose hurriedly, as if caught fraternizing with the enemy. She asked if anyone wanted coffee. When the answer was no, she glanced hopefully at Bee and then evaporated.

Stills remained seated. It struck Bee as a ploy, reverse psychology, as if the detective wanted her to believe she wasn't going to play any power games. And Bee thought that if she herself remained on her feet, she might gain some advantage. So she leaned against the fireplace. "No Bell?" she said.

It took Stills a moment to translate. "Leadership conference," she said. "So you're stuck with me." She chose an expression of concern from her bag of tricks. "How are you feeling, Bee?" she said. Bee shrugged. "I'm sorry for your loss."

Bee crossed her arms. There were these empty phrases to get through, and she'd learned how to play her part. People meant well. Most people. She didn't feel like playing now. "Have you found anything?"

Stills nodded. "That's why I'm here. I figured you'd want to know that Donovan's autopsy revealed no sign of alcohol or drugs."

Bee had to fight the sick feeling in her stomach. Autopsy? She hadn't seen or talked to Trish or Scott since that day at the hospital. She hadn't known there would be an autopsy. Didn't want to think about it.

"Sorry again," said Stills, reading the signs.

"It's okay. I just . . ." Then Bee straightened up. This was actually kind of good news, if there was any to be had. "So he didn't just stumble into the path of the red truck," she said.

Stills held up her hand. "Whoa," she said. "We haven't

heard anything from the lab about the paint chip. But you're right. As far as we can tell, his perception was not compromised by substance abuse."

Did she mean to put a spin on what she'd just said? "So, is what you're saying that it wasn't an accident?" Stills nodded her head tentatively, not sure of the tone of Bee's voice. "As in you think he *chose* to get himself run over?" said Bee. "Is that it?"

Stills tilted her head. "I didn't say that."

"You kind of insinuated it."

"What makes you think that?"

"Because suicide is the only thing that makes sense, as far as you guys are concerned. You don't think a truck or whatever it was could have run him over on Wilton Crescent at the corner like that. It wouldn't have been possible."

Now Stills looked genuinely interested. "Go on," she said.

Bee sighed again. Why was she doing this? She was playing into Stills's hands. But if she was going to try to convince the cop that they were wrong about Donovan, she had to say something. "I went over there. The vehicle had to be coming from Oakland Avenue, right, in order to . . . to, you know, throw him where it did?" Stills nodded. "He'd have had to be a race-car driver to take that turn at speed fast enough to, like, hurl Donovan halfway down the hill. If the driver had been drunk and going too fast, he'd have lost control and more likely ended up in the bush west of where the hit-and-run happened."

Stills looked impressed. "That's how we see it."

"Unless," said Bee, holding up her finger and then immediately dropping it, as if playing at Sherlock Holmes was not going to win her any points. "Unless the driver was parked at the end of Wilton just where it curves into Oakland, parked on the north side of the street facing the wrong way."

Stills frowned. "That seems a little . . . imaginative, don't you think?"

Bee shook her head, deciding to ignore the implied insult. "No one ever parks there, let alone facing the wrong way. It's signposted—'prohibited'—so the spot is always available. It would be a perfect place for waiting."

Stills looked perplexed. "Waiting?"

Was Bee really going through with this? "Waiting. You know, for Donovan to arrive home. The killer would be able to see him walking down from Bank Street, time it perfectly. With one turn of the wheel, he'd be facing directly toward where Turn got hit. And although it would only be like fifteen yards or so, there would be no steering involved. They could just ram him straight on—*pow!*"

She hadn't meant to put it quite so graphically and immediately suffered a queasy feeling in her stomach.

Stills leaned back in her chair. "You think this hit-and-run was premeditated?" said Stills. Bee nodded. "Why?"

Bee sat on the hearth and wrapped her arms around her woozy stomach. "Because I don't think Donovan would have killed himself."

"Not even if he had killed his father?"

"He didn't kill his father."

"Now that interests me," said Stills, leaning forward. "How do you know that?"

"I don't know it. I just know Donovan." She swallowed. "Knew Donovan."

"I gather he had quite a temper," said Stills. She pulled her little notebook out of her pocket and thumbed through a couple of pages. "Incident at school last November."

"He was breaking up a fight, a bully beating on some freshman."

"Thrown out of a baseball game in the National Capital Baseball League for unsportsmanlike conduct *twice* last season. A reported incident at the Cineplex Odeon out at Southbank last August."

Bee shook her head. "Wow, you've really been hard at work. Have you got enough evidence now to prove your case?"

Stills glared at her. "We collect *all* the facts, Bee. We can't ignore that Donovan had anger management problems."

"Which was only ever aimed at douchebags."

"Which Allen Ian McGeary was, I gather."

"Donovan does not *kill* douchebags. He gets angry, yes. And sometimes he lashes out." She caught the look in Stills's eye and quickly added, "Never at me. Never at anyone who isn't a complete . . . oh, forget it. The point is, he gets mad and then he goes straight to remorse. He does not pass go and does not collect two hundred dollars."

Stills looked interested again. "What are you saying?"

"You told me there was a witness. Someone saw Donovan leave his dad's place in a hurry at eight o'clock or something like that. They'd heard a lot of noise and he'd slammed the door. Is that what you said?"

Stills nodded. "At 8:10, to be exact."

"So if they were fighting at eight, I can guarantee you Donovan would not be angry when—*if*—he came back later."

"That doesn't jibe with our witness's report."

"I don't care. You have to know him. It's . . ." She stopped. This was not going well, and stopping was something she should have done approximately fifteen minutes ago.

Callista Stills stood up. Good, she's leaving, thought Bee. But she wasn't. She looked out the window, her hands on her hips.

Just go. Please.

Stills turned around. "His baseball bat was there," she said.

"Are you sure it's his?" Bee was grasping at straws.

Stills nodded. "And what makes us doubly sure is that Donovan's prints are all over it."

"Well, of course, he—"

"And nobody else's."

Bee had no "imaginative" comeback for that. She leaned forward, wrapped her arms around her knees, stared at the floor.

"I'd really like to see your journal, Beatrice."

Bee's head snapped up. "What do you mean?"

"You were writing in a journal when you were in the ICU."

"I don't know what you're talking about."

Stills made no attempt to hide her scorn. She glanced down at her own notebook. "The nurse on duty Saturday, April sixteenth, distinctly saw a brown Moleskine book, approximately five by eight inches in size, in your hands when she had you forcibly removed from the unit." She looked up. "Does that jog your memory?"

This was it. This was the reason she was here.

"He didn't say anything. Just noises. Gobbledygook."

"But you wrote it down. You felt it was worth recording. So maybe we could get something out of it, as well. Maybe even a clue as to who hit him."

Bee shook her head. "He couldn't have seen a thing."

"You don't know that."

"Yes, I do. I went over there again two nights ago. He got hit somewhere around ten thirty."

"That's the earliest time, based on what we know."

"Well, anyway, I went over to Wilton around that time. It wasn't raining like it had been Friday and there was no moon. Moon didn't rise until later. And it was only a quarter of a moon anyway. A waxing gibbous moon—I checked it on Google—that didn't rise until after midnight."

"Impressive," said Stills. "Are you after my job?"

Bee stared at her. She wasn't being flippant. It was a compliment. But Bee couldn't rise to it. Couldn't let the detective get to her.

"I waited right where he was hit. Waited until a car came around the corner from Oakland. They don't come very often. I'm sure you know that." The detective nodded. "Anyway, this driver crept around the corner, worried about oncoming traffic. And even though I had all the time in the world, I couldn't see a thing of that vehicle except the lights in my eyes. I made myself keep watching right up to when the car was even with where I was standing on the curb. Nothing. No license plate, that's for sure. But no color, either. Even when it had passed I couldn't tell the color."

"Keen observation," said Stills, and there was nothing grudging in her respect. "But in all of this research did you ask yourself what Donovan was doing on the *opposite* side of the street from his house? What he was doing about three houses *farther* down Wilton than where he lived, and on the other side of the street?"

Bee just looked away. Hadn't thought of it. She glanced at Stills, who, to Bee's surprise, was not gloating.

The detective sat down again, this time with her legs apart and an elbow resting on each knee. "So why don't you want me to look at the journal?"

Bee stared at her. "Because it's personal."

"Ever heard of obstructing justice?" Bee just stared. "I'm sure a smart girl like you knows what that means."

Bee felt herself unwinding. Why was she doing this? She didn't want them to see her journal because there was personal stuff in there, but she wasn't the one they were after. They were after Donovan. They wanted the case cut and dried. Boy kills his father and then commits suicide by throwing himself in front of a car. Would those few words he had muttered while he lay dying in his bed really convince anyone of anything? What was she trying to prove? What was it she wanted? Could she bargain with them?

"Bee." Stills was looking at her square on, a little impatient now.

"I'll consider it," said Bee. "But I want you to tell me something in return."

"Like what?"

"Who this eyewitness was. These eyewitnesses. Why

you're so sure this is a murder-suicide. That would be a start."

"What, so you can go and cross-examine them?" Stills's face grew solemn. She shook her head. "That isn't the way it works," she said. "This isn't a game, okay?"

Bee could barely breathe. She willed herself not to nod. Not to give the detective the slightest sense of acknowledgment that she had even heard her.

"Don't play Nancy Drew with me, Beatrice. Have you got that? If I have to, I will subpoena that journal. I'd rather not go to the trouble, but if you force my hand, I'll do it."

Bee swallowed. "And what if I just burn it?" She flinched as she said it, half expecting a blow in retaliation. All she got was a challenge.

"That would be an indictable offense, punishable with up to ten years in prison." She let that sink in. "I'm sure, in a case like this, you'd get off lightly. Say, only a year or two." Then she stood up, straightened her jacket, and with one last questioning look at Bee, headed toward the door. She turned as she reached it. "Thank your mother for her hospitality," she said. Bee nodded. She watched the detective open the front door and step out, only to turn one last time.

"Why are you fighting me, Bee?"

Bee wasn't exactly sure. Wasn't sure she could explain it even to herself. She cleared her throat. "Because somebody's got to be on Donovan's side."

Stills shook her head sadly. "I'm not on anybody's side. I can't seem to make you believe that. I just want answers. There are two people dead. Don't you think their loved ones—yourself included—deserve answers? Deserve some justice?"

Bee nodded. *Justice.* That's exactly what she wanted. Donovan deserved that. She believed it with all her heart. And because she did, she stepped up and slowly closed the door on Inspector Callista Stills.

CHAPTER THIRTY-TWO

She showered. Turned the water as hot as she could bear, wanting it to sting, wanting it to penetrate the sharp iron fibers of tension in her every muscle. She leaned into the tile wall and let the water scald her back. She shampooed and conditioned and shampooed again and conditioned again. Finally, she turned off the shower and meticulously wiped down the curved glass walls and door with the squeegee, not leaving a single smear, a single drop of water, just in case it mattered. She wrapped herself in a huge towel and then attacked her hair with a blow-dryer and brush as if it were infested with vermin. Back in her room, her hair pulled back in a tight ponytail, she put on clean clothes for the first time in days: a red kilt, simple black top, and an ivory-colored cardigan she liked the feel of—the comfort of—more than anything else.

She watched a car pull away from the driveway, one of Mom's clients. She went to find her mom in her office and gave her an in-between-clients hug. Her mother held her a little too long but didn't ask how the interview had gone or where she was going. "Let us know if you're going to be late," she said.

Beatrice Northway was the only person she knew who drove the car of her dreams. It wasn't hers. It belonged to her extraordinary globe-trotting great-aunt, who had left the car with Bee while she went off to work with Médecins Sans Frontières, saving people in far-flung countries that Bee didn't always know the names of. At least that's what she thought Toddy was up to. There was something a little bit shady about her. She was a crack shot, for one thing. How many doctors were crack shots? "She might be putting people *in the care* of those MSF doctors, for all we know," her father had once suggested of his peripatetic relative.

There was no way to describe the Nissan Figaro as anything but cute. Ridiculously cute: an escapee from a toy store or a children's cartoon. Something from a fifties Italian movie, where little cars climbed steep and very narrow cobblestone streets. The car should have been black-and-white, because it surely didn't belong in the real world, but in fact only the roof was white, while the body color was called topaz mist, a romantic paint color for such a chubby little cute car. It had none of the amenities one expected in a car other than a barely serviceable radio, but she approached every drive in it with excitement. Not because it was fast or luxuriously appointed or incredibly comfortable. It was none of these things. She loved it because it was unique, and because there was the faintest whiff of her extraordinary great-aunt about the vehicle. A trace of some shady perfume.

She remembered introducing Donovan to the car. He stopped dead in his tracks and gawped. Was this a deal breaker? Would he refuse to be seen in this terminally adorable vehicle? "Amazing," he said. Then he beamed at her. "I bet you gave it a name."

She nodded. "Toddy."

"Because it's like a hot alcoholic drink?"

"No, because of my aunt Toddy. It's her car. I'm just its adoptive parent."

"Toddy the Turtle," he said, which she was going to protest until she realized how perfect it was. "Kind of like Thomas the Tank Engine."

"Is that what you're watching these days on Netflix?" she had asked him.

"Wouldn't miss it. The fifth season—whoa! The affair Thomas has with that racy diesel. Who knew he was gay?"

Beatrice had thought with that outburst maybe their relationship had a chance of working out.

"Is Toddy the Turtle as fast as Thomas the TE?" he asked.

"If I work at it I can get her up to ninety-five," she said.

"Miles per hour?"

"Nope. Only kilometers," she said. "But even when I'm holding up people on a two lane, they always smile and wave when they pass."

He nodded as if he would have been one of those smiling, waving people. "Do you think I'll fit?" That was a good question. At six two, it would be a squeeze. But he did fit. He fit well.

She stood in the driveway and patted the car's hood. "We will miss him, won't we, Toddy?" Unlike Thomas the TE, Toddy had no words of comfort for her.

She drove to Wilton Crescent again. It was 5:00 p.m. Thursday, April the twenty-first. She parked in front of Donovan's place. The sun wouldn't set for another two hours, but there were lights on in his house. She turned off the ignition and sat for a moment. She looked across and down the street to where Donovan had died—well, where the dying had begun so dramatically. The scene-of-crime tape had gone, although she caught sight of a scrap of it fluttering high up in a tree branch. She thought of Trish looking out their front window and seeing that ragged little yellow flag. How long would they be able to bear living here? she wondered.

Trish greeted her at the door. She took Bee in her arms and held her, swaying, for the longest time. Bee held on, wanting to squeeze her back as strongly as Trish was squeezing her but knowing she could never be that strong.

Trish stood back and looked her over. "Good, you didn't bring flowers," she said. "Enter."

Scott wasn't there. He'd missed work for a couple of days, but Trish had assured him she was okay today and he could go. Then she'd gone back to sleep, she said, and only woken up a few minutes earlier, famished.

So they sat at the bar in the kitchen eating pho, and Trish talked about all the people who had come by and what they had brought—especially advice—and the dealings she'd had with the funeral parlor about a memorial service, which had been fine but surreal somehow. It would be later. They couldn't deal with an actual funeral.

"I'm sorry I haven't been around," said Bee when there was a silence long enough to say anything. Trish lifted noodles to her mouth with her chopsticks and slurped them down, then hurriedly wiped her face with a napkin. She looked at Bee, her eyes brimming with emotion.

"Oh, honey, I knew you'd make yourself present when you were ready." She looked at Bee for a long moment. "I hope we'll still see you sometimes."

Bee assured her she would, but she wondered if that was true. Surely all she could possibly represent to Trish now was the loss of her son. She picked up her spoon to drink some of the broth in her huge bowl of soup, paused, and put it down again. Trish looked at her. "Something on your mind?"

"A cop named Callista Stills."

"Ah, Inspector Stills."

"That's higher than staff sergeant, isn't it?"

Trish nodded. "You're thinking of Bell, right?" Bee nodded. "Yep, Stills is his boss. What about her?"

Bee's shoulders slumped. "What has she said to you? About, you know, what happened?" Trish looked away, closed her eyes. "You don't have to tell me," said Bee hurriedly, as if she'd ruined everything by bringing it up. "It's just . . ."

"She's careful what she says," said Trish after a moment of silence. "I mean, she doesn't want to come right out and

say it, but it's fairly obvious they think Donovan killed Al."
She shook her head. "I don't see it."

"Me neither. He was going to talk to him. He was going
to tell him he wouldn't be visiting anymore."

"I know."

"Wait. He told you?"

Trish nodded. "I hope you don't mind. He told us all
about how he was really and truly messing things up with
you and you'd given him an ultimatum."

"Not really."

"That's how he took it, and he was proud to admit it."

"But I didn't want him to break it with Al."

"No, you wanted him to see a therapist. He told us
that, too."

"Oh."

"Bee, I'd been telling him for years he didn't owe his
father anything. Donovan had always been kind of . . . I don't
know, noble about it. If long-suffering counts as noble." Trish
shook her head sadly. There were new lines in her forehead,
darkness under her eyes. She'd obviously gone over and over
this. "I think he thought that he could help somehow. That
his father could be saved, even if it took a long time. Cured.
But Al was beyond saving, and all Donovan was doing was
hurting himself, over and over. The anger . . . the anger was
the worst."

"I know. But I honestly don't think he would ever . . . I
mean I can't believe he could get angry enough to actually . . ."

"Take a bat to him?" said Trish. Bee flinched, then nodded. "I tried to tell Stills that."

"So did I," said Bee. "They say they have a witness but won't tell me who it is or what it was he or she saw happen. I mean, if they saw Turn hit his father, then there's no question, but . . ."

Trish patted her forearm. "He didn't see that. The guy's name is Rolly Pouillard."

"Oh," said Bee. "One of Al's drinking buddies."

"Rolly Polly," said Trish. "That's what Dono called him."

"And he was in the apartment?"

"I guess so. He's the superintendent of the apartment building. Apparently, he and Al were drinking when Donovan arrived. They had been at it for some time. Rolly said Donovan went 'mental' when he saw they were drinking. Which struck me as odd, because God only knows how often Donovan has had to witness his father in that condition."

Bee shook her head. "I know why. Why Turn got upset."

"Because they were going to have the Talk."

"Exactly. Turn had made Al promise to be there and sober. It was serious."

Trish shook her head. "Al and promises . . ."

"So what actually happened?"

Trish had been staring off into the middle distance. She looked at Bee and for a moment it was almost as if she didn't know her. Then she came to. "I guess he smashed things with the bat. Went to town on Al's side table. Broke a ceramic bowl full of popcorn. Then brought it down again and broke some beer bottles and glasses, whatever. Which is when Rolly told him to get out. And he did."

"So he didn't actually hit Al."

"Not according to Rolly. Al got up at one point, lost his balance, and fell. He cut his chin, but that was about it."

"So Rolly didn't see it happen? The murder?"

Trish shook her head. "There's corroboration. Al's neighbor in 306 heard the argument, and when he heard the door slam looked out to see Donovan, or someone matching his description, heading off up the hallway. He's a guy who makes regular complaints about the noise from Al's place, and he's gotten into the habit of writing down the times so he can make a detailed report to the police."

Bee sat staring off into the same distance Trish had so recently scoured, as if there were answers there. There were none, none that she could see. "But nobody saw him hit Al?"

Trish turned back to her soup. Spooned up some broth, then went to pick up her chopsticks and stopped. She had been famished, she said, but Bee watched her put the utensils down again as if her hunger had dissipated.

"We totally do not need to talk about this," said Bee. "I'm sorry."

"No, don't be. You need to know. I need to know. And Inspector Stills needs to know the truth, right, Beatrice?" She said her name as if it were Italian, with the C lengthened into ché, as if she were some princess.

She turned on her stool and took Bee's hands in hers. "So this is what happened, as far as they can tell. At 8:10 the neighbor heard the door to 304 slam, after listening to a lot of noise coming from the apartment. This fellow saw Donovan leave. Rolly stayed on, made sure Al was okay. Rolly was in a bowling league and had to leave shortly thereafter.

He left Al with a good stiff bourbon, according to him. The police checked out his alibi. He was at Merivale Bowling Center from something like eight thirty until after eleven. When he got back to the apartment building, he decided to check up on Al and found him beaten to death. He called 911. The police came and the neighbor, hearing the hub-bub, told them how he'd seen the same boy racing from the apartment again at 10:13 just as he'd seen him go at eight. Again there had been loud noises, what the neighbor called 'domestic violence,' and a door slamming shut. He only saw the boy from the back, but he was in the same clothes he'd seen him in earlier, the clothes Dono was wearing when they . . . when they found him. He was not carrying a bat. The bat was left behind, and the only fingerprints on it were Donovan's.

"It's circumstantial evidence," said Trish. "If Donovan were on trial, a good lawyer could poke holes in the case. That's what Scott thinks. The neighbor left his apartment in between all these goings-on to do his laundry down in the basement. Any number of people could have come and gone in the meantime. The bat was bound to have Dono-van's prints on it since he used it all the time. Someone else could have used it wearing gloves. And Al had some unsa-vory friends."

Bee nodded. "There was a girlfriend, Kali."

"Yeah. But she'd left a couple of weeks earlier, accord-ing to Rolly. He hadn't seen her around anyway. Her clothes — her stuff — were all gone from the closet. She had moved back to the country, up near Perth. They contacted her. She said she was at home that night. She had an alibi and she had no car, either. And apparently Rolly was wrong; she'd been gone for almost a month."

"So . . . ?"

Trish sighed. "So, yeah. It's pretty damning evidence but not conclusive."

Bee thought about what Scott had told Trish. A good lawyer could pick it apart—prove that the evidence was circumstantial, et cetera, *if* Donovan were on trial. But he wasn't going to get a chance to be on trial. "They're going to find him guilty so they can close the case," said Bee.

"They're still looking," said Trish.

Bee knew that was marginally true. They wanted her journal, for one thing. But she was pretty certain that all Stills wanted it for was further proof of Donovan's guilt. And the words in the journal . . . well, you could take them any way you wanted to. But the words "killed him" and "Dad" were right there. That would probably ice the cake.

"What are you thinking about, my lovely Beatrice?"

She came out of her thoughts. Was this a good thing to do? Would it only hurt Trish more? No, Trish wanted what Bee wanted. She wanted to know that her son had not done this thing. "I want to show you something," she said. And from her ever-present bag she pulled the journal and opened it to where the ribbon was. Her finger moved down the page and pointed to a particular word. "Does the name Jilly mean anything to you?"

CHAPTER THIRTY-THREE

"Jilly?" said Trish. Her forehead creased. "This is weird."

"What do you mean?"

"That's a name from a long time ago." Trish cleaned her fingers on her napkin and took the Moleskine from Bee's hand. "What is this?" she said.

Bee looked at her scribbled words. "He was trying to talk. There was a lot of other stuff. Mostly it was just garbled, but I started writing anyway and put down anything that sounded like actual words."

Trish looked at her with a kind of marvel in her eyes. Then she scanned the other words on the page and flipped back to the first page of the hospital papers and her face clouded over. She looked at Bee again. "This doesn't look good."

"Yeah, he said 'killed him,' but he didn't say who did it. Anyway, I won't let Stills see this."

"She knows about it?"

"The 'Winters of Our Discontent' told her about it."

"That must have been around the time she was threatening you with arrest."

Bee nodded, with no pride in her audacity. It had been a horrible scene—dragged out by orderlies like some crazy woman. Well, that's what she was. She shook the experience away. "I guess I must have looked pretty guilty when Stills asked me about it, and so she's really pressing now. Says she's going to get an injunction or whatever." Her eyes appealed to Trish. "What am I going to do?"

Trish stared at the book. Bee wondered if she was hearing Donovan saying these words—hearing his voice. She flipped back to where the entry began. There was a time registered there: 3:04 a.m., Saturday, April 16. Then she flipped farther back before Bee could stop her, but as soon as she saw that what came before was written in prose, she discreetly handed the journal back to Bee. Bee wondered if Inspector Callista Stills would feel the same compunction to resist reading what was clearly personal.

"Do you think the injunction is just a threat?" said Trish.

"I don't know. She's into power games."

Trish nodded. "If she gets an injunction for real, then failing to comply would be reason to press charges. Do you want to go to jail over it?"

Bee shook her head. "It's not just the words—his words, I mean. In the journal there's a lot of stuff about Donovan. About us." She glanced at Trish and then looked away quickly, blushing despite herself. "Not what you're thinking."

"I wasn't thinking anything, Bee. And it wouldn't matter anyway."

"But it does, that's the problem." She had closed the book on her finger. Now she opened it again and flipped back several pages. "Like, for instance, this," she said, and handed the journal back to Trish.

I just wish Al would die. I mean surely his liver is wrecked. Maybe we could get him super drunk and then pour vodka down his throat. Oh God! What am I saying!!! I hate this. I hate that Al bloody McGeary makes me feel like this. And if I feel like this, what must Turn feel!?

She could see that Trish had finished reading the excerpt. She reached out and took it back. "I mean, I guess I could take a razor blade to that page and just take it out. But there's more."

Trish shook her head. "Stills isn't stupid."

"I know. But it's so wrong. I mean it's my *journal*. I can say anything in here. Anything! And it's nobody else's business."

"You're right," said Trish. "I'm sure your mother would have something to say about it."

"What do you mean?"

"I wouldn't be surprised if in her practice she's run into situations where a person who is in her care has kept a diary that would be revealing in a very prejudicial way were it called into question for any reason."

Bee made a wry expression. "You mean if the person was, like, mentally ill, right?"

Trish patted her arm. "Not exactly." Then she smiled wryly. "Well, maybe temporarily mentally ill. But no, I mean that we are entitled to our privacy. A lawyer could probably block the police from getting hold of it."

Lawyers, thought Bee. Was it going to come to that? Not if she could help it. She flipped the book to the last page she'd written on.

"Jilly," she said. "Who is she?"

Trish's expression turned pensive. "Jilly Green was the woman Al left me for."

"Oh."

Trish frowned. "Which is odd, because, as far as I know, Donovan hadn't seen her since he was nine."

Scott came home. Bee made as if to go but he insisted she stay, and Bee phoned her folks to tell them where she was and soon the three of them were all in the cozy front room with a fire on and glasses of wine for Scott and Trish and tea for Bee. The fire wasn't exactly blazing, but it threw up enough light to make the wine look radiant. Bee didn't dare have a drink. She wasn't sure that if she started drinking she'd ever stop. And she was glad she was sober when Trish got around to explaining about Jilly Green.

The more-or-less happy McGeary family, Al and Trish and six-year-old Donovan, had taken a cottage up the valley, near Perth. It was a modest place on a sylvan river. That was how Trish remembered it: sylvan. And Bee pictured a river of greeny-gold with the sun through the trees glinting on it. They met people there, fun people. A lot of back-to-the-landers who lived nearby in a place called Sugar Valley. Folks who lived in handmade houses and threw wonderful kitchen parties and potluck suppers.

"There was a school they built there that doubled as a social center. Sometimes there were dances. We came again the next summer. We looked forward to it all winter," said Trish. She shook her head slowly, contemplatively, and Bee almost thought she could see the sun-splashed river water reflecting in her eyes. "I guess I didn't notice *just* how much Al was looking forward to it."

Trish was sitting cross-legged on the couch. She leaned into Scott. He knew the story. "The whole sordid thing," he said.

They used to get milk from a local farmer: unpasteurized milk and eggs and homemade jam—all sorts of good stuff. Al would go off foraging, as he called it, and come back with baskets full of goodies. For a long time Trish pictured some round-cheeked farmer's wife dressed in gingham, with strong arms from churning butter and an ample backside that would have spilled over the edges of her milking stool. She laughed at the image she was painting. And Bee sensed that she was exaggerating for the sake of the story, because it wasn't hard to see what was coming.

The farmer's wife turned out to be Jilly Green, who was twenty-three when she hooked up with Al. Ten years younger than Trish. "Jilly was married to an awful man," said Trish. "They weren't any old-timey farm family, but a couple of hippies who had more than they could handle taking over her parents' farm. Jilly's brother, Mervin, had joined them to help out, which probably didn't help the marriage any, though it might have saved Jilly's life."

"What do you mean?"

"The husband was abusive." Trish looked down. "I can't remember his name right now. It'll come to me."

"Rory," said Scott. "Rory Tulk."

Trish looked at him with surprise. "How do you remember his name? You weren't even around."

"No, but I listen when you tell me stories," he said. "I am a card-carrying member of that small organization called MWLWTWTTT."

"Which is?"

"Men Who Listen When Their Wives Talk to Them."

Trish laughed and batted him with her free hand and he turned his shoulder to her, protecting his drink. Bee watched with satisfaction: they were both smiling. So was she, she realized. It was possible.

"It's funny," said Trish, "as soon as I met them, Jilly and Rory Tulk, I thought this is a young woman in a bad relationship. I liked her. I thought about getting closer to her so that I could be there for her if she wanted to talk, wanted help. Lend her some of my 'big-city smarts.' For some reason, it never occurred to me that my husband was thinking the same kind of thoughts. Well, not exactly the same kind of thoughts.

"So, jump forward to the second week of August 2006. We pack up the car to go home, back to the city, and suddenly Al steps away from the trunk he's just loaded, turns to me, and says he's not coming."

"You're kidding."

Trish shook her head. "Completely out of the blue. Apparently, Jilly was leaving Rory."

Trish stared at the fire. Scott reached for the bottle of wine on the side table and Trish held out her glass. Bee waited, watching Trish, seeing the memory play out on her face. A trace of a grin found its way to her lips, her eyes, and Bee could only ascribe it to the passage of time and what she had made of herself and her life. That and finding the man who was presently filling her wineglass.

"I can't imagine what Donovan must have thought of that ride home," she said. She shook her head, took a sip of her wine. "Mommy had to pretend everything was fine and Daddy would be coming along later."

"Bastard!" said Scott.

Trish patted his leg. "Oh, it's all so long ago."

"I don't think I would even be able to drive," said Bee.

"When there's a child involved, you'd be amazed what you find the strength to do. That said, I don't exactly remember the drive home. I can't remember, you know, changing gears or anything. Probably drove the whole way in first."

"And then?"

"What's there to say? I guess I tried to get him back. Probably did a good number of those self-destroying things a woman does in such a situation, but he was gone. And, I don't know, one day I woke up and realized that the world had not ended. Not only that, with the passing weeks I kind of liked that it was just Dono and me. I found a good job and I had a fabulous son and really . . . There were reasons to be thankful for having Al taken off my hands."

"And then I came along," said Scott.

"Exactly!" said Trish, and clinked glasses with him. Then

she held up her glass in a toast to the fire. "Thank you belatedly, Jilly Green!"

Bee joined in the toast with the dregs of her citron oolong. It was lukewarm by now and bitter because she'd let it steep too long, but she liked being here and for some reason felt better than she had for days.

"So anyway, to get back to the story—" Trish stopped abruptly. "Do you want me to go on?"

"Absolutely," said Bee.

"Okay, so I decided I was glad to be rid of Al. I mean I *was* well rid of him. There was no decision to have to make. There was just that grudging acceptance that has more to do with pride than anything else—I'd lost him to another girl. And when I realized I was cautiously happy in my new life, even before meeting this charming environmental lawyer here, I filed for divorce. Al was thrilled. He'd wanted a divorce right away, so I got no argument from him. And while we were deciding all that, we made the arrangements for him to see his son. We didn't want to get embroiled in some horrible custody battle and, mercifully, we settled easily on Donovan going out there to the valley one weekend a month: Friday after school to Sunday afternoon, home in time for dinner. It worked for me. And, like I said, I had nothing against Jilly—well, other than the obvious. She seemed like an okay person. A little screwed up—as demonstrated by both her choices of partners—but then who isn't? A little screwed up, I mean." She paused as if she were remembering something else. "No, let me take that back."

"She *was* really screwed up?" asked Bee.

"No," said Trish. "Although Al sure didn't help in that regard. No, what I mean is that she was more than okay. I think she had some kind of magic to her."

Bee stared at Trish. Scott did, too. "I remember you telling me that once," he said. "I thought you must be about the most tolerant and charitable person I'd ever met, as well as being bonkers."

"It wasn't charity. She was . . . something else."

"Magic?" said Bee.

Trish seemed to come out of a trance. "Oh, I don't know. I wanted to hate her, but she seemed, how can I say it, wiser than her years. As if she'd seen things the rest of us couldn't see." Trish took another swig of her wine.

"Well, she couldn't have been all that wise to have married Al," said Scott.

"She didn't. They lived together. He wanted marriage. She was recovering from her first awful marriage, I guess, and waiting to see what would happen."

"To cut to the chase," said Scott, "Al took care of the rest."

"What do you mean?" said Bee.

"Let me see if I've got the order right," said Scott. "Al lost his job at the *Citizen* — maybe it was the commute into the city, but there were days he just didn't make it; he started missing assignments. So he took up freelancing, made drinking his full-time occupation. And within a year, she chucked him out on his ass."

Trish snorted. "It wasn't quite like that. They made it through two years before she, as you say, chucked him out. And the only sad thing about that, as far as I was concerned, was that Donovan liked her a lot."

"Really?" Bee was surprised. "He never mentioned her to me, I don't think."

"He loved going out to that farm. Loved being in the country. I guess I was hurt by that. Ha! I know I was."

"But I appeared on my white charger," said Scott. "Actually, my white Toyota Prius, and suddenly you didn't have time to be hurt."

"True enough. Anyway, because Al was involved, the whole thing went pear-shaped, so there I was, consoling little Donovan again."

Bee leaned forward, rested her elbows on her knees and her chin in her hands. The movement took her closer to the fire and she felt its warmth on her skin. "So he hadn't seen Jilly since . . ." She counted on her fingers. "Since 2008, like, eight years ago?"

"Not that I know of. And I can't imagine he'd keep it from me."

"So why would he have been thinking of her now?"

"The mind's a funny place," said Scott. "He'd suffered a concussion. Who knows where his thoughts were taking him?"

The room grew quiet. There was just the crackling of the wood in the fire, the ticking of the house. Bee glanced at Trish and wondered if she was thinking the same thing that Bee was: Donovan had not mentioned Trish, his mother, in his dying words. But then, if Bee was right, his dying words were not good-byes; they were clues, which is exactly what Inspector Stills suspected.

"She wrote me," said Trish, suddenly breaking into Bee's thoughts.

"Who, Jilly?"

"Yeah. Later. It was a really sweet letter."

"Like a letter letter?"

"Uh-huh, snail mail with a stamp and everything. Her spelling wasn't all that good—"

"Which—admit it—made you feel smug," said Scott.

"A little."

"Way smug," said Scott.

"What did she say?" said Bee. "Was she, like, apologizing for breaking up your marriage?"

"Yeah, sort of, I guess. But mostly she wanted to thank me for . . ." She paused, sucked in her lips.

"Take a deep breath," said Scott quietly after a moment, and rubbed Trish's back in big circles. She pushed against his palm, letting him dig out some of the misery that was in her. "Mostly she wanted to thank me for Dono. How much she'd enjoyed having him around." She stopped, allowed the tears to come, didn't fight them. Bee found it hard to hold in her own tears. Her throat hurt like she'd swallowed glass. Trish sniffed and rubbed her nose on her shirtsleeve. "Sorry," she said. "She told me she hoped one day to have a child of her own, and if he was anything like Donovan, she'd be happy."

If this were a movie, thought Bee, the music would swell right about now. And the dying fire would catch and her tea would be hot again, with a curl of perfect steam rising from it. Then suddenly, Trish sat up straight.

"Wait a sec."

"What?"

"She wrote me again." She handed Scott her drink and, heaving herself up off the couch, she walked over to the kitchen area. Bee watched Trish head toward the desk in the back corner of the kitchen by the doors out to the deck. She sat down in the chair there and started going through one of the drawers.

Bee glanced at Scott, who raised his eyebrows. He didn't know what this was about.

"Aha!" said Trish. "Here it is. Not the letter but something else."

She came back and resumed her seat. From an envelope she pulled a square white card. A wedding invitation, Bee assumed. And that's what it was: an invitation to the wedding of Jillian Amy Green to Matthew Logan Needham. The wedding had taken place in July of 2012 at Saint James Anglican in Perth, Ontario.

Bee looked over the card at Trish. "Did you go?"

"Good Lord, no! But I did send her a gift and a letter wishing her the best. And she wrote back." Trish chuckled ruefully. "I can't find it now, but I remember that the return address on the letter she sent me was 'Mrs. M. L. Needham.'"

Bee couldn't figure it out at first. She took the invitation from Trish. "Who's M. L.? Oh right, her husband's name. Good grief. Do people do that?"

"Women used to. Not content to lose just their maiden name, they went whole-hog and lost every trace of identity."

"Wow" was all Bee could say. She flipped over the envelope that the invitation had come in. The address printed just said Needham.

"Her own folks were dead." Trish shook her head. "Mrs. M. L. Needham. I don't mean to be snotty about it. She was,

I think, basically a good old-fashioned girl who had to go through two terrible relationships—before finding herself a good man."

"Ah, but do you know he's a good man?" said Scott.

"Yes," said Trish definitively. "Because that's what the other letter was about—the second one that I can't find. She wanted to let me know that the former Jilly Green was blissfully happy and expecting a baby. She said she had everything she wanted and couldn't wait to be a mom."

Perhaps it was the mention of the word "mom" that set Trish to crying again. It came softly and she buried her head in Scott's shoulder. The past evaporated, just like that. The stories had happily distracted Trish, and now there was just this most painful and unforgiving present. It was Bee's cue to leave. Quietly she rose from her chair, kissed Trish on the top of her head, and let Scott give her a one-armed hug. She left without a word, but looking back she caught Scott's eye and mouthed, "I'll be back," and he nodded.

She unlocked her car and climbed in. An idea was forming in her mind. Could she go through with it? She started the engine. Yes, she thought. I can.

CHAPTER / THIRTY-FOUR

She woke early, even earlier than her hard-working parents. She dressed in a denim pencil skirt and a simple black V-neck top. She was going for something between country and business. She left a note on the kitchen table:

> *Dearest Momsie and Pop,*
> *Your daughter is feeling remarkably well and has decided to go on an "expotition." I'm not sure if I shall find a heffalump or not, but I'll be home with stories to tell by dinner. Have yourselves an exceptionally useful and happy day.*
> *XOX*
> *Your daughter of all these many years*

She bustled along 417. In the eastbound lane the morning traffic was bumper-to-bumper but she, heading west, could have gone the speed limit if Toddy the Turtle had been capable of it. Behind her the sun was coming up gold, glinting in her rearview mirror, forcing her to dig through her purse for her sunglasses. She merged onto Highway Seven.

She didn't have much to go on. The address on the wedding card had been in Perth, which was roughly an hour and a half out of Ottawa, probably more in a children's-picture-book car. That was fine. The whole expedition could easily be a bust, but at least she'd get a day in the country out of it, a sunny day at that, after days and days of rain.

She made it to Perth, pulled into a Shopper Drug Mart on the highway, and checked the address on Google Earth. The house from which the wedding card had been sent took her through the actual town, which was surprisingly pretty, something you'd never know if you'd flown by on Seven.

Finally she pulled up outside the house and realized as she checked the address again that this couldn't be the newlyweds' place. It was large, impressively old, and expensive. The new hubby's parents, she guessed. Oh well. Nothing ventured, nothing gained. She knocked on the door and a nice-looking woman in her fifties answered. A kind woman, it seemed—kind enough not to be too taken aback by Bee's question. Bee was glad she'd made herself presentable.

"That's my daughter-in-law," said the woman, Mrs. Needham, as Bee had guessed. "I don't know how you ever got this address. They live out at the farm."

"Oh," said Bee. "Do you have their address?"

Mrs. Needham was kind but not imprudent. "What's your name, dear?"

"Beatrice. Bee. Bee Northway." She held out her hand.

"Hello, Bee," said the woman, and shook her hand. "May I ask what this is about?"

Bee tried to think of a good lie but quickly decided Mrs. Needham was not one to be taken lightly. "It's a long story," she said, "but I am going out with a boy named Donovan who used to know Jilly and he . . ." She stopped talking because she had watched Mrs. Needham's forehead crease and then her face cloud over.

"The boy who died?" she said.

It was not what Bee had expected. "Uh, yes." The woman was examining her closely now and frowning. "If I remember correctly, you said you were going out with a boy—as in the present tense."

Bee felt as if she'd been caught in a stupid lie, one she had not intended. "I didn't know that you would have heard," she said. The woman didn't respond right away, but her expression was severe, quizzical. Bee cleared her throat. "I'm not used to talking about him in the past tense," she said. This was all too true. The woman's expression lightened somewhat, but she was wary. Bee held her gaze.

"They were here for dinner on Sunday, Matt and Jilly. She was quite upset. It wasn't just the boy, of course." Bee shook her head. "Jilly . . . knew his father some time ago."

Knew?

Bee wondered what Jilly might have told her mother-in-law about her relationship with Allen Ian McGeary. "Knew" hardly covered it, except in the biblical sense.

"I haven't seen or heard much about it in the news," said Bee, "so I didn't expect it would have, you know, gotten out here."

"We're not exactly in the boonies, dear," said Mrs. Needham. "But you're right. The news came via the jungle drums. Someone out there must have known someone who knew McGeary and word spread that way. Nothing stays secret long in Sugar Valley." She smiled as if to temper this mild rebuke. Then she frowned. "Terrible business."

"Yes," said Bee, hoping she would not recount the whole sordid mess, whatever she knew.

Mrs. Needham was just opening her mouth to hold forth again when a voice called from inside the house. "Ruth, are you ready?"

Mrs. Needham turned and called back inside, "Ready when you are, Henry." Then she turned back to Bee and her expression had changed to one of concern, although there was still a good deal of curiosity in her eyes.

"We've got to run. You'll find Jilly at 2767 Cedar Bog Road. Shall I write it down for you?"

Bee pulled her cell phone from her skirt pocket. "No thanks, I'll just key it in and GPS it."

The woman chuckled. "I'd be surprised if Cedar Bog Road is on GPS. It's a land out of time." She didn't say it with any malice. "It's east of town just off Highway Seven. Maybe fifteen miles past the city limits." Bee keyed in the address. "Have you driven from Ottawa?" Bee nodded. "Then you passed it."

"Thanks so much," said Bee, looking up from her cell phone, which was busily tracking down this "land out of time."

"Ruth?" The voice from inside sounded more insistent.

"She should be in," said Mrs. Needham. "Give her my best."

Bee promised to do so and was thankful for the news. *She should be in.*

As Ruth Needham had supposed, her son's address on Cedar Bog Road was not on GPS, so Bee drove east, keeping an eye open for signposts, blinking into a sun blazing now in the eastern sky at just the height to make her sun visor useless. At one point she saw a sign saying SUGAR VALLEY ROAD, pointing to the right off the highway. She slowed down and almost turned, just out of curiosity. She had this eerie feeling that to do so would be to travel back into Donovan's past. Which is what she was doing anyway. Suddenly she wasn't at all sure what she was up to.

A car beeped at her impatiently. She checked her rearview mirror. A pickup with muddied sides and ridiculously oversize tires. What had Sergeant Bell called it? A lift job. Her hands gripped the steering wheel tightly. She checked the rearview mirror again, watched the vehicle pull up close behind her, impatient. *Shit.* What was going on? She stepped on the gas, trying to milk out a little more speed. The truck driver blasted his horn at her, made her startle and shout out loud. She looked again—several more anxious glances in the rearview mirror—and finally noticed the pickup was black. She breathed out, long and slow. As she rounded a long curve, she could see in her side-view mirror a line of cars and pickups and SUVs strung out like a kite tail behind her. The pickup driver honked again, and she caved into the pressure and pulled over to let him pass. He had a decal on the rear window that said MY DRIVING SCARES ME TOO.

It was not far to Cedar Bog Road, and had she not been going at Toddy the Turtle's slightly whiny cruising speed of 70 clicks, she might have missed it. The sign was on a slant as if it had been plowed into, so that the arrow actually pointed down into the weedy verge of the dirt road. She turned right and headed along the side road with her cell phone sitting on the seat beside her, the address emblazoned upon the screen on a yellow note. It was to prove of absolutely no use for there were no houses. Not ones anyone lived in anymore. There were fields to her left and a forest to her right. She had driven nearly two miles and was beginning to feel distinctly as if she'd made a mistake before the forest dwindled, the view opened up to her right, and she saw a throng of buildings up ahead that she hoped might be inhabited.

As she drew nearer, one new-looking building dominated her vision since it was nearest to the road. She slowed to a crawl and read the hand-painted name on a pristine white mailbox: THE NEEDHAMS it read, nothing more. So be it. She pulled into the driveway. On her left was a herd of old barns and outbuildings that looked as if they'd been put to pasture. Just barely living history, she thought. Once she'd passed the large, new aluminum facility, she saw on her right, hidden from view, an old red-brick farmhouse surrounded by maples, still bare but with the branches bristling—quickening with new life.

She was there.

CHAPTER / THIRTY-FIVE

A dog came bounding toward the car, a big one, but with a wagging tail and curly black hair that made it look more ridiculous than frightening. A Labradoodle, she thought. You could bark as loud and ferociously as you wanted, but with a name like that—not to mention a *face* like that—you're never going to be taken seriously as a guard dog. She pulled in beside a little green Honda with a baby seat in the back. She turned off the motor and looked again at the old buildings to her left, the ancestors: old friends, sapped of color with bad backs, leaning toward one another as if hard of hearing. One or two of them were constructed of logs. Rusted farm implements prowled the edges of this graveyard. She could see their teeth through the long grass.

By contrast, the farmhouse was set back on a pretty lawn, and it looked just the way a farmhouse should, with a wraparound porch and steep gabled roof, newly shingled, by the look of it. The windows, framed in white, were filled with reflected sky. It looked to Bee as if even the shadows on the porch had been freshly painted, they were so crisp and even. A screen door on the side porch opened and a woman came out carrying a toddler. The woman stared toward the car. Bee waved; the woman did not wave back. Bee hoped it was only that the sun was in her eyes and she couldn't see Bee's greeting. At least I'm not arriving bearing bad news—news she doesn't already know, Bee thought. But her heart rate picked up, all the same. This whole idea suddenly seemed inane. She took a deep breath and climbed out of the car.

"Hello?" said the woman as she wandered off the porch onto the lawn.

"Uh, hi . . . Jilly?" said Bee.

The dog took to barking, big time.

"Spinach, down!" said Jilly.

Spinach laughed at the notion of doing as he was told. Or that's how Bee interpreted the series of barks he flung into the cool spring air. She smiled at him, but when she turned back to Jilly, she stopped smiling. The woman looked intently at her, and if there wasn't exactly hostility in her eyes, there was uneasiness. She was wearing clogs and faded jeans and a loose-fitted, wrinkled yellow shirt that might have been spotless one baby feeding ago. She was attractive, but her eyes were ringed with tiredness, probably as a result of the chubby squirming creature in her arms.

"I spoke to your mom?" said Bee. She paused, got no response. "She gave me the address."

Jilly finally nodded. "My mother-in-law. She phoned to tell me you were on your way."

The baby at least was waving at Bee, who returned her greeting. Jilly hoisted the baby up. "This is Cassie," she said. The baby waved some more but then wanted down, and down she got.

"I was a friend of Donovan's," said Bee, figuring that getting down to business might be the best tactic.

"So Ruth said. What can I do for you?" There was no attempt at sharing sympathy for someone they both had loved at very different times in his life. There was, instead, as far as Bee could figure out, suspicion.

"I was with him in the hospital. He wasn't really conscious but he could talk, sort of, and he mentioned you."

Jilly nodded slowly, as if she wasn't entirely surprised. Which was *really* surprising to Bee. Meanwhile, Jilly's gaze never left Bee's eyes. Bee pushed back her hair. It had come out of its ponytail, but she didn't want to fuss with it now. This was not the welcome she had expected, especially not after what Trish had said last night. She had a feeling Jilly was sizing her up, so she stood stock-still and let her. The woman seemed to reach a conclusion.

"Would you like a cup of tea?" she said. There was some warmth in her voice but not enough to boil a cup of water.

"Thanks, that would be great."

Jilly swooped up baby Cassie, who complained and wriggled, which set Spinach to barking again.

There were choices to make about the tea and Bee settled on mint, picked, apparently, from Jilly's own garden.

Bee, sitting on the porch, was to watch the child while Jilly went into the kitchen to make the tea. The suspicion she had sensed earlier was allayed a bit by this show of trust, although it wasn't a task Bee particularly wanted. She wasn't sure what she thought about babies. But she was glad to rest her eyes from the sun under the porch's roof. She fixed her hair, straightened her skirt. Resisted the desire to put on more lip gloss. She could hear a tractor a ways off. Cassie, who was on the lawn, found something to play with, a pebble. Bee worried that she might eat it and choke to death. Gack! What a thought. How soon would she slough off this morbidity?

Soon enough, Cassie threw her stone away—at Spinach, who thought it was part of a game. In place of the stone, Cassie found a twig about as long as her arm, which she commenced talking to while the dog sniffed around at her feet. Watching them, dog and girl, Bee relaxed a little. She wasn't really needed to watch the child; Spinach was doing that. As for Jilly's guarded if not exactly chilly reception, she was not sure what to think.

The screen door snapped and Jilly reemerged with a tray of cups and a plate of fat cookies.

"Not an old family recipe," she said. "I used to bake but these days I'm lucky if I even bathe." Bee laughed, a bit too shrilly, but could think of nothing to say. Jilly placed the tray on a rustic-looking table between the two chairs and sat in the other one. She leaned forward in her seat, her eyes on her daughter. "I'm sure you have a reason for being here, but first I'd like to hear how Patricia is making out."

"Oh, sure. Yeah. I saw her last night."

Jilly glanced at her and then returned her attention to

Cassie. "I can't imagine what she must be going through."
Bee followed her gaze to the child a few yards away, squatting to scratch at the dirt with her newfound friend, Mr. Stick. "Is she bearing up okay?"

Bee nodded. "She's with a wonderful man."

"She is?"

Bee nodded. "Scott's great. Donovan really loved him. He was like a real father." It was a calculated thing to say, but completely true and she had to think that Jilly would be pleased to hear it.

Jilly turned her attention to pouring their tea.

"Honey?" she said.

Bee shook her head and took the cup from her. Her hands were shaking and she hoped Jilly wouldn't notice. She needn't have worried; the woman's eyes had turned back to Cassie, who was heading straight toward a dried-up dog turd. In one fluid movement Jilly had replaced the teapot on the tray, was out of her chair, and in three steps had swooped the baby up and brought her back, wriggling and complaining, while Spinach laughed his doggy laugh to see such sport.

"Sorry," she said, sitting again with the fractious child, to whom she gave a cookie and achieved immediate peace. The baby settled back onto her mother's chest, the cookie in both hands and her eyes filled with contentment.

Now Bee wasn't sure if she was supposed to go on. She sipped her tea.

"I'm glad to hear she found a good man," said Jilly. "She's a nice person." Jilly gently scrubbed some dirt off Cassie's knee. "The other stuff," she said. She shook her head. "I'm going to take some time to absorb it."

"I know," said Bee.

Jilly's hand rested on the wide arm of the deck chair and she stared off at the ancient buildings across the yard. "To this day, I can't believe that I was ever the kind of person who could do that: break up a marriage. What was I thinking? Well, I wasn't. And I paid for it." She shook her head.

"If it's any consolation, Trish is kind of thankful you took Al off her hands."

Jilly looked at her fixedly and then her face relaxed a bit and she rolled her eyes. "I don't doubt that," she said. "Not one bit. But back then . . ." She leaned her head back and closed her eyes. Her face was set, grim and stubborn, not pleased with herself and not about to be coaxed out of it. Seeing her in repose, Bee could see that she was beautiful despite her evident weariness and the cast of her thoughts. Her lips were full, her cheekbones prominent, her skin firm and already tinted—though it was early spring—by the sun, not makeup. Bee had come for information, but Jilly seemed to only now be warming up to her and she was in no rush.

"Trish told me that Donovan loved to come out here," she said.

Jilly's eyes snapped open and Bee half wondered if she had drifted off to sleep. She looked so tired. And there was something else, wasn't there? A sudden shiftiness. The woman lowered her eyes, took a sip of her tea, put down her cup, and looked at her baby. The cookie's perfect roundness had been compromised by small teeth marks, but little of it was gone. It rested in Cassie's plump little hand, which lay at rest on her mother's breast. She was asleep, just like that. Jilly gently hitched her into a more comfortable position. "Yeah," she said. "Dono had fun here. I looked forward to him coming out. We all did.

"My great big lunk of a brother taught him how to play poker," she continued, glancing at Bee to see if this perturbed her. Bee looked startled. "True," said Jilly. "They'd sit at the kitchen table and play for matchsticks: Merv and Al and sometimes another friend or two. I never told Trish. Maybe Donovan did, but I never got any flack from her about it." And now she smiled, really smiled, for the first time, and it was a beguiling thing to see.

"I don't think Trish would have minded," said Bee.

Jilly nodded as if she'd thought as much. She looked out toward the fields. Bee became aware of the tractor sounds again, a long way off. She watched Jilly track the sound, find it, hold it.

"I'd take him places," said Jilly. "I used to deliver baked goods and such over in Sugar Valley and Dono was always game to go along for the ride."

"I passed the turnoff," said Bee. "That's where Al and Trish had their summer cottage?"

"Not quite," said Jilly. "They were farther down the road, where Sugar Creek meets the Black River. But yeah, over that general direction." She gestured to Bee's right and Bee looked that way, across the fields. "Anyway, Donovan and I would trek across the hills. We never bothered with the roads. We'd take the shortcut across our land—we've got a hundred and some acres—right up to the shores of the river. One or other of the folks would come to fetch you if you rang the bell. Donovan loved to ring that bell."

"It sounds cool."

Jilly nodded, then stopped, and the expression on her face seemed to suggest she had stumbled upon another memory, not so pleasing. She abruptly snapped out of it. "Where was I?" she said.

Bee sipped her tea and looked over the rim at her host. "What were you thinking just now?" she said.

Jilly looked at her and the suspicion was there again. The shiftiness.

"Sorry," said Bee. "If you don't want—"

"No, it's okay."

"It's just that I'm kind of hungry to hear about him, you know? I don't exactly know why."

"Really?" said Jilly, and her expression was easy enough to interpret. *Level with me,* her eyes said.

"I'm trying to figure out what happened," said Bee.

Jilly nodded. "You said he spoke to you."

Bee shrugged. "He was only semiconscious. It was garbled."

"But he said my name?"

Bee nodded, and then to save her asking the question she knew was coming, she said, "And other things. Just snatches, but . . ."

Jilly's stare notched down and now her eyes gave away a sadness. "I was thinking how it wasn't all good times. When he was here, I mean. But you probably don't need to know that."

"I'd like to," said Bee. "Anything."

Jilly threw her a sidelong glance, assessing her again. "There was one time," she said. Then she shifted again, as if to relieve a stitch. "Let me start that again. You see, my first husband never took too well to getting ditched."

"Rory," said Bee.

"Trish remembered him?"

"Only that he was bad news."

"He sure was. Bad news when we were married and badder news when we weren't anymore—pardon my English. Al didn't seem too worried, which he probably should have been. Rory was a real roisterer. He had more swagger in him than brains. Heck, I don't know what I ever saw in him." She looked down at Cassie's head with its haze of pale blond hair. "I was a pretty foolish girl. Anyway, Rory made a lot of bluster and fuss and swore this and swore that, but it all seemed to be okay. Then one day, Dono and I were out in the fields on some errand—picking juniper berries, maybe. I don't remember. Anyway, he saw something off in the tall grass. He ran to look and I followed him and then he just stopped. He was looking at something on the ground." Jilly took a swig of her tea, set the cup down.

"What was it?"

"The dog," said Jilly.

"I'm sorry?"

"The dog. He hadn't been around at breakfast. This was a big old Labrador named Minos. He'd go off sometimes. Venture about. Liked to have his little liaisons with the lady dogs."

"And Turn . . . I mean, Donovan found the dog?"

"Yeah. Dead." Bee had known that was coming, but it still made her gasp. "With an arrow through its neck."

"An arrow?"

"That'd be Rory, leaving his mark."

"So he was, like, an archer?"

Jilly raised an eyebrow. "You picturing Robin Hood?" she said.

Bee shrugged. She had been, she guessed.

Jilly chuckled. "He had this high-tech thing. Like something out of *The Walking Dead*."

"And he killed your dog?"

Jilly nodded. "Poor Dono. He loved that animal. I felt so bad for him having to see that. I remember phoning Trish. We hadn't talked much—hardly at all—and I was nervous about doing it. But I needed to warn her, you know. That he might be upset."

"What'd you do?" said Bee. "I mean about Rory; did you know for sure it was him?"

"Oh, sure. Stood to reason. He was a nasty piece of work. But the cops weren't as sure. It was early November, deer hunting season. There were lots of hunters out and about, and even though most of your local hunters ask permission to be on the property, not all of them are quite so civic-minded. Plus you've got your city hunters and tourists who stray, get lost—end up shooting a cow, for God's sake. It happens."

"But this," said Bee.

"Oh, it was Rory, all right. But Rory, see, he could call it a mistake. I mean the land was mine, but he'd been living here with me—my husband and all—so he could claim a right to hunt there, wrongly or rightly, and then just make a big fuss about shooting wild or whatever. He'd spin a yarn."

"So nothing happened?"

"Oh yeah, something happened. The cops who came to the house, I knew one of them pretty good. He'd gone to school with me and Rory. Knew what he was like. Rory was on their books: drunken and disorderly, a few fights, resisting arrest—that kind of thing. But around here that's as it may be—just boys being boys. Still, Harry Cameron—that was the officer—he did me a favor. Nothing official. Just led Rory to believe that maybe a long trip would be a good idea. Head out to Alberta, see if he could get work in the oil fields—something like that. Rory took the hint, and that was the last we saw of him."

The image of the dog with an arrow through its neck made Bee feel nauseous. Turn had never mentioned it. Never mentioned Jilly or coming out to the country. It made her sad in a whole other way, she couldn't figure why.

"My brother Mervin said he'd tear Rory limb from limb if he ever showed up in the county again. But when he did, it was years and years later and nothing much happened."

"So he came back?"

"Sure. Probably got himself fired. He was good at that."

Spinach came up on the porch then and decided to flop down at their feet. Bee reached down and scruffled his neck feathers. He opened his big mouth and panted happily, slobbering drool on the floor. Bee looked up and saw that Jilly was staring intently at her.

"What'd he say about me?" she said.

It took Bee a minute to realize what she meant. "Donovan?" Jilly nodded. "Nothing really," said Bee. "He could barely string two words together. But he managed to say 'Jilly' pretty clearly. I didn't know anyone named Jilly, so I asked Trish and she told me about you."

Jilly nodded and looked somehow wise, as if she could understand why he had talked about her. As if it made sense. And that led to her turning again to Bee. "Would now be a good time for you to tell me what you're really up to?"

CHAPTER THIRTY-SIX

"Like I said, I'm trying to piece together a puzzle," said Bee.

Jilly looked at her through narrowed eyes, then seemed to realize what Bee was saying. "Based on what he told you—Dono?" Bee nodded. "But you said he could hardly string two words together."

Again, Bee nodded. "I know. It's probably insane, but I feel . . . I guess I feel like I have to do something."

The baby whimpered and Jilly soothed her with a kiss on the top of her head. "I don't know much about what happened," she said, her voice low. "All I heard via the grapevine was that Al was dead and so was the boy. It looked like Al was murdered. But Donovan, from what I heard, was run over. I'm guessing there's more to it than that."

Bee took a deep breath. She wasn't sure what she was looking for, but she wasn't going to find out anything unless she confided in someone with her theory, if that's what it was. "Okay, so the cops want to put Al's death on Donovan. He—Al—had his head smashed in by a baseball bat. Donovan's bat, as it turns out."

Jilly made a face. "I can understand the impulse," she said. "But doing it . . ."

"Exactly. Turn—that's what I call him . . . called him—Turn could never have done such a thing. Never. He had a temper, all right, but he . . ."

Jilly nodded. "I hear you," she said. "Go on."

"Turn was there at Al's place. There was more than one witness who saw him come and go and then come back again. And both times he left the place, he was running."

"So it looks bad."

"It looks terrible. And the cops see him getting run over as an accident or maybe even suicide."

"But you don't buy that."

Bee shook her head. "I think whoever killed Al murdered Turn because he knew too much."

"What do you mean? There was something going on? Something illegal?"

Bee shook her head but suddenly realized that this was a whole other avenue of thought. No, she told herself, stick to what you were thinking. "What I meant was that he saw what really happened or something. Except I have no proof other than knowing Turn the way I do."

"And these things he said to you."

"Right. And that."

Jilly considered what Bee had said. "And these words, are they just in your head?"

"No, when I realized he was actually trying to say stuff, I wrote it down in my journal."

Jilly eyed Bee again and seemed to put two and two together. "And you're out here, snooping around by yourself, which suggests you haven't told the cops about what he said."

The cat was now officially out of the bag. "Right," Bee said, and immediately felt stupid. "You see, you could interpret the words in different ways. He actually seemed to be saying, at one point, that he killed his father, but that's not *really* what he said. Only you'd have had to be there to understand that."

"Or have an open mind, maybe," said Jilly. She cocked her head to one side. "So?" she said.

Bee rolled her lips into her mouth and bit down hard. What the hell was she doing! She broke eye contact. Looked away. Looked at the old buildings across the yard, sitting in their shadows—shadows diminishing as the sun rose higher in the late morning sky. She looked again at Jilly. Why would Turn have said her name if he didn't want Bee to know about her—someone he'd never mentioned before? Jilly couldn't be wrapped up in any of this, could she? Not with a new baby and a happy marriage.

The baby whimpered again and Jilly cleared her throat. "I'm not sure how long you plan on taking before you decide to trust me," she said, "but pretty soon Cassie here is going to want my sole attention."

Bee nodded and took the plunge. She reached down into her purse and pulled out the journal. She opened it, handed it over. Jilly took the book in her one free hand. Bee felt she should say something, then stopped herself and leaned back in her chair. Her tea had gone cold. She was leaving a trail of cold tea behind her these days.

Jilly made a *hmm* sound. "Well, here's something," she said. "Kali."

"You know her?"

"Since we were at school. She was just plain Kelly then. Kelly O'Connor."

"So Al met her out here?"

Jilly nodded. "I wasn't entirely surprised to hear they'd hooked up. I could tell she had her eye on him all those years ago when he and I were together." She shook her head. "I've made my mistakes. Two of them, in particular: Rory and Al. But I'd like to think I learned something along the way. Live and learn, right? So I could be accused here of the pot calling the kettle black if I were to say that Kali doesn't have a lick of sense when it comes to men." She sighed. Then she returned her attention to the journal. "Did the cops talk to her?"

Bee nodded. "Yeah. But they don't seem to be giving her much consideration. She broke up with Al over a month ago and moved back here. Nobody'd seen her around Al's place—not even his busybody neighbor, the one who saw Donovan *twice* the evening of the murder." Bee frowned, thinking of Inspector Stills. "Kali had an alibi: doesn't drive, doesn't have a car, and I don't know what."

"Mrs. Billy," said Jilly.

"Excuse me?"

"Mrs. Billy is Ronny Farrow's mother. Has Alzheimer's. She's got a place right near where Kali is staying now.

Ronny was going to put her mom in respite care since she—Ronny—was heading off to Mexico and then, out of the blue, Kali offers to look after her. Doesn't have a job and she'd always liked Mrs. Billy."

"So she was with Mrs. Billy on April fifteenth?"

Jilly shrugged. "Who's to know? The cops sure can't ask the old lady."

"But if Kali was looking after her, then she couldn't have been in Ottawa, could she?"

Again Jilly shrugged. "It kind of depends on when Ronny handed over the old woman into Kali's care. Kali could say she was there—at Mrs. Billy's, I mean—on the night in question and no one can call her out on it. Ronny's a weird gal, a true loner. She just takes off in her old Volkswagen microbus when she's good and ready. Wouldn't have stopped to say good-bye to anyone."

Bee frowned. "So Kali's alibi isn't all that strong?" she said.

"Not as far as I can tell, but then neither is Kali."

"What do you mean?"

"Well, she's hardly someone likely to bash somebody's head in with a bat. Skinny arms. Not much in the way of moxie. She wouldn't be anyone's prime suspect for a violent crime, that's for sure."

Bee had met Kali one of the two times she'd met Al. Well, not met her so much as nodded at her and Kali had nodded back. All she remembered was flaming-red hair.

Jilly, meanwhile, had lifted up the little Moleskine book and deftly turned the page without the use of her decommissioned left hand, holding the sleeping child. Bee watched her eyes hoping for something, anything. And there it was. Her gaze had stopped.

"What?" said Bee.

Jilly frowned. Then closed the book and handed it back.

"You saw something," said Bee.

"Maybe I did."

"Please, Jilly. If there's any help you can give me. Anything."

Jilly took a deep breath and the baby whimpered again. "My advice would be to take this book to the police and let them handle it."

"But they've already made up their minds. They won't—"

Jilly held up her hand, stopping Bee in mid-rant. "Well, you tell them that they need to talk to Kali O'Connor. Again." She placed her empty teacup on the tray and began to straighten the cups there, the Brown Betty teapot, the jar of honey. "She may not have a car, but her new boyfriend does," she said without looking up. Bee stared at her, wide-eyed, waiting—willing her to go on. Finally, Jilly looked up. "That would be Rory Tulk," she said.

CHAPTER THIRTY-SEVEN

Bee was speechless.

Just then a truck rattled down Cedar Bog Road; Spinach leaped up from where he was lying at their feet and raced across the yard barking his head off. Cassie woke up in full howl.

"There, there," said Jilly.

But "there, there" wasn't going to cut it with the baby. "I'm going to try to put her down," said Jilly, getting to her feet.

"I should probably go," said Bee, making as if to stand.

"No," said Jilly, fussing with the child. "I mean, would you stay just a little longer?" She looked fleetingly at Bee.

Bee nodded. She wasn't sure she could stand up anyway. She was in shock.

Jilly rocked the baby on her arm. Cassie's face was red with the exertion of her displeasure at being woken up so abruptly. But already her eyelids were falling. "I'll be back in just a minute," said Jilly softly. "There's something . . . Well, just wait, if you can."

So Bee waited and thought. Kali and Rory, the—what did Jilly call him?—the roisterer. Bee had never heard the word before. She pulled her cell phone out of her pocket. No signal. Not much of one anyway. She'd look up the word later, but she'd gotten the sense of the man from Jilly's story. She imagined him as a brawler with a mean streak in him, a man capable of killing a dog out of spite.

Then a thought came stealing into her brain, demanding her attention. Why *had* Jilly told her that story in the first place? Donovan had come out to the farm over a period of a couple of years, probably many, many times—times enough for he and Jilly to become fast friends. There were probably a hundred stories she could have told Bee about his visits if she'd wanted to wax nostalgic. And Bee had pretty well invited her to remember at will, wanting to hear anything about his past. But something had made Jilly recall this one horrible story of a little boy coming across a dead dog—a murdered dog. Murdered by the very man who now loomed large as a suspect, at least in Bee's eyes, and despite Kali's alibi. It seemed uncanny—too much of a coincidence.

"You okay?"

It was Jilly, staring at her, at Bee sitting on the edge of her chair, her hands gripping each arm as if she were about to catapult herself into action. Bee looked at her, not sure whether to trust her and not at all sure why she would think that. But she had to. Looking into Jilly's eyes, she had to. There was some link there. Some connection.

She stood up, dropped the journal back in her handbag, rubbing her hands down the front of her skirt nervously. "I was wondering why you told me about Rory—about him killing your dog and Turn finding it like that."

Jilly's face seemed to quake a bit. "I knew something was up," she said.

"What do you mean?"

Jilly shook off whatever it was that had made her grimace. "You're upset," she said. "You want to go."

"Yes—I mean, I think I should get back to the cops about Kali and Rory. But I want to know what you meant when you said you knew something was up."

Jilly bent down, picked up Bee's bag, and looked at it. " 'Theater is My Bag,' " she read on the bag's black sides. She smiled and handed it to Bee. Then she took her by the elbow. "I'll walk you to your car," she said.

So they walked, and Bee waited and Jilly did not speak and Spinach came, tail wagging, and walked with them, a loyal escort. They reached the car and, spontaneously, Jilly hugged Bee. Held her, then quickly let her go.

"Sorry," she said.

"It's all right. I just . . ."

"I'm getting to it," said Jilly. "But it's hard. Hard to say." The sound of the tractor suddenly filled Bee's ears again. It must have been there all along, but now it sounded as if it were coming their way. Jilly noticed it, too. She put her hand to her eyes to block out the sun and looked out to the western field. She looked at her wristwatch. Hubby coming home for lunch? thought Bee. Then she looked at Jilly and there was something like fear in her eyes. Not fear, exactly, Bee thought, but what . . . disapproval?

"I knew something had happened," she said. "I mean, before I heard any news of it, I just sort of felt it."

She looked toward the house—no, toward the garden between the house and the long shed. Bee watched her face. There was something in her eyes, a mystery there, and Bee remembered what Trish had said about her being magical.

"I was aware . . . I guess that's the word for it . . . I was aware of Al being here." She looked into Bee's eyes as if for a confirmation.

"What do you mean?"

"Friday. Last Friday evening. I was just cleaning up in the kitchen and I started thinking of Al. God, I hadn't thought of him in ages, but suddenly it was as if he was filling up my senses. I actually stopped washing the dishes and headed out to the yard as if I'd heard someone there. Then when I came in I just stared at the kitchen table. Matt was there doing the books, paying some bills or something. And Al was there, too."

Bee went cold. "I don't understand."

Jilly wagged her head from side to side. "That makes two of us," she said. "It just happens to me sometimes."

"Like a . . . ghost?"

"Sort of. A presence. And then later, after we'd gone upstairs, I heard something. At first I thought it was the baby. I felt as if I'd heard a voice. I went to the window. There was no one there, but . . ." She glanced at Bee, then looked away.

"This is pretty weird," said Bee.

"Don't I know it!"

"Go on."

"Matt and I were getting ready for bed and I said something to him. 'Did you hear that?' I said. But he hadn't heard anything. I listened and . . . well, eventually I just had to come downstairs and check. I went out in just my nightshirt and robe. It was raining. I stood on the porch and looked out toward the woods. I felt somehow as if there was this boy coming through those woods, coming to the house, needing me in some way. I panicked a bit. I mean, I couldn't tell Matt. He's a wonderful husband, solid and trustworthy and loving. I didn't want him to see me in the state I'd gotten myself into." She brought her palms together and raised them to her face, as if in prayer. She bowed her head, closed her eyes. "I know you think this is nuts."

"Maybe I do," said Bee. "I don't know what to think."

"I'm not the hysterical type," said Jilly. "It was just this feeling, is all."

"What did you do?"

"I went inside and tried to phone Trish."

Bee was stunned. "You had her phone—"

"No. I didn't. I hadn't seen her or talked to her in a donkey's age. I got directory assistance, but there was no listing."

"They don't have a landline. Anyway, they were out of town. She and Scott had gone camping."

Jilly nodded. She looked up into the deep-blue sky, took a big breath, and then returned her gaze to Bee. "Anyway, for what it's worth. I wanted you to hear that. God knows why." She threw her hands out to her sides.

Bee wasn't religious, but somehow Jilly's last comment

seemed as good a note to end on as anything. "I suppose he does," she said.

They looked at each other for one more moment and Jilly's eyes seemed to say, This is our secret. Bee nodded—wasn't sure whether to hug the woman back or shake hands or what. In the end, she just fished in her pocket for her keys and headed around the car. She was opening the door when Jilly spoke again.

"Oh, and one more thing," she said. "Rory wouldn't call himself an archer. Around these parts he'd be called a bow-hunter."

CHAPTER THIRTY-EIGHT

Bee glanced down at her cell phone on the passenger seat. Only one bar. She needed to phone Stills, or maybe Bell. Somebody. Bell was more approachable, but Stills was the one she wanted to impress. Then again, Stills was the one who would be more likely to ream her out for pulling a Nancy Drew.

She wanted desperately to be back in Ottawa, but she turned west on the highway because Perth was a lot closer than Ottawa and the sooner she talked to the cops the better. As she recalled, there was a long stretch of nothing between here and home, so Perth was the best option—or earlier, if possible, *wherever she could get service.*

She thought about Jilly's utterly strange confession. "I see dead people," Bee said to herself with full-on irony, but she couldn't dismiss the woman that easily. And come to think of it, she hadn't really said she saw Al or Donovan, only that she sensed them. Very strange. Bee recalled Jilly's initial diffidence toward her, as if she didn't really want to see Bee at all. As if she didn't want to admit to her or anyone that she had this . . . what was it: a gift, a curse?

"ESP," said Bee out loud. "Do we believe in such things, Toddy?" The car was too busy trying to keep up to speed to answer.

Around these parts he'd be called a bowhunter.

There had been a look in Jilly's eye when she said those words, as if this wasn't just some wayward thought. Which is when Bee went cold all over. With a quick glance at the rearview mirror, she swung the car onto the shoulder and slowed to a stop. She grabbed her bag up from the floor on the passenger side of the car and dragged out her journal. She flipped it open to Turn's last words. Not really words at all but an attempt at words—not just some random sound.

Bo . . . Hun . . .

"Oh Jesus," she said. She grabbed hold of the wheel. "Oh Jesus."

A truck flew by, rocking the car and making Bee shout with surprise. She put her hand on her heart and waited a moment. Then she checked the road over her shoulder, put on her blinker, and pulled back out onto the highway.

Toddy the Turtle dawdled along, a dusky sage vision of loveliness on this sunny day, but her driver was not in a lovely state. Not aware of anything but the presence suddenly in her life of a man—a name, at least—she had never heard of before last night.

A history of violence. Wasn't that the expression? Rory

Tulk had a record with the local cops. He killed things. He used to be married to someone who left him to live with Al McGeary. *Talk about motivation.* Okay, it was—she counted on her fingers—ten years ago that Jilly kicked Rory out. But still, he was a hothead.

And he was going out with Kali O'Connor.

A car beeped as it pulled out to pass; she turned to look, prepared to apologize. But the face in the window was smiling with a big thumbs-up. "Cute car!" the woman was saying. Bee couldn't hear her, but she could read her lips and she was used to it.

Kali, née Kelly. Bee had met her just the once. It was at a ball game early last fall, the semifinals. Donovan had tried and tried to get his dad to come and see him play. She'd once suggested that at seventeen he was too old to need his father's support. Wrong. And when she told her mother about it later, her mother said, "Beatrice, my darling, some of my clients in their fifties are still trying to win the love of their parents—even when the parent in question is deceased."

Anyway, at the game, Kali had come along with Al, and it was a rare enough sighting that Bee watched her across the stands as avidly as any bird-watcher scoped an accidental tourist. She was sexy in a slightly sleazy kind of way. Cigarette thin, big boobs, hair and lots of it, as red as cinnamon hearts. Not exactly trailer trash—a bit more style than that in her getup—but kind of used up. "Ridden hard and put away wet," Donovan had said later, an old expression he'd picked up somewhere. "Eww!" Bee had responded. But yeah, that was the impression of the woman. Except, up close, when they finally met, introduced reluctantly by Donovan after the game—up close there was something in Kali's eyes, a kind of green longing that made you want to like her. Her lips were caked with lipstick and would have been sensuous if they weren't cracked. And her face would have been almost glamorous if it weren't for the beer she was wearing inside her flesh. "I feel sorry for her," Bee had said to Donovan driving home that evening. Then she berated herself. "God, what a patronizing thing to say. Sorry." And Donovan had said, "No, feel sorry for her all you want; she's with my father."

And then she wasn't.

Bee glanced down and saw the phone spike two, three bars, four. She glanced in the rearview mirror and saw that she had a trail of six or seven vehicles—too hard to pull off the highway onto the shoulder now—scary. Then she saw a sign up ahead: SUGAR VALLEY ROAD. Aha!

She threw on her turn signal, slowed down, and made the turn left off of the highway. Good.

But Sugar Valley Road wasn't wide enough for stopping. There were no shoulders at all. And soon enough the pavement gave way to a dirt road that wound through wooded land and Bee realized she had made a mistake. "Idiot!" she said to herself. "No problem," herself responded, "just find a driveway to turn around in." She passed a sign tacked to a tree: DRIVE CAREFULLY, ELVES CROSSING.

"Now look what you've gotten us into," she said in her most peevish voice. "Stick with me," herself responded. As if she had any choice.

Meanwhile, this was the place—or near enough—where Donovan's family had fallen apart. And from what Jilly had told her, he would have come here with her, as a middle-schooler, until his life got shaken up yet again, when Jilly came to her senses and got rid of Al.

Donovan had liked coming out here, according to Trish. What wasn't there to like? The road was beautiful. She hadn't seen any houses yet, mind you. Not even elfin ones. But here she was, not five minutes from the highway and she felt already as if she had entered a fairyland. The thought made her shudder.

"This is no time for lollygagging," she said. One of her father's words.

The hilly, winding road straightened out and up ahead she could see a break in the canopy of trees. Then there was a driveway with a sign beside it on the left. A fairly big sign that read: WELCOME TO SUGAR VALLEY SCHOOL. There were elves painted on the sign, presumably the ones she was supposed to avoid hitting. She slowed down to look at the sign. One elf was peeking out from behind the S. Another one was sitting on the word "Valley" so that her legs made the L's. A third elf was holding up the word "School."

"Cute," said Bee.

The road widened here, so instead of turning left into the school driveway, she pulled over onto the right verge and stopped. She didn't turn off the motor, not right away. She looked around for signs of something more dangerous than elves, orcs maybe, but all she saw was gentle meadowland and, past the school and down a hill, the first habitations she'd laid eyes on since she left the main road. The nearest house she could see could easily have been a hobbit house.

It was made of fieldstone and had a high peaked roof, a turret, and a chimney that looked to be straight out of a picture book. "Oh, Toddy," she said, patting the dashboard. "I do believe you've found the place you belong." She smiled and turned off the motor.

As soon as the engine stopped, she heard the wind, and then she heard, on the wind, the sounds of children. She was directly across from the school's driveway and there were children out playing. It was recess, she guessed—correction, lunch hour. The morning had flown by. She cracked her window and the shouts and laughter seeped in. From where she was sitting, she could only see a dozen or so kids. Perhaps that was all there were. It was such a bucolic sight, and the happy sound eased her anxiety. And best of all, her phone was still registering four bars!

She dove her hand into her bag and dug out her journal. Tucked in the back were the detectives' business cards. She considered for a moment who she'd phone but knew it had to be Stills. It was Stills she wanted off her back. And Stills was the lead on the case. She was the one who needed convincing that Donovan was not guilty of anything. She picked up her phone and began to punch in the number, but her progress was interrupted by a bump outside the car. She looked up in time to see a soccer ball ricochet off the car's side and bounce out into the middle of the road. Looking up, she saw a boy, maybe eight, running down the hill toward the escaped ball. Behind him a woman appeared and through cupped hands shouted, "Caleb, do not go out on the road!" Caleb stopped immediately. Good little elf. "I'll be right there," the woman said. Was she their teacher? Bee wondered. She looked lovely. Older than most teachers were anymore, but with the kindest face you could imagine. Her immediate time was taken up by a little girl who had come crying to her with a bloody shin. Meanwhile, Caleb waited patiently, not five yards from the soccer ball and with not a car in sight other than Toddy the Turtle. He was gazing at the car with rapt attention. Ogling it. Well, Bee could solve the soccer ball issue. She stepped out of the car, looked both ways, just to model good traffic safety for young Caleb, and then marched over to the runaway ball.

"Catch," she said, and lobbed it to him.

He grabbed it happily. "Thank you, miss," he said. *God, he's cute.* He turned and headed back up the drive toward the school, then he stopped and turned again. "I really like your car!" he said.

Bee gave him a thumbs-up. He waved and ran to join his classmates and she returned to her car and the half-dialed number. The phone rang and went to a message. Inspector Callista Stills was not able to come to the phone. Bee was invited to leave a detailed message or, if it was an emergency, to phone 911. Well, it wasn't an emergency, but she hadn't thought about leaving a message. So she pushed the little phone icon to end the call. Now she could try Jim Bell, she thought. So she tried with the same result. Damn! Okay, leave a message at least, but not with Bell. So she phoned Stills a second time, and when the beep came inviting her to speak, she said who was calling and began her message: "You need to check on someone named Rory Tulk, who lives in the Perth area. He has a history of violence and a police record and he is currently going out with Kali O'Connor. He and Al McGeary have a past. Call me, please, as soon as you get this and I'll fill you in on the rest. Thanks."

She ended the call. She felt she should say, "Over and out" or "Roger that" or some other official sounding thing. She clasped the cell in both hands and let it sink to her lap. She breathed out, long and slow. Then her head drooped and she closed her eyes, letting the wind slipping in the open window ruffle the edges of her hair. When she opened her eyes, there was a woman standing beside the car, the fingers of one hand resting on the hood. It was Kali O'Connor.

CHAPTER / THIRTY-NINE

Kali approached the open window on the driver's side. Bee wanted to wind the window shut, lock the doors, peel out of there leaving an impenetrable dust screen behind her.

"Aren't you . . . ?" said Kali, bending down to look in the window. For a moment Bee thought she might be able to bluff her way out of it. Why would this woman remember her from one meeting? "Sorry," said Kali. "I can't remember your name, but I sure remember this vehicle."

So much for anonymity.

"Bee," said Bee, lowering the window just enough to reach out and shake the hand that Kali was offering. It was not so much a hand as a jeweler's window-display piece. There were too many rings to count on a hand that was long and slim—more like skin and bone—with nails lacquered porcelain blue and fingertips shaded yellow with nicotine.

"Right," said Kali, who did not exchange her own name. "Huh! How weird to run into you way the heck out here in the middle of nowhere."

Think quickly!

"Are you, like, lost?"

Oh God, yes!

"Yeah," said Bee. "I was looking for Jilly Green? But I must have taken a wrong turn." Kali frowned. Bee's answer had thrown her off, at least for the moment, but maybe it was the wrong distraction.

"So's that who you were phoning just now?" she asked.

"Right! Yeah. Uh-huh. Turns out I missed her road by, like, two or three clicks. Can you believe it?" *Shut up, for God's sake!*

Kali nodded, but the answer clearly hadn't satisfied her curiosity. Time to move into action. "She was expecting me," said Bee, reaching down to turn the ignition key.

"I don't get it," said Kali. "I mean why would you even know Jilly?"

At least she could answer this with something like honesty. She withdrew her hand from the key. "Donovan really liked Jilly. And Trish—do you know who she is?" Bee couldn't help but ask, and wickedly enjoyed Kali's awkward nod. "Yeah, well Trish said that Jilly had been really close to Donovan, too. So I thought somebody should let her know about . . . well, you know . . . about his passing."

There was that phrase again, this time coming out of her own mouth. But it was good in this context. Impersonal. She almost sounded like someone whose heart was not broken in two. She watched Kali's face for any rupture in the facade of her makeup. She'd built up quite a wall of it. Was that a fading of light in her eyes, a throb in the temple, a twitch of the lip? Bee suddenly felt emboldened. "You heard, I guess. About Donovan's accident?"

Kali placed her good hand on the top of the window glass. She nodded. "It's such a terrible tragedy," she said. "I'm so sorry for your loss."

Was her voice shaky or was it just Bee's imagination? "And I'm sorry for yours," said Bee. "How long had you and Al been together?"

Kali made an involuntary motion with her right hand, as if she were throwing away a candy wrapper. Really? "A couple of years, on and off," she said, "but we'd broken up. Did you know that? I mean Donovan would've told you, right?" Bee nodded and watched Kali accept the gesture with some relief. "It was like months ago. Still, it's awful sad," she added, as if she'd only just remembered that it was sad.

"Yeah," said Bee. And now she did turn the ignition key. She was angry, which was only marginally better than being frightened. In the first state, she was consumed with getting away. In the second state, she would have to be very careful not to run over Kali O'Connor. Several times. She wasn't sure why. She was guilty of something, that's all Bee knew.

The car revved to life and Kali stepped back from the window. Glancing at her, Bee could see she was worried. Good! Let her stew. She turned her eyes to the front and grabbed the gearshift. Glancing sideways, she could see that Kali was saying something to her. Bee cupped her left ear.

"Do you want to come over?" she asked.

About as much as I want to go over Niagara Falls in a coffin.

"Got to run," said Bee. "Thanks anyway."

She pulled forward and then turned out into the road until she was facing the school's driveway. She could just run up there a car length or two and avoid having to do a three-point turn. This was a very good idea because her three-point turns often ended up being five- or six-point turns. In a flash she saw herself going off the dirt road into the grassy ditch. She opted for the driveway. The little sage-green car leaped ahead, forcing Kali to jump aside. The woman screamed and Bee slammed on the brakes. She stared at Kali, looking for evidence of some injury. Kali was tottering backward, grabbing at her right leg. *Did I really hit her?* No, she would have felt it. Kali screamed again.

Get the hell out of here. Go. Go.

She threw the car into reverse, but when she hit the gas the tires just spun.

"Help!" cried Kali at the top of her lungs. "Oh, help, please!"

Bee was petrified. The whole thing was a show—had to be?

Do not fall for this!

She tried again, and the engine roared. Good. But just as she was about to turn to check the road, she saw the kind teacher and several children, Caleb among them, appear at the top of the driveway. Which is when Kali made her move. She fell. She stumbled toward the car, bounced off the back end, and sprawled on the ground, holding her leg and howling.

It was a bold move. She ended up lying right up against the left rear tire—half under the back end of the car. There was no room for Bee to maneuver. She pressed down hard on the brake, put the car in park, and threw her hands up in the air. Then she reached forward, turned off the key.

She pulled the hand brake and clambered out of the car.

Kali's caterwauling had been pitched to override the sound of the engine. Now she contented herself with moaning and rolling around as the teacher arrived on the scene.

"Get back," the teacher said to her flock of elves. Then she hurried toward Bee, her face filled with concern. "What happened?" she asked.

Bee stuttered, trying to answer, but the teacher blew right by her and was soon kneeling by Kali's side, her hand resting lightly on the woman's shoulder. "Kali," she said. "Where does it hurt?"

Bee watched, struck stony silent by what was happening. She'd stage managed enough amateur theatrics to recognize a really bad performance. Surely, it was a charade. But part of her wasn't sure. Had she hit Kali? No! Toddy would have shuddered at contact. And in that moment she thought of Donovan and what had happened to him and she broke down. Her butt was leaned against the door. Now her bones melted and she slithered down the door until her backside met the gravel of the roadway.

The next thing she knew, the nice teacher was attending to her. She was squatting in front of her, a hand on her shoulder. "It's all right, dear," she said. "I don't think anything's broken." Bee sniffed, and out of thin air the teacher pulled a tissue. Or it might have been from her pocket; the thing is, it was there and immediately put to use. Bee was sobbing. The accident may have been phony, but Bee's reaction was not. Which is why she wasn't sure at first what it was the teacher was saying. It sounded a lot like she had asked Bee to drive Kali home.

"What was that?" she asked.

"Could you drive Kali home?" said the teacher patiently, as if Bee was one of her young students, one of the dumber ones. She wasn't condescending, just serenely capable of bringing even the dullest mind around.

No! No! No! No! No!

"It's just down the way a bit, near the river. I'd go but for the children . . ." She didn't plead; she didn't need to. She was one of those rare people who saw nothing but good in her fellow human beings, and her eyes had surely found Bee's inner very-nice person.

"I guess so," said Bee. She gazed into the warm eyes of the teacher and hoped those eyes were smart enough to see the panic in her own eyes. Hoped that the inner ear of this lovely woman could hear the voice screaming inside Bee that she did not want to do this. She really, really, really did not want to be alone with Kali.

"Oh, that is so kind," said the teacher, actually clasping her hands together.

Two of the older kids had come, at the teacher's request, to help Kali off the ground. Bee, on her feet again, marveled at how poor Kali's acting skills were. At one point she actually limped on the wrong foot.

Didn't anybody see that?

It didn't matter. The show must go on. The other

schoolchildren, who were not supposed to come too close, had gathered around on every side. Bee was surrounded. If she tried to make a break for it now, she would definitely hit someone, maybe several little someones. It would be like bowling! In her mind's eye she pictured the driveway littered with wounded elves. Unfortunately, none of them would be the woman moaning and crying crocodile tears onto the shoulder of a chubby twelve-year-old.

Bee watched as they guided Kali to the passenger door. Watched her like a hawk. Waited for her to look at Bee and see the contempt she had for this trumped-up injury. But as she watched her, Bee realized something: the hobbling might be fake, but the tears were not. This woman was on the edge, desperate, wrestling with hysteria. And it had nothing to do with being hit by a car. One of the lads who had stepped up to help let go of her, but not before asking Kali to steady herself with her hand on the roof of the car. Which is when Bee saw the cell phone in Kali's hand. A pink one with a starry pattern on it. She wasn't sure when it got there. When she was lying on the ground under the back end of the car? Before the teacher arrived? If she had made a call, it couldn't have been a long one. And who had she called so surreptitiously? Bee didn't expect it was 911.

CHAPTER FORTY

Bee collected her wits. They were strewn all over the place.

"Did you lose something, dear?" asked the nice teacher. Bee looked at her. She'd been staring at the ground as if she had lost some real thing. "Just shaken up," she said.

The teacher squeezed her arm gently. Then stepped away. "I'm sure she'll be fine once she gets home. Don't you worry. Nothing's broken."

Bee wanted to argue that she would worry if she wanted to, and it had nothing to do with Kali's leg. Something was broken—her confidence. Which is when the teacher smiled at her and said, apparently without the slightest shred of irony, "You know, it's so lucky you showed up."

And with that she rounded up her young elves and headed up the drive. The performance was over. Bee took one last deep breath. She was going to have to do a far better job of acting than Kali if she was to get through this. Kali suspected something, but what could she possibly suspect of Bee? Bee's excuse, that she had gotten lost on her way to Jilly's farm, was a reasonable one, whether Kali believed it or not. Then again, mentioning Jilly might have been the big mistake. Stick to that story anyway, she told herself. Then she climbed back in the car.

Kali was silent, staring straight ahead. Without an audience she wasn't even going to be bothered to whimper.

"I'm so sorry," said Bee. "How's the leg?"

Kali managed a tight little nod. "It'll be okay. I just want to get home, you know?"

"Yeah, yeah. Of course." Bee knew the feeling. She turned the key and the trusty little car started up. She backed out onto the road and headed south.

"It's left at the fork up ahead," said Kali. Her hands folded into fists.

The fork was just over the hill and around the bend. From the top of the hill, Bee caught a view of the river over to the left, and beside it, along its bank and climbing into the low hills around it, a scattering of houses between the trees. There was a tall escarpment behind the trees, as if part of an ancient wall that had encircled this enchanted community millennia ago. Magical-looking houses, probably made of candy, thought Bee. Houses fit for hobbits and other denizens of Middle-earth. And maybe witches who threw children into the oven when they were fattened up.

The right fork led around the escarpment to the Black

River Bridge, three and a half miles along. That must have been where Donovan had holidayed as a kid. "Left!" said Kali in a panicky voice.

"Sorry," said Bee, swinging the wheel around hard so that Kali was jostled against the door. "Sorry," she said again once she had the car under control. It wasn't an apology that would have stood up had she been wired to a polygraph.

The road, such as it was, petered out to a trail, ruts in the grass, mud from the rains of last weekend that had dried and cracked in the warmer weather. The car wobbled down toward the river.

Say something. Allay her doubts.

"I'm going to have quite a story to tell Jilly," she said. And regretted it immediately.

"What story?"

"This," said Bee too loudly. "Running into you, I mean." And then she laughed, and her own hysteria exploded into the little car. "Oh, sorry. That sounds awful."

"It's just up ahead," said Kali, pointing to a little cottage on the right, not three yards from the road. It was tiny, constructed of weathered blue cedar clapboard with empty flower boxes and lopsided shutters and a moss-covered roof that was more moss than shingles.

"I didn't mean to laugh," said Bee, pulling the car up to the picket fence outside the cottage. "Honest. I guess I'm just really strung out."

"Yeah. Tell me about it."

There was a sign, carved in wood. FRANCESCA'S END, it read. The sign was as dilapidated as the house. The paint had gone from the carved letters, leaving only the impression of them. The fence had once been white. It was missing teeth, and the gate, which opened inward, was half unhinged and leaning drunkenly. Bee stopped so that the car door could swing open into the gateway. She turned off the motor and was immediately aware of the pounding of her heart. Or was it Kali's? The whole car seemed to rock with the pent-up anxiety inside it. Bee could see the river, about a hundred yards farther down the track, straight ahead. To her right was meadow grass, bending back with a breeze coming off the water. She was thinking of a getaway, pushing this horrible woman out the door and then swinging around in a circle through the grass and back onto the road. A getaway that would be severely hampered if she turned into the meadow and found herself up to her axle in mud.

"Well?"

"Pardon?"

Kali glowered at her. "Aren't you going to help me out?" She made a face meant to indicate she was in pain, in case Bee had forgotten what this whole business was about.

"Oh yeah. Right." She opened her door and stepped out. It seemed cooler down here. Cooler and very isolated. The seven dwarves had obviously gone off to the mine earlier that day and Snow White had presumably already eaten the poison apple because there was no one singing while she did her housework. There was no one at all. Birds. Birds and wind. And behind it, the faint rushing of the river. That was all.

She looked down the road and there was a boarded-up place and, next to it, presumably the house of the woman who had gone to Mexico. The one with the demented mother. Oh! A demented mother was good! That meant there was someone living with Kali now. Mrs. Billy. She might have Alzheimer's, but Kali could hardly murder Bee in the old woman's presence, could she?

Bee rounded the car and squeezed through the opening between it and the fence. She opened the car door. Kali didn't move.

What, thought Bee, does she expect me to carry her?

Kali just stared straight ahead; the pulse in her lean and stringy neck was bounding. What is she up to? Bee wondered. And the answer came to her as soon as she asked the question.

She's stalling. Playing for time. Which means . . .

"I don't have all day," said Bee, and her voice sounded harsh, just plain nasty.

Kali's head swung around to glare at her. "You should have thought of that when you ran me over."

Whatever acting Bee had intended to do, she abandoned it now. "I didn't run you over. This whole thing is bullshit." Kali winced as if she had thought her act was convincing. "Just get out," said Bee. Then she turned and looked up the road, back toward the fork. He would be coming. She was sure of it now. Kali had called Rory. Who else would she call? Somehow in the mayhem up at the school she had called him. "Now!" she shouted and watched Kali jump in her seat.

And then Kali was out of the car, all right, in one swift motion, and there was nothing wrong with her limbs, skinny as they might be. She lunged at Bee and pushed her hard, both her hands to Bee's chest, ramming her toward the cottage. The pebble-stone pathway was slippery with moss and Bee lost her footing. She regained it, but Kali was hitting her now, pounding on her back and arms as Bee turned away, trying to defend herself.

She's a lunatic, thought Bee. And desperate.

Kali was swearing now, thrashing her way through obscenities even as she thrashed at Bee, who cowered, covering her head, crouching in the sopping weeds that lined the path. There were rocks in the grass; one the size of a fist glistened with dew and Bee grabbed it up. It was as if the stone had been plugged into a power source because she no sooner plucked it from the ground than it seemed to take off, carrying her fist upward into Kali's belly. The woman doubled up and fell backward. Bee threw the rock down and scampered over Kali's thrashing legs.

"Don't go!" the woman shouted frantically.

But Bee slammed the passenger door shut and skittered around the car to her side.

"You just wait. You hear me? Fucking wait!"

Bee opened the driver's door, and as she glanced at Kali, she saw her trying to get up—but this time she really was injured. It stopped Bee for a moment. What was she doing? Who was she, this girl gone crazy? It didn't matter; every fiber in Bee's body screamed to hightail it out of there. She started the car and drove away, straight down the road toward the river. There had to be a turning point, and yes—there it was, on the left, a drive leading up into the trees. She pulled in, threw the car into reverse, and pulled back onto the road. Then she threw the car into drive and roared ahead, the car's back end slewing side to side in the drying dirt, the tires spinning and then catching and flinging the car forward.

Kali was waiting. She had made her way out into the

middle of the road, one hand clutching her stomach, the other held out in front of her. Bee sped up. The distance between them shrunk, fifty yards, twenty-five yards. The woman wouldn't move. Bee swore at the top of her lungs, one ragged, filthy word dug up from the very bottom of her own despair and fury, a sound coming from her that loosened the teeth in her mouth and resounded in her skull as if there were nothing in it but bone and emptiness.

Then she slammed on the brakes.

She stopped right at Kali's feet.

The woman stared at her, her body heaving, her mouth gaping open, her eyes mad with fear. She leaned forward, one hand on the car's chrome insignia. The other arm hung limp at her side, injured in her fall, perhaps. The car growled. Well, not quite—more like muttered excitedly, as if to say, I'm not the kind of vehicle you do this in but it is rather bracing! Slowly, hesitatingly, Kali began to move around the car toward the driver's side. She was limping, but this time it was evidently for real. Her hands never let go of the car's hood, as though she had to maintain contact with it to stand upright as well as to hold it there. The madness had gone from her eyes. There was pleading there now. If we could just talk, her eyes seemed to say. Bee waited, her hands grasping the wheel, her mouth open trying to take in enough air to soothe her racing heart. Her eyes never left Kali's eyes. She was inching her way down the side of the car, as if there were a path there, not more than a foot wide, and a chasm to the other side. And, oh, her eyes were talking. I can explain, said her eyes. It wasn't me, said her eyes. I'm a victim, too, said her eyes.

And all the while Rory is on his way!

Bee waited and watched, her own eyes tracking the woman as she came up to the driver's door. Again, as before on the shoulder outside the school driveway, she bent down until her face was framed in the window. Up close her face was ravaged, tearstained, pathetic in its need. She took the handle in her right hand and placed her left hand on her knee.

It was now or never. Bee tromped on the accelerator and the Figaro leaped in response, dirt flying from its back wheels. She almost heard the snap of Kali losing her grasp on the door handle, but she didn't look back. Heard a shout of pain—a broken wrist? Don't think. She concentrated on the road. Only when she made the fork did she slow down and look back. Kali was sitting on the ground, her head in her hands. And even from so far away Bee could see her shoulders heaving.

Bee sped up the hill and past the school driveway, picking up speed on the straightaway, hoping that all the little elves were safely in school. She wanted out of this place. She wanted Inspector Callista Stills and Staff Sergeant Jim Bell and all the cops in Perth and Ottawa and . . .

She glanced at the passenger seat. Her phone. She slowed down, stopped. Put the car in park. She lurched across the passenger seat and grabbed her bag from the floor. She searched through it. Not there. It had been on the seat. It was gone. She swore and threw the bag on the seat. Then she reached across the passenger seat and explored the space between it and the door.

"Please, please, please!" she prayed to the god of lost things. But it was not there. *She* had it. Kali O'Connor.

CHAPTER / FORTY-ONE

Bee leaned backward in the driver's seat, suddenly overcome with fatigue. What now? Kali had asked her who she'd called. She had lied. She'd told her Jilly. But she'd inputted Stills's number. So when Kali looked, the last number Bee had called would be Inspector Stills. *And Kali had met Inspector Stills.*

Stills had interviewed her. The woman was going to freak out. Was that bad? Not really. In fact, it was great! Kali had been frightened back there. Now she would be truly, deeply frightened. If she had anything to do with the murder, it would serve her right. Maybe she'd make a run for it. That wasn't Bee's problem. She just wanted Donovan's name cleared. No, who was she kidding! She wanted justice. She wanted his killer to be brought down!

Bee sat there, her mind racing. Stills would phone. Bee tried to imagine Kali standing there holding the phone, it jangling in her hand with its ringtone of Groucho Marx singing "Lydia the Tattooed Lady." And there would be that number on the screen, that name. What would she do?

Her thoughts were interrupted. Up ahead a car was coming her way. The first one she'd seen since she'd turned onto Sugar Valley Road. Not a car. A truck. And as it neared, she saw that it was a red truck moving fast, sending up a dust storm behind it. A truck with an urgent destination.

For one moment, Bee froze. Then she threw her car into gear and stepped on the pedal. The car complained and she remembered the hand brake. She released it and the car shot forward, clinging to the right verge of the road. The truck loomed large. It sat high on its springs. *A lift job. A red lift job.* The front fender way off the ground, the license plate speckled with mud, but readable. She read it. Sounded out the letters and numbers. *Remember that.*

She couldn't see inside the pickup, the windows were tinted. Gleaming black in the noonday sun. She prayed that Kali hadn't given Rory a description of her car.

Then she had to stop praying or trying to pierce the blackness of those windows with her eyes and concentrate on the road, because the vehicle would be upon her any second. She pulled over as far as she could, over to the edge of where the narrow road fell away to rock and bramble. She daren't move any farther over. Daren't go any faster. Then—*whoosh!*—the truck passed her, pebbles pinging off her car's sides and windshield.

"Thank you, God," she shouted, "I owe you big time!"

She pulled out into the middle of the road, raced though the next turn and the one after that, until at last she saw the highway straight ahead.

"Yes! Yes! Yes!" she cried. And didn't slow down until she was perilously close to the intersection, where she slammed on the brakes.

She sat, held up by a long line of speeding traffic passing by on the highway. Biding her time, catching her runaway breath, her finger hammering on the steering wheel, her eyes flitting to the rearview mirror, seeing only dust.

He doesn't know my car. Kali recognized it, but she wouldn't have had time to tell Rory about it when she'd called him. The only thing she'd have had time to tell him was that she—Bee—was there in Sugar Valley and something needed to be done with her. He can't turn around, thought Bee. There's no way. Not until he gets to the school, at least. But he won't stop there; he'll race on to Kali's.

Rory owned a big red pickup. It all fit horrifyingly together. She glanced again in the rearview mirror, still waiting to turn onto the highway. She imagined a towering dust storm pulling up behind her as she waited to zip into the traffic. Her eyes focused on the dust storm in her head until the dust settled and she could see the vehicle again in her mind's eye and read the license number she had memorized.

RUCO 467.

"Oh!" she gasped, throwing her hand over her mouth. She felt like she was going to be sick.

Are you, he had said.

And she had asked him, Am I what?

See, he had said.

And she had looked around the intensive care unit as if there were something she was supposed to get for him.

Oh!

She closed her eyes and moaned. Her neck felt too weak to hold up her head. It fell forward on her hands gripping the steering wheel fiercely. Her hair, loosened almost entirely from its ponytail in her fight with Kali, now fell around her face like a curtain. And she was back in the hospital, back in the space capsule with Donovan, her notebook on her lap, her hand waiting to write, grasping at every syllable. She could hear his voice in her head, insistent, pleading.

CHAPTER / FORTY-TWO

The car dealership looked like the Holy Land must have looked to Joshua. Milk and honey and Chryslers. She made her way through the parking lot of shiny new cars and pulled up at the front doors. She climbed out and there was already someone waiting, a man with a crew cut, a striped tie, and a grin on his face. "I sure hope you're looking for a trade-in," he said. She looked back at Toddy the Turtle, who had never looked so down at the mouth, her mossy sides covered with dust and grime.

"I need to use your phone," she said.

The salesman set her up at his desk and showed her how to dial out, then wandered away to gaze out at the lot—or longingly at the Figaro, she figured. Bee punched in the number and it was picked up after only one ring.

"It's me, Beatrice Northway."

"Where the hell are you?"

"Perth." She looked on the desktop and saw a neat little stack of business cards for sales coordinator Maury Beamer. She read off the dealership's name.

"So you're buying a new car?"

"No."

"I've been trying to reach you for fifteen minutes."

"And no one picked up?"

There was a pause. "You and your cell phone have become separated?" said Stills, with a slightly ominous tone.

"Yeah. Kali has it. Kali O'Connor."

"What the—"

"Let me explain!" cried Bee, loud enough to draw the attention of the salesman. She waved at him. He held up his hands as if she had a gun and it were a stickup. Then he walked away. Bee turned her attention to the disgruntled voice at the other end of the line, explaining what had happened.

"Didn't I warn you not to do this?"

"Do what?"

"Play Nancy fricking Drew!"

"It wasn't like that, and it doesn't matter anyway. Here's a license number—have you got a pencil?" Stills grunted. "Ontario plates: RUCO 467."

"And this is?"

"Rory Tulk. Kali's new boyfriend since she left Al."

There was a pause. "Go on."

"It's a red pickup. A red GMC Sierra." She paused for effect. "With a lift job."

Then Bee decided now might be a good time to take

a breath since she wasn't sure she had done so since Stills picked up.

"So what are your plans now, Ms. Northway? Thinking of making a citizen's arrest?" The voice was testy, but maybe there was some grudging respect.

"I was thinking of eating," said Bee.

"Better idea, stay put. Are you safe there, do you think?"

Bee looked around. There were five people in the showroom, three of them salespeople as far as she could tell: Beamer, one other guy, and a woman. There was an elderly couple looking at one of the four cars on display. None of them looked like Justice League of America candidates. "I guess," she said, the doubt evident in her voice.

But Stills wasn't listening for shades of feeling. "Good. Stay safe," she said. "You hear me? We're on this."

"Okay."

"Give me your number there?"

Bee read the number off Maury Beamer's business card. But even as she did, she knew she couldn't stay here.

"I've got to eat," she said. "I'm starving."

Stills made an exasperated sound. "What's the address?" Bee told her. "Listen. I've pulled the place up on Google Earth. There's an OPP station about five clicks west of you on the right. The Ontario Provincial Police."

"I know what the OPP is."

"Hooray for you. Go there. I'll phone ahead."

"Okay," Bee said, and hated how meek she sounded.

"I'm serious, Bee."

"I know you are."

"Stay out of trouble. You got that?"

The elation of having reached the detective and passed on her report seeped away like air out of a punctured tire. Bee felt weak and powerless. It was physiological, she knew that: adrenaline payback time. "Got it," she said. Then Stills signed off and the phone went to a dial tone. She hung up.

"Cavalry on the way?" said Maury Beamer cheerfully.

"I guess."

She would get lunch on the way. She had seen fast-food places when she'd entered town that morning. The cop shop must be in there among them somewhere. Then she thought of Perth's pretty little downtown. There would probably be a bakery or something there where she could get a bowl of soup and a sandwich on freshly baked bread. Down-home cooking. Which is why it came as a surprise to her that her hands, with a will of their own, turned the car left onto Seven. Eastward and home. She wanted to make herself a grilled cheese sandwich in her mother's sunny kitchen and then curl up in bed for a year. With all the doors locked.

She felt bereft, as if Stills had deprived her of victory. Instead, the inspector had chastised her, cautioned her. She felt no sense of accomplishment, only a gnawing sense of emptiness. She had been in the middle of something half an hour ago and now had been cast aside. She turned on the radio, CBC-2, and some achingly beautiful classical piece poured into the car. She switched to CBC-1. It was the noon phone-in. They were talking about mold. She switched back to CBC-2. If you were going to be depressed, you might as well soak in it. And this piece was as good a backdrop to sorrow as she could imagine. She sobbed. She swore at Inspector

Stills as if she were in elementary school again and the nasty teacher had taken away her guinea-pig feeding privileges.

She didn't want justice. Not really. What she wanted was Donovan. She wanted him back, right now, beside her, banging out the beat to a song on the radio—though not this one. She felt utterly alone.

The music was by Arvo Pärt. It was a requiem for someone or other. There was a bell in it that just kept chiming throughout the whole piece, and that bell carved a little chapel in her brain where she could huddle in her solitude, wondering how if she was this lost she would ever be found again.

Then she looked in her rearview mirror and the narrow, cold little world into which she was in the process of crawling exploded. There was a red pickup on her tail.

Stay put, Stills had told her. Stay safe. Stay out of trouble. Why had the detective's message not registered? Well, it had, actually. There was no better place to stay safe and out of trouble than home.

Even if home means passing through Mordor?

Oh, she had thought of that. She knew she would have to pass the exit to Sugar Valley Road, but it had been half an hour or more since Tulk had raced past her on his way to Kali. If he'd wanted to give chase, he would have turned right around and been back on the highway in less than ten minutes. That's what he would have done, she had thought. He'd seen the vehicle she was in. Not exactly a race car and completely recognizable.

Why don't I have a blue Toyota?

So he'd have raced up to Seven and turned east at warp speed and kept going knowing he could overtake her before she got anywhere near Ottawa. By the time he gave up and doubled back, she'd be closer to civilization—or at least halfway, Carleton Place—where she could pull into a big box store parking lot and disappear. Okay, she hadn't really thought it through, but this . . . Where had he come from?

She heard the engine behind her roar and when she checked her rearview mirror, he was gaining on her, shortening the distance between them so much that she couldn't even see the cab of the pickup.

He's going to ram me. He's just waiting for a break in the traffic so no one will witness it.

He honked his horn. He honked it again and again and again and then pressed his hand down on it and held it there until Bee cried out.

"Stop it!" she shouted. Then she hurled a garbage-bag-load of curses at the air. If only curses were nails.

She shoulder checked and he started to swerve left and right, left and right, honking the horn again, throwing on his emergency flashers, inching closer and closer. He was clearly insane.

She clutched the wheel tightly, holding on to her sanity as much as the road. *He's not going to waste his time ramming you. He's going to make you fly off the road all by yourself. Shatter you. Break your own damn neck.*

She glanced to her right: flooded woodland as far as she could see. No houses, no places of business, just swamp. There was a decent shoulder, but pulling over would only make his job all the easier, putting her right up against the drop-off into the mire. They rounded a long, slow curve, and as they came to the straightaway she saw traffic approaching in the westbound lane. He'd have to stop acting crazy. It wasn't going to serve his purpose for her to die with witnesses to say she was pushed. Sure enough, he turned off the flashing lights and stopped his weaving. He even dropped back a car length or two.

One, two, three vehicles flashed past and then the road was clear again as far as the eye could see. She heard his engine roar and he pulled out to pass. For a tiny moment she dared to believe that that's what he was doing. She was driving so slowly, the poor guy just wanted to get by.

If only!

He stayed even with her in the wrong lane and then began to edge closer and closer to her flank. She held her own, refusing to budge. If he wants me off the road, he's going to have to hit me. Then a better idea occurred to her. She checked the rearview mirror: empty. Good.

One, two, three. Brake.

The Figaro's tires squealed and its little sage-green rump swayed perilously, but the Sierra flew on by and had to pull back into the eastbound lane because of oncoming traffic.

"Who's trailing who, fucker!" she cried.

He slowed down. She held her distance. There was a car coming up behind her now. Tulk couldn't just stop, could he? There would be a pileup—a turtle sandwich. But as long as she kept her wits about her, maybe she could dart onto the shoulder at the last minute. They came to a passing lane and the car behind her raced by. The passenger in the car waved, a big smile on his face. "Love it!" he mouthed. Another stretch of nothing but road. A peninsula through a sunken place of motionless, naked trees. Then Tulk pulled over onto the shoulder to let her pass, and what else could she do? She sure wasn't going to stop! She flew by him, Toddy's engine churning out enough power to almost get the needle up to the speed limit. Tulk fell in behind her again and in a moment was back on her tail, honking and flashing his lights and threatening at any moment to put her over the edge, if not literally then at least mentally.

Up ahead—way ahead—she saw a tractor-trailer coming. A massive-looking thing: an eighteen-wheeler. She caught the silver glimmer of sunlight on its impressive grill. The idea came to her from some dark recess of her unconscious. It wasn't sane, but when a madman is sitting on your rear bumper, there aren't a whole lot of sensible solutions available.

Can you do it?

She would have to try.

Will it work?

Possibly not, in which case she would be dead anyway. And with that encouraging thought still in mind, she swerved into the westbound lane, destined for a head-on collision with thirty tons of steel.

She heard the air horn and marveled at how quickly the distance closed between her and the tractor-trailer.

Now!

She swerved onto the westbound shoulder, almost lost control but managed to keep the car from tipping over into a watery grave. The eighteen-wheeler flew by, his air horn deafening. The car, now stopped, shuddered from the truck's drag. And far ahead she saw the red Sierra round the next long, slow curve.

She gasped for breath but there was no time to rest. A couple of cars passed and then there was a break, long enough for her to scream into a U-turn and head back west. She had a plan.

CHAPTER / FORTY-THREE

She had passed Cedar Bog Road only minutes earlier, seen the bent-over sign out of the corner of her eye as she held off the maniac badgering her, pressing her, wanting to kill her. She knew that Tulk would take the first opportunity he could to turn around and come back for her, and the way he drove, he'd catch her long before she could reach the car dealership, let alone the OPP station in Perth.

Why had she ignored Stills?

What was wrong with her?

Did she have a death wish?

Well, there wasn't time to think about it now. She needed to get to a phone. She needed to get off the damn highway—the sooner the better. So she swung onto the dirt road and raced down it toward the Needham farm, hoping that the dense tangle of brush along the cedar fence was high enough to hide her escape, should Tulk already be heading back this way. She pulled into the yard and made sure to drive close to the house so that the shed shielded the car from the road.

The dog came bounding out of somewhere. But the yard was otherwise empty. The little green Honda was gone. She turned off the Figaro, got out, pocketed the keys, and closed the car door.

"Hello," she called.

Spinach barked and came to give her a lick. Bee ruffled his ears.

"There's nobody here, is there?" she asked him.

He barked again, clever dog.

"Are you going to growl and bite me if I try to go in the house?"

Spinach laughed his doggy laugh, his tongue lolling out. Probably the worst watchdog ever. She headed toward the back door, the one that led into the kitchen. She was hoping that it would be unlocked. Her own home back in Ottawa was not only locked but equipped with burglar alarms and video surveillance. Somehow she didn't think that Cedar Bog Road was a high-risk area for burglary or that Jilly Green was the kind of person who locked doors.

And she was right.

She held the screen door open with one hand, turned the handle of the inner door, and pushed it open. She stood on the threshold, leaning in.

"Hello?" She waited. The dog whined behind her, trying to nose his way in, but she stopped him with her knee. "Uh-uh, Spin," she said. Then she called out again. "Is anybody home?"

Nothing but the ticking silence and the smell of tomato soup. There was a pot of it on the stove. The aroma drew her in. She closed the door behind her. Spinach was not amused and let her know it.

The stove was off but there were dishes in the drying rack by the sink: bowls and round spoons. There was a loaf of bread on a wooden board on the counter, and a knife beside it. Feeling like Goldilocks, she cut herself a piece. Then she crossed to the stove and dipped it in the warm soup. In three bites the bread was gone. Because the soup was neither too hot nor too cold but just right, she figured her next step would be to find a bed that was just right and wait until the three bears returned. But the thought of a bear was enough to forcibly remind her of the man who seemed determined to deal with her, one way or another. A man she had yet to actually lay eyes on but who was monstrous, nonetheless. She had no doubts at all that he had killed Donovan in his red machine. And working backward, she could only imagine he had killed Donovan's father as well, smashed his face in with a bat. And now he was looking for her.

There was a phone in its cradle on the counter by the back door. She picked it up but was not sure what to do. Did she dare to phone Stills? No. She was too far away to be of any help, and Bee wasn't sure she could take being scolded one more time, whether she deserved it or not.

So she dialed those three numbers her mother had taught her about as a child. Dialed and let it ring and ring and ring. She walked to the back door. Pulled it open, stood looking through the screen. Spinach was nowhere to be seen. The phone rang and rang. Bee couldn't see the road from where she stood, so she stepped out onto the porch. There was only Toddy standing in the yard. When she looked north, she could see a stretch of the road beyond the large utility shed. She trained her eyes on it. The line opened.

"You have called 911," said the dispatcher, "where is the emergency?"

"Oh, thank you, thank you. Cedar Bog Road," said Bee.

"Do you have a number on Cedar Bog Road?"

"No . . . No, I've forgotten it. But it's the first house on your right about a couple of miles or so from the highway. Highway Seven. East of Perth."

"And what is the nature of the emergency?"

"Someone is trying to kill me. I'm being chased by a lunatic."

"So you require law enforcement?"

"Yes! Please! He tried to run me down and I got away, but he's after me."

Did she imagine the pause that followed this remark? Because, hearing her own voice, she sounded like a lunatic herself.

"Where are you calling from, please?"

"I told you. Oh, you mean whose place? It's the Needhams' farm. They're not here. There's no one here. This man is a psychopath. Please hurry."

"Yes, ma'am. I have already contacted the police. Help is on the way. But please stay on the line, I have more questions."

"A red GMC Sierra," said Bee.

"Is this your vehicle, ma'am?"

"No! It's his—the lunatic's. License plate RUCO 467."

"This is the person who you say is after you?"

Who you say. She hated the sound of that. "I'm not making this up," said Bee.

"No, ma'am. I appreciate—"

"Oh shit!"

"Ma'am?"

"There's a car coming."

"Can you make out whether it is the vehicle in question?"

Bee had only caught a glimpse of it through the trees far up the road, but she could hear it now and doubted from the roar and the cloud of dust that it was going to be the little green Honda.

"It's him. I've got to go."

"Ma'am, please don't hang up."

"You don't understand. I've got to hide."

"Take the phone with you, if you can."

"Sorry. I . . ." Bee didn't finish. Her thumb pressed STOP and she slid back into the house and closed the inner door. She locked it. Shit! She should have stayed on the line. Should she redial? No. No time. She looked around the kitchen. There were three doors. She raced to the first and pulled it open—some kind of a pantry. She opened the second—stairs down to the basement. She shuddered.

Spinach was barking furiously now at the approaching car. Bee whimpered and fled to the only other door, one that led into the entrance hallway. There was the front door to her left, with curtains and an antique umbrella stand. A colorful rug made of rags lay in front of it on the dark wood floor. She checked the door; it was locked: a ceremonial entranceway. She peered out into the yard just as the red pickup wheeled in. The dog raced around it. Oh, if only he were vicious!

She watched Tulk pull up behind the Figaro and stop. She waited for him to step out, wanting to see him — wanting to see what she was running from, what she was up against. He didn't open the door and her curiosity gave way to panic. She turned. To her left was a living room, straight ahead was a steep and narrow flight of stairs to the second floor. She tore up the stairs, then stopped. The knife! The one in the kitchen she'd cut the bread with. She should get it. She turned to go back down and then stopped. Who the hell did she think she was kidding! There was no way she could do anything to a person — even a killer — with a bread knife. So she raced back up the stairs hand over hand along the polished oak railing, cursing for having wasted precious seconds dithering. She heard a car door slam. Heard a voice raised at the barking dog. Heard the dog yelp. She yelped herself.

And then there was silence.

She stood looking around. There was a hallway along the banistered stairwell. There was one door to the right of the stairs at this end and one at the front of the house. Across the hall, there were three doors. Against the wall, right at the landing, was an old pine table about as wide as a school desk but with raised sides and back, and with a single drawer. There was a large ceramic bowl sitting on it, the outside ochre, the inner surface off-white and crackled with age. A pitcher sat in the bowl. A washstand.

She heard the kitchen door rattle. Heard a hand slam against it and a voice yell, though she couldn't tell what he said. Then she heard hard footsteps on the porch. She listened. Heard the footsteps return. *Heard the unmistakable sound of the door being opened.*

She heard it close behind him. Heard footsteps tromp across the kitchen's pinewood floor. There was a runner down the upstairs hall, a faded mossy-green carpet. She slipped out of her flats, picked them up, and on tiptoes started toward the front end of the house. The attempt to conceal her passage failed. The old floorboards creaked under her weight. She stopped. At least she was out of sight were he to look up.

He was in the downstairs hallway now. Had he heard?

"Hey, bitch," he said. "Didn't know I used to live here, did you?" he said. His voice was pitched to intimidate: a big voice, rough around the edges. Silently Bee lowered her shoes to the floor and reached for the pitcher in the bowl on the washstand.

"Jilly still keeps the key in the same place. Imagine that. All these years later."

Bee picked up the pitcher in two hands. Not heavy enough.

"You in the living room, bitch?" *So he hadn't heard.*

She heard him clump across the hall, a man in serious boots. Gently she placed the pitcher on the floor beside her shoes.

"Hello? You in here, Miss Busybody?" More clumping, in the living room this time. "Now whyn't you just come on out. Make it easier on everybody."

She picked up the ceramic washbowl in both hands. It had the circumference of a basketball hoop, must have weighed the same as a sack of potatoes. She held it firmly and turned to face the stairs, two yards away.

"Not here," said Tulk. "Which means you're upstairs."

More clumping and then he stopped. "You up there, girl?"

He took a step up, the stairs complained. Another step. She grasped the ceramic bowl more tightly. He stopped. Couldn't see her yet, nor she him.

"You come out and we can have a talk," he said. "If I have to hunt you down, I'm just going to get madder and madder and, ooo-ee, that won't be pretty."

He took two more steps and she knew she could wait no longer. She crossed the floor to the top of the stairs.

"Well, what do you know?" he said looking up at her. "Finally we meet."

He wasn't a big man, she figured, even accounting for the foreshortening of looking down on him from this angle. He was broad across the shoulders, though, with large hands, one of which had grabbed the railing when he saw her holding the washbowl.

"Planning on throwing the crockery around?" he said. "Hell, I was afraid you'd find Matt's rifle, maybe even his shotgun. Must be up there somewhere. Not that I'd know, but it stands to reason."

Without taking his eyes off her, he ventured up one more step. She stood perfectly still, her right foot toeing the edge of the landing.

"Picked yourself a woman's weapon, huh?"

She raised the bowl above her head and watched him take a step backward. The stairway was narrow; there was no way she could miss.

"Like I said, we should talk. Pretty girl like you don't

really want to be messing with me. You never know what I might do."

Tell him you've called 911. Tell him they're on the way and he'd better run for his life.

She tried to talk. She opened her mouth but there were no words there for this man. Nothing she could say. His face was unshaven, his hair a rat's nest. His eyes looked haunted. She wanted to think he had been losing sleep over what he'd done. Maybe he was even drunk. Wanted to think that he was suffering in some way, in excruciating pain. But she wasn't prepared to talk to him.

Then he made his move. Reaching along the railing for a higher purchase, he launched himself up two steps at a time and then another two steps until he was halfway up. She hurled the bowl at him, howling with rage as she did it.

She couldn't miss and she didn't!

He turned his shoulder, but the weight of the bowl and the force of her throw made him lose his footing and he stumbled back, fell to a knee, cursing and yowling with pain. She didn't waste a moment watching to see if it was enough. Nothing was enough. She darted back to the washstand. She couldn't lift it but she dragged it to the top of the stairs just as he started back up. She got behind the cabinet and heaved it with all her might.

It rocketed down the stairs, gaining momentum, and one sharp edge caught him right in the gut, sending him hurtling down, trying to hold the thing like it was an animal to wrestle with. He landed on his back and the washstand rolled over him and crashed on the floor in the hallway below.

Tulk lay half on the stairs and half on the floor. He was

twisted so that his torso was front-side down. She watched, saw his hand twitch. Heard him groan. He was hurt but not hurt enough, and she had to move *now* because there was nothing left to throw at him.

Forgetting her shoes but not the pitcher, she skittered down the stairs, grabbing hold of the railing like it was a lifeline. She slowed her flight, suddenly horrified at the idea that she might trip and end up falling on top of him. She reached the bottom and stepped gingerly between his legs, having at last to let go of the banister. There was just his torso to climb over and those arms flung out to the side.

Carefully, she stepped as far as she could and as soon as her left foot was planted, her right followed — taking a giant step. She lifted her left leg to follow and his hand suddenly darted out to grab her ankle. She screamed and he pulled, not just to pull her over but to pull himself upright. His face was bloodied. He must have caught a corner of the table or the newel post on the way down. He snarled at her as she tried to pull away and she saw a tooth was missing, his gums slathered with fresh blood. She threw her back against the stairwell wall for support, switched the pitcher to her right hand, and kicked out at him with her captured foot. But now his other hand came up and grabbed her calf and he pulled himself toward her. He looked up at her, grinning like a death's-head.

"I got me one helluva view up your skirt," he said triumphantly through his bruised and bleeding face and bloodied tongue. And she brought the ceramic pitcher down on his head with every ounce of energy she possessed.

As soon as she felt his grip lessen, she pulled herself away with a mighty shout and tore through the kitchen, through the outside door, where Spinach met her, barking his head off. He danced around her as she made her way across the yard, the gravel digging into her naked feet. She got to the Figaro and fished for the keys in her skirt pocket. They weren't there. Not in either pocket. She glanced back toward the house in time to see the screen door fly open and Rory Tulk stumble out like a drunkard. She turned and saw his pickup. It was her only option. She couldn't run, not far enough, not in bare feet across the farmyard. So she groped her way around the hood, aware suddenly that she was whining—keening—like a mad person. She reached the driver's side door and prayed that it was open. It was. She hauled herself up on the runner bar and heaved the door open.

"Nooooo!" he shouted. "Get the fuck away from my truck!"

She clambered in and slammed the door behind her. She searched and found the door lock and cried with relief to hear the solid click. Then her eyes saw what she could not have dreamed of seeing. The keys. He'd left the keys in the ignition—probably for a fast getaway. She glanced toward him. Tulk was shambling across the yard. Spinach was barking like crazy and growling and darting at Tulk from every side to nip at him. He swung his arm at the dog, who was too smart to get caught again. The dog dashed behind him and in trying to hit Spinach, Tulk fell over, twisting like a top and landing hard on his side.

Bee turned the ignition and the vehicle rumbled under her. She revved the engine. High. Exhilarated and terrified by the sound of it. All that power that had scared her to death when it was chasing her.

The last sound Donovan had ever heard outside of that space capsule at the General. The last sound he had heard in the real world.

She reached down to the gearshift and put the truck in drive, felt it tug at her arms as it bounded forward. Then she swept out into the yard and pulled the vehicle in a tight circle, spinning out, and raced toward Tulk lying helplessly on the ground. The dog sprang away. Tulk's face looked like something from a horror movie, his chin thick with blood, his face contorted, his eyes wide with terror.

She slammed on the brakes three feet from his body. By then he'd thrown his arm over his eyes. Now he moved it and looked up at his own truck hovering above him. He tried to stand and she revved the motor, her foot hard on the accelerator and the brake. The truck shuddered under her, wanting to move, wanting to crash forward and crush him. The motor was screaming, and it took every fiber of moral courage she possessed to keep her foot on the brake.

Then she saw him turn his head northward. He was up on his knees and two hands like a four-footed animal staring toward the road, and although the shed was in her way, she was pretty sure what he was hearing. She let her foot off the accelerator and then she heard it, too. Sirens.

Without turning off the vehicle, she opened the driver's door very slowly, never taking her eyes off Tulk. The sirens were louder now, nearer. Tulk turned to stare at her and then rolled onto his back, beaten, and covered his face with both his hands. She stepped out of the truck and jumped down to the ground. She walked in a wide circle around him as the

344

police cruisers arrived, two of them. He was crying—bawling like a baby. She watched him, his body heaving. And something broke in her. The very last shred holding back her own welter of pain and loss, and she started crying, too. She leaned her hands on her knees and cried for all that was wrong with the foolishly optimistic idea of being alive.

CHAPTER FORTY-FOUR

Beatrice D'Amato Northway sat in the back of one of the police cruisers. New experience after new experience. Rory Tulk sat in the back of the other, the only difference being that he was handcuffed. She doubted that this was a new experience for him. An ambulance had been called. Inspector Callista Stills had been called. She was en route. No one was going anywhere until she got there.

The cops had allowed Bee to use the washroom in the farmhouse. One of them, a woman, accompanied her and waited. "Tanis Cowan," she said, sticking out a hand to shake. Bee took it, amazed at how little strength she had left. The greeting didn't impress Rory Tulk, who banged on his car-door window until one of the cops gave him the stink eye. "If you've got something that'll stick to Rory, this'll all be worthwhile," said Constable Cowan.

Bee was picking her way carefully in her bare feet. "Does everybody know everybody out here?" she asked.

Cowan grinned. "Couldn't say but we tend to know the baddies."

There was a small washroom in the front hall. Bee splashed her face and brushed her hair and found a headband in the bottom of her THEATER IS MY BAG bag and came out of the little room feeling almost human, the wreckage at the base of the stairs notwithstanding.

"My keys!" she said.

Cowan grabbed her as she made to pick up her car keys from the debris. "We'll have to get the inspector's okay on that," she said.

"Okay," said Bee, a bit weirded out. "Can I at least get my shoes? They're up on the landing." She was about to pick her way through the pine and ceramic carnage, but Cowan wouldn't let her go. "Sorry again, miss. Can't have you contaminating the crime scene," she said. Then she pulled a pen out of the breast pocket of her flak jacket and strung it through the handle of the pitcher with which Bee had clocked Rory Tulk. She picked it up, still intact, not even a chip out of it. "Are your prints likely to be on this thing?" she asked. Bee made a face, nodded. "Good, then hold it for me, will you?" Bee took the pitcher and waited in the hallway as the policewoman made her way up the narrow staircase. She came down a moment later with Bee's flats and handed them to her.

"What do I do with the pitcher?" said Bee.

"Ah, just put it down. I figured giving you a chore was easier than putting you in cuffs."

"Really?"

"It worked, didn't it?" She looked around. "Heard a lot about this place. Looks like Jilly's been doing a number on it," said Cowan. "Used to be a regular stop-off on OPP rounds."

"Really?" Bee looked around at the staid wallpaper, the framed prints of flowers on the wall, the cotton print curtains, the polished front door. There was a drop cloth at the back end of the hall, and paint things. It was a work in progress.

"Jilly's brother, Mervin. Mixed with some pretty bad types."

Bee said, "So did Jilly."

And Constable Cowan said, "You got that right."

They walked through the kitchen and started back toward the cruiser.

"Jilly Green made some mistakes, but she's always been one of the good ones," said Cowan.

"Did Mervin reform?"

The constable shook her head. "Died in a fire few years back. Gang-related stuff."

Bee looked around. "Here?"

Cowan scratched her head. "Not sure. You could ask Harry Cameron over there. He'd know. Some kind of raid."

But Cameron was on the radio again and Bee said it didn't matter, so Cowan led her back to the cruiser. "Now that you've got your shoes, we can't take any chances on you doing a runner," said Cowan with a smirk. The flats were not the kind of thing you wore in any kind of footrace, but Bee wasn't about to argue. Cowan apologized as she deposited her back in the police cruiser with doors you couldn't open from the inside. A prison on wheels.

"It's okay," said Bee. Truth was, she felt safe in the vehicle.

Half an hour into the wait, Jilly arrived home with the baby. They wouldn't let Bee out of the car to speak to her. Bee watched the woman, Cassie on her hip, fish her cell phone out of her handbag and phone someone. Rory started pounding on the back window of his cop car when he saw Jilly. She walked over to stare at him, her face filled with sadness, which only made him pound all the harder until Constable Cowan led Jilly away. Bee watched her say something to Cowan, who shook her head. Jilly turned to Bee and shrugged. Bee sat mutely, her hands in her lap, feeling guilty as hell for having brought such danger here. But Jilly's eyes did not seem to judge her; they were filled with concern. Wait until she sees the wrecked antiques, thought Bee. Jilly waved with her fingertips as she left, and Cassie waved, too. Bee managed to wave back, although the energy it took to lift her arm surprised her. She watched them head toward the house and was rewarded with Jilly turning once again to blow her a kiss. Bee had so much to say to her, so much explaining and apologizing to do. And thanking. Meanwhile, Spinach leaped about his master and tried to tell her the brave part he had played in the adventure.

It was three o'clock before a big brown unmarked car pulled into the yard, driven by Sergeant Bell with Inspector Stills riding shotgun. The ambulance had arrived and, under strict police guard, the attendants were dealing with the worst of Tulk's injuries, which apparently included a broken arm that needed stabilizing. They bandaged up his face. There would be stitches needed.

Bee wondered if Stills was making her wait. She had only glanced at Bee, her face expressionless, before speaking to the officers. At great length. Then she and Bell and Cowan and Cameron, who seemed to be the one in charge of the scene, headed toward the house. Bell glanced back and smiled at Bee, hunched his shoulders, his way of letting her know he was on her side, but what you gonna do, eh? At least that was what she hoped it meant. It might also have meant, Who knows how long it will be until we let you out? Maybe your time in the back of the cruiser could be time struck off your prison sentence for being an idiot.

Finally, Stills came out of the house and headed toward Bee's cruiser. One of the officers opened the door and the inspector stuck her head in. "If we let you out, are you going to take off?"

Bee shook her head before realizing this was Stills's idea of a joke. She climbed out and they walked across the yard away from the melee of vehicles parked every which way. A loud rumbling out in the field indicated a tractor heading home. That's who Jilly must have phoned, Bee thought. She had never considered farmers with cell phones. Actually, she had never really thought about farmers at all—not since Old MacDonald in kindergarten. E-I-E-I-O.

She was expecting a major dressing-down from Stills. She was expecting that somehow Stills would lay that obstruction-of-justice threat on her now, except it wouldn't be a threat anymore, it would be a criminal charge. She wouldn't argue. There had to be some price to pay for what she'd done today. She'd been lucky enough to avoid getting killed. Anything short of that seemed fair. She imagined finishing her last few months of high school in a cell. Well, at least she could study without distraction.

But Stills didn't waste time rebuking Bee. "We've got ourselves a serious problem," she said. "There is all kinds of forensic evidence linking Kali O'Connor to Al McGeary's apartment, but she lived there for a couple of years so that's of no use to us in making a case. It remains to be seen, however, whether we've got even one tiny thread of evidence linking Tulk to the place. The apartment building has two CCTV cameras, one in the lobby, one in the back entrance. Neither of them is operational. Rolly Pouillard is not exactly the world's best superintendent. So there's no proof of Tulk entering the building at all." She looked at Bee, her eyebrows raised. "You see where I'm going with this?" Bee nodded. "On top of that, the next-door neighbor who saw Donovan leave his dad's apartment, not once but twice, did not see or hear anyone else enter or leave the apartment other than Rolly Pouillard."

"The neighbor was doing his laundry, wasn't he?"

"He was. But that doesn't help us, right? A good lawyer could poke holes in any charge we might try to bring against O'Connor and Tulk."

"What about the paint chip?"

Stills turned to Bell, who shook his head. "There wasn't enough of it for the CSI wonks to determine the make."

"But the color—"

"The chip had to be used up—emulsified—in order to do the chemical analysis, but we have accurate color photos of it that oughta give us something like a match."

Bee nodded. "Could you look at the truck's bumper? See where the paint chip came from?" Bell's look of incredulity was almost comical. His gaze wandered over to the vehicle in question and, following his gaze, Bee saw what a wreck the bumper was, mud stained and cracked in so many places. "Oh," she said. Then she looked at Stills, examining her eyes, looking for a bright side to any of this.

Stills seemed to read her mind. "We've sent officers to pick up Kali for questioning. Our one big hope is that, faced with all of what's gone down today, she'll crack. A confession would make things a lot easier."

Bee nodded. She thought of the woman she'd fought with earlier. How she had wrestled like a crazed dragon lady one moment and entreated Bee so pathetically the next. And there was that final vision of her when Bee stopped the car at the crossroad and looked back down the lane to Francesca's End to see Kali sitting on the ground, beaten and hapless. A horrible thought occurred to her.

"I hope she's still alive when they get there," she said.

Stills looked at her sharply. "What do you mean?"

Bee shook her head. "I don't know what a person looks like before they try to off themselves, but when I last saw her . . ."

Stills looked at Bell, who immediately got on his cell phone. He walked away from them, left them in an uneasy silence.

"Hey," said Stills. Her hand gently touched Bee's arm. Bee looked at her. "You still think this is the line of work you want to get into?"

Bee saw a glint in the detective's eye. It was as much of a smile as she was going to get.

CHAPTER / FORTY-FIVE

Kali was alive when they found her. She was packing. She threw open the cottage door when she heard the cruiser arrive, expecting to see Tulk in his big red Sierra. That's what Bee heard from the cops later. Apparently, Kali stared and stared at the police, hardly able to take in what the arresting officer was saying to her. She just dropped her suitcase and stood there on the threshold of the cottage.

"What about Mrs. Billy?" Bee had asked.

"Her alibi, you mean?" Stills had said. "Apparently, Kali shuffled her off to respite care at a local nursing home as soon as her usefulness was over."

That was the report Bee got from Stills, who had become a little friendlier of late. If her manner had hovered around freezing before, she was a few degrees warmer than that. But you'd still want to wear a muffler and gloves in her presence.

On Monday, April the twenty-fifth, ten days after the tragic events at Allen Ian McGeary's apartment and on Wilton Crescent, Kali broke. There had been long sessions with Stills. Stills sensed that Kali wanted to talk and only needed enough encouragement. Kali kept saying it wasn't her fault, and Stills kept saying tell us your story, until finally she was ready to let it all out.

Monday was also the first day Bee ventured back to school since that terrible rainy weekend. She thought she was ready for the kind of reception she was going to receive. There had been news over the weekend that the police had made arrests in the murder of both Donovan and his father. Names were named, so Bee thought she wasn't going to have to suffer the stares and whisperings behind hands of those who assumed she had been dating a murderer/suicide victim. That's what she thought anyway. She did get some of that; folks who didn't keep up with the news or chose to ignore it because their own version of what happened was more interesting. She got the girl who burst into tears the moment she saw her, her sympathy like a tidal wave of emotion that threatened to submerge Bee. She got the classmates whose eyes she felt watching her, waiting for her to break down. She even saw one girl in English who had her cell phone in her palm the whole length of the class, ready to catch every tear when Bee did finally break. There was even one ghoul who came up to her at her locker and asked her if she'd seen Donovan's body after the accident.

There were those people, yes, and then there were the ones who nodded at her as they passed and said with their eyes that they were thinking of her but expected nothing from her. And there were friends who ran interference for her, a girl she hardly knew from her geography class who had copied out everything she'd missed and only wanted to give it to her, no strings, no gossip. It was a long day, but she managed to get through it, exhausted but relatively unscathed.

And there were Daisy and Max and Jen, the best friends a girl ever had. And there were her parents. It would be all right. And it would never be right.

So it was a surprise to answer the doorbell not half an hour after getting home that first Monday back at school and find Inspector Stills standing there.

"She talked." That was all Stills had to say for Bee to open the door wide and invite her in. They sat in the kitchen, where Bee had just made herself some cinnamon toast. Stills passed on the cinnamon toast but accepted the offer of a coffee. "Do you want anyone to be here?" she asked. "Your mom or dad?" Bee sat across from her and shook her head, wondering if Stills was about to read her her rights.

"What happened?"

Stills began.

Kali had phoned Al to let him know she was coming sometime early in the evening of April fifteenth to pick up the last of her things. She'd hinted it would be best if he were out; she promised to leave her key. It was worth a try, but she wasn't surprised to find him there. She was, however, surprised to see him sitting in the middle of what looked like a minor explosion. He was well into a bottle of Jim Beam, but not so much that he couldn't recount with some amusement the scene that had produced the broken glass and pottery and popcorn that surrounded his corner of the homely apartment.

"What'd you say to him?" Kali had asked when he told her about Donovan going off like that with a baseball bat. "Now why would you think I had to say anything to set him off?" Al had asked. And she said, "Because it's what you do, Al. It's all that's left of the famous wit with which you used to write newspaper columns. This is you at your wit's end."

Bee started. "Kali said that?"

"Pretty well word for word," Stills said. "Seems that one of the things that drew her to McGeary in the first place was that she had dreams of becoming a writer herself. Anyway, he tried to get her going, but she was not interested. She was beyond caring is how she put it.

"She hadn't left much behind in the place, but there was one big item, a flat-screen TV in the master bedroom, that was hers. She undid the connections and then phoned down to Rory on her cell. He was waiting in the driveway out front of the apartment building. She warned him, 'Don't get into it with him, okay? Don't let him rag you.' Rory said he was good. He just wanted out of there. But I guess as soon as he arrived, Al started in.

"'If it isn't the old cuckold himself,' Al said the minute Rory came through the door. Kali figured Rory had no idea what a cuckold was, but he didn't like the sound of it and he recognized the tone well enough. But he was as good as his word. He sloughed it off and went to get the TV. Al kept up the verbal hounding the whole time. Just sitting there in his chair, 'like an invalid king'—that's what she called him. But I guess Al saved the best for when Rory came out of the bedroom laden down with the television.

"'Well, off you two lovebirds go,' Al said. 'And Kali,

I truly hope you have better luck with him than Jilly did. Major problems in the sack, is what she told me.' Kali had her hand on Rory's arm. 'Don't listen,' she told him. 'He's a drunken bum. He's nobody.' She tried to hustle Rory out the door, which she said wasn't easy when he was carrying a flat screen. And then Al says, 'My oh my, Jilly, she had some great stories to tell about your sexual impotence, Rory Tulk.' Kali said Rory's face was getting redder and she could feel the anger just buzzing in his body, but she almost had him out the door when Al delivered the coup de grâce: 'Which is why Jilly was so amazed to find herself pregnant.' "

"What?" said Bee.

Stills nodded. "That's what he said, according to Kali."

"Was it true?"

"Was what true—Kali's statement, or that Jilly was impregnated by Rory Tulk?"

It hadn't occurred to Bee that Kali might have made up her story. "The getting-pregnant part."

"Who knows? It's the kind of thing a creep like McGeary would have up his sleeve for causing maximum damage. And it sure helps to explain what happened. Rory came right back in that apartment, put down the television, and called Al a liar. Told him what he thought of him and all, but Al had his sword sharpened. 'Of course I was sleeping with her before you two broke up,' he said, 'but not long enough for the child to be mine. Oh ho, what a shocker that was!' Kali tried to drag Rory off. He wouldn't move. He had murder in his eyes, she said. So if she couldn't move him, she figured she'd try and get between them. Try to stop Al. She went over to him and told him to just let it go. What was he trying to do?

Why couldn't he for once in his miserable life just keep his ugly mouth shut, et cetera, et cetera. But Al didn't even look at her. He just watched Rory, saw the storm building. 'Of course, there was no way she was going to *keep* that baby of yours,' said Al. 'Here she was finally getting out from under Mr. Five-Second-Lover and she's expected to saddle herself with his brat, for God's sake? No way! Luckily, I was there to help her arrange to get rid of it. Eh, Rory? Think about that. You almost had yourself a child there and you never even knew it.'"

"And he went ballistic," said Bee. It wasn't a question.

Stills nodded, drained her coffee. "That's Kali's story. There was the bat Donovan had left just lying there, and Rory didn't hesitate to pick it up and lay into Al."

Bee stared at her plate of toast. She hadn't touched it. She picked up a slice and then returned it to the plate. "It's so evil," she said. "Not Rory. He's just . . . just stupid. But what Al did."

"No," said Stills. "It's suicidal."

Bee stared at her. Stills shrugged. "Think about it. Sometimes a weak man like that who's lost everything wants to end it but can't really bring himself to do it. But if he happens to have a skill set like McGeary . . ."

Something was bothering Bee. A *lot* was bothering her. The story was devastating. But something had occurred to her as she listened. What was it? Right!

"And nobody heard any of this?"

Stills shook her head. "That's what I wanted to know, as well. We went back to double-check with the neighbor, Sayyid Shan. He was back and forth, down to the basement, doing his laundry, but he only heard and saw Donovan. I grilled Kali about that. She said Al never raised his voice. Not once. This place has paper-thin walls so any kind of shouting match becomes a matter of public record. Al kept it all quiet. Just sliding the knife in. No fuss, no muss."

"But what about Rory?"

"According to Kali, he didn't hardly say a word. He just picked up that bat and went to town. Probably knocked him out with the first strike so there'd be no shouting from the victim. And unlike the breaking of the bowl and the bottles and the glasses, a body doesn't make a lot of noise when you pummel it."

Bee shuddered and wrapped her arms protectively around her chest.

"Sorry," said Stills.

The scene was vivid before Bee's eyes. And to her shock she found herself imagining what it must have been like for Kali. "She—Kali—didn't *she* cry out? Try to stop it?"

Stills tipped her head and raised her eyebrows. "In your own brief encounter with Mr. Tulk, did you try reasoning with the man? Did it seem a likely avenue for downgrading the situation?"

Point taken. Bee closed her eyes and sighed. Then she opened her eyes again and stared at Stills. "Poor woman," she said.

And Stills, to her surprise, nodded.

CHAPTER FORTY-SIX

"So they . . . what? Just left?"

"Yeah. They got out of there. Lucky for Tulk he'd been wearing his work gloves to carry the TV so no fingerprints on the bat—or on anything. I guess Kali did some quick thinking. They'd walked in on a scene of violence and only added to it, not created it. She checked the hallway, saw it was clear and then they booted it—didn't run into a soul until they were out in the driveway. They were loading the truck, Kali looked up and—bam!—there was Donovan walking up the driveway toward the front door. They stared at each other—she and Donovan. She said she couldn't bring herself to say anything but she watched Donovan take it all in: the clothes, the basket of bathroom stuff, the flat screen, which he knew was hers. He just nodded. 'See you,' he said apparently, but he couldn't have known just how soon."

"That must have been when he saw the license plate number," said Bee.

"What do you mean?"

Bee suddenly realized there was information she'd been withholding from Stills.

Stills seemed to realize it, too. Her eyes narrowed. "When you saw that red Sierra, it wasn't just the color or the lift job that let you know it was the vehicle in question, was it?" Bee shook her head. "I thought you'd seen the vehicle and taken down the license. But you *recognized* the number, as well." Bee nodded and watched Stills's face cloud over. "He told you the license number. Donovan. He said it in his coma or whatever state he was in."

"Yeah, but I didn't know it."

"What do you mean you didn't know it?" Stills was building up a head of steam. "I told you I wanted to see that journal of yours. If we'd had a license to go on that whole crazy scene out at Sugar Valley could have been avoided." Bee got up and turned toward the hall. "Where are you going?" Bee didn't answer.

She came back a minute later with her bag and fished out the journal. She showed Stills the page of scribbled notes. Pointed at a passage:

Are you . . . Then a bunch of stuff.

See . . . More stuff.

Oh . . .

Stills took the journal from her and flipped to the next page, flipped back. "This is all you had?"

Bee nodded. "He said it a bunch of times, but I had no

idea it was a license plate number, and neither would you have." Then she took back the journal and closed it. She rolled her lips inside her mouth. She flicked at her cold cinnamon toast for a moment, waiting for the lecture. When none came she looked up and Stills was eyeing her quizzically. "You want to know why I didn't give it to you," said Bee. Stills nodded. "Because if you just read the words he said, it sounded as if he might have killed his father, but I knew that's not what he meant when he was talking."

"Jeez! How much did he actually say?"

Bee pushed the Moleskine toward the detective. "There's other stuff in there, personal stuff. Stuff that would have looked really incriminating."

Stills found the list and glanced through it but seemed to lose interest. She closed it, put the elastic ribbon over it, and handed it back without another word.

"And so Donovan goes up to the apartment," said Stills, "and walks in. And sees what happened . . ."

She stopped and let Bee digest the scene all over again, from Donovan's perspective. Bee remembered one time she'd been with him and he'd dropped off something at his dad's while she waited in that same driveway where Tulk had parked, the drive that swung in from the westbound lane of Carling Avenue. When he came down that day he'd been angry about something. Something his father had said or done.

"What are you thinking about?" said Stills.

Bee looked up and told the inspector her memory. "We drove away but Turn—Donovan—was so edgy I pulled off into a restaurant parking lot and asked him what was up. He didn't want to talk. He wanted to walk. And so we left the car there and headed down to the river.

"It's weird," Bee continued. "That part of Britannia is so soulless, but you're, like, just a few blocks from the Ottawa and it's so beautiful. The river is so wide there, and there's a good pathway that goes for miles and miles. Parks and kids and bicyclists and in-line skaters and joggers and geese and . . . well, it was a good antidote and soon Donovan began to loosen up. There was a place he wanted to show me.

"I guess he went down there often when he was visiting his father. There's this kind of miraculous sculpture-like thing. Somebody had piled stones on top of one another along the rocky shore and made them into columns that stood in the shallow water on a great wide shelf of granite. The stones were as big as shoe boxes or pizza boxes and as small as pocketbooks or fists. The columns were random in size, but there must have been twenty or more of them, rising out of the water like some prehistoric city. Found art. No plaque or explanation. Several afternoons of work, maybe, wading about and rearranging the earth a little to capture a passerby's attention and make them smile." Bee remembered watching Donovan's face. He had looked happy.

"You think that's where he went?" said Stills. Bee gazed at her, impressed.

"When he'd broken the glasses and all that?" said Bee. Stills nodded.

"Yeah," said Bee. "That's what I figure. He headed off

to the river and cooled himself down. Walked it off. Because he had to go back and have the talk, see. Had to finish what he had started. But first he needed to get himself to a place where he could bear to walk back into that horrible apartment—that trap. Because that's what it had become to him. And that's what it was that night."

She looked up at Stills. She was afraid she was going to cry, but she needed to hear the end of the story.

"You want me to go on?"

Bee nodded.

"Okay, so O'Connor and Tulk followed him up to the apartment. Kali tried to talk to Donovan. She tried to tell him they hadn't done it, they just found him like that. He didn't believe it for a minute. He tried to leave and Tulk stopped him. There was a scuffle and Donovan got away, slamming the door behind him."

"And getting what's-his-name—Shan's—attention."

"Right. While Kali had the sense not to follow. Not right away. Rory was going to chase after Donovan, but she heard the door open down the hall, heard Shan call out to Donovan, yell at him. So they sat tight. Waited until the coast was clear. Then snuck out."

"And drove to Wilton Crescent to kill him, knowing he'd go home."

Stills nodded. "That about sums it up."

Bee stared at the table. Could feel the tears pricking her eyes. Feel the anger and sadness rising in her like opposing armies battling it out in her head, her heart, her gut. She looked up at Stills. "Might as well tell me everything," she said.

And Stills leaned back in her chair. "Well, yeah. I could. But she wants to tell you."

Bee's eyes narrowed. "She who? Kali?" Stills nodded. "She wants to tell me how she killed my boyfriend? Is she some kind of sadist? Why does she think I'd ever want to see her face again?"

Stills held up her hand. "I hear you," she said. "And for the record, she said more or less the same as what you said just now. But she asked if she could see you, and I'm passing that on for you to consider."

Bee looked away, wiped her cheek. "She's in jail, right?"

"The Ottawa-Carleton Detention Center, for the time being. Out on Innes Road."

"I don't want to go to jail. I don't want to be anywhere near her."

"She'd be behind glass. You'd be talking to her on a phone. Twenty minutes is the maximum time they allow."

"No," said Bee.

"Okay," said Stills. "It's not a straightforward thing, in any case. You'd have to fill out a visitor's request form. There'd have to be a security check. I could expedite the process, but still—"

Why was the inspector doing this? "Didn't you hear me? I said no."

"I did hear you, Bee. I get it."

"Go in there so she can make up a story about how it wasn't her fault?"

Stills shrugged. "It's totally your call. She's signed a confession already. There's no need for this to happen. As I said, I was just passing it on." Bee nodded just once. A curt acknowledgment that she understood and none of her anger was aimed at Stills. "If it makes any difference, she's made our job a whole lot easier," said the detective. Then seeing the flash of rage in Bee's eyes, she threw up her hands. "I know, I know. That doesn't give her any rights. None. Except . . ."

Bee waited. Watched as Stills lifted her empty coffee mug and then put it down again. "Except what?"

"Except," said Stills, "you said it yourself a while back: 'Poor woman.' Your words. Am I right?"

Bee's shoulders fell. This was the last of it. The last bit left of the mystery. Stills could tell her. Right now. She already knew; Bee could see it in her eyes. She could tell Bee the last tragic remnants of the story and then it would be over. Or would it? Would one last glimpse of him — of Donovan — help to bury him, help to give her some rest? Or would it backfire and only make her want to throttle his murderers? Would she become embittered for life? She didn't want that. She wanted it all just to go away. She looked at Stills and saw something in her eyes she hadn't seen yet: a glimpse into the whole strange and awful world that the detective lived in day in, day out. A world populated by evil and foulness, but also by blundering stupidity, wrong lifestyle choices, and horrendous mistakes in judgment. Split-second decision making that could have gone either way. Maybe not if you were one of the Rory Tulks of the world. But was there anything inherently wicked about Kali O'Connor? What was Stills saying to her by not saying? She didn't know. And she didn't know why she was even considering the question posed to her. She looked at the detective and the glimpse inside her head was shut down. The inspector's face was perfectly neutral. She'd shut the door. And for some reason Bee hated that even more than what she'd been asked to do. She nodded almost imperceptibly.

"What?"

"I'll do it."

CHAPTER / FORTY-SEVEN

She was dressed in orange just like on TV. Her face was makeup free; her red hair, looking anything but lustrous, was pulled back tight in an orange scrunchie, as if it were part of an inmate's uniform. She looked haggard, a woman who'd gone from thirty-something to fifty-something in a week. Maybe murdering people did that to you. Her hands, Bee noticed, were ring free. All those rings confiscated. Why? Was it a suicide-watch thing, like not letting prisoners have belts or shoelaces? What were you supposed to do with a handful of costume jewelry—knock yourself out?

She picked up the phone on her side of the glass. Bee picked up hers. "Thank you for doing this," said Kali. Bee said nothing, did nothing, nor did Kali seem to expect a response from her. "I wanted you to know that I liked Donovan." She paused. Bee's head buzzed with terrible things to say, like, If this is what you do to people you like . . . et cetera. She held her tongue.

"Did he ever say anything about me?" Kali asked. Bee's eyes narrowed, her gaze set at just past incredulous and verging on piercing. "No, I guess not," Kali added quickly. "I'm sorry." Her head drooped—perhaps because Bee's laser-beam eyes had melted the front half of her cerebral cortex.

"This is harder than I thought it was going to be," said Kali, fidgeting in her chair, her voice over the phone muffled, as if coming from a long way off. She didn't look up. And then it was as if the line had gone dead, and yet there she was, only a plate of bulletproof glass away.

Bee cleared her throat. Kali looked up. "You wanted to see me," said Bee, her voice as steady and dispassionate as she could make it.

Kali nodded. "I wanted you to know that I tried to stop Rory from . . . from doing what he did."

"Which thing?"

Kali looked perplexed for a moment and then said, "I had nothing to do with what happened to Donovan."

"How would he have even known where Donovan lived if you hadn't told him?"

Kali's shoulders sagged, defeated. "I know. Let me just tell you what happened and then it's done and you'll never have to see me again."

So she began. How they waited inside the door of Al's apartment only long enough for the next-door neighbor to close his. Then they took off. Reaching the street, they saw Donovan a long way off, crossing the road, the median, making a dash to the south side. They got in the pickup. Carling is divided into east and west lanes where the apartment is, and being on the north side they had to turn west and drive a ways, then make a U-turn at the first light they came to. It was raining. The roads were slick. The traffic was Friday-night busy. After a moment they caught sight of him still running, looking back now and then. He stuck out his thumb. Before they could reach him, a van stopped and picked him up. They followed the van all the way down Carling to Bronson, turned right, then down Fifth to Bank, then south. The guy dropped him at the corner of Wilton.

"I jumped out of the truck," said Kali. "I told Rory I'd handle it myself. He said he'd pick me up later and took off up Bank. I took after Donovan. He had his hands tucked in his jeans and his hood up, his head down, hunched over against the rain. I called to him. He didn't turn. I ran to catch up to him." She stopped and Bee saw the woman's vision shift. She wasn't in the visiting room any longer. She was there in the cold rain on Wilton Crescent.

" 'What do you want?' he said when I finally caught up to him. 'We need to talk,' I said. He shook his head. 'What you saw back there at Al's. You have to know what happened.' 'I know what happened,' he said. 'No you don't,' I told him. 'You think we killed him, but it wasn't like that. He killed himself.' That got his attention. 'With a baseball bat?' he said. 'No,' I said. 'I mean, yes, but he brought it on. You know how he does that.' "

Then Kali told Bee what Inspector Stills had already told her: Kali's signed statement about Jilly being pregnant with Rory's child and aborting it and Al telling the story in a way that was guaranteed to make Rory go crazy.

371

"He listened," said Kali. "Dono listened. He didn't stop walking, but he listened and nodded. He knew what I was talking about, all right, when I said Al brought it on himself. 'It was like he wanted it to happen,' I told him. 'As if he was too weak to end his miserable life himself and so he farmed out the job.' That's when Donovan stopped. We were almost at his place. He looked at me with this . . . I don't know . . . kind of sad look."

Bee put her hand up to stop Kali. "What were you hoping for?" she said. "That Donovan was going to take the rap for it? Was that the plan?" Kali looked down at the counter in front of her, its edge chipped and stained. "Well?"

Kali looked up and shook her head.

"I mean, you had Rolly as a witness. He'd seen Donovan break stuff earlier."

"That was before we got there. We didn't know Rolly had seen anything. Or anyone else."

"Yeah, but you *did* know the guy next door saw Donovan leave in a hurry. Did you think you could convince Donovan not to mention you'd been there or something? Like, 'Oh, we didn't mean to kill him, so you won't tell on us, will you?' "

Kali shook her head. "I'll tell you what I was planning if you'll listen."

Bee glared at her as she tried to rein in her anger. After a moment she nodded curtly.

"I wanted him—Dono—to know what happened. How it happened. How Al baited Rory. But I'd already made up my mind to give myself up."

That caught Bee off-guard. She downgraded her glare but not her suspicion. Kali sniffled, took a tissue from a box on the counter. She looked inquiringly at Bee, as if she were waiting for permission to proceed.

"Go on," said Bee.

Kali sniffed again, wiped her nose. "As soon as Rory dropped me off—as soon as he drove away and I could think again—I knew we had to turn ourselves in. Except I also knew that Rory wasn't going to go for that. No way. All I could think was to tell Dono to phone the cops and give them Rory's license plate number and my new address and phone number out in the valley." Bee's eyebrows drew together. "It's true, so help me God," Kali said, and crossed herself as she said it. "There was no way I could've talked Rory into giving us up."

"How do you know?"

"Because I *tried*," she wailed. "I tried the whole way we were following that van with Dono in it." She paused. "Anyway, you've seen what he's like." Bee nodded. "I swear it. I tried, Bee, and I failed, and so I had to get the word to the authorities and I wanted Dono to do it. To phone them right away."

Bee just stared at her. And Kali stared back, daring the girl to call her a liar. "It's what Donovan said next that I needed you to hear—hear from me personally."

Bee waited. Couldn't bring herself to speak. Could barely bring herself to breathe.

"I told Donovan about what Al had said and he started nodding his head as if it made sense somehow—as if he knew perfectly well how Al would do that. Then he looked at me for a long time and he said, as God's my witness, 'I killed him. It was me. I did it.'"

Bee froze, but only for a moment. Then she went as if to put the headset down but Kali stopped her. "No, please, Beatrice. *Listen* to this. He explained what he meant." Bee fixed her headset. "He said before he left, the first time, he told his father he was never going to see him again. His exact words were, 'You are dead to me. Do you get that? From now on you are dead to me.' Then Dono looked at me, his eyes kind of sad and soft, and he repeated it. 'I killed him,' he said. Then he turned and walked into his house." She stopped and folded her hands on the counter.

Bee stared at her, her mouth hanging slightly open with this new shock. "What do you mean he walked into his house?"

"Exactly what I said. He walked in and shut the door. Turned the dead bolt and everything. I was that close, I heard it."

"But—"

"He came back out. Yeah. I know. But right then he was gone, and I . . ." She took a deep breath. Then her eyes glided up to look at the clock. There wasn't much time left. "I didn't know what to do. Rory had said for me to wait for him, he'd pick me up. I looked around; the street was deserted as far as I could tell. There were parked cars. No people. I saw lights twinkling through the bare trees on the other side of the street. I walked over there so, you know, Rory could see me when he came back. I could see this pond or whatever it was below and the canal beyond that and the lights along the Queen Elizabeth Parkway; they were shining in the water. I felt a kind of peace, knowing that the nightmare was going to be over soon. He'd phone—Dono—and he'd tell

374

them the story and, hopefully, tell them I had done what I could to stop it. I was ready for whatever they'd throw at me. I'd screwed up bad but I never, *never* meant for what happened to happen. I'm not sure if you know this but I begged Al—begged him—over the phone not to be there when I came for my stuff. I knew what he'd do. I just never knew it would be so . . . so . . ." She looked up, stripped of hope and hopeful all at the same time.

Bee could feel the poison draining from her. The woman on the other side of the glass was, just as she'd suspected, pathetic, not evil. That didn't change the facts. Donovan was dead. That would never change. But hating Kali O'Connor seemed to be a fool's game.

"What do you want from me?" said Bee. "Am I supposed to forgive you?"

Kali shook her head. "No. That's not it."

"And I *still* don't know what happened to him," said Bee.

Kali's face hardened. She nodded—seemed to brace herself. "So I was standing over on the other side of the street and then I hear this door open. I turn to look and it's Dono. Coming over to me. He comes over, crosses the street, and says do I want to come in, have a coffee or something. I can't believe it."

No, you can't believe it because you don't know Turn. Bee wanted to shout at the stupid cow but buttoned her lips, needed to know the end—could see it coming.

"He's like, 'It's cold. Why don't you come in?' And I'm trying to think, is this some kind of a trap? But then I think, how can it be a trap? I've already told him to call the cops. And I figured maybe he'd done that already. So I ask him.

And he shakes his head, explains how his phone is charging up and then he'll do it. And I can't believe why he hasn't done it yet. Then he must have read my mind or something because he says, 'Or, you know, you could. If the call comes from you, it would look better. And you'd be safe in the house until they got here.' Safe from Rory, I guess he meant."

Bee watched Kali's face. She looked kind of stunned, as if she still couldn't figure it out—would never figure it out.

"So I said to him, 'Thanks. Yeah.' And he smiles and turns to go. And then I hear the truck and see the lights and . . ."

She broke down then, and because Bee did not want to join in on *anything* Kali O'Connor did, she sat as still and cool as a rock, her back straight, her hands on her knees, watching the woman cry. She knew she would come to feel something like empathy for this wretched creature, but right now she only wanted to watch her suffer. She didn't like herself for wanting this, but it didn't matter. She didn't have time for her right now. Her mind was on Donovan. His last act was one of kindness—of reaching out. Just like he had returned to Al's apartment to check up on his father. Two right things that turned into the wrongest thing he ever did, through no fault of his own. And Bee knew something else. She knew that despite everything else—all the feelings roiling around in her—Kali had given her a gift of this memory. Someday maybe she would thank her.

EPILOGUE

The second week in May, Bee Northway and Trish Turner went antique-store hunting and found a ceramic washbowl pretty much identical to the one Bee had hurled at the head of Rory Tulk way back, when, in the middle of a nightmare, she had found herself alone in someone else's house having to fight for her life.

Matthew Needham, Jilly's resourceful husband, had been able to fix the old pine washstand, good as new apparently. Jilly hadn't said anything about the bowl when they talked on the phone, but Bee was pretty certain neither Matt's resourcefulness nor Jilly's magical powers, whatever they were, extended to pottery.

So Bee phoned Jilly and told her that she and Trish would like to drive out to visit her. Trish wanted to meet Cassie. Jilly suggested they meet Matt, too, and bring Scott, and so the whole thing became a Sunday luncheon.

It was a good day. Bee was learning how that worked — that there *could* be good days. You were allowed good days. It didn't mean you were horrible. It didn't mean you'd forgotten anything. And it didn't mean the bad days were over. Your job was to breathe in the good days and breathe out the bad.

She needed to see the farmhouse again. She knew that. And she needed to see it when there were good people and a good baby and a good dog there to help dislodge the awfulness of what had happened — an awfulness that still kept her up at night sometimes.

Jilly was a bit distracted on the visit. She looked tired beyond the tedium of motherhood. She couldn't always hold Bee's eye, and that was disquieting. Bee already felt terrible; she couldn't bear to feel even more guilty. She had lured a monster to this place — *back* to this home, where he had once lived and then been banished from. That hadn't been her plan, but that's what had happened. A place that Jilly was lovingly fixing up in what spare time she could manage. And then here was this terrible memory of her earlier life contaminating it — wrecking the joint.

But the meal was good and Scott managed to make things jolly. He insisted that Bee act out her triumphant defeat of Rory Tulk and managed, somehow, to turn that horrifying experience into something hilarious. He played the part of Tulk himself and hammed it up terribly while she stood at the top of the stairs with the brand-new old washbowl in her hands. Jilly had called up to her, pleading with her not to throw it, if she didn't mind. It was bizarre, really. Psychodrama.

Life went on. It had a habit of doing that, Bee had noticed. July came and final exams and late acceptance to her second-choice university. She and Daisy took a road trip there. Life began, inexorably, to become normal. It was a counterfeit of normal, really. It was not a kind of normal you wanted to look at too closely or in too bright a light. But still . . .

Then one rainy August morning, Jilly phoned her. They danced around salutations, asking about school plans, the baby, the farm, and then Jilly cut it off.

"Listen, there's no way to make this sound anything but weird, so I'm just going to say it, okay, and then . . . well, whatever will be, will be."

Bee wasn't sure what to say. She looked through her store of useful responses and could only come up with "Sure."

"So, I've been seeing Donovan," said Jilly. "You know . . . like I told you." Now, Bee really could not speak. "I assume you're still there," Jilly continued, "and I appreciate that there is no reasonable reply to what I just said." She sighed nervously. "Here's the thing. I've sort of been his guide or something. I won't hear from him for weeks and then suddenly he'll show up needing help—needing my attention."

"I'm not sure I understand."

"Yeah," said Jilly, "well, I can't say I'm surprised. But there it is. I guess I'm just delusional or something, but all I can do is play along. So I give him advice—or not advice so much as encouragement, you know?"

Silence.

"And, okay, I'm going to cut to the chase, because I can tell this is going nowhere." She sounded exasperated, but Bee didn't sense that she was exasperated at Bee so much as at the task she had given herself. Embarrassed, even. "I think he's gotten through."

"Gotten through?"

"Yeah, you know. He's There, if you know what I'm saying."

If you know what I'm saying. There was no phrase in the English language that made less sense to Bee at that moment than "if you know what I'm saying."

"And here's the thing . . ." Jilly paused and Bee could hear over the line the baby crying. "I'll be right there, sweetheart," Jilly called out to her daughter. Then her voice returned to the phone. "Sorry, Cassie just woke up. I'll make this short. He—Donovan—is going to contact you."

Bee froze. For a moment she was horrified and then she was furious. She did not need this! Life was hard enough. Life was just sorting itself out and here was this bonkers woman out in the boonies telling her that her dead boyfriend was . . .

"I'm sorry," said Jilly.

"What did you say again?"

"He's going to find a way to contact you."

"Jilly, listen, I—"

"I know. You think I'm not playing with a full deck. Maybe you're right. But trust me on this. He's going to get in touch with you this Saturday."

This was another jolt. "Saturday. Saturday, August the thirteenth?"

"That's right. Is it a special day or something?"

"Yes," said Bee. "It's my birthday."

"Well, then. That explains it."

"It doesn't really explain anything."

"Of course it doesn't. I only meant that he would pick that day. It makes sense."

"And what am I supposed to do with this? Like do I need to hang out by the phone all day? Or is he going to show up at the door with a bouquet of flowers? Should I dress up? Wear his favorite top?" Bee waited, heard nothing but the baby crying and calling for her mother. "Sorry," she said. "I didn't mean to be rude, it's just that—"

"I deserve it," said Jilly, sounding crestfallen. "Believe me, I didn't want to call. Been putting it off. I like you, Beatrice. From what I've seen, you're a good person. And I can only imagine what you're thinking right now: I'm a crackpot— a meddlesome fruitcake, a witch with a screw loose. Like I said, I did not want to even make this call. But I owe it to him. Okay? Can we just leave it at that?"

Bee nodded and then cleared her throat. "Okay. But Jilly, all kidding aside, what *am* I supposed to do?"

Jilly said. "Don't *do* anything. He'll find you. You can't prepare for it. He's not going to appear at the party, if you're having one. He's not going to freak you out. I'm sure of that much. There will be some sign and you'll know it when you see it: know it's him. That's all I've got."

"Okay," said Bee. "Uh, thanks . . . I guess."

"You're welcome."

"And Jilly," Bee said loudly. It took a second for her to reply; she must have been putting the phone down.

"Yeah?"

"Give Cassie a hug from me."

"Will do."

"Good-bye."

But Jilly had already hung up.

Daisy and Jen had thought maybe it should just be the girls, but Bee wanted Max there, too, and Jen's new friend, Rifat. No, it would not be weird. And since it was her birthday, she got to make the call. There was going to be a party. She was overdue for a party. And the party was going to be at Daisy's cottage up in the Gatineau. After that, she'd change the picture on her desktop, the one of them sitting on the rock at that cottage.

She hadn't told anyone about Jilly's call. There was a good chance that her friends would think she was losing it, so she'd kept it her secret. But she did wear the top he liked best. It was purple. She didn't wear much purple; maybe that was what made it stand out. She was going to have a good time. She had made up her mind. She and Turn had only ever celebrated two birthdays together: hers in August, his in October. They had no traditions. She didn't anticipate missing him any more than she did any other day that he came to mind. And yes, he came to mind a lot, but it was bearable. That was maybe the saddest part.

And so they partied. They swam and ate and drank and played Twister, at Daisy's insistence. Her cottage was a repository of games of all kinds for all ages from all eras.

For some reason, Bee kept checking her cell phone. Ridiculous.

There was music playing nearly all the time. Until suddenly, just after eleven, it went off. So did the lights. A blackout.

"But there's not even a storm," said Jen.

"Somebody didn't pay their electric bill," said Max.

"I'll find the candles," said Daisy.

Bee could scarcely breathe. She felt the cottage close in on her, as if the air was being sucked out of it. "I'm going out on the deck," she said.

The moon shimmered on the lake. It wasn't scary—not outside. Except maybe a little. "A blackout," she said quietly to the night. "Isn't that just, like, a little too clichéd?" Standing on the deck alone, she soaked up the darkness and the cool. "I'd have expected better from you, Turn."

Then there was music again. Daisy had found her parents' mammoth old battery-operated radio, and the song was Tor Miller's "Carter and Cash." Bee smiled. Turn had loved that song.

They had been driving somewhere in Toddy the Turtle and it had come on the radio. Turn immediately cranked it up and started banging his fists on his knees, almost in time. He joined in the chorus:

"And all the while the world / It hit me with the sweetest sound—"

"No," she said, laughing.

"What do you mean, no?" he said, raising his voice over the music.

"It's not 'the sweetest sound,' it's 'the *speed* of sound.'"

"No way," he said. So they listened closely for the next chorus.

"See," she said. "I told you."

"Bah," he said.

"It's true."

"Maybe, but it *should* be the sweetest sound."

"Why's that?"

He didn't answer right away. He wanted to listen to the song and he bopped around in his seat so much she wondered whether he'd drive Toddy right off the road. When it was over, he turned the radio off.

"You're just sore," she said. "You hate losing. Even a lyrics-recognition contest."

He laughed. "I'm not sore. Not one bit."

And she knew he wasn't. He was happy. Really happy. And she was happy right then, too. She was often happy with him, but right then she was deeply happy, maybe because of the song.

Inside Daisy's cottage, the song blaring out of the tinny little speakers of the ancient transistor radio ended and the news came on, only to be turned off right away. And it was quiet again. Blackout quiet. The others were chatting, but sotto voce. The raucous part of the party had been drained off and there was just this warm glow to it now. Or maybe it was just that you don't ever want to talk too loudly in the dark.

So there was the lake and the cicadas and some night bird. There was the gentle lapping of the waves on the rocks down below. "And all the while the world," Bee sang quietly to herself. "It hit me with the speed—" No, she thought.

Turn was right. She started again. "All the while the world, it hit me with the sweetest sound . . ."

She stopped again, swallowed hard. She looked around, not afraid, just filled with wonder. Then she closed her eyes and felt him—felt him behind her, so close that she was quite sure his arms were around her even now, holding her, holding her up. "Thank you," she said.

ACKNOWLEDGMENTS

In an unguarded moment, I divulged to the writer Monique Polak a scary incident I had been through—something I was having trouble coming to terms with. We hardly knew one another but sometimes you reach out to another writer knowing they'll just *get* it. She assured me I'd write about it one day, which shocked me at the time. It wasn't a throwaway line; there was something about her quiet confidence that heartened me, pushed me eventually, to take a deep breath and dive in despite my trepidations. Thank you, Monique, for knowing.

With two exceptions, all of the characters in this story are fictional. The two exceptions are the kind teacher Bee meets at Sugar Valley School, who is modeled on my dear friend Coral Nault, longtime teacher at Brooke Valley School. She has only just retired but the work she has done is a testimonial to her dedication, to which I add this small tribute.

And the helpful cop, Constable Tanis Cowan, is a very real, very good soul, though it's hard to imagine her in uniform! While far from retiring, Tanis is moving on to new endeavors and I wish her all the best.

It's become popular of late, in book acknowledgments, to thank all the people in the biz that help one's book come into being. The trouble is that once you start naming names, the list can get pretty long pretty fast: agent, publisher, editors, publicists, and so on. I hope they all know that I honor what they do. Thank you, one and all. I do want to include a shout-out to my dear friends at Vermont College of Fine Art, in the Writing for Children and Young Adults program. My fellow instructors and the extraordinary students I have the great pleasure to work with—and stay connected to after they graduate—are the gift that keeps on giving and a continuing source of inspiration and strength. Love you all!